# A Thousand Years of Darkness

*What if the President of the United States was trying to topple the nation—and you found out about it?*

---

**Charles W. Sasser**

**For all Americans:
May we learn to live free**

Deadly Niche Press

Denton, Texas

This is a work of fiction. Names, characters, places, and incidents are products of the author's imagination or are used fictitiously and are not to be construed as real. Any resemblance to actual events, locales, organizations, or persons, living or dead, is entirely coincidental.

Deadly Niche Press
An imprint of AWOC.COM Publishing
P.O. Box 2819
Denton, TX 76202



Manufactured in the United States of America

ISBN: 978-0-937660-74-4

Author's website: www.charlessasser.com

## What they're saying about Charles W. Sasser

"As for the writing, it's near perfect, flows smoothly and has that certain flair that all of us who type for a living seek to achieve..." *PACIFIC FLYER* on *Predator: The Remote-Control Air War over Iraq and Afghanistan.*

"The most gripping scenes in the book document...emotion in the seconds just before the Hellfire missile arrives on target..." *THE NEW YORK REVIEW OF BOOKS (NEW YORK TIMES)* on *Predator: The Remote-Control Air War over Iraq and Afghanistan.*

"A gripping combat memoir...honest and exciting...a roving tale, full of sharp detail and told in the harsh language of soldiers baptized in fire..." *KIRKUS REVIEWS* on *Taking Fire*

"Bustles with danger, intrigue, and surprise. Rapid-fire action from beginning to end." Clive Cussler on *First Seal*

"Tough, raunchy, gritty, but surprisingly tender... If you never made it to 'Nam,this book will take you there... unbeatable!" *MILITARY HISTORY Magazine* on *The 100th Kill*

"Outstanding! Exciting! Gut-grabbing...!" *LEATHERNECK Magazine* on *One Shot—One Kill.*

"A grim, authentic window to a world of horrors only hinted at in the tabloid headlines..." *PUBLISHER'S WEEKLY* on *Homicide!*

"A powerful emotion-packed mystery..." *CONCISE BOOK REVIEWS* on *No Gentle Streets*

"A model of good historical writing..." *LEATHERNECK* on *Hill 488*

"Abundant action, a fast pace and an unusual ethical dilemma..." *PUBLISHER'S WEEKLY* on *Dark Planet.*

## Books by Charles W. Sasser

**Fiction:**

*A Thousand Years of Darkness*
*The 100th Kill*
*Liberty City*
*The Return*
*Sanctuary*
*No Gentle Streets*
*Dark Planet*
*The War Chaser*
*Operation No Man's Land* (as Mike Martell)
*Detachment Delta: Punitive Strike*
*Detachment Delta: Operation Iron Weed*
*Detachment Delta: Operation Deep Steel*
*Detachment Delta: Operation Aces Wild*
*Detachment Delta: Operation Cold Dawn*
*OSS Commando: Final Option*
*OSS Commando: Hitler's A-Bomb*
*No Longer Lost*
(Novella, in *The Foxy Hens Meet a Romantic Adventurer*)

**Nonfiction:**

*None Left Behind*
*Homicide!*
*Always A Warrior*
*Raider*
*Patton's Panthers*
*Warriors* (contributor)
*First SEAL* (w/Roy Boehm)
*Fire Cops* (w/Michael Sasser)
*Magic Steps to Writing Success*
*Taking Fire* (w/Ron Alexander)
*The Soldier of Fortune* (contributor)
*The Walking Dead* (w/Craig Roberts)
*One Shot—One Kill* (w/Craig Roberts)
*In Cold Blood: Oklahoma's Most Notorious Murders*
*Last American Heroes* (w/Michael Sasser)
*Doc: Platoon Medic* (w/Daniel E. Evans)
*Arctic Homestead* (w/Norma Cobb)
*Crosshairs on the Kill Zone* (w/Craig Roberts)
*Going Bonkers: The Wacky World of Cultural Madness*
*The Shoebox: Letters for the Seasons*
(by Nancy Shoemaker, edited by CWS)
*Devoted to Fishing; Devotionals for Fishermen*
*Predator: The Remote-Control Air War over Iraq and Afghanistan (w/Matt J. Martin)*
*The New Face of War* (Time/Life series contributor)
*True Detective* (Pinnacle true crime series contributor)
*God in the Foxhole*
*Shoot to Kill*
*Smoke Jumpers*
*Sniper Anthology (contributor)*
*At Large*
*My Mom is My Hero* (contributor)
*Hill 488* (w/Ray Hildreth)
*Encyclopedia of Navy SEALs*

# PART I

*"If the lights that guide us ever go out, they will fade little by little, as if on their own accord... We therefore should not console ourselves by thinking that the barbarians are still a long way off. Some peoples merely let the torch be snatched from their hands, but others stamp it out themselves."* — Alexis de Tocqueville

## Census Worker Murdered in Cemetery

***(Tulsa)**—Ron Sparks, 41, a federal census official in Oklahoma, was found stripped naked hanging from a tree this morning in a rural cemetery in northeastern Oklahoma with the word "Fed" scrawled on his chest with a felt tip pen. The witness who found the body at the Akins Cemetery told reporters that Sparks was naked, bound head and foot with duct tape, blindfolded with more duct tape, and gagged with a red rag. The Department of Homeland Security and the FBI are investigating whether anti-government elements may have committed the homicide...*

*A statement issued by Homeland Security blamed "Southern populist terrorism whipped up by such as Zenergy News Cable and talk show personalities like Rush Limbaugh and Jerry Baer for fomenting anger, fear and vitriol." In Washington, Senate Majority Leader Joe Wiedersham (D-Ill) expressed concern that conservative talk show hosts like Baer might be contributing to a poisonous anti-government sentiment.*

*"I think people in positions of power or influence inciting hate and violence need to be held accountable," he said. "Political hate speech is just as dangerous as any other form of hate speech..."*

# Chapter One

## Tulsa, Oklahoma

A raw-boned laborer in his thirties, out of work during the deepening recession, grabbed a coffee and a muffin at McDonald's and found an empty booth at the back where he could keep an eye on the parking lot. Joshua Logan wore frayed jeans, steel-toed boots, a blue chambray shirt and a *Tulsa Oilers'* baseball cap.

Outside, some kid with a ring through his lip, green-spiked hair and baggy convict jeans was "loose changing" customers. A woman who looked faded and tired led her little boy by the hand around the young beggar and climbed into a pickup truck. Logan was pretty sure neither of them was a Fed.

He craved a cigarette to go with his coffee and muffin, but he had quit cold turkey after a pack went up to seven dollars. He sipped coffee until he spotted Morris' old blue Ford follow a tan Toyota onto the parking lot. A black woman in a red hat got out of the Toyota and came into Mickey D's. Morris sat in his car looking nervous.

Morris had awakened Logan at five a.m.

"Things are about to get hotter than an Arkansas bitch in August," Morris warned when Logan answered his bedside phone. "Meet me. You know where."

Morris and Logan often had coffee at Mickey D's when they worked construction together. The urgency in Morris' voice told Logan this might have something to do with Ron Sparks' hanging.

As Logan watched, Morris got out of his Ford and looked around some more. He was a short man as thin and nervous as a starving squirrel. He wore threadbare jeans like Logan's and a T-shirt that proclaimed *God and Guns for America*. He was still standing by the open door of his Ford when two plain black SUVs whipped in through the *Out* drive. Logan recognized them immediately. All Federal Home Security vehicles were painted black.

Tires squalling, the SUVs sent the dude with the lip ring and spiked hair scrambling out of the way. Morris dived for his Ford. Not quickly enough. The SUVs disgorged beefy plainclothesmen armed with M4 assault rifles. The parking lot erupted in rifle fire. The black woman in the red hat screamed as she waited for her breakfast wrap at the McDonald's counter.

The takedown was accomplished so quickly and with such cold efficiency that Logan's mouth was still agape when a couple of the Homies broke away and stormed the Golden Arches, rifles ready at port arms. They meant business. Like they knew Morris came here to meet someone.

The Mickey D's breakfast trade worked in Logan's favor. He ducked through the lines and reached the opposite door by the time the Homies burst in and splayed themselves to either side of the doorway, eyes sweeping.

"Everybody stay put!" barked a command. "Don't anybody try to leave!"

Logan ducked out the door without being spotted and fled down the back side of the building. At the corner, he flattened himself against the wall and chanced a quick peek around it. Homies were bunched up at Morris' Ford, looking down at Morris lying on the pavement in a spreading pool of blood. Logan heard one of them laugh.

*Bastards!*

Four or five vehicles were lined up in the Drive-Through lane. A young woman behind the wheel of the first vehicle stared at Logan with terror-filled eyes. He brought a finger to his lips to swear her to conspiratorial silence. She kept staring.

Logan glanced back toward the door. He would never reach his parked vehicle unobserved. Feds played by different rules than local cops. They'd probably kill him, whether he was armed or not.

For an instant, he thought of carjacking the young woman since he would never be able to reach his own vehicle. Unwilling to put her through the trauma, however, he took a deep fortifying breath and sprang from hiding. He sprinted across the Drive-Through and back parking lot toward a little wooded-bank creek that ran behind the Arches into a nearby neighborhood. The muscles in his back contracted against expected gunfire.

He threw himself face down in tall grass beyond the curb and crawled desperately toward the stream, pulling and pushing with his toes and elbows. He rolled over the side of the creek into the rocky streambed. Only a trickle of water ran through it. It had been a dry summer.

He scrambled to his feet and parted the underbrush to see if his flight had been noted. The young woman in Drive-Through broke line and gunned her car toward 193rd Street. A Homie ran out and yelled at her, but she was already in traffic and picking up speed. In these unusual times, people kept their mouths shut and saw nothing.

Logan doubted anyone else noticed him. Most were transfixed on the shooting and had not been looking in his direction. His first impulse was to run, using the creek as a conduit to get the hell out of Dodge. Dogs barking in the nearby neighborhood persuaded him to wait a few minutes until things calmed down.

His heart rate and breathing quickly returned to near normal. While he watched, an unmarked Tulsa Police car drove up and parked on the perimeter where a Homie was stretching yellow crime scene tape. Anyone with street savvy could always spot an unmarked cop car. A fit Indian-looking detective wearing jeans and a brown sports jacket over a knit shirt got out and, with a noticeable limp, walked up to a Homie who seemed to be in charge. The Homie had long arms and a face as dull as an old ax blade. The detective had eyes as hard and cold as blue flint.

It was obvious the two didn't like each other. Logan thought for a moment the Tulsa detective was going to punch out the Homie's lights. He was disappointed when he didn't.

Dogs in the adjacent neighborhoods were calming down. Logan slid from hiding and trotted up the rocky streambed. Time to get out before he ended up face down like Morris.

# Chapter Two

## Tulsa

Detective James Nail had been nearby working a case when the shooting went down. He got out of his unmarked at Mickey D's, hitched up the 40mm Glock-22 concealed beneath his brown sports jacket and walked up to Anthony Kimbrell, Regional Director of The Department of Homeland Security. His limp was the result of a gunshot wound to the knee several years ago. He looked around with unspoken disapproval: Blue Ford on the far side of the parking lot, driver's door ajar, bloody corpse all torn apart by gunfire sprawled face-down on the pavement, shattered window glass sprinkled on and around the body, rifle-toting Feds in SWAT black standing around, crime scene tape cordoning off the lot to keep back a smattering of curiosity seekers. Gawkers at a crime scene could be arrested for obstruction.

Nail started around Kimbrell to take a closer look. Kimbrell blocked him. The detective dropped his head like a cage fighter about to throw a punch.

"You're jumping my call, Nail," Kimbrell snarled. "This is a federal matter."

"You're on my turf, Kimbrell."

"We trump local yokels, Nail. It's a new day. Why don't you get back in your buggy and go write some poor fucker a traffic ticket?"

Homeland Security had formed after Nine-Eleven to protect the United States against terrorist activity. It had since gobbled up the FBI, CIA, the National Guard, Border Patrol, Coast Guard, Secret Service, Immigration, FEMA, and several other agencies to become the Big Dog in the nation when it came to law enforcement and intelligence gathering.

Nail resisted an urge to plant a fist square in the middle of Kimbrell's smirk. Instead, he splayed one big-knuckled hand against the Homie's chest, pushed him aside, and walked up to look at the dead man. The stench of urine and fresh blood saturated the air. The guy must have pissed himself when he died.

"Nail, this is a crime scene," Kimbrell protested. "I could charge you with obstruction of justice."

"Who is he?" Nail asked, indicating the body.

Kimbrell stood silently fuming. Then, grudgingly, "Fucker's name was Greg Morris. He's one of the organizers of that underground bunch of peckerwoods called The Defenders who strung up the census worker in the cemetery over in Sequoyah County."

Nail nodded. "Bit of an overkill, wouldn't you say?"

The body was nearly ripped in two. Bullet holes riddled the Ford's open door and windows. Nail observed an AR-15 rifle with clip inserted lying inside on the front passenger's seat.

"Did he return fire?" he asked.

Kimbrell stepped in front of Nail and thrust a cell phone at the detective. "I have your lieutenant on the phone."

Nail ignored him. "Were you one of the shooters, Kimbrell?"

"We'll send the city copies of our reports."

"Kind of irregular, isn't it? Investigating your own shooting?"

"Fuck you."

Nail moved around him again. No spent cartridge casings from the AR-15. It hadn't been fired.

"Why do you suppose a Defender would drive around with an illegal firearm in plain sight when he knows the Feds are on their asses?" Nail wondered.

"Because they're a bunch of stupid anti-government crackers? Take the fucking phone, Nail, and get off my scene before I have you arrested."

Nail took the phone. "Nail here," he said.

Lieutenant Jack Ross's voice: "James, let them have their scene."

Nail looked squarely at Kimbrell. "Lieutenant, they assassinated this poor bastard in cold blood."

"James, you're butting a stone wall. It's both our asses, so leave it alone. That's an order, Detective."

# Chapter Three

## Tulsa

Foliage rimming the little creek that ran behind McDonald's turned into concrete for flood and erosion control as the stream wound around the base of a hill into a housing addition. It became a large, open aqueduct. A sewer these days, what with city budget cuts to accommodate the tanking economy. Joshua Logan waded filthy water up to his knees. Plastic Coke bottles and beer cans banged against his shins. Twinkie wrappers and Burger King bags resembled jellyfish.

Black-and-white city cop cars prowled the streets in the aftermath of the shooting. The Homies had apparently somehow identified Logan as Greg Morris' intended contact and were determined to chase him down. The ambush had gone down too smoothly for the Homies not to have had sources. Who had Morris told about their unscheduled emergency meeting this morning?

A police cruiser stopped on a viaduct that spanned the creek, waiting in a line of rush hour traffic for the light at the intersection to turn green. Logan ducked underneath the span and crouched in the dark. After the traffic started moving again, he climbed the concrete bank and peeked over the top. The cruiser turned left at the light and headed back toward McDonald's.

Logan was wet and muddy. Water sloshed in his shoes. He was sweating. He reached for his cell phone, thought better of it. Asking other Defenders to come to his rescue would only place them in jeopardy. Homies would be monitoring electronic signals in the area. Logan was on his own.

He hadn't so much as a Saturday Night Special with which to defend himself.

He slid back down the bank into the water and hurriedly made his way downstream, intent on getting out of the area as fast as he could. The creek cut from the housing addition toward East Admiral Boulevard, a busy street this time of morning. Dogs barked from some of the houses. They could smell fear.

The creek flowed into an older working class neighborhood where Logan felt more comfortable in his soiled and wet laborer's clothing. He was approaching another viaduct punched underneath Admiral when blue lights lit up as a cruiser pulled a vehicle to the side of the road. Cops were stopping anyone in the vicinity who looked suspicious.

Logan cowered in the viaduct directly underneath the traffic stop. He heard a car door open and the sounds of a police radio. Policemen often turned up the volume when they got out of their cars in traffic. Logan realized the dispatcher was talking about him.

"*...white male thirty-five to forty years old, wearing old jeans, a blue shirt and an* Oilers *baseball cap... Subject belongs to a militia organization called the Defenders... Consider armed and dangerous. Wanted by Homeland Security for the murder of Ron Sparks...*"

Traffic passing over his head did not quite drown out the thumping of his heart in the confined space. A semi-truck rattled the bridge. The angry honk of a horn... Somewhere a factory whistle... Normal sounds on a morning not so normal.

The cruiser's flashing blue lights reflected in the dirty water of the shallow stream. Logan craved a cigarette. His hands trembled. He felt trapped in the sewer, like a 'coon in a creek with hounds baying on its trail. He resisted the urge to break and make a run for it.

*Mustn't do anything stupid.*

After a tension-filled two or three minutes during which Logan was certain the cop must overhear his ragged breathing, he heard a car door slam. The blue lights went off. Logan thought the cop was leaving. He crept to the opposite opening of the viaduct and peered out.

He was unable to get a look at the roadbed above. Three kids playing hooky from school were skipping stones on the creek about a block away. Logan heard them laughing and shouting.

One of the boys looked up and noticed Logan hiding in the viaduct. He pointed excitedly; the other two honored his point. All three began waving their arms, pointing and jumping up and down to attract the attention of the cop, who apparently hadn't driven on after all. Logan had no choice but to run for it.

He bunched his legs and charged from the viaduct, like a cottontail punched out of a hollow log. He hadn't taken more than a half-dozen steps before the mechanical *Kraa-a-a-ck* of a pump shotgun being charged stopped him in his tracks.

"Freeze, asshole, or you're dead meat!"

## Bill Will Ban Violent Words, Symbols

***(Washington)***—*In the aftermath of a federal official being hung in Oklahoma, a crime blamed on violent anti-government rhetoric, Congress is calling for a return to civility by passing a law that will ban the use of violent words and symbols from national discourse. Pointing a finger as though it were a gun or telling a rival sports team "we're going to kill you" could become criminal offenses...*

*"Violence caused by reckless and irresponsible speech is a major alarm going off," said Speaker of the House Barbara Teague (D-CA). "We need to tone down the rhetoric. If the people won't do it themselves, then government must do it..."*

# Chapter Four

## Washington, D.C.

Dennis Trout occupied his post as Senate Majority Leader Joe Wiedersham's Chief of Staff mainly because he happened to be Wiedersham's brother-in-law. While he waited for Wiedersham to get off the phone, he cracked an office window blind to look out over the Capitol grounds and the Washington Mall. He had hardly had coffee yet and these damn Tea Baggers were already marching up Constitution Avenue toward the Capitol. Their homemade signs buffeted the morning air.

**Roses are Red, Violets are Blue**
**Anastos' is a Commie, Wiedersham is Too**

**America's Greatest Threat is Congress**

**I Love My Country; It's Government I'm Afraid Of**

Senator Wiedersham sat with his expensive Balmorals oxfords propped on his Louis XIV oak desk, cell phone pressed to his ear. His twelve hundred dollar Brooks Bros. suit and two hundred dollar haircut never fit just right on his corpulent frame. He was about fifty. Trout had taken perverse pleasure in a description of the Majority Leader broadcast by a commentator on Zenergy News Channel. He had copied it word for word in his notebook: "*...an obsequious weasel with all the moral core of a cheap streetwalker and the philosophical understanding of a ventriloquist's dummy. He makes 'greasy politician' sound almost flattering in comparison...*"

The shadow of the Capitol dome stretched all the way out to Third Street where a line of helmeted SWAT-type Homeland Security police were lined up to block the Tea Partiers. They were armed with automatic weapons. Armored riot vans sat parked in the traffic circle.

From what Trout had seen so far of the Tea Party Movement, it was composed mostly of grandpas and grandmas and hicks from the sticks who brought their kids and grandkids with them. They came to Washington with their crude signs and listened to speeches by Right-wingers such as Jerry Baer or Congresswoman Michele Bachman, afterwards breaking up to feed their kids ice cream and catch buses to see the sights. If they only knew what was *really* going on in government, they'd come armed with pitchforks and torches.

The official line in Washington was that the Tea Partiers were "violent" and "traitorous" bottom suckers feeding on "a virulent strain of anti-Americanism." It always astonished Trout at the contempt the average politician in Washington harbored for the common people. But, of course, Trout kept such thoughts to himself. He was a pragmatic man who knew which side his toast was buttered on. Marilyn was always there to remind him of how much he owed her brother; Joe was going to take him all the way to the top.

Trout listened in on his brother-in-law's phone conversation while pretending to be absorbed in the scene playing out on the Mall and in front of the Capitol. Protesters were starting to push close to the security line.

"A bunch of ignorant Homer Simpsons, a bewildered herd!" the Majority Leader spat into his cell phone. "T-shirts and baseball caps," he mocked. "Sundresses with bra straps sliding down their arms. Fuchsia bandannas and American flags wrapped around their heads. Jerry Baer's Tea Baggers. You half expect to see them wearing face paint and foam fingers and shouting, 'Hook 'em, Horns!' They'll leave a ring around Washington that even Mr. Clean can't wash out."

He laughed at his wit. A short, quick bark of disgust.

"Jerry Baer is beginning to look like Mr. Big out of a James Bond movie," he continued to the person on the other end of the phone. "Somebody's going to jam a CO2 pellet gun up his ass and he'll explode like a fat blimp."

He barked again and hung up.

"Dennis, move away from that fucking window," he snapped. "Get me the Director on the hook."

Dutifully, Trout moved to the end of the Senator's desk and used the land line to dial Vladimir Gonzalez. The Director of Homeland Security answered on the first ring. Trout handed the receiver to Wiedersham and returned to the window. Outside, leaders of the Tea Party protest halted at the security defense line on Third Street. The rest of the march piled up behind. Trout saw some people breaking out thermoses of coffee to pass around.

"What the fuck's the holdup?" he overheard Wiedersham demand of Gonzalez.

Wiedersham was one of the most powerful men in Washington, a Beltway mover and shaker, an important figure in the larger global community. "Nobody fucks with me," was how he liked to put it.

"Demonstrations are outlawed in Washington," Wiedersham shouted into the phone, hauling the Director's ass over the coals. "What part of 'outlawed' don't you understand, Gonzalez...? It's Southern populist terror... Fuck it. *Make* an incident."

Wiedersham's face was so red it looked about to explode.

"They're rioting in the streets," he raged. "These Tea Baggers have to be stopped before we have people hanging in cemeteries all over the country.... Gonzalez , quit your stalling, man. We *own* the fucking media. They're with us. They won't print shit unless we tell them to."

He hung up and swiveled in his chair to face Trout across the office. "Get away from the window," he ordered again, impatiently.

Trout turned away from the blind to face his brother-in-law. He had a bad feeling in his gut. Wiedersham and he simply looked at each other, not speaking, waiting. They didn't have long to wait. Trout flinched when he heard a sudden roar from the distant crowd, followed by popping sounds. Like firecrackers, but which Trout knew were not firecrackers.

He closed his eyes and dropped his chin on his chest. He felt sick.

## Tea Party Riots in Washington

***(Washington)***—*A Tea Party march protesting high government deficits and the National Health Care Act erupted in violence in front of the U.S. Capitol this morning when gunshots rang out from several points in a crowd estimated to number at least ten thousand. In self-defense and out of fear for their lives, Capitol Police and Homeland Security Police returned fire. Three Tea Party members were reportedly killed and four wounded. One Homeland Security officer suffered a sprained ankle. Fifteen leaders of the march were arrested and charged with inciting to riot...*

# Chapter Five

## Tulsa

Detective James Nail's daughter, Jamie, 19, lived in a modest second-floor apartment on Cherry Street, the closest thing Tulsa had to Greenwich Village or the French Quarter. Off-duty after the abortion at Mickey D's, James Nail limped up the outside stairway to his daughter's door. He wore his Glock-22 strapped butt forward underneath his jacket and his shield on his belt. He let himself into the apartment using his key. He walked through the kitchenette—dirty dishes in the sink—to the cluttered living room. Messy, like her mother. He heard the shower running.

"Girl, you *know* how I hate to wait!" he sang out.

"Oh, Daddy!" came the cheery, gurgling-water response.

"It's your mother's birthday. We only have a couple of hours to shop before I go on duty."

"Daddy, you're divorced. You don't have to remember Mama's birthday."

"If *she* hadn't been born, we wouldn't have *you."*

"You old silly. You're such a romantic. Even if you buy her a present, she won't let you come in the house."

"You can say it's from the milkman."

Jamie giggled. "There's coffee on. Pour cups. I'll be just a minute."

Nail returned to the kitchenette. The pot was on the stove. He poured a cup and looked in the frig for cream. Leftovers from days before, a banana turned black... Again, the mess made him think of Connie. She divorced him three years ago after Jamie turned sixteen and started driving.

"You've changed, James. You're not the man I married."

*No shit, Dick Tracy.* For God's sake, he wasn't toting up numbers on a spread sheet or calling on clients to sell widgets and gadgets. *His* clients were generally dead, shot or stabbed or ground up in a wood chipper, dumped in old septic tanks, boiled, burned, dissected...

"You come home smelling like death. I can't stand it anymore. I don't think you feel *anything*."

He located evaporated milk still in a can. He scraped crust from around the opening and made his coffee blond. Before carrying the cup to the table, he opened a closet door and looked inside. Ragged men's jeans and political-slogan T-shirts cool with campus radicals. One had the likeness of Che Guevara wearing his revolutionary black beret. Another displayed President Patrick Wayne Anastos' campaign slogan: *Hope and Change.*

"What are you doing, Daddy?"

He hadn't heard the shower turn off. She wore a terrycloth robe with a towel wrapped around her long black hair. Her face glistened with diamond water droplets. Amazing how much she looked like her mother when Connie was nineteen. Except for the seawater blue eyes; they were like her father's.

"I was making sure he wasn't hiding in here," Nail said.

"Rupert's afraid of you, Daddy."

"Because I compared him to a rare bird?"

"I don't think a yellow-bellied scum sucker is actually a bird."

"You think?" He fanned through the other T-shirts. "I'm still not convinced his skinny butt isn't hiding in here."

"Rupert is not skinny. He's—"

"—scrawny?"

"I was going to say revolutionary *lithe.*"

She dried her hair. He poured another cup of coffee and slid it across the table to her place. She took a hurried sip and dashed back to the bedroom. Nail heard her getting dressed.

"You're so old-fashioned, Daddy," she called out from behind the door. "People like Rupert with courage and foresight are helping President Anastos bring social justice to America."

"We should have sent you to Oral Roberts University instead of TU."

"The capitalist system is broken, Daddy. We must change the future in order to restore hope."

Nail sighed. Like a lot of Americans, he was too busy with a job and day-to-day life to pay a lot of attention to politics. On election day, he had had two dead bodies in a northside Kentucky Fried Chicken and a suspect exchanging bullets with cops. The polls were closed by the time he took the perp into custody.

He sipped his coffee. "Damn, daughter. This oil spill you call coffee would melt a ten-penny nail."

"It'll put hair on your chest," she teased back.

"Then what happened to Rupert?"

She laughed, refusing the bait, and came out in jeans and a blue low-necked T-shirt. At least it didn't have a slogan on it.

"Rupert won't drink it either," she said.

Nail pushed his cup aside. "That's one thing we have in common."

"You have to give him a chance, Daddy."

"I will—as soon as he gets a job."

She sat down and smiled patiently across the table. "He has a job."

"Community organizer is not a job."

"Daddy, let's call a truce and go shopping?"

Jamie purchased a bracelet for her mother's birthday, Nail a sweater he thought she might like, as long as she didn't know it came from him. Jamie hooked her arm through his elbow and they strolled to the Food Court for cold drinks while she rambled on about an event at school during which a student got his nose ring caught in his girlfriend's earring.

"Daddy? Earth calling Dad. You're not listening."

"Of course I am, kiddo. You know how transfixed I am over dudes wearing nose rings and high heels."

She giggled. She was accustomed to his sarcasm. They purchased Cokes and found a table next to one of the TVs turned to a news channel. The screen showed protesters at the U.S. Capitol Building being dispersed with tear gas and gunfire. An elderly woman overturned her wheelchair in the panic and people stampeded over her. The crawl at the bottom of the screen listed the death toll at three.

"Kiddo, about Saturday?" Nail ventured.

She looked up at him, a soda straw between her lips. "What about Saturday?"

They'd had these conversations before, he the over-protective parent, she the newly-emancipated daughter guarding her independence.

"I suppose Rupert will be out at the ORU Center with all the other crazies waving their signs?"

"Daddy, Rupert is not crazy. People are justifiably outraged. Jerry Baer is the reason the rednecks hung that census worker in the cemetery."

"I suppose Baer put the noose around the guy's neck?"

"He's *responsible* with his hate rhetoric. We have to let him know he's not welcome to spread his venom in Tulsa."

# Jerry Baer: They'll Destroy Me

***(New York)**—Jerry Baer, the most-listened-to personality on U.S. TV, said he feared for his life and expects to eventually be destroyed, one way or the other. He became a media sensation through Zenergy News Cable and a popular TV program that placed him at the top of his enemies' list. Senator Joe Wiedersham's (D-Ill) introduction of the FAD (Fairness of Airwaves Doctrine) Bill was initiated in response to widespread fear over hate-speech and Baer's unfounded allegations that President Patrick Wayne Anastos' White House is full of Marxists and communists.*

*"It's unpatriotic at this time of war and economic crisis to criticize the government," Wiedersham said. "We're simply not going to tolerate those who stand in the way of national security and progress..."*

*Baer follows a long tradition of paranoia-peddling dating back to the Great Depression. Like "Lonesome Rhodes" in* A Face in The Crowd *(1957), Baer has a special loud-mouthed, alarmist knack for keeping riled up the uneducated, God-fearing, flag-waving, NASCAR-loving, country music-listening trailer trash in more backward regions of the nation.*

*"Everything in Washington is all screwed up," Baer railed on a recent show. "The pot is boiling with political correctness, economic takeover by the government of private businesses, abuse of civil rights, corruption and an administration determined to trample the Constitution in order to 'fundamentally transform' our country. We're under attack by our own government. A witch hunt has already started for dissenters, seditionists and obstructionists. And I'm not going to shut up about it. They can ban me from the airwaves, outlaw what I say, slander me and charge me with sedition—and I'll still speak out. From prison or on street corners if I have to. The only way they can destroy me is with a bullet to the head..."*

# Chapter Six

## Washington, D.C.

Dennis Trout paused inside the doorway to *The Fountains* on 6th Street to let his eyes adjust to the club's low light. His boss, Majority Leader Wiedersham, would rather be caught in a Wal-Mart or a McDonald's than in a place like this. *The Fountains* was tucked back in a strip mall behind a camera store and a bail bondsman. Bail bonding thrived in D.C. Not because of politicians, who were rarely ever brought to task for their misdeeds, but instead because the city was about seventy percent poor African-Americans.

It was "Happy Hour" and the place was jumping. Trout spotted Judy at the far end of the bar. She waved. He dodged through the crowd of working class stiffs toward her. It was a joint with eats, a honky-tonk, as Judy called it, but he didn't have to worry about being recognized here. He had removed his coat and tie and left them in his BMW to avoid looking too much out of place.

"Darling," he muttered to the Lady Clairol blonde as he pecked her lips and collapsed on the stool she had reserved for him. He slumped with his elbows on the bar and ordered a Whiskey Sour from a barmaid wearing a short skirt and apron and in her red hair a blue ribbon that looked as bedraggled and unwound as he felt.

"What's wrong, dumpling?" the blonde asked.

Trout sighed. "I guess you heard what happened in front of the Capitol?"

A blank look on her face.

"Maybe not," he said. Her TV tastes ran more toward *Oprah* and *As The World Turns*. "The Tea Party people?"

"Oh. You were at the riot?" she said, squeezing his hand in sympathy.

"It wasn't really a riot."

"It wasn't?"

Her unawareness of current events astounded him. It shouldn't have. After all, her innocence was part of what attracted him to her—other than her spectacular boobs and good legs. She was about thirty, a few years younger than Trout. Tonight, she wore faded fisherman's jeans frayed at the thighs and cuffs, a low-cut lace blouse that revealed a lot of cleavage, and the gold-plated locket on a neck chain that Trout gave her. Her mouth was too wide, her nose and her brain too small.

She wore too much makeup. Trout's wife Marilyn, had she known about Judy, would have described her as low class.

The barmaid with the droopy ribbon returned with his drink. "Here you go, honey."

"Do you have a table available?" he asked, looking around.

"There's an empty one in the corner," replied the barmaid, whose name tag introduced her as *Brandi*. "You folks going to eat?"

Trout picked up his whiskey and Judy's martini. "Do you have a menu?"

Brandi pointed. "It's up on the wall."

"Of course it is."

Judy followed as Trout wended his way through the noisy patrons to a round, bare table in a dim corner. He moved his chair across from Judy's and tossed off a long draught from his glass and waited for the liquor to hit his stomach and spread its relaxing warmth through the rest of his body. Judy waited, watching him. She knew his routine by now.

"Damn!" he exclaimed, shaking his head. He finished off the drink and lifted a finger at Brandi for another one.

"You drinking on an empty stomach," Judy pointed out.

"I have to be at least half-drunk before I go home. Marilyn has something planned for us tonight with her society friends."

"Politicians?"

"Everything in Washington is about politics. We're all mad. Sometimes I feel like I'm trapped in a Lewis Carroll novel."

Judy was lighting a cigarette. She looked puzzled.

"Lewis Carroll," Trout snapped. "*Alice in Wonderland.*"

"I ain't stupid," Judy protested.

"Put out that damned cigarette. That's one vice I can't stand."

She stamped the cigarette out on the edge of the table and flipped the butt on the floor. "What vice *can* you stand?" she asked.

He took her hand. "Sorry, baby," he said. "If you only knew what it's like in that pit of professional parsers, bullshitters and liars. They can't get through a single day without bending or breaking the truth. God forbid anyone calls them on it. They rally around each other like a pack of wild dogs, howling and snapping while they try to hide from the people that they're robbing the people of everything they have."

"Why do you stay then?" Judy asked.

He finished off his second drink and couldn't lift his eyes to meet hers. Truth was, Washington politics and the power that accompanied them could be the most potent addiction on the planet. Being close to the seats of power was like living above all the petty limitations that curbed the appetites of ordinary citizens. Even teenage interns expected to be seated at the best tables and deferred to by their mentors' chauffeurs.

Although Trout kept promising himself he would make the break someday, he doubted he ever would. Marilyn's father had been a senior congressman from Illinois until he died last year after forty years in the House. Marilyn and her brother Joe both stumped for President Anastos' election, Wiedersham as campaign advisor. Trout had met Marilyn and Joe through his own father, who served two terms in Congress before he got disgusted and moved back home to Iowa. Trout's old man was an anomaly in the Beltway—an honest man with principle. Thinking of his father sometimes embarrassed the son at what he had allowed himself to become.

"Dennis," Senate Majority Leader Wiedersham preached, "you watch yourself, play ball with the right people and don't do anything stupid like screwing a senator's wife and you're on the fast track. Things are not going well in Illinois' Ninth District. The DNC has mentioned you as a possible candidate."

With that promise looming in his future, Trout was honest enough to confess he wasn't about to run off to Bugfuck, Oklahoma, with a bleach-blonde he had picked up in a bar one night. Things were good enough for him just like they were. Judy was his pressure valve. A roll in the rack, a good Lewinsky, and he was ready to charge back into the ring with the big boys.

She was also the only person he could really open up to, who would listen and then, most conveniently, forget; she wasn't the sharpest knife in the chef's drawer.

He ordered a third drink, straight whiskey this time.

"Hittin' it a little heavy, ain't you, honey?" Brandi observed.

"Just keep 'em coming until I say enough," Trout retorted.

He sat there seething, elbows on the table, glaring into his glass of amber liquid. He was accustomed to using Judy as his sounding board following a few drinks. After relieving his conscience with talk, he would further reduce stress by escorting her to the studio apartment he rented for her over by George Washington University and banging her brains out. If she thought she was being used, she never complained.

Suddenly, he opened up in a single blast: "They killed those people in cold blood. They were nothing but a bunch of ordinary people. They manufactured the incident. The newspapers and cable are going along to show the Tea Party Movement plotting to overthrow the U.S. Government—"

Shock immobilized Judy's over-painted face. Trout caught himself. He might have gone too far this time in revealing to an outsider that his own government was guilty of outright murder. There was a big difference between telling a bimbo *that* and complaining to her over being slighted or insulted by a senator's aide or bitching about a bill introduced by some congressman to redistribute pork money.

"Who're *they*?" Judy asked.

He had said enough. "They. Them. What the fuck's the difference?" He tossed off his drink and moved the subject around to Judy's pending trip to Oklahoma.

"When will you be returning to Washington?" he asked.

"After the funeral. My kinfolk is all gonna be in Tulsa for it."

Ron Sparks, the census official found hung in the cemetery, had been Judy's cousin.

# Chapter Seven

## Tulsa

James Nail drove past the giant Praying Hands at Oral Roberts University and parked his pickup truck in the service lot across the road from the massive stadium. He got out, belted on his holster with the Glock in it, drew on a blue vest with POLICE stenciled in gold lettering on the back, flipped a ball cap marked TPD onto his head and he was ready. He stuffed a few extra quick-tie plastic cuffs into his vest pocket. Radicals like those expected to protest the appearance of conservative TV talk show personality Jerry Baer had a bad habit of throwing things at police and forcing confrontations.

The long driveway to the stadium had been cordoned off for Baer's arrival. People were already starting to gather. Task Force Lieutenant Jack Ross, supervisor for the event, stood in full uniform at the top of the broad granite stairway that led into the convention center, looking straight down the corridor where other uniformed cops were stationed at intervals to keep the crowds pushed back and the drive clear. Lieutenant Ross was taller than Nail, a few years older, rather thin and solemn, with his bill cap pulled low to shade his eyes from the late afternoon sun. He gave Nail a friendly nod. Ross had been Nail's first supervisor years before in Patrol Division.

"I hated to call you in on your day off," Ross apologized. "But I needed every available cop, uniformed or not. If you have a hot babe on the string, I'm sure she'll wait."

"I wish."

Lieutenant Ross tipped his head toward a grassy knoll that lay behind and to the right of the swelling crowds that lined the corridor. Several hundred noisy activists wearing either ACOA (Association of Community Organization Activists) red T-shirts or PEIU (Public Employees International Union) blue Tees were creating a ruckus and thrusting signs about as though they were weapons.

**BAER THE BIGOT**

**STOP THE HATE!**

**DESTROY NAZIS!**

"The clans are gathering," Ross observed.

"More like the venal herd," Nail replied.

"I didn't realize you knew big words."

"My ex-wife is a school teacher."

A teacher on the near edge of the grassy knoll lined up her fifth graders in choir formation and led them in a chant to the tune of *Jesus Loves Us:*

*Umm-Umm-Umm,*
*Patrick Wayne Anastos.*
*He said we must be fair today.*
*Equal work means equal pay.*

*Umm-Umm-Umm,*
*Patrick Wayne Anastos.*
*He said that black, yellow, red or white,*
*All are equal in his sight.*

Ross grimaced. "All we need is a granite Anastos statue where the faithful can fall down and worship the messiah."

Nail scanned the demonstrators for his daughter. He quickly picked out Rupert Madison, community organizer and Jamie's boyfriend. Red ACOA T-shirt, red do-rag tied around long, scraggly hair, red placard bearing a yellow hammer and sickle with President Anastos' picture underneath it and the inscription **HOPE 'N CHANGE**. Nail could never understand what Jamie saw in this piece of garbage.

He was starting to feel relieved that he didn't see Jamie when he spotted her in the middle of the protestors. He turned his head away. Her mother Connie had been a "progressive" rabble rouser in college. Jamie had taken after Connie in politics as well as in good looks.

Lieutenant Ross ducked into the ORU Center to check on inside security, leaving Nail to man the supervisory post outside the big double doors. Since the auditorium was already filled to capacity, the overflow waited merely to catch a glimpse of "the Thomas Paine of this generation" when he arrived. Police had stretched rope barricades the entire length of the drive to the stadium door.

The fifth graders and their teacher continued to chant "*Umm-Umm-Umm Patrick Wayne Anastos.*" Rupert and his bunch grew louder and more obnoxious. Jamie, though somewhat more subdued than her fellow demonstrators, still seemed to be having a serious good time shouting and stamping her feet.

The sudden surge and roar of the crowds at the turnoff onto the campus from Lewis Avenue announced the arrival of Baer's cavalcade. A pair of black Suburbans with tinted windows appeared, moving slowly along the opened corridor toward the stadium's back doors. People cheered and waved every time a smiling Jerry Baer stuck his head out the back window of the lead vehicle and waved.

Nail had never watched the guy on TV. He was therefore surprised to discover that the hero of America's Tea Party Movement was a rather round-faced doughboy in his forties with unruly hair sticking out like bristles all over his pale scalp. He more resembled a baker or a used car salesman than the phenomenon that had the political community's underwear caught in the cracks of their asses.

Things seemed to be under control so far. The demonstrators were louder than ever, but appeared content to play to the Six O'clock news channels. The twin Suburbans stopped at the bottom of the broad granite stairway. Nail's narrowed eyes scanned the crowd for trouble. Anything could happen these crazy days in America.

A brace of tough-looking bodyguards with pistols on their hips jumped out of the trail car and stationed themselves fore and aft of Baer's vehicle. A cheer went up from Baer supporters while protesters went into a frenzy, yelling obscenities and threats and jabbing their placards and signs in Baer's direction. Baer alighted from his car wearing blue jeans, a white dress shirt, gray sports jacket and his trademark white sneakers. Waving and laughing with *his* people.

A well-built young woman who appeared to be in her early thirties got out of the car behind Baer. She wore navy blue form-fitting slacks, a white blouse, and a blue ribbon that set off her curly black hair and olive complexion. Pretty girl. Nail assumed she was Baer's wife.

Cops expected any threat to Baer would most likely originate from the protestors. Nail noticed Baer's head suddenly tilting toward the sky. A look of horror traced his smile into a death rictus. The detective snapped his eyes skyward in time to see a medium-sized Bell helicopter sweep in low above the domed roof of the ORU Convention Center. It bore the Channel 6 News bird on its fuselage. Nail hadn't heard it because of the constant roar of the crowd.

The chopper came in at full throttle and air-skidded to a halt above Baer's stopped vehicles. Two men wearing ski masks, sleeveless bullet-proof vests, and harnesses to keep them from falling out were crouched in the chopper's open doorway. Both were armed with squad automatic weapons instead of TV cameras, SAWs like those carried by troops in Iraq and Afghanistan. The jailhouse tat of a dragon on a bare arm from shoulder to wrist seared itself into Nail's memory.

*Oh, God! Jamie!*

Nail charged down the granite steps, his hand darting for the Glock at his belt, ignoring the helicopter as his eyes searched for his daughter. Let the bodyguards protect Baer.

The scumbags in the chopper opened fire, the sound of their weapons like the magnified ripping of sailcloth. Stunned silence in the crowd for two or three heartbeats, people trying to digest what was happening. Then panic set in. Hellish screams of terror and tramping feet as people ran over each other in sudden blind flight.

Nail raced downrange past the hood of Baer's suburban, toward where he had last seen Jamie. Bullets clanged into the vehicle, gouged a line across the pavement ahead of him, and ricocheted in all directions. He heard a shout of pain and surprise as Baer slammed to the ground, his writhing body spewing blood, painting a pinkish stain in the air.

Nail dodged to one side and emptied a full clip from his Glock at the helicopter as it darted around the sky like a dragonfly. At least it gave the assholes in it something to think about.

Salvos from the helicopter cut a swath through the massed protesters. Nail glimpsed Jamie's yellow shirt. A long-hair next to her went down hard, leaving another little pink cloud where he had been. Nail lost sight of Jamie when she dropped to her knees to help the wounded man.

So desperate was he to reach his daughter that nothing else mattered. He sailed over Baer's convulsing body and dodged around one of the bodyguards. A gunman in the chopper opened up again in his direction.

*"Jamie!"*

She popped up out of the protestors to look directly at him just before he collided with Baer's panic-stricken wife and knocked her to the pavement. He stumbled and fell on top of her. Lead sprayed the pavement around them, chipping concrete, ricochets shrieking. Something slapped against his head.

*"Jamie!"*

Everything went black.

## Terrorist Attack in The Homeland

***(Tulsa)****—Eight people were slain and seven wounded by automatic weapons fire in what federal authorities are calling a domestic terrorist attack. Among the dead are Rightwing TV personality Jerry Baer and one of his bodyguards. Federal authorities say they do not believe Baer was the primary target since five of the dead and two of the wounded were there to protest Baer's appearance at Tulsa's ORU Center.*

*"Baer was collateral damage," said Anthony Kimbrell, Regional Director of Homeland Security. "This was Rightwing terrorism from what we believe to be the same anti-government band that lynched one of our people in the Akins' cemetery. Baer just happened to get in the way."*

*The helicopter attack by machineguns occurred as an estimated 10,000 appeared to hear Baer's usual harangue against the U.S. Government. The helicopter was later abandoned at privately-owned Riverside Airport; it had been reported stolen earlier that day.*

*President Anastos issued a statement from the White House condemning the shooting and describing it as "abominable, a disgrace, proof that certain violent elements in our society who disagree with the progress we are implementing will stop at nothing... There must be recognition on the part of every American that change toward social justice and a more fair and equitable society will not be won without struggle. We are going to have to change our conversation, we are going to have to change our traditions, our history, we're going to have to move into a different place as a nation.. ."*

*The U.S. Congress is calling for increased gun control and further restrictions on hate speech, on large assemblies that might threaten the peace and stability of communities, and on inflammatory talk radio and TV. Senate Majority Leader Joe Wiedersham (D-Ill), a former Anastos campaign advisor and author of the Fairness of Airwaves Doctrine (FAD) Bill, said he and Speaker of the House Barbara Teague (D-CA) will support bills to temporarily restrict First Amendment guarantees during this crisis.*

*"We have hard-core, Rightwing elements declaring war on the United States of America," he warned. "It's a crisis with which we must contend firmly before it erupts into anarchy."*

# Chapter Eight

## Tulsa

Regaining consciousness, Detective James Nail opened his eyes to subdued lighting, lime-green walls, a muted TV on a stand, and the smell of hospital disinfectant. He attempted to sit up. Lacerating pain behind his eyes knocked him back in bed. He lay trying to blink away explosive star flashes of light.

His eyesight returned after a few moments. Lieutenant Jack Ross approached the side of the bed. He was still in uniform and appeared thinner and even more solemn than usual.

The bandages encasing Nail's skull felt tight enough to restrict brain function. He attempted to speak. Nothing came out.

"A bullet grazed your skull," Ross explained, standing above the bed. "You'll be all right in a couple of days."

"Jamie?" Nail finally croaked.

Ross seemed unwilling to go there.

"*Jamie?*"

Another explosion of pain behind his eyes. Lieutenant Ross rested a hand against Nail's chest. He slowly shook his head. He didn't say anything; he didn't have to.

The detective turned his head away and lay staring at the ceiling until dawn. For many years he had seen survivors of murder victims fall apart, wounded beyond recovery, some even committing suicide, others living the rest of their lives as though they were also dead. Had Connie thought to check on him, she would have found a man more emotionless than ever. Long ago he had learned that the way to cope with tragedy was to not think about it. Blocking off the mind was an old cop's trick learned from the mean streets of the city.

Lieutenant Ross kept vigil from his chair across the room while cops came and went in ICU. They stepped up to Nail's bedside and looked down at him. Most touched his arm or squeezed his shoulder. Nail barely noticed. The black cop known as Big C stood by his bedside for a long time.

Nurses entered to examine the patency of his IVs and take vitals. A doctor making rounds looked over his chart on the computer monitor.

"Does he know?" the doctor asked Ross.

The lieutenant nodded. The doctor left.

A sullen red sun rose out of a gray dawn to cast reluctant rays through the hospital windows. Lieutenant Ross jerked awake when sunlight touched his face. He got up to pull the shade.

"Leave it," Nail said.

They were the first words he had spoken since he learned of his daughter's fate. He continued to stare at the ceiling. Ross walked over.

"I went by Connie's house as soon as I could," he said.

Nail knew his ex-wife would blame him, irrationally.

"What do we know about the perps?" he asked in a voice as hard as kerosene.

Ross took a deep breath. "You want me to turn on the TV news?"

"I want you to tell me what we know."

"I've seen more evidence at a drive-by shooting," Ross said. "We found the helicopter and News Chopper Bob's body abandoned at Riverside Airport, along with two SAWs and spare ammo. The chopper was apparently hijacked an hour before the incident. There aren't any witnesses. The airport was closed for repairs and workers given the day off to go to the Tulsa County Fair. That's about it. TPD is out of the loop. The Feds are conducting the investigation."

Nail's eyes narrowed.

"They're already blaming Rightwing militia terrorists," Ross said. "They're saying the Defenders did it."

"Baer's dead, right?"

"Baer got in the way. At least that's the spin."

"What do you think?"

Ross shrugged. "I wouldn't believe the earth is round if it came from Kimbrell."

"Can you get me the files?"

"Tulsa Police has been ordered to stay out of it."

"Jack, they killed my daughter."

"Kimbrell wants to question you when you're able."

"Screw him."

"James, you're one tough old bird," Ross said with feeling.

Display of emotion made such men uncomfortable.

An exchange of conversation outside in the hallway saved them further embarrassment. Officer Schwartz, the uniformed cop guarding the door, a courtesy and precaution extended all hospitalized policemen injured in the line of duty, stuck his head inside.

"There's a woman here says she needs to talk to James," he announced.

"He's not talking to reporters," Ross objected.

"I'm not exactly a reporter," intruded a woman's voice. A slim young woman dressed in jeans and a red shirt squeezed past Schwartz in the doorway and entered the hospital room. She was rather swarthy with black, curly hair and dark eyes. Nail thought she looked familiar.

"Detective Nail, I'm Sharon Lowenthal."

"Have we met?"

"In a way."

She carried an arrangement of flowers in one hand and a Bible in the other. Lieutenant Ross shifted on his feet. "Well, uh, James, you obviously don't need backup. I'm going home to crash. Just tell Schwartz if you need anything."

He started out with Schwartz in tow.

"Jack, the files?"

"You'll get 'em." He hesitated at the door. "You know Deputy Johnson in the county jail? He called the station saying they've got a prisoner wanting to talk to you. His name's Logan. Joshua Logan."

"Never heard of him."

"Johnson says the guy won't talk to anyone but you. The Homies have a hold order on him. He's one of the Defenders."

That caught Nail's attention.

"Apparently he was at the McDonald's shooting and saw you there," Ross added. "That's all I know."

He tipped his head to Nail's visitor. "I'm outa here."

"Jack?"

Ross looked back.

"Jack, this is not over."

"Didn't figure it was," he said. Schwartz closed the door behind them.

"Detective Nail," the woman said when they were alone. "I came to thank you for saving my life."

# Chapter Nine

## Tulsa

A nurse popped in to Nail's room to see what was going on. Sharon Lowenthal handed her the arrangement of flowers and asked her to find a vase. Nail nodded that it was okay. The nurse bustled out.

"Refresh me on how I saved your life," Nail prompted. "I seem to have forgotten."

She approached his bedside. "I'm not surprised. I thought you were dead. You took a bullet meant for me."

He touched the bandage that helmeted his head, vaguely recalling having collided with someone in his desperation to reach Jamie when the shooting started.

"That was you?" he asked.

"If you hadn't grabbed me and thrown me to the ground," she explained, "I would have been killed along with Jerry and the bodyguard."

Tears brimmed her eyes.

It also occurred to Nail that if he hadn't crashed into this woman, he might have reached Jamie in time to save *her* instead.

Sharon sat on the edge of his bed. She placed the Bible in her lap and took his hand in both of hers.

"I'm so sorry about your daughter, Detective Nail. I've been praying for both of you."

Tears landed on his bare arm. He withdrew his hand and stuck it underneath the sheet. He looked away. He didn't want this stranger seeing the raw anguish talking about Jamie wrung from the depths of his wounded soul.

The nurse provided a welcome intercession by returning with the flowers in a vase. She smiled awkwardly while she placed the flowers on Nail's bedside stand, then quickly departed. The interruption allowed Nail time to regain his detective's composure. He felt hollow again. His face hardened. Sharon stood up with her Bible.

"Thank you for what you did," she said, looking rebuffed.

She seemed so completely sincere and open that her very presence generated a certain peace and warmth. Unexpectedly, Nail didn't want her to leave.

"I'm...I'm sorry about your husband," he offered.

She looked at him. "My husband?"

He noticed she wasn't wearing a ring. Her eyelids squeezed tight. She opened them again.

"Jerry isn't...wasn't my husband. I worked for him. Carl Patton and I produce *The Jerry Baer Show* on Zenergy Cable News. I also edit Jerry's monthly magazine *Truth*." She choked up. It took her a moment to recover. "Jerry was a good friend."

Neither spoke again for a long minute, each grieving in his own way. Grasping for something to say, Nail ventured, "They won't get away with it."

She studied him. "From what I see in the drive-by media," she said, "they've already gotten away with it."

"I *will* hunt them down."

Nail gingerly swung his bare legs over the side of the bed and sat up to face her. This time there was no sudden burst of pain. Sharon moved to steady him, but he waved her off. He felt a bit light-headed. She sat on the bed next to him.

"Are all cops so independent?" she asked.

He grimaced. "Only those who get shot in the head."

He noticed her eyes were red and swollen. She probably hadn't slept. She stared at her Bible.

"You don't believe they were Rightwing terrorists like they're saying, do you?" she said.

"Do you?"

"Jerry Baer received at least a hundred death threats every week from people wanting to shut him up. This goes deeper than you'd ever believe."

"I don't give a damn if it goes to the threshold of Hell. Somebody is going to answer for it."

"I heard you were one stubborn man."

He stood up, weaving on his feet. Sharon rose and grabbed him around the waist.

"What are you doing?" she cried in alarm.

"I'm breaking out of this joint."

"You can't even walk. There's a policeman outside the door."

"Schwartz and I go back a long way."

"Where will you go? What will you do?"

"Find who did this to my daughter."

She seemed to suddenly make up her mind. "I can help."

"I work alone."

"Don't be pig-headed. Lean on me. I have a rental in the parking lot. I'll drive while we talk."

He hesitated. She had almost as much at stake as he.

"I feel a draft," he said.

"Hospital gowns don't have backs."

"Jeez Louise!"

"I won't look. Wrap yourself in a sheet. I'll take a peek out in the hallway. By the way, where are we going?"

"I have to get some clothes from my apartment."

"And then?"

He hesitated.

"You have to talk to me if we're going to be accomplices in The Great Escape."

He glanced at the Bible she carried. He nodded thoughtfully. She was serious.

"Your average scumbag doesn't steal a helicopter and bring along buddies armed like Marines," he said. "My cop's blue radar is pinging. The hanging in the cemetery, the shooting at McDonald's, and now *this*... Cops don't believe in coincidence."

## Happy Meal Banished

***(Washington)***—*President Anastos' administration is noted for its bold public health and environmental stance. A new bill making its way out of committee will ban McDonald's from putting toys in Happy Meals as an enticement to children. The measure is designed to help fight obesity in young people.*

*President Anastos is considering signing an executive order to ban sweetened beverages like Coca Cola from being sold or consumed on all federal, state and local government property...*

# Chapter Ten

## Takoma Park, Maryland

Dennis Trout was still peeved over last night's Paul McCartney concert at the White House. His brother-in-law was an arrogant, pompous piece of work who fit right in with the Parliament of Whores in Washington. Joe Wiedersham would do anything in order to maintain power, no matter how shady, unethical or downright illegal. No man's ass was too dirty for him to kiss if it furthered his personal ambitions.

So what did that make him, Dennis Trout, who kissed the ass of the man who kissed dirty asses?

Trout didn't want to go there, not this early in the morning. He put on coffee in the kitchen and made his way to the downstairs bath where he brushed his teeth, shaved, splashed water on his face and finally studied himself in the mirror as he toweled off. There was little youthful idealism left in the face that looked back at him. He was already starting to bald, forcing him to let his sandy hair grow longer in a comb over to conceal it. *You, sir,* he self-mocked, *are no John Kennedy.*

He swigged directly from a bottle of Maalox. Someone once observed how there were more sour stomachs in Washington, D.C. than in any other capital of the world.

Marilyn had been waiting for him when he walked through the door yesterday evening after a longer-than-intended "Happy Hour" at *The Fountains* with Judy. She was already dressed to the nines. Still a handsome woman with her raven hair and green eyes. Gained a few pounds. Cultivated a dirty motor mouth, which only seemed to make her more acceptable to the politicians who made up the inner circle with which her brother Joe ran in Congress and at the White House.

"Damn you, Trout."

She called him by his last name when she was pissed.

"We'll be late for the special Paul McCartney concert at the White House with President and First Lady Anastos," she accused. "It's the event of the season, an opportunity for the President to notice you. You're behaving more like an insufferable little prick than a future U.S. congressman."

"I thought Paul McCartney was dead."

That set her off. He closed his ears and mind and let her rant, a skill he had learned over the years of their marriage.

After the McCartney concert—apparently, he wasn't dead—Senator Wiedersham and the President disappeared into the basement War Room with other senators, congressmen and White House "czars." From across the room, Marilyn shot her husband a look that expressed her disappointment in him. The look suggested he wasn't kissing enough ass to be included.

A portly man in his sixties arrived late and was immediately ushered downstairs. Talk had it that multibillionaire George Zuniga, one of the richest men in the world, and an avowed Marxist, had funded Anastos' campaign for the presidency. Trout had run across him several times and found little about him to like.

Not having been invited to the War Room reinforced in Trout's mind his status as consummate outsider. No matter how long he put up with Wiedersham's crap, he was never going to make the true inner circle of power, never be much more than a glorified gofer. Even if he were selected to run for the Illinois 9th District seat, he would still be holding down a brother-in-law job.

"Somewhere, deep down, Dennis, you have a conscience," Wiedersham once admonished him. "That's a dangerous thing to have when you're trying to do what's best for the world."

His major fault was that he *might* have a conscience?

He had drunk too much last night at the White House. Now, nursing a hangover, he burped at himself in the mirror and took another bolt of Maalox. On his return to the kitchen for a mug of coffee, he stopped and looked up the carpeted stairway to see if Marilyn was stirring. The hallway lights were still off. Good. He liked to have mornings to himself with his coffee and the cable news channels before he threw himself back into the rat race. He added honey and flavored creamer to his coffee and padded to his study.

Politicians lived and died by the daily news cycle. Trout retrieved his notebook from its hiding place in one corner of the bookshelves that lined the walls, sank into his favorite easy chair, raised the leg rest, and turned on the wide-screen TV. Even if he wasn't an inner circle guy, he could generally tell what was going on in the inner circle by the spin politicians fed the news media and the media dutifully regurgitated.

This morning, there was some more brief handwringing over Judy's cousin found hung in the cemetery, a recap or two about the terrorist attack at the ORU Convention Center in Oklahoma, and some heads talking about how the Tea Party Movement was producing extremist militias with the mindset of Timothy McVeigh. Most of the chatter this morning, however, was about the American Petroleum oil spill in the Gulf of Mexico that was pouring a couple of million gallons of crude into the Gulf every day and polluting the coastlines of Louisiana, Alabama, Mississippi and Florida, killing pelicans and mucking up the fishing industry. An environmental disaster, no doubt, but why all the coverage today after the spill had been on-going for more than six weeks?

Trout listened closely, sometimes scribbling furiously in his notebook.

Anastos' speech delivered last evening prior to the McCartney concert led the news cycle on every channel, charting what was apparently to be the government's new approach to the spill. The President appeared on screen from the Oval Office: Mr. Cool, chin arrogantly tilted, big ears like antenna to catch the populist murmur, head moving side to side in his now familiar "teleprompter wag." Something about the guy annoyed Trout. He suspected Wiedersham's own regard for Anastos extended no further than as a means to advance his personal ambitions.

"It's not the presidents who rule the world," Wiedersham liked to say. "It's the power behind the presidents."

"We have laid out a battle plan, uh, that we feel will successfully, uh, bring this greatest disaster in the history of our nation to successful closure," Anastos declared in exaggerated hyperbole from the TV screen. "What we, uh, have here is the moral equivalent of war against the, uh, oil spill that is assaulting our shores. In the same way that, uh, our view of our vulnerabilities and our foreign policy was shaped profoundly by Nine-Eleven, I think this oil spill disaster is going to shape how we think about the environment and energy for many years to come, and, uh, one of the biggest leadership challenges for me going forward is going to be to make sure that we draw the right lessons from this disaster and, uh, that we move forward in a bold way. I won't accept that we can't change our energy plan to wean the nation off its ruinous dependency on oil."

What the media talking heads said about the President's address was more revealing than the speech itself. In an age when "truth" was relative, almost everyone could be bought and sold like whores—the press, Hollywood, universities, unions, education... It seemed everyone was willing to line up for research grants, favorable legislation, insider tips, access, social perks, pork from the public trough...

Trout took a long swig of coffee. Damn, he was getting cynical! He switched channels.

Junie from *Table Talk* was spouting off as usual to a mainstream news anchor. "I say seize AP's assets right now. Take over the country. I don't care. Issue an executive order. Call it socialism, call it communism, call it anything you want."

The news anchor, who had once confessed over the air that just being in President Anastos' presence "makes shivers run up and down my leg," also demanded government action.

"Mr. President, I want to see the boot on the neck of AP tonight. I want to see finger pointing whether it's in your personality or not, to act kind of like a dictator and call the shots."

Trout had seen both Junie and the anchor several times in the Russell Senate Office Building conferring with Senator Wiedersham and other Progressive politicians. They had been bought and paid for.

Another channel aired a clip from yesterday afternoon showing a raucous mob of ACOA and PEIU union demonstrators on Pennsylvania Avenue. Although such gatherings had been outlawed in Washington, Trout saw no signs of black-clad Homeland Security Police. Just ordinary cops standing back out of the way to guarantee the demonstrators their First Amendment rights. The rowdy demeanor of this bunch, the atmosphere they created, the tenor of their protest signs throbbing against the backdrop of the White House made sharp contrast to the nonaggressive behavior of the Tea Party march that ended in bloodshed in front of the Capitol Building.

**THE PEOPLE MUST ACT**
**STOP THE OIL CAPITALISTS**

**RALLY TO STOP OIL CAPITALISM**

**PROTECT THE ENVIRONMENT**
**SPREAD THE REVOLUTION**

**THIS SYSTEM HAS NO FUTURE FOR YOUTH**
**THE REVOLUTION DOES**

Duane Smith appeared with a bullhorn to speak to the demonstrators. Smith, a community organizer and former Black Panther, was President Anastos' environmental czar.

"The President is on your side," he assured the mob. "The President wants to do what is right, but what he needs is the will of the people behind him. We have to start from the bottom up. The President needs the right atmosphere to do what he knows is right."

The mob went wild, shouting and screaming and stabbing with their banners.

"I think something has shifted this week," Smith shouted. "When we look back on the Anastos presidency, I think we will see that this week marked when Progressives became Progressives again."

Something *was* shifting. Trout could feel it. He wasn't exactly sure what. Maybe, if he were honest with himself, he didn't want to face up to what it was.

Senator Wiedersham's fierce countenance popped up on another channel. Red power tie, costly suit that didn't quite fit, narrow eyes glaring. "The way to cure this crisis is to give us more authority to act on behalf of the people..." he was saying.

Trout flipped channels and landed on the Zenergy News Network. He let out a bitter little laugh. Zenergy was "the enemy." He felt like a traitor for watching, but it provided a different take and some relief from the orchestrated collective baying of what that character Jerry Baer referred to as "the drive-by media" before he got waxed in Oklahoma.

A Zenergy reporter was interviewing a group of people in Detroit who had lined up for blocks to receive free government cash from the economic stimulus packages passed by Congress. It was a sad sort of comic relief against modern reality.

"Why are you here?" the young newsman asked a group of overweight women.

"To get some money."

"What kind of money?"

"Anastos money."

"Where's it coming from?"

"Anastos."

"And where did Anastos get it?"

"I don't know. His stash. I don't know where he got it from, but he's giving it to us to help us. That's why we voted for him. We love him."

Whereupon the women began dancing around, waving their arms and chanting, "Anastos! Anastos! Anastos...!"

Trout heard Marilyn up and about. He changed channels again. Marilyn hated Zenergy even more than her brother did. The flip landed on a CSPAN special featuring the head of the Communist Party of the USA giving a speech at a Columbia University campus rally. He was a portly man with gray hair in a ponytail, an old hippie, standing with a microphone on the august marble steps of higher learning, surrounded by students.

"The capitalist oil spill is the result of a system not fit to be caretaker of this planet," the old hippie harangued the rally goers, who responded with roars of approval. "The oil spill crisis will help provide the revolution we need. In building the New World Order, we're building it on the kind of principles we all want to live with. The Revolution is real. And we have to take up this real battle."

Trout wrote in his notebook: *They're building up the crisis of the oil spill the same way they did when they created a crisis of Health Care and nationalized it, when they nationalized the big banks and took over General Motors. They aim to nationalize energy...*

Marilyn entered the study, accompanied by her poodle Reggie, whose white hair was dyed a shocking pink. Trout was propped back in his easy chair sipping his coffee, notebook stuffed out of sight. Marilyn's raven hair was mussed and she had sleep in her eyes. Only the matching-Reggie-pink dressing gown she bought in Paris at the price of an average workers' monthly salary saved her from looking frumpy. She didn't bother taking a chair. She was on her way to the den to watch TiVo reruns of *Oprah* or *Whoopi.* That she tarried along the way was only because she had something on her chest other than a C-cup bra.

"Trout, you're about as assertive as a Chihuahua," she forthrightly accused.

He sipped his coffee and continued staring at the screen.

"It was embarrassing after the concert," she continued in an injured tone. "All the wives noticed you were the only one excluded from the meeting with the President and Mr. Zuniga. I could have died, literally died."

"Paul McCartney was excluded."

That was small consolation.

"If you have no backbone to stand up for yourself, I'll have to do it for you," she snapped. "I just got off the phone with my brother. I gave him a piece of my mind. A future congressman from Illinois ought to be treated more respectfully. Mr. Zuniga is very powerful and influential and can direct your political career like he did the President's."

She sniffed and wheeled to depart, that sycophant Reggie on her heels. She paused in the doorway and looked back.

"Joe offered us a hot tip on investments. It came directly from Mr. Zuniga," she said. Trout knew she was rubbing his nose in the fact that *she* had more access to the inner circle than he. "He suggested we buy oil shares."

He frowned. Because of the oil spill, the President had already suspended deep sea oil drilling off the coasts. Private investors would be left out in the cold if he nationalized America's energy industries.

"Not *our* oil," she clarified with another sniff. "That would be stupid. *Brazilian* oil. Joe said to sink everything we can in shares of Petrobras. It'll make us billionaires."

She left with Reggie. Trout rubbed his eyes wearily. He thought of Judy. Bugfuck, Oklahoma, might not be so bad after all. He got up and padded in his house slippers to the bathroom to take another shot of Maalox.

## U.S. Provides Oil Aid

***(New Orleans)***—*Due to environmental damage caused by the American Petroleum oil spill in the Gulf of Mexico, the White House is expected to announce today that the U.S. moratorium on deep water oil drilling will continue indefinitely. However, Secretary of State Linda Johnston said yesterday that the U.S. will provide financial aid to Mexico and Brazil to drill in the Gulf to help offset any energy shortfalls...*

*In the meantime, hundreds of people are starting to congregate on oil-stained beaches around the Gulf coast to protest oil drilling. Protestors carry signs demanding President Anastos seize control of the oil industry...*

# Chapter Eleven

## Tulsa

Sharon Lowenthal drove Nail in her rental Saturn to his apartment on South Lewis in order for him to change out of his hospital gown and purloined sheet into something more appropriate. Weak and dizzy, he sat at his dinette table to rest after exhausting himself changing into jeans and a yellow button-up shirt, over which he drew a light tan windbreaker to conceal the S&W .38 revolver stuck in his waistband. Homeland Security had seized his bloody clothing and police-issued Glock 22 as evidence.

"Do you want something cold to drink?" he asked Sharon.

She surveyed the one-bedroom efficiency as though considering the probability that the only thing in the frig if it was as Spartan as the rest of the place was a partial gallon of milk past its expiration date.

"Coke?" she requested.

He started to get up.

"I can find it," she offered, rising. He dropped back down at the table.

She opened the frig door. A sour odor assailed the kitchen. Something in a bowl had mold growing on it. There was one bottle of Coca Cola, open and flat. She settled on the last Mountain Dew and slammed the frig shut before anything alive escaped.

"We can share a drink?" she asked.

He shook his head.

"I take it you aren't married?"

"Divorced."

"I'm sorry."

"You?"

"Also divorced."

"Sorry."

"Why? You think I'm an old maid or something?"

"Don't be so touchy." He clambered to his feet, bracing himself against the back of the chair. He started to remove the bandages from his head but thought better of it. "Let's go."

"To where?"

"The county jail downtown."

"Joshua Logan?"

She drove them downtown. Nail slumped in the passenger's seat with his eyes closed, nursing his headache. Sharon turned on the radio and caught a live broadcast being delivered by President Anastos from a D.C. high school gym.

"The old order has been shaken," he was saying in his rich baritone, "the old ideas and institutions are crumbling, and, uh, a new generation is called upon to remake the world..."

Nail opened one eye. "You can't get away from that man."

She glanced at him. "Remind you of anything from history?"

"Only that I have a headache and he's making it worse."

He switched the radio to Classic Country FM 99.5. Linda Ronstadt crooning *Blue Bayou.*

Sharon stopped at a red light. "What will we learn from Joshua Logan?"

He shrugged. "That's why we're talking to him."

She waited for him to continue. He didn't. She prompted, "You said there were connections between Ron Sparks and the shooting at McDonald?s...?"

"We don't have diddley yet. It's a cinch the Homies aren't about to tell me anything. I'll have to start from the outside and work my way toward the center."

"Don't you mean *we*?" she corrected. "I have a stake in this."

He said nothing. The light turned green. She pulled on through the intersection.

"I need to help in this, James. I was with Jerry almost from the beginning. What he knew and what he said got him—and your daughter—murdered."

They were almost to the jail.

"It's too soon to speculate," Nail pondered. "The way you work a homicide is like you throw a bunch of marbles on the ground. You start picking up the marbles one by one until you get to the center."

"And Logan is—?"

"Marble number one."

Nail studied her as she looked for an open meter in the courthouse parking lot.

"I'll get to the center one way or the other," he said.

She stopped the car in the middle of a lane in order to meet his steady gaze. "*We* will," she said.

* * *

The county jail consumed the entire sixth floor of the district courthouse. By the luck of the draw, Deputy Johnson happened to be on duty, manning the security desk in front of the electronics door to the cellblocks. He was too old and too fat to work the streets anymore.

"Man, you look like—" Johnson began when Nail got off the elevator. He saw Sharon and amended the last of his statement to "—awful."

"Good seeing you too, Johnson. This is Sharon Lowenthal."

"Meecha," Johnson said. "I'm Jewish too. 'Johnson' don't sound like no Jew name, but it is. Johnski."

He laughed heartily.

"You know how to get on the right side of a girl," Nail said.

"That's what my three ex-wives say. You got my message about Logan."

"You want to bring him out?" Nail asked. "We can use one of the interrogation rooms?"

"No can do. The Feds came and picked him up about two hours ago. Custody slip says they taking him to the Homeland lockup in Oklahoma City. I've transported prisoners there before. They don't let no other law enforcement in that joint. They meet you out front and that's as far as you go."

Nail had had run-ins with Oklahoma City before, trying to interrogate homicide suspects in cases the Feds considered sensitive.

"Logan knew they was coming for him," Johnson added, "so he left this for you."

He opened a desk drawer and extracted a sealed envelope with *Nail* scrawled on it. Inside was a sheet of lined legal yellow paper filled with barely-legible handwriting. Sharon read it with Nail.

*Det. Nail. I seen you at McDonald's when the feds kilt Greg Morris so I thought you a straight arrow. One of the cops told me who you was when they arrested me. I don't got much time. They coming for me cause I know some things, like how the Defenders didn't kill Ron Sparks and who did. I know it sounds crazy, but it ain't. Ron was what you call a double agent who knowed things from somebody he knew in Washington, D.C. He was supposed to infiltrate the militia cause the militia is the only ones standing up to fight. Understand what I'm saying? He was working for Homeland, but he was really with us. Det. Nail, the commies ain't going to let me live either, sure as God made little green apples they ain't. Not much time left. I hear them coming for me...*

The letter ended abruptly. Nail took it to mean Logan had had only enough time to slip the envelope to Deputy Johnson before Homeland Security took him away.

"Anybody else read this?" Nail asked Johnson.

"I put it in my pocket so the Homies wouldn't see it."

"Much obliged."

"Nail, I'm real sorry about...your daughter and all."

# Chapter Twelve

## Tulsa

Sharon suggested Nail return to the hospital to complete his treatment. He shook his head.

"I'm apt to run into Kimbrell and take his head off. Drop me at my apartment. You have a place to stay?"

"I took a room at the Kensington."

He thought about it. "Is Baer's security still in Tulsa?"

"Ernest was sent home to Iowa to be buried. Herb, the other bodyguard, escorted Jerry's casket back to New York. They were good friends. Do I need security?"

"Whoever these people are may have intended to kill you too," he said bluntly.

They went quiet, she in sober reflection, he in dark and revengeful thought.

The route to Nail's apartment led past the ORU campus, which Sharon had avoided earlier on the drive downtown. Both glanced at the dome-topped stadium where so much blood had been spilled and where their lives had been suddenly changed forever. The stadium and parking lot were still roped off with yellow tape bearing warnings every few feet along its length: *Homeland Security. Restricted Area.* Tears filled Sharon's eyes. Nail's jaw hardened and his eyes narrowed.

"Do you think they'll try again? To kill me, I mean?" Sharon asked when they reached his apartment building, a red-brick, four-story structure left over from forty years ago when the area was known as The Restless Ribbon.

He got out of the car, but his equilibrium faded. He staggered against the open door for support. Sharon rushed around and slipped underneath his free arm.

"Lean on me."

"I'm all right."

"Don't be stubborn, Nail."

He relented. He fished in his pocket for the key to his apartment and handed it to her. She opened the door and locked it behind them before letting him down on the sofa.

"You don't have a cat or dog? Maybe a parakeet?"

"Mice."

"Yuk! Is it too late for breakfast?"

"There's a Burger King down the block."

"You're in no condition. I'll fix us something here. If you have something?"

"There are some cans of tamales and beans in the cupboard. Above the sink."

She smiled when she looked. The cupboard was as bare as Old Mother Hubbard's except for the can of tamales, one of pork and beans and a Campbell's chicken noodles.

"As long as I have a can opener, we eat," he said. "It's in the drawer by the stove."

She removed cans, employed the can opener on them, turned on two burners and found some pots below the oven.

"Jamie..." The catch in his throat made him pause. "She wasn't much for cooking either."

Sharon looked around the cramped apartment. "I can't believe she stayed with you."

"She had her own apartment over by TU. If you think this is bad, you should have seen hers. Just like her mama."

He watched her at the stove in her jeans and red shirt, a spoon in one hand, tending the pans. It had been a long time since a woman cooked for him. It was a nice feeling, even under the circumstances.

There was an old-fashioned percolator coffee pot on the back burner. She shook it, found it half-full and turned on the burner.

"You didn't answer me. Do you think I'm in danger?" she asked without looking at him.

"You said this runs deep. How deep?"

"Did you ever watch Jerry Baer's show?"

"He was some kind of conspiracy nut."

"I suppose that makes me a conspiracy nut as well. I telephoned Zenergy News this morning. Carl Patton is running *Best of Jerry* next week with a special on Thursday for the funeral. Judge Galliano will fill in until I return to New York. I fully intend to take up where Jerry left off by continuing to expose these people for what they really are."

"Which would be?"

"Marxists," she said without embarrassment. "Communists."

Nail shook his head. "I thought the Cold War was over."

She was stirring beans with a spoon. She seemed unoffended by his disbelief, as though she had been through it before.

"Did you know Virginia erected a statue honoring Josef Stalin?" she asked.

"You're kidding, right?"

"Communists are cool these days. Public schools ban American flag T-shirts, but you can wear one with Che Guevara on it. Actress Cameron Diaz toured Central America carrying a purse with a Soviet red star on it and the slogan 'Save the People.'"

He shrugged. "Hollywood is full of dimwits."

He recalled that Rupert had left a Che Guevara T-shirt in Jamie's closet.

"Those who don't know history are doomed to repeat it," she said gently, as though trying not to indict him for his ignorance of current world affairs. "Most everyone thought we had beat the Marxists, but they never give up. That's what Jerry was doing—educating America on our history and where we're heading."

She tasted the beans. "Do you have condiments?"

"In the cupboard to your right. Both the salt and pepper."

She had a nice smile, a little sad because of things, but still nice.

"We used to view communists as dangerous to the Free World," she continued. "Now, communists are teaching our kids history. Kids know about 'social justice,' but they've never heard of the gulags or the mass slaughter in the Soviet Union, China, Cambodia, and wherever else Marxism is implemented. They can give you the name of Michael Jackson's monkey and the titles of Lady GaGa's albums, but most of them never heard of Vladimir Lenin or Pol Pot. All the networks are producing programs commemorating the anniversary of Michael Jackson's death while America is burning and the emperor is fiddling."

Nail thought her a bit melodramatic. The United States was the only permanent, dependable nation in the world. It was too big and powerful to fail. America would *never* accept communism.

"Do you want to eat on the sofa?" Sharon asked.

He got up from the sofa to take a seat at the table. "I go formal when I have guests."

"Which by the looks of things isn't too often."

She dipped tamales and beans on his plate, took a share for herself and sat down. He started to dig in, but she stopped him with a sharp look.

"What?"

"Let's say grace." She bowed her head and took Nail's hand in hers. He hesitated, then bowed his head. He hadn't talked to the Big Guy in a long time.

She finished the blessing and let Nail's hand go. "Now, we eat. Today *is* Sunday, right? Don't you go to church?"

"I'm usually working on Sunday." He kept his head and eyes lowered as he ate determinedly past the lie. Coffee percolated. Sharon jumped up and poured two cups. "Cream and sugar?"

"Black and hot."

She walked to the frig and seemed to brace herself for another foray inside it. Sighing, she turned back. "I suppose I'll have mine black and hot also."

When she returned to the table, Nail said, "You read what Logan wrote about commies. Pardon me if I find that hard to swallow."

"No harder than this coffee. How long has it been in the pot?"

"No more than a week at most."

She rolled her eyes before returning to her subject.

"I'll call New York to send me DVDs of Jerry's shows. The man insisted on exhaustive research. He didn't merely offer his opinions. He provided facts and evidence to back them up. He's the Thomas Paine of our generation. The Tea Party movement started with him. He's the major reason why the Anastos administration is trying to shut down opposition media."

"So the commies *are* coming?" he asked derisively.

"Do you recall when Nikita Khrushchev came to the United States?"

"I wasn't even born. You weren't either, unless you're a lot older than you look."

"If that's an off-handed compliment, thanks. This is how Khrushchev said it would happen: 'You Americans are so gullible. You won't accept communism outright, but we'll keep feeding you small doses of socialism until you finally wake up and find that you already have communism. We won't have to fight you. We'll so weaken your economy that you'll fall like overripe fruit into our hands.'"

"You're beginning to sound like Big C Brown."

She lifted a brow.

"One of the biggest and meanest detectives you'll ever meet and an old friend who goes back to the first war in Iraq," he explained. "Big C is always talking about black helicopters, concentration camps, foreign troops in Tulsa and Albuquerque, a secret army, commies in the White House..."

"You're making fun of me, James."

He threw out his palms. "I'm listening." It was better than talking about other things that only further depressed them.

"In 1963," she went on, undeterred, "the Communist Party USA listed the goals it must accomplish in order to turn America socialist.

You tell me which of them it has accomplished so far or is about to accomplish."

Her passion intensified as she set down her coffee cup and began ticking them off on her fingers one by one:

"Capture one or both political parties;

"Gain control of the media;

"Exert influence over book reviews, editorial writing, and news content;

"Dominate key positions in radio and TV to make programming decisions;

"Infiltrate churches and replace revealed religion with social religion;

"Exclude public prayer on the grounds that it violates separation of church and state;

"Discredit the U.S. Constitution by labeling it inadequate and old-fashioned;

"Discredit America's founding fathers;

"Ban private ownership of all firearms;

"Infiltrate and gain control of labor unions;

"Nationalize healthcare, banks, energy and other institutions;

"Destroy the family as an institution by encouraging promiscuity and easy divorce;

"Collapse the economy...

"Feel free to stop me at any time."

Mel Gibson in *Conspiracy Theory* was a nut, but it turned out he was right. Still, that there was a communist cabal working under the auspices of the U.S. Government to subvert and take over the country made no sense whatsoever. Nail shook his head in denial. It was all too overwhelming. Next thing he knew, he'd be out with Big C looking for black helicopters and secret extermination centers.

Sharon was not going to let him off the hook. Like she could read his mind.

"Anyone who believes in Marxists is labeled a conspiracy kook wearing a tin foil hat and lumped with people who see UFOs and Bigfoot," she said. "It was Marx' idea to discredit and delegitimize opponents by marginalizing them. If that didn't work, you sent them to re-education camps or liquidated them."

Nail was ready to let it drop and move on. "If they—whoever *they* are—wanted Baer dead, why didn't they simply assassinate him without making such a big production of it? All those other people didn't have to die."

Sharon sighed. "You have to know and understand Marxism. Marxists thrive on fear and intimidation. They have to create a threat, an enemy at the gates, in order to justify draconian measures for the public safety. You can see the spin in the drive-by media. News sources depict the militias and Tea Parties as threats to the peace, safety and freedom of the country. That justifies building a private domestic anti-terrorism force and taking measures like the Fairness of Airwaves Doctrine to close down opposition. Murdering Jerry is another step in our government's reign of terror to take over the nation. We're all fools if we think they're going to stop with this."

Nail stared deep into his coffee, still unconvinced. "Right now, I'll settle for nabbing the maggot with the big tattoo."

She gave up. "So where do we start since Logan is out of reach?"

"I'd like to take a look at that chopper, but I'm sure they won't let us near it. That leaves us with a couple of minor league marbles like Rupert."

"Rupert?"

"My daughter's boyfriend. He's a community organizer for ACOA and PEIU. I'd like to know who ordered him to bring out the troops to be fodder at ORU when this thing went down."

"And the other lead?"

"We might be interested in who shows up for Ron Sparks' funeral."

"You're not dismissing Joshua Logan's note?"

"You can't dismiss anything when you're starting from zero," he said. "We begin with Rupert after you wash dishes."

"We start tomorrow morning," she corrected him. "Even God rested on Sunday—which I suggest you do in your condition. I have a feeling we're going to need every advantage we can get."

She pushed away from the table and gathered dishes for the sink. He watched her. It seemed he may have taken on a partner.

"I suggest we take a drive to the Kensington and pick up your luggage," he said. "You'll be safer here."

## Murder Conspirator Slain in Escape Attempt

***(Oklahoma City)***—*The suspect jailed in a murder plot to assassinate undercover Homeland Security Agent Ron Sparks, who was posing as a federal census taker, was shot and killed Sunday afternoon while being transported to a more secure federal facility in Oklahoma City. Anthony Kimbrell, Regional Director of Homeland Security based in Oklahoma, said Joshua W. Logan, 38, died on the scene yesterday after he attempted to forcibly escape from two agents who were driving him from Tulsa to Oklahoma City for confinement and trial...*

# Chapter Thirteen

## Tulsa

"Welcome to the New World Order, sleepyhead."

The aroma of frying eggs and bacon and boiling coffee. Nail sat up in bed, not sure where he was for a moment; he was accustomed to batching it with coffee and a bagel for breakfast. Sharon leaned casually against the door frame to his bedroom with her arms crossed and a half-smile on her lips. She looked scrubbed and refreshed in a pair of form-fitting black slacks, medium high heels, and a blue blouse with a ribbon tied at the throat. There was a matching blue ribbon in her hair. She had already made a run to the Safeway, judging by the smells coming from the kitchen.

"I hope you don't mind," she said, still smiling. "I used your shower after I cleaned two dead crows and a Petri dish from your frig. I'm happy to report that nothing attacked me in the process."

He looked her over. She used makeup sparingly. She didn't need it. "That shower never did for me what it does for you," he said approvingly.

"Thank you, sir."

Last night she insisted that the patient sleep in his own bed. She had washed and dried a sheet and a pillow case in the Laundromat next door before building her nest on the sofa. She must have been up and about for some time, although Nail was sleeping so soundly he hadn't heard her.

"The smell from the kitchen is enough to clog arteries within a three-block radius," he commented, smiling his appreciation.

"You don't look like you have cholesterol issues."

He sat bare-chested in bed, wearing only the bottom of an old pair of Army sweats. Sharon's presence in his bedroom—well, *almost* in his bedroom—made him suddenly uncomfortable. She walked to bedside to inspect the bandages on his head.

"I picked up some fresh gauze and antibiotic cream," she said. "We need to change the dressing after you shower and get dressed."

She turned and walked out, smiling back over her shoulder. "Hurry. Breakfast is almost ready."

She waited to ruin his day until he limped from the shower wearing khaki trousers, hiking boots, a white button-down short-sleeved shirt and carrying a gray summer sports jacket over one arm. The little .38

S&W was tucked into his belt. She set a plate of food in front of him at the table and took her place across from him before she sprang a copy of The Tulsa *World* on him.

He shot her a quizzical look. He was hungry, ravished; he took it as a good sign. Then he lost his appetite when the headline jumped out at him.

**Murder Conspirator Slain in Escape Attempt**

His jaw tightened. He looked up. She was watching his reaction.

"What do you think now?" she asked.

"Cops don't believe in coincidences."

"Neither did Jerry Baer."

He didn't think he was hungry after such a jolt, but he cleaned his plate and swigged another cup of coffee. Made fresh this morning. Nail had some calls to make. Sharon cleaned the table and washed dishes while he worked the phone. He started with Lieutenant Jack Ross.

"Where the hell are you?" Ross demanded. "Schwartz said you left the hospital yesterday morning with your bare ass flapping in the breeze and he hasn't seen you since."

"I had things to do."

"Obviously. With the pretty young woman?"

"I do have a life, believe it or not."

"Kimbrell's been asking about you after he couldn't find you at the hospital."

"Isn't it funny how his name keeps popping up every time there's a dead man. Jack, what do you know about the Homies capping Logan?"

"Only what's in the news last night and this morning. James, I'm advising you to get in touch with Kimbrell. Talk to him man to asshole."

"Jack, how about the ORU file?"

"Kimbrell is threatening to issue a material witness warrant for your arrest."

"I'll ponder it."

"We can't hold your home address from him much longer. You're officially on medical leave. How's your head?"

"Fine. The file?"

"Remember Toby, runs the Quik Trip on Lewis Avenue? Helped us in the Morgan girl murder? I'll have a squad car take the file by there. There's not much in it. The Homies are keeping all the working reports under lock."

"I owe you one, Jack."

"No more than I owe you and Big C over the years. That reminds me. Big C needs to talk to you."

"I'll call him when things settle down."

He hung up. Sharon shot him an inquiring look from the sink where she was elbow deep in dishwater suds.

"I love to see a woman in the kitchen where she belongs," he said, trying to lighten up things.

"Barefoot and pregnant too, I suppose."

Neither of them was in the mood for more banter. Nail picked up the phone again. He had been putting off calling his ex-wife. He dialed. She answered on the fourth ring and he could tell she had been crying. He heard voices in the background. At least she wasn't going through this alone.

"Connie...?"

That was as far as he got. She went off on him, screaming and shouting into the phone. He finally had to hang up. He dropped his chin in his palms and sat staring at the phone. Sharon dried her hands and came up behind him to place a hand on each shoulder. She smelled of *Dawn* soap.

"She's blaming me for... for Jamie," he said in a strained voice. "She had a hell of a birthday."

"James...? James, she's grieving."

"Sharon, I tried... I couldn't get to Jamie in time."

He batted his eyes.

"I blame myself," he said.

## Federal Judge Strikes Down Oil Ban

***(New Orleans)****—U.S. Federal Judge Orville Fielding struck down the Anastos administration's ban against deepwater oil drilling in the Gulf of Mexico following the disastrous AP oil spill that continues to leak about two million gallons of oil daily into the Gulf...*

*The White House promised an immediate appeal...*

*White House spokesman Dewey Gubbins said President Anastos "is not trying to put oil companies out of business... He believes either Big Oil act more responsibly or it will leave government no choice but to take more control..."*

# Chapter Fourteen

## Washington, D.C.

Senate Majority Leader Joe Wiedersham was hosting an important meeting in the conference room of the Russell Senate Office Building, the exact details of which Dennis Trout had not been made privy. He was routinely excluded from such meetings even though he had been his brother-in-law's chief of staff for the past three years. Wiedersham normally called the meetings before major legislation was introduced—like the TARP bailout funds for General Motors and Goldman-Sachs, the Healthcare and Finance Bills, FAD—or when the President was about to sign new Executive Orders to impose additional federal regulations on the nation.

Trout nursed his resentment and tried not to show it as, like a good gentleman's gentleman, he escorted arriving participants to the big soundproof conference room down the hall from Wiedersham's office and made sure there were fresh *hors d'oeuvres* and coffee and that the bar was stocked with drinks and mixes. His eventually becoming *Congressman* Trout depended on playing ball with the Big Boys, getting his toast buttered on the right side.

The meeting, Trout noted, and which he later recorded in his notebook, seemed restricted to some of the top players in the continuing economic crisis. One of the first to arrive was veteran Congressman Frank Barnes, chair of House Ways and Means. Openly gay, he was flaming down to his limp wrists and a lisp. A year ago, he got caught up in a scandal involving his "partner" operating a homosexual prostitution ring out of Barnes' Washington apartment. Barnes naturally had the support of the Washington establishment. The media dutifully glossed over the incident and Barnes won reelection from Massachusetts. Voters, Trout had discovered with growing cynicism, paid little attention to what went on in the rarified air along the Potomac. All they cared about was that their representatives bring home the bacon and keep the entitlements coming.

Duane Smith arrived in the company of Speaker of the House Barbara Teague and Senator Harry Roepke (D-PA), who headed the White House Economics Commission. Ms. Teague's losing battle to retain eternal youth included Botox injections that turned her face into a big-eyed mask in which only the lips and eyelashes were capable of movement. Harry Roepke wore a wig and had his nails, hand and foot, done weekly at taxpayer expense. Smith, the White House Environmental Czar, was also president of the powerful Public Employees International Union, PEIU, and had recently assumed a position on the Board of Directors for the SIDA Corporation.

Curious, Trout had conducted some research on SIDA. It was not listed publicly anywhere, but he discovered a document on Wiedersham's desk touting the Serious Infectious Diseases Association as an enterprise created "to design and develop novel countermeasures to prevent and treat serious infectious diseases with an emphasis on biological warfare defense and...to develop population control measures through military application in a crisis." Whatever that entailed.

Two or three other senators and congressmen and a like number of industrialists completed the small congregation of movers and shakers. George Zuniga kept the others waiting and the meeting held up until he arrived with his bodyguard. Wiedersham met them personally to escort them to the conference room.

Trout thought Zuniga one scary-looking dude. Brushy gray brows arched like the overhang of caves inside which lurked dangerous black eyes that coldly surveyed his surroundings like carnivores casting for prey. A broad nose. Meaty lips that resembled bloated leeches and looking as if they might drop off his face if he smiled. His accent was thick and sinister. Somewhere in eastern Europe from which region Christians thought the Antichrist might appear. Trout always thought the Antichrist would be younger.

It was said the wealthy financier required no invitation to the White House; he dropped in unannounced anytime he felt like it.

Zuniga and Wiedersham walked past Trout as if he were a permanent fixture, like a wall or a door. Trout obediently fell in behind. The burly bodyguard looked him over suspiciously before taking up his station outside the door to the conference. No sound leaked out of the room. Trout started to return to his office. Wiedersham stopped him.

"Hold up, Dennis. Mr. Zuniga, I'd like to introduce Dennis Trout, my chief of staff as well as my sister's husband."

Zuniga's dark eyes appraised Trout. His expression remained unchanged.

"Zee next congressman from the state of Illinois?" he said in his thick accent.

A thrill of delight ran up Trout's spine. He actually blushed. Joe must have put in a word for him. "Well, sir. Not yet."

"Are you zee team player, Dennis Trout?"

Trout glanced gratefully at Wiedersham. "I like to think I am, sir."

"Zen you most certainly *will* be considered to be zee next congressman from Illinois. Someone from my office will contact you soon with zee details."

He entered the conference room. Wiedersham tarried with Trout. "You can't lose if Zuniga funds your campaign," he whispered. "How do you suppose Anastos became President?"

Zuniga's bodyguard held the door open for the majority leader.

"Well, come on, Trout, for God's sake," Wiedersham chided. "You're on the team now. Act like it. And don't disappoint me."

Pleasure and surprise flooded Trout's soul, temporarily cleansing it of the resentment stored against his abusive and self-centered brother-in-law. He was so grateful he could have kissed the man's hand. Or his ass—except he was already doing that.

Trout felt as though his rear end was wagging like Reggie's as he trailed Wiedersham into the mahogany-paneled room where Zuniga had already claimed his seat at the head of the table. Handout reports, ballpoint pens, laptop computers, coffee cups and cocktail glasses garnished each place at the table, arranged earlier by Trout himself, who at the time never suspected he would be invited to use them. Wiedersham impatiently indicated a place for Trout to sit with him near George Zuniga at the head of the table.

Trout sat down, feeling awkward and out of place but at the same time immensely thrilled. Wait until he told Marilyn. He himself was a player now, not just some glorified gofer. Dennis Trout was on his way up. His toast was finally getting buttered. *Congressman* Trout. He liked the feel of it on his tongue.

Wiedersham stood up.

"President Anastos sends his regards," he announced, "but he cautions, along with Mr. Zuniga, I'm sure, that we not be too visible at this stage. FAD hasn't been passed yet and Zenergy News is still snooping around—although, I must say, one fewer in force than a few days ago."

That elicited a round of restrained mirth. Trout joined in guiltily, realizing that the reference was to the death of talk show guru Jerry Baer, who had been the administration's chief nemesis. Wiedersham spoke another minute or so in welcome and reminded everyone that all notes must be deposited in a burn bag before leaving the room. Then the congregation got down to business.

Ground rules and objectives had apparently been established in prior gatherings, so there was no need to restate them. Everyone seemed to be of one accord and on the same page. Trout felt as though he had walked on in the middle of a conversation. The single topic for today's meeting seemed to be the American Petroleum oil spill in the Gulf and how it could be used as a springboard to—and Trout gasped mentally when he finally understood—further depress the economy. It took him a while longer to understand *why* they wanted to collapse it.

"If Judge Fielding's ruling against us stands and allows the oil rigs to resume operation," Science Czar Harold Golden pointed out, "it will delay Cap and Trade until next year or even later. The EPA won't move far enough fast enough to allow us to nationalize oil, gas and coal. We can't afford to wait. This is our time. We have to move on it while the poker's hot and we have the people worked up to do something about the environment."

"Judge Fielding won't be a problem," Wiedersham reassured the assembly, with a quick look at Zuniga. "His ruling is already under Supreme Court appeal, on a fast track for a decision by next month. Fielding has a few skeletons in his closet which I'm sure well-directed news sources will discover and use to discredit him. If that doesn't work..." He shrugged.

Trout wondered what he meant by that.

"Louisiana alone will lose twenty thousand jobs if the drilling ban holds," Environmental Czar Duane Smith put in. "Gas prices will necessarily skyrocket to five bucks a gallon, seven when we push through Cap and Trade and carbon taxes. My people are ready to take to the streets to protest."

Sam Shrader laughed. He was chief of the Office of Information and Regulatory Affairs with almost unlimited power to impose regulations to laws passed by Congress.

"Never let a good crisis go to waste," he quipped cheerfully. "We don't care if they're our people or *theirs*, just so long as they're out there forcing us to take action to restore harmony."

House Speaker Barbara Teague with her porcelain-cast face was the only woman in the room. She followed the exchange by bobbing her head back and forth, her face smooth and blank from injections, making her appear totally clueless.

"There are thirty three oil rigs in the Gulf," she interjected. "If the President's suspension lasts only six months, it'll be too late for the oil companies to recover. AP and Big Oil will lose billions of dollars. The rigs will have to be leased out. It costs ten million dollars to move one of those things. If they move out, they won't be coming back."

George Zuniga bobbed his massive head. "Ms. Teague, it is up to you in zee House and Majority Leader Wiedersham in zee Senate to twist arms and push through legislation to nationalize energy. We are on a time table that must be met before zee next Presidential election and before zee obstructionists have time to organize resistance."

"We are well aware of the time table, Mr. Zuniga," Wiedersham said. "We are on track."

All at once it dawned on Trout what Marilyn meant about investing in foreign oil. More than twenty billion dollars in U.S. economic stimulus funds had been "lent" to Petrobras, the Brazilian nationalized oil company, for it to pursue deep sea oil drilling off both its own coasts and off U.S. shores. Trout was willing to wager a million dollars against an oil-dead pelican that Petrobras would be leasing the Gulf oil rigs. He was also willing to accept even greater odds that George Zuniga had made heavy investments in Brazil oil himself. He, and everyone who followed his lead in the venture, stood to make a ton of loot if President Anastos' ban held and the rigs went to Petrobras, even more if the administration made good on its efforts to nationalize America's energy industries.

"We'll never have a better opportunity," lisped Congressman Frank Barnes. "I think, really, what we're seeing now, we're seeing the start of the end of the capitalist system. I say good riddance. It hasn't helped people on the planet. Although I do have certain reservations that the speed of our methods—"

George Zuniga cut him off. Even his well-fed laughter had a sinister quality. His lips, Trout noted, did not fall off after all.

"Opportunity," he said. "That's what vee have to keep in mind. It is well to understand that if vee do not want zee world's wealth controlled by people with money, then zee alternative is to have zee world's wealth controlled by people with guns. What vee are doing is necessary at this stage to crumble zee government into our hands."

Muttered agreement passed through the room. In this assemblage, it was *In George Zuniga We Trust*. Trout ducked his head, unsure about whether to join in or to be appalled at the candor with which they were discussing engineering the economic meltdown of the United States. For some reason he thought of Michael Douglas' line in *Wall Street:* "Corruption is why you and I are prancing around in here instead of fighting over scraps of meat out in the streets. Corruption is why we win."

Senator Wiedersham leaned over toward Trout. "I hope you're well-invested in Petrobras, *Congressman* Trout," he said with a sly grin.

Trout grinned back, conscience assuaged. This was one of the happiest days of his life.

# Chapter Fifteen

## Tulsa

Nail and Sharon picked up the ORU police file Lieutenant Ross left with Toby at Quik Trip. They were on their way to Cherry Street where Rupert rented a pad a few blocks from where Jamie had lived. Sure enough, there was nothing of substance in the file, not even autopsy or ballistic reports. Disappointed but not surprised, Nail wheeled a left onto Cherry Street and then turned off onto side streets to avoid passing Jamie's apartment. He was sure Connie would be there either today or tomorrow to pack up their daughter's things.

Rupert lived in a seedy neighborhood of rooms for let by the night or by the hour. It was afternoon by now, the sun well up without a cloud in the sky. Nail wore a bill cap with an *AAA Quarter Horses* logo on it to conceal the smaller bandage Sharon used to dress the bullet graze to the side of his head. He could tell he was getting stronger.

As luck would have it, Rupert Madison happened to be stepping out the door of the shabby rooming house he shared with a half-dozen other downtown types with long hair, nose rings, face tats, stashes of grass in the kitchen and revolution on their fried brains. Rupert was dressed down in a red T-shirt with Mao on it and ragged ride-low ex-con jeans. He started to bolt when the tan Saturn whipped to the curb and he recognized Nail.

Nail jumped out of the car. "I'll pound your ass into the pavement when I catch you," he promised.

Rupert hesitated. Sunlight glinted off the ring in his nose. Nail walked up to him, Sharon close behind looking pale and uncertain.

"Man, you don't hafta come on me like this," Rupert whined. "I feel as bad as you do. She was my lady."

Nail clenched a fistful of Mao's T-shirt face and frog-walked Rupert into the narrows between the rooming house and a falling down privacy fence. Rupert reeked of marijuana smoke.

"James...?" Sharon whispered, looking around to see if there were witnesses.

Nail slammed Rupert against the side of the house and switched his grasp from Mao to the ring in Rupert's nose. He twisted it until tears of pain ran down Rupert's cheeks.

"We can have a conversation once we've established the ground rules," Nail said. "If you lie to me, Ru-pert, I'm going to stuff one of those fence posts up your ass. Do we understand each other?"

"But Jamie—"

Nail yanked on the nose ring. Rupert howled and rose on his tiptoes.

"Don't ever say her name in front of me again. Who ordered you to organize the demonstration at ORU?"

"Man, shi-it! That's what I do. I'm a community organizer."

Nail put an extra twist into the ring. Rupert howled some more and dropped to his knees in agony. Nail pulled him upright again with the ring.

"Let's start again," Nail suggested patiently.

"Man, I don't know who it was. That's the truth. It might have been the union. I got a phone call and this dude says roust out the troops, there'd be buses to haul 'em. That ain't unusual when Baer shows up someplace. The man's a hate magnet—"

"This voice on the phone tell you something was going to happen?"

"Man-n-n-n! They'll kill me if I say something."

"I'll rip this ring out of your fucking nose."

Tears streamed down Rupert's face and dropped on the grass. He was starting to blubber.

"He warned there would be a helicopter and for me to.... Man, ease up, you're killing me."

"Not yet." Nail tightened his grip on the ring. "For you to do what?"

"Okay. Okay. I didn't know they were going to shoot *us*, man, and that's the truth, else I'd never have gone for it. I thought it was for Baer."

"What did he tell you to do?" Nail repeated.

"Some of my people was supposed to tell the cops when they started asking questions that we heard stuff being yelled from the helicopter."

"What kind of stuff?"

"You know, like, 'This is for Timothy McVeigh,' and, like, 'Remember Waco.'"

"And you told the Homies that even after they shot up your people? And my daughter?"

"Shi-it, man! You think I wanna be dead too? I swear that's all I know. I'll have to split town if they find out I been talking to you. Now will you let me go?"

Nail released him. "Remember the fence post," he warned as he turned and limped away with Sharon trailing, she too astonished to speak until after they got in the Saturn and drove away. Nail headed south toward Floral Haven Cemetery where Ron Sparks' graveside services were about to begin.

"Do you believe him?" she finally asked.

"Sure. Didn't you notice?"

"Notice what?"

"He was so scared he wet his pants."

"Heavens! What do you think so far about what I've been trying to tell you about commies and our government?"

"We still don't know anything until we track down the voice on the phone that called Rupert. Which isn't going to be easy."

"Who do you think? ACOA? PIEU?"

He shrugged. "Somebody knows the shooters."

Sharon changed her approach. "What are we looking for at Ron Sparks' funeral?"

Again he shrugged. "We're just fishing right now."

"What are we using for bait?"

"If Sparks was really with the Defenders, there might be some militiamen there."

"Aren't the Defenders murder suspects? How are we going to recognize them?"

"If you're going to argue with logic, skip it. Keep your eyes and ears open. I've solved homicides like this when the killer showed up at his victim's funeral."

"Why would a killer do that?"

"Because. I don't know. They're all a little weird?"

He took Memorial Drive. A lot of traffic this time of day.

"James, would you really have... ? You know, the fence post?"

She looked amused. Nail looked grim.

"There's nothing I won't do to get to whoever did this to my daughter. *Nothing.*"

## Supreme Court Defines "Freedom of Expression"

***(Washington)***—*Supreme Court Justice Dianne Cagle said the U.S. Government would have the legal right to censor or ban political books, magazines and speech on radio, TV and the internet once the far-reaching Fairness of Airwaves Doctrine (FAD) bill is passed by Congress and signed into law by President Anastos.*

*"In the exercise of our First Amendment rights of freedom of expression, every person should respect the rights and reputations of others," Cagle said. "The right of freedom of expression does not extend to political propaganda against the U.S. Government or its representatives; to propaganda for war; incitement to violence; hate speech; advocacy of hatred that constitutes ethnic incitement; vilification of others; incitement to cause harm; biases on any grounds of discrimination specified, implied or contemplated..."*

# Chapter Sixteen

## Tulsa

Nail drove the Saturn between massive stone pillars that framed the entrance to Floral Haven. The cemetery might have been a well-manicured golf course except for headstones and various theme monuments—artificial waterfalls, angels, Jesus ministering to a sheep and a cow... Nail steeled himself. Jamie's funeral was this coming Thursday; her mother wanted her interred here at Floral Haven.

A narrow paved drive twined through the cemetery toward where a pavilion was erected over an open grave. Parked cars lined the road. A considerable crowd of mourners had already gathered. Nail saw Homies in dress black uniforms with rifles, waiting to administer the traditional twenty-one gun salute to a fallen soldier and comrade.

The sun was shining and women with sun-brellas were being escorted toward the pavilion. There was some low laughter, even lower voices, and a few sniffles. The scene recalled for Nail how his grandmother, who had raised him from the age of five in the hills around Tahlequah in the Cherokee Strip, used to drag him to every funeral in the county, whether or not she even knew the deceased. It was a social event. Nail had grown up horrified by waxen faces in satin-lined boxes and the scent of cut flowers. Ironic that he would have become a cop investigating violent and unnatural deaths.

"Let's get it over with," he said, turning off the ignition and getting out of the car.

"You want to tell me what we're looking for or not?"

"Clues."

"Meaning?"

"Follow me, kid."

"All you have to do is whistle."

"You a fan of old Humphrey Bogart movies?'

"Isn't everyone?"

They wended their way through tombstones towards the gathering. Sharon took his arm so they would fit in more naturally. Both avoided looking at the headstones, which reminded them of their own all-too-recent losses. From long habit, Nail's eyes scanned the crowd for anything that looked out of place. He readily picked up on a couple of men in sports coats whose shifty eyes and stand-apart attitudes didn't seem to belong. The men immediately locked on Nail and Sharon. It was like they expected him to show up and were waiting.

Nail directed Sharon's attention to them. "The two jokers this side of the old schoolteacher with big hair. Don't look now, for Pete's sake."

"How am I supposed to see the jokers if I don't look?"

He told her about Kimbrell's threat to obtain a material witness warrant for his arrest.

"How did they know you'd be here?"

"Speculation. Same as I would have done."

"Can they really arrest you?" she asked, then immediately answered her own question. "Of course, they can. They're the government. They know you're as stubborn as a pig and won't let this rest. Somebody doesn't want you nosing around."

"The feds could hold me indefinitely."

"Or you could end up 'escaping' like Joshua Logan."

"You wanted in on this. Well, you're in—up to your pretty neck."

She discreetly shot a look at the suspected undercover Homies. "Being us stinks. Let's get whatever we came for and get out of here."

A podium had been set up for the guest book. Nail pretended to sign in while he checked the names and addresses of guests. The only one that really caught his eye was an address in Washington, D.C.

"Logan's note inferred Sparks had a political contact in Washington that fed him information," he said.

He handed Sharon the pen so she could look at the name while she pretended to sign in.

"Judy Sparks-Taylor," she noted.

"We might want to talk to her."

"How do you propose we figure out which one she is, Sherlock?"

"That's why I'm the hero and you're the sidekick."

The two men were still watching them.

Nail searched the mourners for anything that might give away the Washington visitor. His eyes settled on a young bleach-blonde in jeans and sandals who wore too much makeup. Judging from the obit in this morning's Tulsa *World*, Sparks' relatives were likely poor whites out of the Cooksons and Ozarks. The bleach-blonde hung with a small group of other men and women and small children, most of whom also wore jeans or overalls. She had "Judy Sparks" written all over her, although it seemed unlikely she could be anyone's political contact in the capital.

It occurred to Nail that his hiking boots and base ball cap with the quarter horse logo on it might also label him as much the hayseed as jeans and sandals. At least he wore a jacket, if only to conceal his handgun.

He memorized Judy Sparks-Taylor's Washington address, then maneuvered to keep the crowd between Sharon and him and the two men while he discreetly attempted to have a brief word with the blonde. Someone clasped his shoulder from behind. It required all the self-discipline he possessed not to wheel around and plant one on the interlocker's jaw.

"James?" said a familiar voice.

Nail allowed himself a small grin of relief. He turned around. A big black man in a suit and tie grasped his hand in a giant mitt.

"Damn!" Nail said, glad to see his old friend. "The people you run into in places like this. Sharon Lowenthal, meet Corey Brown. Big C. I think I told you about him."

Brown bowed politely. His hand engulfed hers. "*Everybody* know Sharon Lowenthal and Jerry Baer," he said. "It a real honor, sister. Schwartz say you was pretty."

Other than being an enormous man, more than six-and-a-half feet packed into an athlete's body, Brown's other notable characteristics were a head shaved as slick as a bowling ball and the deep blue-black coloring of a Zulu warrior. He was a handsome man with thick lips and a long, thin nose slightly crooked, as though once broken and never properly set. Boxers had noses like that. There was something in the dark humorous eyes that immediately engendered trust.

"You're African-American!" Sharon exclaimed in surprise.

"American," Big C corrected her with a smile. "I was born in Mississippi, grew up in Oklahoma."

"It's just that when James said... You know? Black helicopters and everything. I expected someone different."

Big C chuckled, the sound of a lawn mower starting up. "I read *Truth* magazine and watch Jerry and you on Zenergy," he said. "You done convert our friend here to the truth yet?"

"I'm working on him."

"He stubborn."

"I suspect it runs in his friends as well."

"Could be," the giant replied affably. The top of Sharon's head barely reached his chest.

"Big C was Jamie's godfather," Nail explained to Sharon. Both men looked at their feet. When they regained control of their emotions, Nail went on. "C and I were partners on the SWAT/TAC Squad."

Big C squeezed Nail's shoulder. "James here one of the best police snipers you ever see. He made this shot one time—"

Nail shook his head for C not to go on. Sharon regarded both of them curiously.

"I keep finding out new things," she said.

"He got layers like a cabbage," C said. "You have to keep peeling 'em off. Dude save my black ass in the old days. Took a bullet for me."

"Now I'm stuck with him for the rest of my life, 'cause that's the rule," Nail said. "C, you didn't say what you're doing here."

"Ron had a cousin from D.C."

"Judy Sparks-Taylor. How did you know Sparks?"

Instead of answering, Big C turned his head to check on the two Homie plainclothesmen.

"James, them feds are here to arrest you," he warned. "I find out hour ago a warrant issued. Jack Ross call and say I see you, tell you stay hid until he get it sorted out."

Kimbrell hadn't wasted any time. One of the two Homies took a folded magazine from his back pocket and opened it. James saw the title: *Truth.* The Homie looked at the magazine, looked up.

Sharon tensed. "My picture is on the masthead," she said. "James, I think it's time to go."

"C, you got an idea which of these people is Judy Sparks?" Nail asked, not taking his eyes off the feds.

"I be looking at everybody come in," Big C said. "I figger she the cheap-looking blonde in jeans."

"Joshua Logan wanted to tell me something about Sparks," Nail said. "But he's dead now."

"Folks have a habit getting that way lately."

Sharon tugged at Nail's jacket sleeve. "James..."

Big C looked back over his shoulder. The two feds were walking toward them.

"Slug me, James," Big C suggested quickly. "When I go to grab your arm, you go hit me right on the chin hard as you can."

"What?"

"Do it. But maybe not *that* hard. James, you got my cell number, right?"

The feds broke into a trot, weaving their way purposefully through the mourners. Big C grabbed Nail's arm, as though to detain him.

"Now!" he hissed.

"Sorry, pard." And Nail unleashed a hard fist that caught his big friend on the point of the chin. Brown dropped to the ground. Sharon emitted a muffled, surprised scream. Nail grabbed her hand and bolted with her toward their rented Saturn. The crowd reacted with astonished cries. Someone yelled, “Halt!”

A quick glance over his shoulder revealed to Nail what Big C had in mind. Acting half-dazed from being slugged, the big cop lurched to his feet and plowed into the feds as they rushed by in pursuit, bringing both of them to the ground with him in a tangle of arms, legs and curses.

Sharon ducked around to the other side of their car and jumped in. Nail kicked over the engine and jammed the gas pedal to the floor. The Saturn fishtailed, squalling rubber.

“You know how to show a girl a good time,” Sharon managed as Nail squealed the vehicle onto Memorial, barely avoiding a collision with a honking delivery truck going one direction and a low-rider full of illegal Mexicans going the other.

# Chapter Seventeen

## Tulsa

The enraged Homies would never be able to prove Big C bumped them down deliberately. By the time they untangled themselves and reached their vehicles to chase Nail and Sharon, the tan Saturn was already gone in the heavy traffic on Memorial. They would not get within a mile of Nail now, not with his kind of head start. Local police would be of little help; few of the TPD cops would seriously try to hunt down one of their own, not on some phony "material witness" warrant.

Holding his face with both hands, Big C clambered to his feet and staggered around in a daze. Through splayed fingers he spotted the busty bleach-blonde looking horrified from all the excitement. He stumbled his way toward her. People were exclaiming over his injury, but no one offered to help, their reluctance to get involved perhaps due as much to his size as to his race.

He dug a fingernail into his skin so blood leaked between his fingers by the time he reached the blonde. She attempted to get out of his way, but he intentionally tripped and plunged into her, bringing her to the ground with him. The ruse had worked once with the Homies.

Effusive with apology, he struggled to his knees and had to wrap his arms around the woman's shoulders to keep from falling again. Denzel Washington couldn't have given a better performance. Once a personal contact was made, it brought out the Good Samaritan in people whose souls weren't already corrupted and hardened. The blonde braced herself to support Big C against her body.

"I all right, miss," he wheezed. "Let me catch my breath. I'm a cop."

He managed to extract his badge case. Flashing the shield made him the good guy automatically. He felt the blonde relax. He was on his way to gaining her confidence.

"I'll call you an ambulance," she offered.

"No, no. I be okay. Don't let go just now 'cause I sure enough fall flat on my face. It's a face enough to stop traffic like it is."

People gathered around out of curiosity. The funeral ceremony went on hold. Only the Homeland Security Honor Guard remained in place since no one authorized it to break ranks. Someone handed the blonde a handful of tissues. She used them to apply pressure to the cut on Big C's cheek.

"It ain't hardly nothing," she diagnosed. "That was a bad man that hit you?"

"Bad to the bone," Big C agreed, hamming it up. "I come pay my respects to Ron and I recognize that dude wanted on a felony warrant."

"What do you reckon he was doing here at the cemetery?" she asked.

"I was asking him just that when he catch me off-guard. It won't happen again."

"You sure enough you don't want to go to the hospital?"

"I stay. Won't nothing keep me from paying respects to a friend."

"You was friends with my cousin?" she asked.

"Buddies. What with us both cops and all."

Which was true, in a way. Big C had become acquainted with him through the Defenders.

Big C pretended to be more unsteady on his feet than he anticipated, which prompted the girl to insist he continue to lean on her. They introduced themselves. Judy presented assorted uncles, aunts and cousins, most of whom seemed shy, stand-offish and backwards. The only thing the scene needed to complete it were dueling banjos.

Funeral services resumed after a few minutes. A preacher stepped solemnly to the head of the waiting casket. A small summer cloud came up and spat rain. Everyone who could crowded underneath the awning. There was no room for Big C and Judy. The sprinkle of rain felt cool on Big C's shaved head. Judy clutched Big C's arm and shed tears as the casket lowered into its final resting place.

Big C wondered about the blonde. On the surface at least, Judy didn't appear keen enough—or deceitful enough—to be the Washington spy Ron Sparks had alluded to. She was too open and unassuming.

Nonetheless, even though he felt he might be wasting his time, C decided to go ahead and play out his hand, see what he could get out of her. She might not be nearly as dimwitted as she appeared. Besides, she was probably smoking hot underneath all that makeup, and he liked her.

# Chapter Eighteen

## Tulsa

Nail bee-lined for his apartment after escaping from the cemetery. He pulled to the curb a block away and sat in the car with Sharon until he was sure no one was staking it out, waiting for him. Logic dictated that another material witness warrant would soon be issued for Sharon now that Kimbrell knew she was with the Tulsa cop. She hardly batted an eye when he informed her of his reasoning.

"Jerry warned these kinds of things would happen once you start exposing the truth," she said.

"Slip under the wheel and keep the engine running," he told her. "I'll get our things from the apartment. I'll only be a few minutes."

"My bag's already packed by the table."

"I like a girl ready to go."

He exited the Saturn and walked down the side of the street to his apartment building. Not many cities had sidewalks anymore. Deciding it was safe, he hurried upstairs. He returned to the car ten minutes later with Sharon's bag and his old parachute bag packed with clothing and necessities. No telling when they'd be able to return. He tossed the bag in the back seat and got in on the passenger's side, dropping a small FedEx package on the seat between them.

"This came for you while we were out. Overnight express left it at the door."

She glanced at the return address. "It's the DVDs of Jerry's show I promised you and the new copy of *Truth* distributed yesterday. I had to call in changes to my piece after... after ORU. Am I driving?"

"A woman'll be less conspicuous."

"You could hide on the floorboard."

He wasn't sure if she was teasing or not. "Head north on Peoria and catch the Keystone Expressway toward Mannford when we get downtown."

"Won't they be looking for you?"

"Life is full of chances."

Nail breathed a little easier once they hit the Keystone and headed west out of the city on the heights paralleling the Arkansas River.

"I take it you have a plan?" Sharon said.

Nail grunted. He stared out the side window. Within the space of the past few hours, he and this woman he barely knew had become fugitives together wanted by the law. Perhaps it would have been best for both of them if he had remained in the hospital to answer Kimbrell's questions. Except, he suspected Kimbrell wanted him out of the way and would have locked him up, no matter what.

"So what have we detected so far, Detective?" Sharon asked, one hand on the wheel, the other punctuating the air. "We don't seem to be collecting many marbles."

Nail pulled back from her sweeping hand. "Are you Jewish or Italian?"

"Jews talk with their hands too."

"Huh!" he grunted. "All right, so we're not on the fast track."

"What do you call a fast track? I've been shot at, ended up in a strange man's apartment with mice, became an accessory to police brutality by threatening to run a fence post up a witness' posterior, got in a brawl at a cemetery, and now we're being chased by the federal government."

"I live a dull life."

He was trying to work it all out in his mind. Nothing made sense.

"Sparks got himself off'd in a cemetery and the feds laid the rap on the Defenders," he mused. "Rupert gets his marching orders over the phone so they can lay the blame on Rightwing fanatics when they were actually after Jerry Baer..."

Sharon lifted an eyebrow at him. "*They?*"

He flung his arms wide in frustration. "So I'm beginning to sound like I should be wearing a tinfoil hat. Kimbrell is up to his ass in all this. I'm willing to wager he gets his marching orders same as Rupert. Do you realize how wacky this sounds?"

"Like a man starting to wake up?"

"For God's sake, Sharon, we're talking government conspiracy here. It happens in Venezuela. Maybe in the Ukraine. But not *here* in the land of mom's apple pie."

"One of the things Jerry and I had to contend with on his program," she said, "was to understand that people in government are no different from anyone else when it comes to what they're capable of doing. They can be spiteful, nasty and deceitful. Because they think of themselves as The Enlightened doesn't mean they *are* enlightened. The only difference between a thief in Congress or the White House and a thief on the streets is that the latter snatches your purse while the former snatches your freedom."

Nail shook his head. His cell phone rang. He dug it from the pocket of his jacket and checked the number on the screen. Big C.

"You all right, C?"

"Man, you about took my head clean off."

"I'm passive-aggressive."

"James, where can I find you?"

"The Safe House?"

"That's the only thing my ex-wife didn't take. Her lawyers couldn't find it."

"Meet us there?"

"It be later. I'm with Judy Sparks. Tell you about it when I see you. Watch out for black helicopters. They starting to circle."

## Open Letter to the Tea Party

***(CPI)***—*"Your kind—mostly white folks beholden to an absurd nostalgic fantasy of what America used to be like—are dying. We just have to be patient and wait for your hearts to stop beating..."*

# Chapter Nineteen

## Washington, D.C.

President of The United States Patrick Wayne Anastos was working up the troops from the podium at the Kellogg Conference Center. Arrogant chin tilted up and out, looking down his long nose, the tell-tale wag of his head from left teleprompter to right teleprompter pacing his delivery. More than three hundred AmeriCorps platoon and company commanders from all over the nation stood in ranks and formations across one side of the convention center. A mass of ACOA members and union leaders and representatives filled the rest of the coliseum, cheering and whistling, punching fists in the air and chanting, "*The One! The One*!"

The President's rich baritone voice probed and soothed, stimulated and caressed.

"Workers of the world unite isn't, uh, just a slogan anymore. The system we have now is broken down and, uh, we can see it everywhere, from the oil spill in the Gulf and the arrogance on Wall Street to the pollution of our atmosphere and the, uh, desperate conditions of our citizens in obtaining equal social and economic justice. The free market system is not working, it is not going to work. Americans just haven't, uh, recognized it yet. So we need to create a new one for them..."

His words echoed from loudspeakers all over the convention center. Several hundred throats picked up his energy and threw it back at him. "*The One! The One! The One!*"

"I am absolutely certain that generations from now," the President resumed, "we will be able to look back and, uh, tell our children that this was the moment when we began to provide care for the sick and good jobs for the jobless; this was, uh, the moment when the rise of the oceans began to slow and our planet began to heal. This was the moment, this was the time when we came together to remake our world. We are the ones the world has been waiting for."

*"The One! The One!"*

Fists clinched, The One bent down into his mike. "Fired up!" he shouted into it to make the sound of his voice reverberate and echo.

"*Yeh! Yeh!*" thundered the response. His AmeriCorps disciples wore green *AmeriCorps* T-shirts, black ball caps and black trousers bloused into military combat boots. They stamped their feet in the cadence of troops marching through a conquered city.

The President's voice whipped his audience into a frenzy of excitement. *"Ready to go!"*

*"Yeh! Yeh! Yeh!"*

*"Fired up!"*

*"Yeh! Yeh!"*

*"They can't stop us now!"*

*"The One! The One! Yeah-h-h-h!"*

## Government to Stop Conspiracy Theories

***(Washington)***—*Speaker of the House Barbara Teague (D-CA) and Senate Majority Leader Joe Wiedersham (D-Ill) promise to introduce a bill to stop conspiracy theories against the government. They say this can be accomplished by legally banning the transmission of conspiracy theories through the internet, TV, radio, print, or by face to face conversations. The bill will also provide for cognitive infiltration of suspected conspiracy-oriented groups and for recruiting private parties to engage in counter-speech...*

# Chapter Twenty

## Washington, D.C.

Dennis Trout was still on a high after the meeting in which he was finally accepted by his brother-in-law's political insiders. He and Wiedersham returned to the senator's lavish office to discuss details of the meeting and the role Trout was to play in events currently unfolding. Wiedersham settled into a long and windy monologue on how fortunate Trout was to have a mentor like him. Liz, who ran the outer office, hurried in and handed the senator a sealed manila envelope. She was buxom and attractive in a matronly, premature gray sort of way. Trout sometimes wondered if she and Wiedersham might not be playing hanky-panky, as Judy would put it. Wiedersham's long-fled ex-wife must have suspected the same thing; Liz' name had come up in the divorce proceedings.

"A messenger from the White House brought this over," Liz said and hurried back out, closing the door.

Wiedersham extracted a magazine from the envelope. On the cover appeared a depiction of President Anastos riding a donkey over a cliff. Trout recognized the magazine banner: *Truth*. Jerry Baer's rag.

Wiedersham read the note accompanying the periodical and turned to a page marked with a Stickem. He looked up, thought about it, and then handed the note to his chief-of-staff. It was a memo from White House Press Secretary Dewey Gubbins.

*Joe. P.14 by Sharon Lowenthal. Zenergy News is leading with a similar story tonight on prime time. The President is uncomfortable. He wants to know what's going on with the FAD Bill. D.*

"Call over there and tell that fuckhead Gubbins I'm on it," Wiedersham instructed Trout.

While Trout was on the phone with Gubbins, Wiedersham read the designated piece in *Truth*, tossed the magazine open on his desk in disgust, and got on the other line. Trout hung up his phone and edged over to the Louis XIV desk and read the headline: **One Year Ago.** When Wiedersham didn't object, Trout picked up the copy and scanned the article.

"She's not going to let Baer die quietly," Wiedersham was saying to someone on the phone. "There's speculation that she's taking up Baer's mantel. We can't afford to take shit from her any more than we could from Baer. They created the fucking Tea Baggers and now they have people organizing all over the country to make a run for the mid-term elections. That can really gum up the machinery. Do you know where she is?"

Trout overheard only one side of the conversation, but he assumed Wiedersham was laying into Vladimir Gonzalez, head of Homeland Security.

"How do you know she's still in Oklahoma? Who the fuck is Kimbrell...? Yeah? What cop...? We don't give a rat's ass about some Podunk cop or his dead daughter. You tell Kimbrell what the President wants is for him to find that woman."

# One Year Ago
## by Sharon Lowenthal
## (*Truth* Magazine)

*Jerry Baer was savagely murdered this week. He was not "collateral damage" in a Rightwing attack on innocent ACOA and PEIU demonstrators, as the mainstream media claims. He was a deliberate target by entities determined to silence the Thomas Paine of our generation. His was undoubtedly the most influential voice in America in the resistance to One World Government. The Tea Party and other similar grass roots movements were largely mentored, inspired and created by Jerry Baer. He predicted his own death just days before he died in a hail of rifle fire in Tulsa, Oklahoma. He had too much influence and had to be stopped.*

*One year ago, Jerry said you would not recognize this country by now. Can you believe what has happened in this single year?*

- *That government has taken over our automobile manufacturers and many of our banks and financial institutions?*
- *That government through the oil spill crisis is moving to nationalize the energy industry and enact a massive Cap and Trade climate bill that will destroy the economy?*
- *That top-level advisors in the White House are avowed communists?*
- *That the White House's most frequent visitor is a labor union president who has repeatedly exhorted, "Workers of the world unite?"*
- *That the U.S. President himself said that now is the time to establish a One World Government?*
- *That there is a movement led by our own government to end the dollar as the world's reserve currency?*
- *That, through expanded eminent domain laws, government can seize your house and business in the public interest and give them to private entities?*
- *That the President's science czar has called for sterilization of people through drinking water and forced abortions?*
- *That there is a proposed FAD bill for government to take over journalism?*

- *That a multi-trillion dollar stimulus spending bill written by community organizers and union bosses instead of Congress will put the country into such debt that it may go bankrupt?*
- *That Americans peaceably assembled in Washington, D.C. to exercise their First Amendment rights were deemed terrorists and fired upon?*
- *That government would establish a private army along the lines of Adolf Hitler's Brown Shirts?*
- *That private citizens like Jerry Baer can be assassinated when they became a threat to government takeover of our country...?*

# Chapter Twenty-One

## Tulsa

After Ron Sparks' funeral ceremony ended, Big C Brown expressed reservations about driving in his condition, saying he was still dizzy. Judy offered to drive his car for him to the downtown precinct station. It would provide him the opportunity to subtly interrogate her on what she might know about her cousin and his activities in Oklahoma that led to his gruesome death.

She found and applied a band aid to his self-inflicted scratch. He told her he felt much better and offered to buy lunch to thank her for her kindness. They ended up in a little open-air taco place on the west side of the Arkansas River opposite Tulsa River Parks. Big C was a charming man with a dry sense of humor. Although she seemed sad at first because of the funeral, batting back tears, she was soon giggling and chatting with the big cop. Small talk mostly. Big C didn't want to press her too soon too hard and have her clam up on him.

Afterwards, they took a walk across the pedestrian bridge that spanned the river. It was covered to protect strollers from the weather. They stopped halfway across and leaned elbow to elbow on the railing to watch brown water cataract across the low water dam. They made a curious pair, the bald black giant and the tiny bleach-blonde who wasn't much taller than past his elbow.

"How you ever go from Oklahoma to Washington, D.C.?" Big C asked casually in their get-acquainted conversation.

"I married this soldier named Sam Taylor stationed with the Arlington Honor Guard," she replied. "I stayed in Washington when he took off with some bitch prettier and younger than me. I danced for a spell. I tended bar. I waited tables. A girl on her own has to get by."

"Nothing wrong with that."

Once she got going, she was like the Energizer Bunny and just kept going on and on. Completely guileless. A quality Big C found oddly attractive. They walked to the River Park end of the bridge and bought Sno Cones. He had strawberry, she lime. She linked her arm through his elbow as they retraced their way back across the bridge.

"I suppose I might have done come back to Oklahoma," she explained, "except I got myself tied up with a married man. Dennis is an important man in politics. Sometimes he thinks I'm stupid, which I ain't. I'm just not quick and ain't had that much education. Truth is, Corey..."

They walked some more while she searched for the right words, both of them gazing upriver toward Sand Springs.

"Truth is, I've done fell in love with Dennis," she finally continued with obvious pride that a poor country girl like her could hook up with a man like that. "I miss him already. Do you care if I smoke?"

She extracted a pack from her purse. Big C didn't smoke, but he carried a lighter with the inscription *2nd Cav* on it from when he and Nail went to the first war in Iraq. He lighted her cigarette. She blew smoke and smiled at him as smoke threaded from her nostrils.

"It's a nasty habit," she admitted.

"We all got our habit, Judy. What do Dennis do in Washington? A congressman or something?"

"He's Chief of Staff for Senator Joe Wiedersham. Do you know who he is?

"Senate Majority Leader."

Wiedersham had been ubiquitous on all channels pushing the FAD Bill and speaking up on behalf of the President about the oil spill crisis. Cousin Judy, Big C realized, must have been Ron Sparks' inside Washington contact, whether she was aware of it or not.

"Dennis wants to be a congressman," Judy said, searching Big C's expression to see if he believed her.

Big C made no comment. As far as he was concerned, ninety-nine percent of politicians gave the other one percent a bad name.

"Dennis ain't like them others," Judy went on, as though reading his thoughts. "He says sometimes you got to do things that ain't so good so you can do good for the most folks. I done got a real education on politicians since I been in Washington. Dennis likes to talk to me about things. Sometimes it can be real scary. Nobody there trusts anybody else. Dennis says they'd rather screw you than say howdy-do. But Dennis is smart too. He keeps notes and stuff and writes them down in his notebook. He takes it with him almost everywhere. One time he told me he knows too much about what's going on, so he keeps the notebook as insurance in case they try to screw him over."

"Sounds like smart thing to do. You ever read anything in it?"

"Huh-uh. No, sir!" She shook her head vigorously. "I beg him to get out of politics so we can move someplace else."

"But he stay."

"It's just temporary," she said too quickly. "One term in Congress, then he's getting out and divorcing Marilyn."

She sucked on her cigarette, her cheeks caving in and her lips puckering around the cylinder. She left lipstick on the filter. She looked troubled.

"You talk to your cousin Ron often, did you?" Big C asked.

"Ron and me was always calling each other on the telephone," she said, brightening and then growing sad in almost the same instant. "We grew up together and was real close. Like brother and sister."

"Did you ever meet any of Ron's friends, people he worked with or anything?"

She squeezed his arm. "Just you."

"When was the last time you talk to Ron?"

She answered immediately. "Like two days before it happened, you know. Ron called me and said he was scared. I knew he was doing something with some militia people. Working undercover, I think."

"He scared of the militia?"

"I guess so. There was something about this guy who was on to him and would cause trouble."

"Did he say who?"

"It was something like Kimbrough. Maybe Kimble."

"Kimbrell?"

"That's it."

She stamped out her cigarette butt and took his arm again. "My flight to Washington leaves in three hours. You want to walk some more first?"

# Chapter Twenty-Two

## Keystone Lake, Oklahoma

The fishing cabin Nail and Big C called the "Safe House" dwelt in timber on the banks of Cottonwood Creek that flowed into Keystone Lake west of Tulsa. The rutted road that cut down to it was so overgrown that Nail missed the turnoff on the first pass and had to turn around and go back. The ruts snaked across a field and through a stand of elm and a persimmon thicket. Shade from old growth oak surrounding the cabin prevented weeds and grass from overpowering it. Entwined branches made the cabin almost invisible from the air, especially during the summer. A couple of window shutters rattled in the breeze that crept up the narrow creek from the open lake. The cabin looked neglected. It needed paint and maintenance. No one had come fishing here much lately.

Nail and Sharon got out of the Saturn. "We need to return it to Avis," he said.

Sharon looked around. "What will we do without a car? Ride mules?"

"This *is* Oklahoma," he teased. He pointed to a rickety shed off to the right of the cabin. "I have an old pickup truck stored. Big C and I use it to run errands and pull stumps. It'll get us around and the Homies won't have it on their radar."

She took a few steps to the side and made a face as she looked around. "Where's the outhouse?"

He laughed. "There's plumbing. And electricity."

"People in New York and Washington think everybody lives like this between the Mississippi River and the Rockies. It reminds me of *The Shack.*"

He didn't understand. They walked to the cabin and Nail dug the key from underneath the door stone.

"*The Shack* by William Young," Sharon explained. "It's a Christian book. A man's daughter is murdered in an old shack in the woods. He returns to the scene years later, where he meets God—"

She caught herself. Dismay swept her features. She touched Nail's cheek with her fingertips.

"James...I'm sorry. I didn't think."

He shook her off. "We both have our wounds," he said.

The interior of the cabin was almost as rustic as the exterior. It had two bedrooms, each equipped with a bunk bed. There was also a small toilet and a shower. The living room with its worn sofa and a couple of ratty easy chairs merged with a kitchen that consisted only of a table and a stove fueled by a propane tank. Canned goods were stacked against one wall. Sharon looked them over.

"Have you always been a gourmet chef?" she asked.

"Wait until you taste the crappie."

She took another look at the cans. "What's a crappie?"

"A fish."

"Will we catch fish?"

He straightened from inspecting the TV-DVD player. A picture came on the screen. "We may not have time," he said.

He walked out the back door and down a steep path to the creek. She followed. The creek ran slow and deep and dark with mud flats on either side. Doves cooed. Cicadas burred. The air was rich and thick and earthy with scents.

"You *never* smell anything this wonderful in New York!" she exclaimed.

"We used to bring Jamie and Charlie fishing here when they were kids," he said, his hands stuffed deep into his pockets while he gazed downstream as though he half-expected to see them canoeing toward him. "Charlie is Big C's son, a couple or three years older than Jamie. He just went on the Dallas Police Department."

Sharon walked up and stood next to him. He took her hand absently, as if it were the natural thing to do, and led her to a big fallen log in the grass overlooking the water. They sat together on the log in a long silence. A beaver slapped its tail upstream. He opened his fingers to release her hand, but she left it where it was. Simple human contact sometimes made things better.

"This is a good place to fish or just sit and not think about the world," he said.

They felt comfortable with each other. Conversation was not necessary when two people were linked by shared tragedy. The sun was getting low and resting on treetops to the west. A whippoorwill questioned the approach of nightfall.

"Big C said you took a bullet for him," Sharon said after awhile. "Was that how you got the limp?"

"It was a long time ago."

"When you were a sniper?"

"Yes."

He didn't want to discuss it. She let it go. They sat on the log and waited for sunset.

"Are you originally from New York?" he asked conversationally.

"The Bronx," she said. "A traditional Jewish home in a traditional Jewish borough. Mom and Dad moved to Miami Beach ten years ago."

"I've heard people from the Bronx talk," he commented. "You sound more like... Oh, maybe Idaho or Indiana."

"I worked on my accent when I decided to go into broadcasting. I was a DJ on a morning drive pop music show in Des Moines before I married and moved back to New York."

"How long were you married?" When she failed to answer right away, he added, "I'm sorry. That's personal and none of my business."

"I'm over it. We just went different ways. I was a Jew for Christ, he was Italian Catholic. The old, old story of too many differences."

"You met Jerry Baer in New York?"

"After my divorce I was producing a late night radio show called *On the Edge*, a liberal Progressive would-be countermeasure to Rush Limbaugh, Sean Hannity and Jerry Baer." She laughed self-consciously. "You wouldn't have liked me then. Many Jewish women grow up defensive with a victim mentality that points them politically left. I belonged to Women's Lib and Code Pink. I did it all, except burn my bra. That was going *too* far."

She blushed and covered it with another laugh.

"So what happened to change you?" he asked.

"Jerry Baer. I started listening to him on the radio before he went to TV. He made a lot of sense. He opened my eyes to the reality of where our country is headed. I couldn't work for *On the Edge* anymore. One night I ran into Jerry at an event. He was there with his wife Irene."

She choked up. "I became real close to her and Jerry. And their children. They have to be taking this hard. I should probably be there with them."

"I'm sure Irene will understand."

"I've spoken to her on the phone. Poor thing. It must be like her worst nightmare coming true. Jerry tried to prepare her for this eventuality, but that's something no woman wants to face before it happens."

They sat on the log and held hands until she had control of her tears.

"Anyhow, that's how our partnership started," she went on presently. "Jerry took me with him when he moved to Zenergy TV. What about you? I hardly know anything."

Nail found himself telling her about his coming up in the Cookson Hills around Tahlequah, raised by his Creek Indian grandmother in Cherokee country after his parents died from a logging truck crashing into their pickup truck. He enlisted in the army when he was seventeen, served as a platoon squad leader with the 2nd Armored Cavalry during *Desert Storm*, the first Iraqi war. That was where he met Big C, who was also from Oklahoma. Combat experience cemented the two soldiers from Oklahoma into a firm friendship built on trust and common ground.

When the two soldiers redeployed stateside, they got out of the army and applied for the Tulsa Police Department, where they were accepted and attended rookie school together. Big C was Jamie's godfather, and Nail was Charlie's. Big C and Charlie moved in with Nail and Connie for awhile after his wife Latisha ran off with an ex-convict from Granite. Nail in turn moved in with Big C and Charlie after Connie decided her life with a cop wasn't "fulfilling." The two cops always joked that before either married again he should seek the other's advice and permission. Big C bought the "Safe House" as much for the in-between-marriages times as for fishing.

"Your grandmother...?" Sharon asked.

"She died while I was in Iraq."

"I'm..."

"I'm sorry too," he said with a tinge of bitterness in his voice. "I was in the army six years. I've been a cop for nearly twenty. Sometimes I wonder what it was all for. My country is getting harder and harder to recognize."

"I know," she said, looking up the creek with him toward where the sun was red through the treetops. "Jerry gave ordinary people a voice. We mustn't let that voice die."

## Food Safety Modernization Bill Succeeds

***(Washington)***—*In order to ensure Americans' safety when it comes to their food supply, Congress has proposed a Food Safety Modernization Bill which authorizes the Federal Food and Drug Administration (FDA) to oversee how farmers grow fruits, vegetables and livestock. The bill includes safety rules governing soil, water, hygiene, packing, which animals may be kept on which fields and when, and the sale of produce through so-called "farmers markets." It also increases inspections of food facilities. For the first time, government will make sure that food is safe from the field to the consumer...*

# Chapter Twenty-Three

## Keystone Lake

James Nail was up and dressed at sunrise; it was his favorite time of day. Last night Sharon changed the bandage on his head and assured him that he was healing properly. Before going to bed, she paused at her bedroom door, having switched into a pair of light sweats bottoms and a baggy T-shirt. Without a word, she returned to where Nail sat splay-legged on the sofa, thinking. She bent quickly and kissed him on the cheek. It surprised him. By the time he recovered, she had disappeared into her room and closed the door.

The morning sun felt warm on his face as he strolled down to the creek and stood on the bank to watch big catfish roll while sand bass chasing shad churned the creek's surface. He pulled down the brim of his *AAA Quarter Horses* bill cap to shade his eyes, but the cap refused to fit right because of his bandaging. He ripped the tape off his head and touched the wound gingerly with his fingertips. It wasn't much more than a bullet burn. The cap fit after that. It certainly fit better than the pieces of the puzzle surrounding his daughter's murder.

Over the years he had lost count of how many homicide cases he had worked. Multitudes of mangled bodies with their dead eyes startled and frozen in terror at the moment of death from gunshot, knife wound, drowning, bludgeoning... People killed each other out of passion, revenge, greed, occasionally for the pure hell of it. He had killed twice himself. Not murder, but killing.

The first time was a ski-masked armed robber heisting a *Wendy's*, for God's sake. Nail was waiting for him with a twelve-gauge shotgun when he ran out. The dude got off one shot with a Saturday Night Special before Nail let him have a round of Double Aught.

The second scumbag was a serial strangler of young women. He was holed up with a .380 in a Seven-Eleven on North Apache and had Big C dead to rights. Nail, sniper on the scene, jumped out in the open and yelled to distract the shit bird inside the store. The guy shot him instead, in the lower leg, shattering the bone and his knee. Big C dragged Nail out of the line of fire and pressure-bandaged his leg. Nail refused to be evacuated until he finished his job. Five minutes later, he got a clean sight picture through the scope of his 30.06 bolt-action Winchester and took off the top of the perp's skull.

He never dreamed in his worst nightmares that he would be investigating his own daughter's murder. Things were much different when you had a personal stake in the outcome. He felt overwhelmed, inadequate, a state of mind he had never entertained in any other case. In previous homicides, he ferreted out the suspect and arrested him. Case closed. Justice.

In this case, however, he was beginning to comprehend that it was more complicated than all his previous homicides combined. As Sharon said, it ran deeper than he could ever imagine. With implications of political corruption, of an evil network of *Dr. No* types who seemed to encompass the globe. Who committed crimes with cold, deliberate calculation and were powerful enough to casually eliminate with impunity anyone who got in the way.

There were so many pieces to it that he hardly knew where to start. First, there were the dead: Greg Morris at McDonald's; Joshua Logan attempting to escape; Ron Sparks hung in the cemetery; Jerry Baer, Jamie and all the others at ORU. Second, there were those populating the case and complicating it: Rupert; Judy Sparks-Taylor; Director Anthony Kimbrell; the shooter with the tattoo in the helicopter; the Defenders; ACOA; PEIU... Although Kimbrell appeared to be a common denominator, Nail couldn't help looking upon him as little more than a bit player on a big stage whose strings were pulled by a puppet master.

Damn! He was getting another headache just thinking about it.

Big C arrived driving a red Ford pickup truck and wearing jeans, boots and a green T-shirt that made him look like a model for the Incredible Hulk. Nail and Sharon met him outside as he drove up.

"That was something, what you two reprobates pulled off at the cemetery," Sharon congratulated them.

Nail grinned at C. "I hope I didn't give you a black eye, pard?"

"I already got two black eyes."

Nail glanced at the road that led out through the trees to the main blacktop. "You weren't followed?"

"Bro', how long we be fighting crime and evil and you ask that?"

Nail slapped him on the back. "Sorry."

Big C ran a massive hand across his shaved head and flashed bright ivories at Sharon. "You much too fine to be hanging with home boys like us," he teased. "He probably got you in the house cooking and cleaning. You ain't had lunch, right? I brought take-out."

Take-out *hamburgers*. Sharon laughed as they retreated inside from the mosquitoes. "How would James and you eat if you couldn't open a can or stop at a drive-through?" she asked.

Sharon reheated fries. James cleared the table of unopened cans, the contents of which they had initially planned for lunch. Sharon recited grace. While they ate, Big C filled them in on what little he had gleaned from Judy Sparks-Taylor during their afternoon together.

"She Ron Sparks' cousin all right," he said. "She having a fling with this married dude works as chief of staff for Senate Majority Leader Joe Wiedersham. Dennis Trout his name. At least we know who fed Ron Sparks information from Washington—except I don't think she *know* she the contact. She... Well, she naïve and trusting. I like the girl and don't want see nothing happen to her."

He paused to think it over. He took a long draught from his Coke cup before proceeding.

"What I figger is somebody in the Defenders snitching to the Homies. Ron told Judy two days before he killed that Kimbrell suspected him of double cross and going over to the militia. I figure Kimbrell had him hung and try to lay it on us Defenders. Morris and Logan seen it happen and went on the run with the Homies chasing to shoot them up. I still don't know how this all fit in with ORU, but I got an idea it do."

"If we're right, C," Nail speculated, "Kimbrell may be up to his neck in this but we'll still need his snitch inside the Defenders to turn on him to prove it."

"Same ones kill Ron could be the ones in the helicopter," Big C added.

Nail dared not be too hopeful, not at this early stage of the probe. His mind shifted to another revelation that had surprised him as much as anything else his friend had divulged—that Big C was apparently a member of the militia known as the Defenders.

"Being in militia ain't something you go spreading around, not even to best friends," Big C explained. "Militias is organizing all over from Texas to Florida to Arizona and the Southwest and Middle West. I see President Anastos on CNN saying government is going to end the militia's reign of terror, that people deserves to be secure in they homes from domestic terrorists as well as from foreign terror. Like *we* the ones shooting down folks."

The Defenders, Big C went on, knew Ron Sparks was a Homeland Security agent from the beginning. Greg Morris brought him into the organization. The commander of the Defenders, Colonel Josiah Mosby, objected at first.

"He's a patriot like the rest of ya'all," Morris argued. "He's seen the inside workings and knows how it's rotting. He wants to resign from Homeland, but I think he can better serve us by being our eyes and ears inside the enemy camp."

Sparks was about thirty, lean and serious with a large nose and nearly-black eyes.

"My great, great grandparents survived the Jewish holocaust," he said at his initiation. "I'm Jewish, I'm an Okie, but most of all I'm a loyal red-blooded American. I've seen some of what they're planning for us and I just can't go along with it and keep quiet. Paul Revere said it best: *They're coming! They're coming!* We had better be prepared."

Sparks had proved his worth and his loyalty. Two days before his hanging, he spoke to the Defenders at their meeting in Akins about disturbing developments his "contact" in Washington had passed on to him.

"President Anastos and his cronies have directed more than ten billion dollars in economic stimulus funds for recruiting and training a secret civilian army loyal only to them," he revealed. "AmeriCorps was supposed to be a civilian *unarmed* federal service organization. You know, plant trees, fight forest fires, organize communities to be good little Progressives... Instead, more than three hundred thousand young AmeriCorps Green Shirts are currently being trained as a military arm in remote secret camps all over the United States."

The Defenders fell unearthly silent as Sparks continued his message. Most were farmers and hill people from eastern Oklahoma's Green Country, with a few like Detective Corey Brown from the nearby cities of Tulsa, Muskogee and Fort Smith.

"Why does government require a civilian army of Green Shirts on top of Homeland Security?" Sparks asked rhetorically. "Who are the enemies they expect to fight with such a large force? Tea Parties? Conspiracy nuts? People who carry 'Don't Tread On Me' flags? Jerry Baer? Zenergy News Cable? Militia groups? The American people...?"

Now in the Safe House, Nail sat at the table with Big C and Sharon silently pondering Ron Sparks' warning. Sharon slipped outside to the rented Saturn to retrieve the FedEx package left at the door of Nail's apartment. While she was gone, Big C said, "I taking some earned leave from the police department. I got an idea how to set up a little sting to flush out the snitch in the Defenders so we can ask him some questions."

"C, what about the blonde? Judy? She's going to be in trouble when they figure out she was the one passing information to Sparks that she apparently learned from what's-his-name. Her lover."

"I thought about that. I don't know. If they not picked up on her yet, she may be safe. Maybe Trout think she too stupid to understand what's going on."

"Is she?"

"She ain't stupid," Big C said, sounding defensive.

Nail nodded reflectively.

"You could have did worse for a partner," Big C said after a moment.

"We've always been partners, C."

"I was talking about Sharon."

Nail looked toward the door through which Sharon had gone. "For her sake," he said, "it might be best to turn ourselves in. I owe her that. I'm getting her in too deep."

"The sis in deep already, James. You think Kimbrell going to let you walk right out again? Least he going to do is keep you and her lock up someplace. You think because you a cop it make any difference to this peckerwood? I ain't risk a friend on what these people may or may not be capable of."

They saw Sharon through the window as she left the parked Saturn and returned to the cabin in the sunshine. Big C leaned across the table and lowered his voice.

"I bet she suppose be killed at ORU too. How long you think she last on her own? What you owe her, bro', is keep her alive."

# Chapter Twenty-Four

## Keystone Lake

Nail had always considered Big C to be an intelligent and rational man. He was also a conspiracy freak. Like, China would send in foreign troops to enforce martial law; secret internment camps were being built to imprison dissidents; private ownership of guns was about to be outlawed; the government was compiling a list of Americans deemed dangerous; black babies were being poisoned in the ghettos; voter fraud and intimidation stole elections... Freemasons; Bilderbergers; New World Order; One World Government; Illuminati; black helicopters...

"Even if you paranoid," Big C would quip, "it don't mean they ain't out to get you."

It disturbed Nail that Sharon seemingly agreed with C.

"We are under attack by our own government," she declared grimly. "Anyone like Big C or Jerry Baer who connects the dots is branded a paranoid kook who has to be discredited. First they ignore you, then they ridicule you, and if that doesn't work, there's the gun and they win."

She extracted the copy of *Truth* from the FedEx parcel and thrust it upon Nail. "Read this," she ordered. "After that, I want us to watch Jerry's DVD together."

Nail begrudgingly took the magazine into the living room and settled at the end of the sofa, reading in sunlight shining through the window. His brow knitted in concentration while Sharon and Big C continued weaving their dark intrigues together at the kitchen table. He finished *One Year Ago* and read it again carefully. Sharon was standing there when he looked up.

"Only one year," she said, "and they are well on their way to 'fundamentally transforming the United States of America.'"

He stared at the magazine in deep thought, his previous assumptions challenged not only by Sharon's article but also by the events of the past week. Sharon turned on the TV, slid in a DVD, and sat next to Nail on the sofa. Big C occupied the easy chair. Light inside the cabin was afternoon dim and yellow and the blue light from the TV screen flickered off their faces. Doves outside cooed and a meadow lark issued its tri-noted plea for companionship.

Nail immediately recognized the fifty-year-old doughboy with the pale hair and pink skin who exploded on the screen with charm, enthusiasm, sincerity and intelligence. Nail glanced and saw tears flowing down Sharon's cheeks. She batted at them with her hand. He started to take her hand, but didn't.

"This was taped only a few days before..." She stopped at that.

They were soon engrossed in Baer's personality and the show's content.

"Welcome, America, to the Jerry Baer Show. This is my producer, co-host and friend Sharon Lowenthal." There she was on the screen with Baer, smiling and looking gorgeous. "Tonight we are going to expose how individuals within our own government are collapsing America economically and socially and replacing the Constitution with a shadow government that is almost ready to take over. Don't accept my word for anything. Listen to *them*, their own words. If you want the truth, America, if you can handle the truth, come on. Follow me."

Bumper music and the show's screen logo faded into a film clip of President Patrick Wayne Anastos at a microphone with his ubiquitous teleprompters in place. An adoring drive-by media telecaster had once commented how Anastos "could read a grocery list and mesmerize. The power of his voice alone makes people want to run out to the nearest supermarket and buy peanut butter, jelly, cookies, soup and everything else on the damn list." In truth, however, while his baritone voice *was* rich and compelling, he appeared haughty and condescending before the camera and his speech was interrupted by irritating pauses and "uh's."

"This, uh, Supreme Court never ventured into the issue of redistribution of wealth," he was saying. "The tragedy of the Civil Rights Movement was that the Civil Rights Movement became so, uh, court focused I think there was a tendency to lose track of the political and community organizing activities that, uh, are able to put together a coalition of power through which you bring about redistributive change. I refuse to, uh, allow America to go back to the culture of irresponsibility and greed that made an economy with, uh, soaring salaries for some and shrinking working class incomes. I did not run for office to, uh, help a bunch of fat cat bankers on Wall Street."

For the next hour, Nail sat glued to the set, astonished at the historical depth of Baer's knowledge, taken aback that almost none of this was appearing elsewhere on TV or in the newspapers. It was easy to see why the political ruling classes might have wanted to hush Baer. Clip after clip, politicians caught off-guard and therefore more candid than they might otherwise have been indicted themselves to support

Baer's assertion that Washington under the Anastos administration was full of Marxists scheming against the American people.

One clip showed House Speaker Barbara Teague with her Botox'd face frozen like that of a deer caught in a trucker's headlights. "I think we've had enough of capitalism. I think we need more regulation of society."

A rumpled, heavyset man appeared on the screen, identified as Senate Majority Leader Joe Wiedersham. Nail exchanged looks with Sharon and Big C. This was the man from whom Judy Sparks-Taylor through her lover Dennis Trout had apparently obtained certain sensitive information that she passed on to her cousin in Oklahoma.

"The need for de-development presents economists with a major challenge," Wiedersham was saying. "I believe basically the system is broken. It is basically a bankruptcy of free marketing and a refutation of the principles of Reagan and Thatcher. Economists must design a stable, low-corruption economy in which there is a more equitable distribution of wealth. Redistribution of wealth both within and among nations is absolutely essential if a decent life is to be provided for every human being."

A clip of Congresswoman Nadine Walters followed. "The dumbest poor creature on Capitol Hill," Sharon editorialized to Nail and Big C.

"And guess what this liberal would be all about," poor Nadine confessed on TV. "This liberal would be all about socializing..." Uh oh! Bad choice of words. She caught herself and stared into the camera while she tried to think her way out of the trap. "Uh, what I really mean would be about basically taking over and the government running all your companies for the good of everybody."

Baer came back on, with Sharon sharing the set with him.

"Listen to them, folks," he exhorted. "They're not even bothering to hide their intentions anymore. The masks are coming off. They think we're a bunch of pasty-white, NASCAR-watching, gun-toting, pickup-driving reactionaries with racist tendencies sitting slack-jawed in front of our televisions, too stupid to know we're being spoon-fed in every aspect of our simple, dreary lives. It's the responsibility of the elites in society to manipulate the general public and tell us how to vote, what to eat, who to love and hate, what to think and when to think it. In their minds, man cannot govern himself. We aren't enlightened enough to make our own decisions."

The scene changed to a late-night network TV host. "We can't get sixty percent of people to agree on anything," he ranted. "Sixty percent doesn't even believe in evolution. Sixty percent doesn't even have passports. They're stupid. It's up to President Anastos to drag them into the New World Order."

The TV Sharon appeared. "It doesn't make any difference which political party is in power," she said. "Republican or Democrat. Both parties are full of Progressives leading us down the same path, one only at a slower pace than the other."

A printed quote came up on the screen to support her statement:

*The argument that the two parties should represent opposed ideals and policies...is a foolish idea. Instead, the two parties should be almost identical, so that the American people can throw the rascals out at any election without leading to any profound or extensive shifts in policy. Then it should be possible to replace it, every four years if necessary, by the other party, which will...still preserve, with new vigor, approximately the same basic policies. Professor Carroll Quigley.*

"Seventy percent of our economy is now run by government," Baer resumed. "It'll be the same no matter which party is in power. The nation has been leading to President Anastos since the 1930s. Folks, if you haven't heard about Cloward and Pivens, it's time you do some homework. Their goal for the country is to collapse it internally and create a crisis that requires emergency measures by government. Progressives are already in position to control everything. Folks, our country as we know it is being destroyed."

Next appeared a scary-looking man with black eyes staring out of caves, thick lips, and an Eastern European accent. Baer introduced him as "George Zuniga—the richest and most dangerous man in the world."

"What if a small group of world leaders were to conclude that zee principal risk to the earth comes from zee actions of rich capitalist nations?" the unsettling man asked rhetorically. "In order to save zee planet, the group decides that zee only hope for zee planet is that zee industrialized nations collapse. Isn't it our responsibility to bring this about?"

Baer climbed onto a stool and dropped his head into his hands. When he looked up again, his face was haggard and dead serious.

"More banks have failed this year than in all of the last decade," he lectured. "The country is in debt eighteen *trillion* dollars. We suffer from double-digit unemployment. The economy is entering a spiraling freefall. Government borrows five billion dollars every day from China just to keep afloat. Sooner or later, the world will realize that our debts can never be repaid. There'll be a worldwide panic against the dollar, the results of which will be fatal and irreversible to the Republic. We are deliberately being made to collapse."

He jumped to his feet, pacing across the set. A crusader warning his countrymen.

"Societies need government," he continued, sweating and punctuating the air with jabs and chops. "Government elevates men to power, and men who seek power are prone to corruption. Corruption spreads like a plague. Out of lust for money, power and sex, for their own gain and their evil ideology, such people will replace equal justice with social justice. They will trade individual freedom for an all-powerful, all-knowing government that will forsake the creative potential of individuals for a two class system in which the elites rule and everyone else is a serf. Throughout history, we have seen this slide into tyranny. As we slept, a corrupt and expanding network was being built to replace our Republic the moment it was weak enough to fall. While we slept, our servant became our master. *Now* is the time the master will act. *Now,* while they have the power, they will destroy America and take it over from the inside."

Nail was stunned, speechless. He felt Sharon watching him.

The camera zoomed in for a close-up of Baer's worn face.

"Someday people will ask, 'Why didn't somebody warn us?' Somebody *is* warning you, folks. We're under attack from enemies both foreign and domestic. It's all wrapped up in political correctness, the economy, corruption in Washington, our involvement in overseas wars, radical Islam, allowing illegal immigration for votes, Marxists in Congress and the White House.

"The next step is force. Soldiers will be coming. A witch hunt has already started for dissidents, those who will oppose a socialist takeover of our country. If the elites have done their job right, there will be almost no fight left in the public. People will welcome the tanks when they roll in to restore order. We will submit to searches, give up all our Constitutional rights—and forget about our neighbors who have been dragged away to disappear."

The man appeared to be in agony. Sweat beaded his forehead and trickled down his face, soaking his collar. This man on the screen was now dead, murdered along with Jamie Nail. Ice ran down Nail's spine as Big C's warning finally sunk in as to what he owed Sharon—to keep her alive, even though she seemed determined to take Baer's place as the next Thomas Paine sounding the alarm.

## President Touts Second Bill of Rights

***(Washington)****—In his crusade to initiate reforms to provide new goals of human happiness and well-being, President Anastos said it is time to amend a Second Bill of Rights to the U.S. Constitution, as first proposed by President Franklin Roosevelt. The new Bill of Rights cements a pact between government and citizens that, under government supervision, would guarantee equal standards of living. The Second Bill of Rights will include:*

*The right to guaranteed employment and pay;*

*The right of every family to a decent house;*

*The right to adequate medical care and the opportunity to achieve and enjoy good health;*

*The right to adequate protection from the economic fears of old age, sickness, accident, and unemployment;*

*The right to a good education;*

*The right to rest and leisure...*

# Chapter Twenty-Five

## Washington, D.C.

Chief of Staff Dennis Trout—perhaps it would soon be Illinois *Congressman* Trout if everything went well—hadn't had a swig of Maalox since yesterday. He was thinking about it now though, on the phone with his wife. He had no idea what might have set her off this time. As best he could determine, she was raising hell for no other reason than that she was married to him. She should have been ecstatic with joy. After all, he *had* achieved insider status—and found a possible sugar daddy to fund his campaign in Illinois.

His stomach rumbled and he opened a desk drawer to find his Maalox. He was trying his best to placate the bitch. He didn't want to piss her off, which in turn would piss off her brother and cause him, Trout, to lose everything he had kissed ass for these last years.

Whatever her other complaints, she quickly moved on to the issue of his having neglected to feed Reggie this morning before he left for the office. Marilyn had had an early spa appointment.

"I won't forget again, Marilyn, I promise. Say, why don't I take you out to *Komi's* for dinner." *Komi's* was her favorite dining. "Not tonight. Tomorrow evening, okay? I'm working late tonight."

He held the phone out from his ear. It seemed to vibrate from her on-the-other-end fury. The damned thing would explode if she knew he was actually meeting his mistress instead of working late. Judy had returned from her little foray into *Deliverance* and Trout needed his ashes hauled in the worst way. It took so little to make the blonde happy—a stolen night now and then when he was horny or needed a bedpost to talk to. She was so simple.

He finally got off the phone on a final refrain from Marilyn. "Damn you, Trout!"

Liz in the outer office transferred an incoming call to Trout for screening before he passed it on to Wiedersham. It was that idiot from Homeland Security again. Vladimir Gonzalez. Another ass kisser looking to get his toast buttered. Trout thought him a pompous little man with a little man's complex. A Russian immigrant's grandson who claimed direct descent from Vladimir Lenin via a Venezuelan his mother married.

"Hold one, *Officer* Gonzalez," Trout said politely but with deliberate slight.

"*Director* Gonzalez."

"Hold one, *Director* Gonzalez."

Trout knocked once, then opened the door that separated his much, *much* smaller office from Wiedersham's. Wiedersham didn't like to be buzzed like some Michelin tire dealer from the Midwest. He was on the other line. One *Vigotti* shoe propped on top of his desk and his *Armani* suit looking cheap enough on him to have come off the rack at Wal-Mart. He held up a finger to Trout and laughed his odd bark at whoever was on the phone.

"It'll be out of committee in two weeks latest," he was saying. "It may take some arm twisting, but Teague assures me we have the votes in House and I have them in Senate. The web'll be ours along with other communications."

"It's Gonzalez," Trout announced when Wiedersham clicked off his phone and sat up in his chair.

Wiedersham scowled.

"He says it's important."

The Majority Leader took the call. Curious about what the two might be up to, Trout took his time going through the *Out* box on the table next to the door. Wiedersham transferred all his routine crap to Trout for him to take care of—such as the RSVP to the media formal dinner to be held Saturday night. Trout gofer'd the mundane for Wiedersham so his brother-in-law could gofer for the President. With a wry smile, Trout speculated on how *everybody* in D.C. was a gofer for somebody else. Even the President of the United States.

Wiedersham was less cautious about his Chief of Staff overhearing his conversations now that Trout had won insider status. Nonetheless, out of old habits of distrust, Wiedersham turned his back and lowered his voice, which made him sound like Marlon Brando in the old *Godfather* movies. Trout pretended disinterest, but he was mentally taking notes.

"Power is a matter of whose balls you can squeeze," Wiedersham had once explained. "It's who's banging who, who's cheating on his income tax, who's a closet fag, who's in bed with which lobbyist, who's stealing campaign funds... Collecting that kind of dirt is like money in the bank. You can call your own shots. Everyone has something to hide. You find out what it is and use it when you need it."

"*Blackmail?*" Trout had blurted out in astonishment. That was during his early idealism stage.

"Politics. Like insurance."

Wiedersham's *Vigotti* banged on the top of his desk. He snapped into the phone, "How could Kimbrell have lost them? Gonzalez, you could replace that doofus with Barney Fife and be ahead of the game... Of course, that cop knows something or he wouldn't be snooping around with her. They have to be stopped, the sooner the better...We can't have that loud-mouthed cunt taking Baer's place and rousing the rabble... Just get it done."

# Chapter Twenty-Six

## Washington, D.C.

They had banged until they were both sweaty and out of breath and tangled in sheets. The bedside light was back on. Trout noticed he was starting to develop a little paunch from soft living and too little exercise. Judy didn't seem to mind either it or his balding scalp. She wasn't like Marilyn. She caressed his forehead, wiping off sweat, and then kissed him there.

"Want a beer, darling?" she asked.

She was smiling, gorgeous but as brainless as a cow.

"What do you have?"

"Bud or Bud Light."

"Bud Light."

Senate Majority Leader Wiedersham would never drink a beer unless it was imported. Pretentious ass!

Judy got out of bed, as naked and innocent as a baby in her nudity. She padded into the bathroom first and left the door open. He heard her brushing her teeth and taking a leak.

"For God's sake, Judy! Close the door."

He hated hearing women use the bathroom.

At a newsstand on the way over he had picked up a copy of *Truth* with the caricature of Anastos riding a donkey off a cliff. He had only briefly looked at the issue before when it arrived on Wiedersham's desk. He opened it now to the *One Year Ago* article by Sharon Lowenthal and read it carefully while Judy finished in the bathroom and went to the kitchenette for beers. No wonder Wiedersham and the White House had their shorts in a bunch.

It was a little troubling to Trout as well, in what it portended for his own career if this Lowenthal woman continued Jerry Baer's campaign. Deep down where he sometimes thought he no longer had a *down*, he was disturbed and a little frightened by the changes Anastos, George Zuniga and the White House "czars" were about to foster upon an unsuspecting nation. A lot of change that left very little hope.

He was staring up at the ceiling, hands behind his head in deep thought, when Judy returned with two beers in plastic promotion glasses from Taco Bell, on them colorful images of Spider Man. Classy. He sat up in bed with the sheet covering his legs and accepted one of the beers. Judy snuggled under the sheet with him. She tapped her plastic glass against his.

"Over the gums and down the hatch, watch out, belly, here she comes."

Trout took a sip.

"Judy, what happened in Oklahoma at the cemetery? What do you know about this man Kimbrell?"

## Pentagon Prepares for Economic Crisis

***(Washington)***—*Speaker of the House Barbara Teague announced today that the U.S. Government is preparing for widespread civil unrest. The defense intelligence establishment, she said, is looking at the threat to national security caused by the worldwide economic downturn.*

*The Pentagon has launched a year-long exercise called "Unified Quest." A Pentagon spokesman said they are looking at responses that may be necessary during a national collapse that could force the military to keep "domestic order among civil unrest and deal with fragmented global power."*

*White House spokesman Dewey Gubbins said a crisis could mean the suspension of Posse Comitatus that prevents U.S. troops from acting against U.S. citizens...*

# Chapter Twenty-Seven

## Green Country, Oklahoma

When Big C came outside the cabin at first light, Nail had Sharon's rental Saturn pulled up to the shed's open door with battery jumper cables running between it and the old green Chevy pickup inside.

"I'm going to try to kick it over," Nail said, ducking under the cables and climbing into the pickup. The pickup whined and gasped, but it finally caught and began rattling along until it finally leveled out and ran smoothly. Big C disconnected the jumper cables and hung them on a nail in the shed.

"You got wheels, man," he said approvingly. He stopped and looked down the mostly-overgrown road. "Maybe we should get some food and guns and block off the road and shoot any sucker trespass until this shit over."

"What makes you think it's ever going to be over?"

"They *ain't* no God if them motherfuckers win."

Big C took his leave immediately after a breakfast of coffee and beef hash from a can. He shook hands with Nail and they nodded at each other; there was no need for words between them. Sharon hugged the black cop.

"Go fishing or something," Big C advised. "I call you in a day or so after I get the sting set up."

He mounted his red Ford pickup and headed toward eastern Oklahoma and "Green Country."

Up until recent years, banks were reluctant to lend money to people east of the Grand River in that swath of northeastern Oklahoma known variously as the Ozark foothills, the Cookson Hills, the Cherokee Strip, or, in the hyperbole of the Bureau of Tourism, "Green Country." The Cookson Hills had a legacy of outlaws and violence. From Indian Territory days into the Twenty First Century, infamous and not so infamous badmen and badwomen had fled into those rugged hills to rely on the close-mouthed and suspicious inhabitants to protect them from the law. Here hid out Jesse James, the Daltons, Belle Starr, Al Jennings, Ma Barker, the Kimes Boys, and Charles "Pretty Boy" Floyd. Nearly every old barn from Sallisaw to Pryor carried with it a story that "Purty Boy" once hid his car in it.

It was not surprising, therefore, that militia might have sprouted and flourished where people were a unique, independent breed suspicious of authority, quick to temper, backward by urban standards, and slow to accept outsiders and the outside world. Yet, even here, times they were a'changing. There had been a time when a black man ignored at his own peril the hand-lettered sign on a back road to nowhere, *Nigger, don't let the sun set on your black ass.*

In Sallisaw, Big C borrowed a phone at a service station to telephone Lieutenant Jack Ross and let him know James Nail was in a safe place.

"We trying to stay off of cell phones except in emergencies," he explained. "Feds can trace them by satellite they want to."

"Kimbrell and his Homies are sniffing around like garbage flies," Ross told him. "Wherever James is, tell him to stay there. I've arranged to carry him on medical leave as long as we can. There are plenty of witnesses to what happened at ORU without bringing James in. But they're still playing bloodhound when it comes to James and that girl."

"They trying to stop Sharon before she get back on TV where it harder to shut her up," Big C said. "James ain't likely to give up till he got somebody by the balls—and Kimbrell ought be afraid them balls are his."

Big C took I-40 east from Sallisaw and turned north on the Central High road to a crossroads known as Akins, in the cemetery of which Ron Sparks had recently been lynched. From there, roads into the Cooksons got rougher and rougher until some weren't much more than graveled trails through the woods. There were farms with decent houses next door to unpainted shacks with half-naked kids playing in the dirt. If the commies, environmentalists, anti-modernists and various other wackos had their way, Big C thought, everybody in America would be living in shacks. Except the people's keepers, of course.

Colonel Josiah Mosby lived in a rundown double-wide mobile home near the isolated community of Bunch on Big Sallisaw Creek. He claimed to be descended from John Singleton Mosby, the famous Confederate leader of Mosby's Rangers. He assumed the honorary "Colonel" after he and Greg Morris organized the Defenders. As far as Big C knew, Josiah had never actually served a day in the military.

When Big C alighted from his pickup, three dirty-faced little boys in shorts tore around the end of the house chased by two black-and-tan hounds, a goat, and three geese. The elder of the trio, about nine, waved. But instead of mobbing Big C with rough affection as they usually did when he came calling, they stampeded onto the wooden add-on porch. Alice held the door open for them. Mosby's half-Cherokee wife gave a febrile wave and ducked back inside with the children. The Colonel came out and closed the door behind him. He shook hands rather formally and the two men walked to a wooden bench underneath a shade tree and sat down. Big C, puzzled by the strange behavior of friends, stared at the trailer.

"Don't mind them, Corey," Mosby said. "Ol' Ranger died last night from tangling with a 'coon he treed. Alice and the kids was attached to that dog. So, what's going on? Heard anything more about Sparks being hung in the cemetery? What reason could Logan and Morris have to do something like that?"

"They didn't do it. The Homies executed Ron," Big C said. "Somebody in the Defenders snitched him off."

The Colonel bent over and hung his head and clasped his hands around his bony knees. He was about forty, more lean than thin, with the big hands and big nose and small head common to many hill people.

"How was Logan and Morris mixed up in it then?" he asked.

Big C shrugged. "Either they saw who killed Ron or they know who the snitch is," he speculated. "You and me talked before, Josiah. Maybe we oughta take look at that new guy from Muskogee, uh—?"

"Tom Fullbright."

"Seems our problem start after he show up. Don't he pal around with Luther Hawkins? Colonel, if you call a meeting of the Defenders, say for Friday night, I think we can flush out our forked tongues. Besides, I know a lady the Defenders might want to listen to."

They discussed the details. The Colonel suggested holding the gathering in the old abandoned church at Akins. Big C didn't think it a good idea to congregate so near the cemetery where Sparks ended up dead.

"All right," Mosby conceded. "There's a one-room schoolhouse at Bunch that ain't been used for school since I was a kid. I'll pass the word to the men."

"Make sure Fullbright and Hawkins show up."

They stood up.

Usually, Alice brought out lemonade. Big C cast another glance at the trailer. The two hounds lay draped across the porch steps, blinking against flies and with their tongues lolled out. Alice peeped out through parted curtains. She closed them when she saw Big C looking at her.

"They really taken Ranger hard," the Colonel said.

# Chapter Twenty-Eight

## Keystone Lake

Sharon tugged on Nail's hand after Big C left. "James, you promised we'd go fishing. I don't think I can bear another can of hash or pork 'n beans."

He realized what she was trying to do, take his mind off Jamie, and it was okay. He didn't know how he would have made it through these last days after his daughter's death without Sharon, who was valiantly endeavoring to get them both past their mourning period. Even through his grief, he found delightful the graceful way she walked and the way her hands swept and dived through the air when she talked.

They scrounged a couple of fishing poles from the cabin. Nail turned over a rotted log and found some juicy grubs for bait. They walked together to the creek and sat on the fallen log. They caught a couple of fat channel cat, some bluegill and a crappie. Nail cleaned and filleted them. Sharon promised they'd have fresh fried fish for dinner.

"With a can of pork 'n beans," she added with a laugh.

They both kept busy the rest of the day to keep their minds occupied. It was too painful when they slowed down and began to think. Nail cleaned his truck and took a walk in the woods, old memories of better times with Jamie flooding his thoughts. Sharon remained in the cabin working on another article for *Truth.* Nail tried not to think about her either, the way she kissed him goodnight on the cheek. They were merely two needy people drawn together by loss. Romance was the last thing either needed.

She fried the fish for dinner. They kept the conversation light and airy, self-consciously so. After nightfall, mosquitoes or no, they sat on the log by the creek underneath an amazing canopy of stars and held hands. She lifted her face to the stars and sighed deeply.

"Oh, look!" she exclaimed, pointing. "A shooting star. Quick. Make a wish."

"I don't believe in wishes."

"I'll make a wish for both of us then."

She closed her eyes tightly, then opened them again. "It's done."

"What did you wish for?"

"It won't come true if I tell you."

"You can tell me *if* it comes true?"

"Yes. Afterwards." Her face was still uplifted.

They were quiet for awhile. He felt comfortable with her. He liked the feeling.

"Looking up into the heavens puts everything in perspective," she said presently. She continued after he failed to respond. "We humans are so infinitesimally small. Mankind's problems, even though global, pale in comparison to the universe. James, even if we try real hard, no way can we possiblly comprehend the meaning of *infinity* or *forever.* How can anyone gaze into these marvelous heavens and not see the face of God?"

He looked up and all he saw was the face of his daughter.

## Oil Ban Judge Dies of Overdose

***(New Orleans)****—The body of New Orleans Federal District Judge Orville Fielding was found this morning in a French Quarter alley, dead of an apparent overdose of amphetamines. Witnesses and acquaintances stated they knew the judge was addicted to "speed." Adele Raineau, a well-known Bourbon Street prostitute, said Fielding had visited her earlier in the night on a "personal matter."*

*Judge Fielding made news when he struck down President Anastos' ban on deepwater oil drilling in the Gulf of Mexico after the AP oil spill disaster. The ban was under appeal by the U.S. Justice Department.*

*Following the announcement of Fielding's death, Judge Walter E. Durant said he would immediately reinstate the ban to halt any drilling in the Gulf for at least a year...*

# Chapter Twenty-Nine

## New York City

Senate Majority Leader Joe Wiedersham gave his chief of staff Friday and Saturday off and two Broadway tickets with the stipulation that Trout meet a man at a Park Place address on Friday afternoon. The man's name was not important, Wiedersham explained with a mysterious smile, only what the man had to say. Trout telephoned Marilyn and tried to sound apologetic about not coming home. Surprisingly enough, Marilyn wasn't upset. In fact, she seemed almost cheerful, an unusual condition of equilibrium for her.

She said. "My brother told me this is vital to our career."

What did she mean—*our* career?

Trout hung up and called Judy to take a cab and meet him at Dulles. He didn't particularly like New York and certainly didn't relish spending time there alone. He didn't particularly like D.C. either. He couldn't recall anyplace he really liked.

Judy showed up at the airport looking like a common hooker with lots of cleavage and a short skirt with her thighs showing. "Like it?" she beamed.

"Ummm."

"You said I should wear something nice."

"I hope you brought something else," he fussed. "I'll dress you from now on."

"The only thing you want is to *undress* me. I got jeans in my carry-on."

"Go to the *Ladies* and change now. For God's sake, wipe off some of that makeup. You look like a..."

He caught himself.

"A *what?*" she demanded.

"Just change. And hurry."

She returned shortly in jeans. Pouting. She had seemed strangely distracted since her return from Oklahoma. They hardly talked to each other on the flight. He stretched his legs in First Class and picked up the latest issue of *Newsweek*. The cover story: *We're All Socialists Now*. He cast it aside and took Judy's hand.

"I'm sorry, honey," he said. "I've been under a lot of stress."

She withdrew her hand. "If'n you want another Marilyn," she sulked, "you should have stayed in the hog pen."

"What the hell is that supposed to mean?"

"You know what it means."

She still wasn't talking to him when the cab dropped her off in front of their Manhattan hotel and he continued with the taxi to keep his appointment. He'd send her some chocolates, the Wal-Mart kind she liked with the cherries. She had probably lost *her* cherry when she was twelve and out playing doctor in the barn with her brother or cousin in Oklahoma. If she wasn't happy by tonight, he wasn't getting any and may as well have come to New York alone. What was it with women that they had to be so fucking difficult, always thinking of themselves?

Park Place from Ground Zero north was packed with a demonstration in progress, thousands of people jammed into the concrete-and-glass canyon to get blasted from microphones on a hastily-raised platform. It had something to do about unions and banks. It seemed everyone in America was pissed off about something and getting more pissed off every day.

Trout's cabbie was pissed off because he had to detour. He cursed in Arabic.

The man who greeted Trout on the eighth floor of the Park Place building was about fifty or so and, in a crowd, would have been as unnoticeable as an old rusty well bucket, to use a Judy euphemism. Until he opened his mouth, at which time he spoke with authority and conviction. The man said to call him "John," first-name-only, but Trout knew from the moment he walked into the little cubbyhole that this wasn't really John's office, that John wasn't his name, and that John had probably been dispatched by George Zuniga to vet the new guy to see if he were a congressional candidate worthy of being backed by the wealthiest, most influential and most powerful man in the universe. In fact, that was what John told him before frisking him with the skill of a NY street cop, apologizing profusely while explaining that they couldn't afford to take any chances with a hidden wire or recorder.

"What we discuss today is between you and me, whether we come to an agreement or not," John warned politely. "You seem to be a promising young fellow. Sit down."

He indicated a chair in front of a bare-topped desk. Trout accepted it. John took the swivel chair behind the desk and leaned forward with his elbows on top of the desk and his hands tented below his chin.

"Let's not waste each other's time," he suggested. "We'll get directly to why you were summoned here."

*Summoned?* Well, he *had* been summoned. Trout smiled. He was an old hand at kissing ass. When obsequious was called for, he could out-obsequious even his brother-in-law. He *really* wanted to be a congressman.

"Drink?" John asked, scooting back and taking a bottle and two glasses from a desk drawer. He poured. They lifted their glasses. "To hope and change," John toasted.

They sipped. John regarded Trout through heavy eyebrows.

"If you *are* selected as one of our candidates—and you come with top recommendations—rest assured you *will* be elected," John began.

"How can you promise that?" Trout asked, curious. "I hope I'm not being too forward?"

"Not at all. There's no need for us to be guarded with each other, *Congressman* Trout." A thrill ran up Trout's leg. "A very wise man once said, 'It's not who *gets* the votes that counts, it's who *counts* the votes.' Suffice it to say that everything is in place to bring about a complete transformation of the United States of America, as Anastos promised. All we need to ensure that our policies and programs are implemented is to have enough good people ready to take over the House and Senate when the time comes. There are eighty seats in the House and eight in the Senate up for grabs in November. We already have a majority, but once we install far-sighted Progressives like you in all those contended seats there won't be anything to stop us.

"Incidentally, after this election, there will be no future elections in which the outcomes are in doubt. *We* will control voting—or at least the counting of votes. Congressman Trout, you may be on the ground floor of the most historical movement the world has ever know. Indeed, the rise of the oceans will slow and the planet begin to heal. Hitch your star to those who really count, who can change the world for the better. We're Aristotle's men of gold who rightfully should rule to bring about a new, brighter, more equitable age of civilization. It's our destiny."

Trout liked John. He relaxed and had another glass of brandy. John chuckled. Trout tittered. They chatted about various other topics. Trout had a feeling that John knew *everything* about him.

"How's your wife Marilyn?" John asked out of nowhere.

Trout nodded, noncommittal.

"And Judy Taylor?"

John chuckled at the look on Trout's face. "We do our homework," he said. "For dinner tonight, may I suggest you take her to The Pig Out Café in the Bronx. She'll feel more at home there."

The cheap shot annoyed Trout, but he restrained himself. He wondered if John knew Judy's maiden name was Sparks and that she was a cousin to the Homeland Security agent hung in the cemetery?

That she had been at her cousin's funeral when Sharon Lowenthal and the cop escaped from Kimbrell's men? Trout volunteered nothing, however. It was none of Wiedersham's business; it was certainly none of John's or his boss Zuniga's.

John moved on, surprising Trout further with a candid discourse about the nature of government and political power, at least according to George Zuniga. Trout wondered why John bothered to explain it to him. Perhaps to test him? To see where he stood?

"Are you aware that twenty-six percent of Americans want authoritarian control, need to be told what to do?" John asked in a conversational tone. "Most of the other seventy percent will go along with almost anything. They can be controlled by tapping into their deepest fears and dreams, as long as the illusion of freedom and Constitutionality is maintained.

"A man named Edward Bernays believed that opinion can be regimented and democracy administered by an intelligent minority. Marx taught that you first identify what it is you want to control—in this instance, the U.S. Government. You earmark and organize people who consider themselves to be oppressed victims. Blacks, Hispanics, gays... You also infiltrate and corrupt powerful institutions such as unions, politics, education, churches, the media..."

He laughed without humor.

"We've been manipulating them for our own purposes for decades under the guise of liberalism and compassion, waiting for the right time. Well, our time has arrived. Now we turn all these groups against each other and create chaos. It doesn't matter whether the chaos comes from the Right or the Left, as long as we have rioting and violence in the streets. People will be howling for government to step in and do something to stop it."

"And we are waiting in the wings to accommodate them."

John beamed at him. Apparently, Trout had provided the proper response. He swallowed any misgivings he might have initially indulged and beamed back.

"Out of chaos will come the new social order," John said. "When it comes, it will come fast, like—how does that phrase go?—like a thief in the night."

He chuckled, then sobered. He stood up and stuck out a hand to shake Trout's, ending the session. "We'll be in touch," he promised.

Trout assumed he had passed the test as to what Zuniga and Wiedersham expected of him once he was bought and paid for.

## Congress Passes Finance Bill

***(Washington)****—After an all-night meeting, Congress passed the Finance Reform Bill in response to the worst recession crisis since the Great Depression.*

*The law allows government to take over companies that threaten the economy. A powerful council of regulators would be on the lookout for risks across the finance system.*

*Senate Majority Leader Joe Wiedersham (D-Ill) said the new law "sends a clear message to the country that financial recklessness from Wall Street to the consumer on Main Street won't be allowed to spread joblessness across the country..."*

# Chapter Thirty

## Green Country, Oklahoma

The first part of their drive from the Safe House to Green Country passed in broody silence, Nail and Sharon each deep in thought. Jamie and Jerry Baer were being buried today, Jamie in Tulsa's Floral Haven and Baer in New York. Nail had cell-phoned Connie last night to try to explain why he couldn't attend their daughter's funeral. She didn't want to listen; she hung up on him. Sharon in turn spoke with Irene, Baer's wife, who responded with warmth and understanding. She cautioned Sharon not to return to New York.

"Jerry wouldn't quit over threats," Nail overheard Sharon say. "Neither will I."

For the trip, they dressed in jeans and T-shirts to better blend in with the ambience of Nail's old rusty Chevy pickup. A couple of farmer types on the road. Nail found a spare baseball cap for Sharon with the logo *Six Chuter Inc* on it. She twisted her hair into a curly ponytail that she let hang out through the cap's back opening. He liked the way she looked—a mixture of saucy and tom boy.

They dropped the rental Saturn off at *Avis* in Tulsa before proceeding together in the pickup. The Homies might be wise to the rental but not likely the Chevy. They stopped for lunch in Sallisaw at a *Kentucky Fried Chicken.* At least, Sharon observed with an attempt at levity, lunch didn't come in a can. Afterwards, they headed north into the hills to meet Big C at a restaurant in Stilwell. That was all the information he provided when he called last night.

It might have been a pleasant outing but for the shadow of today's funerals hovering over them. They passed through some road construction heralded by a big sign that read *Project Funded by The American Recovery and Reinvestment Act.* There were some sawhorses and orange road cones, but nobody was working.

"The beneficence of the Anastos administration," Sharon commented in disgust. "Like some dictator reminding the little people of how much he's doing for them."

Off the main roads, Sharon was intrigued by the Oklahoma countryside, an eclectic mixture of shacks, mobile homes on rural lots, prosperous farms and ranches, and the occasional 19$^{th}$ Century antebellum plantation house.

"I'm a city girl," she exclaimed over one stretch of poor road lined by a series of hillbilly-type dwellings with yards full of chickens, hound dogs and kids. "I didn't realize Americans still lived like this. Maybe I did, but I hadn't seen it up close."

"This is the *real* America where values mean something," Nail said. "All these folks are poor, but they're proud. All they want is to live and be left alone."

"Is this how you grew up, James?"

"Not too far from here. They tore down the old home place."

As Nail drove, Sharon absently jotted down on the back of an insurance form from the glove compartment a list of book titles she thought Nail should read to further his understanding of what was happening to America. He had admitted that he didn't keep up with current events. Like most Americans, he was too busy with life to pay much attention to the constant squabbling of politicians in distant Washington D.C. He had been chasing murderers, working odd hours, keeping up with Jamie. He rarely watched TV, read few books outside professional manuals, and didn't believe a word the Tulsa *World* printed.

"If we get a chance, we'll stop at a bookstore on the way back and pick up some of these books," Sharon offered.

"Young lady, when am I going to have time to read? We're in the middle of working the most important case of my career."

"It's not exactly going at a Sherlock Holmes pace," she observed.

"I won't quit."

She clasped her hand over his on the steering wheel. "I well know that," she said.

She handed him the list of titles when they located the café in Stilwell where they met Big C:

*Atlas Shrugged*
*1984*
*The 5,000-Year Leap*
*Rules for Radicals*
*Culture of Corruption*
*How Evil Works*
*Going Bonkers: The Wacky World of Cultural Madness*
*Lenin, Hitler and Stalin...*

Over coffee, Big C informed them of what he had in mind. "At the Defenders meeting tonight, I like Sharon to be the speaker. They really impressed with her. For sake of morale they need to hear what she have to say. Most of them watch Jerry Baer. You'll be safe there.

"We got two new men come in the Defenders right before Ron Sparks did. Colonel Mosby and I trust the rest of the unit with no question. It just a hunch, but we think one the new guys was planted to spy on us and on Ron, make sure he doing the job Homies sent him to do. During the meeting tonight, Colonel Mosby and I gonna slip word to these two guys that ya'all staying the night in a motel in Sallisaw. One will think ya'all in the Callahan Motel, the other that ya'all in the Sallisaw Motel. I already signed your names into a room at each, but ya'all ain't gonna be at either one. Kimbrell want you two as bad as we think he does, Homies will be on the way. We sit back after the meeting to see which motel the Homies raid—and we got the guy who snitch to Kimbrell. If you right about all this being connected, James, we could find out who hung Ron and shot up the folks at ORU."

So far they had little else to go on.

The sun was setting in breathless scarlet behind a row of elms that bordered an abandoned one-room schoolhouse near the community of Bunch when Nail and Sharon arrived with Big C following in his own pickup. Whippoorwills were already echoing each other while crickets and frogs warmed up in the wings. The lot around the sandstone-sided WPA Great Depression-era building was grown up in weeds, among which a sizeable number of vehicles were parked in unstudied disarray. The Bunch township sometimes rented the schoolhouse out for various civic and social functions, although not too often, judging by its rundown condition.

Some eighty or more men crowded into the one long room, gossiping and laughing and waiting for Colonel Mosby to call the meeting to order. Most were whites or Indians with a few black men thrown in from Tulsa or Muskogee. Militiamen suffered a reputation enhanced by the media for being backward Neanderthals armed with God, guts and guns. The atmosphere inside the schoolhouse failed to support the reputation. Nail found the gathering jovial and friendly, more like an old-time cake walk or a brush-arbor revival than a clandestine rendezvous to plot against the government. Sharon agreed that this wasn't at all what she expected.

A local minister opened with prayer. Colonel Mosby led the Pledge of Allegiance. Someone else read passages from the U.S. Constitution. Excitement rippled through the seated congregation when Mosby introduced Sharon and people recognized her from TV. Nail and Big C took seats in the front row when Sharon mounted the little stage up front to the makeshift lectern.

"We not setting the trap on the snitches tonight until you two safe someplace else," Big C whispered to Nail.

Sharon gave a command performance, considering how little time she had had to prepare. She reasoned, she challenged, she cajoled, she mesmerized, her graceful hands swooping and dipping to emphasize and italicize. Her words were as sharp as rapiers one moment, soft and purring and judicious the next. She had learned from the best: Jerry Baer. The rough cut men seemed not to take a collective breath for minutes at a time. When they did breathe, it was as a single organism. In her jeans, t-shirt and ball cap, she had them in the palms of her hands. They loved her.

Something outside caught Nail's attention. He turned his head to listen. The windows were open to let in air. He heard nothing but the distant hoot of a barn owl. He must have the jitters. He shook his head when Sharon noticed and shot him a questioning look. She immediately resumed where she had left off, drawing her audience with her into a world where conspiracy theories were based on facts and hard evidence.

"People are in place to take over this government," she was saying. "Their tactic is to intimidate and scare, divide and conquer. Radical Marxists and others from the Progressive Left have been granted permission to act up in the streets, to march and riot and protest for social justice. They need you to get angry, to be racist, to grab a gun and fight back. They *want* violence, they want us at each other's throats. They must convince people that the Tea Parties and the Conservatives are the radicals, not them, and that you are a threat ready to explode. The more unruly the Left becomes, the more we react, the better these people like it. Government, they claim, will have to take away rights and clamp down in order to restore order. People in the middle will beg for government to do something, anything. Just keep us safe. It's a trap—"

*A trap!* Something snapped in Nail's mind. The nightly serenade of nocturnal insects and tree frogs was at once soothing but, when it ceased unexpectedly, was like an alarm going off to the ears of the experienced outdoorsman. Nail should have caught it sooner.

The serenade had stopped.

# Chapter Thirty-One

## Ozark Mountains, Arkansas

Dark figures appeared at the windows on either side of the building, the light inside reflecting off snout-like countenances that Nail recognized as men wearing gas masks. His hand streaked for the .38 snub he carried in his belt. He heard Big C shout, "Get down!"

Stun grenades exploded in bright flares that blasted out glass in the opened windows, rattled the walls and slapped people off their feet. Tear gas followed, issuing toxic clouds of smoke and mist. Trapped men yelled and coughed. The attack was swift and well-coordinated.

Nail desperately looked around for Sharon, his eyes burning and almost blinded. He caught sight of a ball cap with a ponytail. She knelt up front with both hands covering her eyes and face. Smoke swirled. Nail sprang to his feet to go to her. An explosion knocked him over a row of folding chairs. He landed on his head. The gun flew from his grasp. Pain shot from the wound he sustained at ORU and down his spine.

There was a reason they called those damn things *stun* grenades.

A brief rattle of gunfire, sharp and deafening in enclosed spaces. Stomping and crashing about. Yelling and screaming. Hacking and coughing up tear gas. More gunfire. Not from the Defenders, who, unsuspectingly, had secured their weapons in their cars and pickups.

Nail had no idea what was going on. Now unarmed, he crawled on elbows and knees toward where he last glimpsed Sharon, carrying his head low to the floor for the fresher air there. He reached the lectern and felt all about. His eyes seemed scalded with boiling water. All he saw were blurred shapes appearing and disappearing in the churn of smoke and mist.

Someone kicked him in the back, knocking him flat on his face. Arms grabbed him from both sides and from behind. Half-blinded, Nail wrenched free and lashed back at blurred forms. His knee connected with somebody's groin; he heard a satisfying yelp of pain. He kicked viciously at other man-shapes.

Although he accounted well for himself, he was outnumbered and quickly overpowered. His captors flipped him back onto his belly and locked his hands behind his back with plastic tie-strips. Men on each arm hoisted him to his feet and rushed him out of the schoolhouse into the fresh night air. He gasped to fill his lungs with it.

"Okay, we got them!" exclaimed a voice gone Darth Vader through a gas mask.

Nail was ushered at a run from the school. There was no more shooting. The only sounds were of running feet, a few shouted commands, and muffled cries from tear gas victims. Even the whippoorwills had hushed.

Flames erupted from the windows of the schoolhouse. Nail smelled gasoline and felt the heat. He had last seen Sharon near the lectern. Frantic with fear and concern, he struggled with his captors, but succeeded only in knocking them off their stride. Although he still couldn't see, he had the impression of being half-dragged through a collection of parked vehicles. A large number of men were running all around him. Doors slammed, engines roared to life.

A commanding voice shouted, "Redeploy! You know where to go."

Nail felt himself lifted by his bound arms and tossed into the back of what he assumed to be a van or SUV. He bounced off another passenger who was apparently in the same state of bondage. He was so overwrought that he barely heard his fellow captive's surprised yelp. He continued to kick at his tormentors until they captured his legs and tied them together with rope, so tightly he felt his circulation cut off. Secured hand and foot, all he could do was lie there wedged between the other prisoner and the side of the van. The double doors slammed. He heard them lock. The engine kicked over and the vehicle lurched forward, immediately picking up speed and jouncing over rough country roads.

"James, are you all right?"

His head hurt like hell, but he forgot all about the pain in his relief at hearing Sharon's voice.

"Oh, God! It *is* you," he whispered back. "I was so afraid—I mean, the fire and everything."

"I'm glad to see *you.*"

"Under the circumstances, maybe neither of us should be so glad."

"You think we're being arrested?"

"More like abducted."

"James, I'm scared. Terrified."

"Now's the time for it if you can get an extra wish on your falling star," he said.

As Nail's vision cleared, he determined they were being transported in a utility van with small windows in the rear doors and none on the sides. The van stopped after awhile and one of the two men up front came back and tossed a blanket over the prisoners. Nail guessed it was to conceal them from any nosy local cops.

"What are you doing with us?" Nail demanded. "I want to see Kimbrell."

The man emitted a harsh laugh. "You don't want to see Kimbrell."

They started up again. Nail succeeded in dislodging a corner of the blanket by shaking his head back and forth. At least now he could see enough from the van's floor to tell dark from light. They left gravel roads and were soon speeding along a freeway. Headlights of passing traffic washed the inside of the van. There was nothing within reach of the cop's hand that he could use as a weapon or as a tool to cut his bonds.

They passed through a small town, slowing, and Nail saw through the rear window the name of the town on a stalk-like *Love's* sign: Roland. "We're on I-40 heading east toward Arkansas," he relayed to Sharon, whispering.

"Shouldn't they be taking us to Tulsa? That's where the warrants were issued."

"I guess we're not in Kansas anymore, Toto."

"I always despised that wimpy little dog."

"How about Dorothy?"

"James, will you listen to us? We're babbling."

Nail attempted to use his teeth to remove the blanket from Sharon's head, unsuccessfully.

"James, I'm *really* scared."

He felt her body trembling against his.

They reached the Ozarks after an hour. The van lumbered uphill and picked up speed on the down slopes. Nail thought they were headed north and east, maybe up toward Mountain View. He moved as close as he could to Sharon to try to comfort her. After awhile, she stopped trembling and dozed off from exhaustion. Nail remained awake and alert for an opportunity to escape, although the possibility of that seemed slim at the moment.

Since he had nothing better to do, he pondered over what could have gone wrong at the schoolhouse. Big C had assured him that only he and Colonel Mosby knew about Sharon's and his pending visit. The snitches should have found out only that evening along with everyone else, certainly not in sufficient time to contact Homeland Security for a raid on the schoolhouse. Yet, the Homies knew exactly what they came for. The attackers made their way directly for Sharon and him the instant stun and tear gas grenades began going off. Nail knew they had been set up.

But by whom? Where was the leak? Had the Homies tapped their cell phones through the National Security Agency? These days the feds didn't need a tap warrant to listen in on private conversations.

All this brought up another nagging question. Why weren't Sharon and he shot at the scene instead of snatched if Kimbrell wanted to get rid of them? That would be the easy solution: Kill them and claim they were part of a militia plotting to overthrow the government.

Further consideration opened another avenue of exploration. Zenergy and perhaps even some of the government-tamed news outlets might begin to connect the dots if Nail and Sharon were killed in a Homeland Raid. It would be too obvious. Jerry Baer murdered—and then a week later his apparent heir successor killed.

The same reasoning applied to Nail, who was known to be investigating the case on his own and whose daughter was slain with Baer. Nail and Sharon had fled from material witness warrants, apparently afraid for their lives at the hands of the Homeland Security agency that had killed two previous militia members under questionable circumstances. The conclusion was sobering. Sharon and he were already fugitives. Instead of being murdered in the open to become martyrs to their cause, they were about to disappear and never be seen or heard from again.

"James?" Sharon whispered, stirring.

"Huh?"

"Were you asleep?"

"Like a baby."

"Who are these people? Are they from the government?"

"They're here to help us. The check's in the mail."

"What are we going to do?"

"I don't see we have much choice except to go along for the ride."

"This is not going to end well," she decided. "James, will you pray with me?"

"If you think God is listening."

"He's better than wishing on a star..." She hesitated, then began to pray. "Dear Precious Jesus, our Savior in Heaven, son of the Living God..."

The long ride and the steepness of the driving terrain suggested they were deep in the Ozark Mountains of either north central Arkansas or Missouri when the van slowed and geared down to turn onto a rougher road. Nail heard gravel crunching underneath the tires. They traveled several miles like this with tree branches slapping against the sides of the vehicle before it stopped and the engine cut off. It was near dawn. From his restricted point of view, Nail saw gray sky and a pine bough hanging above the windshield.

Sharon began to hyperventilate as she struggled with approaching terror. She must have reached the same conclusion as Nail had. He struggled against his tethers, but it was no use.

The back doors flung open. Summer heat and humidity flooded into the air-conditioned cargo bay. Nail cocked his bound legs for a last desperate stand, intending to kick out the teeth of the first man who touched them. He would not go peacefully into that good night. Someone jerked their blanket off and jumped back before Nail could get a good shot at him.

"Ooo-whoo!" whistled a young cocky character wearing the AmeriCorps uniform of black jeans, boots and green T-shirt with the crossed-shovels AmeriCorps emblem on it. "She's a looker on TV, but she's even hotter in person. 'Hello, America,'" he mocked, mimicking Jerry Baer's distinctive voice. "'Welcome to *The Jerry Baer Show'* ...Oh, I forgot. There ain't no *Jerry Baer Show* no more."

His comrades laughed. They were likewise uniformed. Several carried rifles and sidearms. An older man stepped forward. He appeared to be in his thirties and transported himself with some authority. He was muscled like a bodybuilder, with blond hair cut military style.

"Move over, shitbirds," he snarled at the others.

Nail's legs were still cocked, but he froze in astonishment. The colorful tattoo leaped out at him even in the poor light of dawn. It decorated the blond man's left arm from bulging biceps to wrist—a dragon previously burned indelibly into Nail's memory.

## Citizens Train as Pro-Government Militia

***(Washington)****—The White House confirmed Friday that it has begun military training for civilians in what White House spokesman Dewey Gubbins called a first step in assuring law and order in the nation. AmeriCorps, he said, will provide most of the manpower. Recruiting centers are to be opened in seven major locations nationwide...*

*"We must no longer rely on just the military," President Anastos said. "We must have, to attain our national security objectives, a civilian defense force just as powerful, just as strong, just as well-funded and well-trained as the military...*

# Chapter Thirty-Two

## Bunch, Oklahoma

Big C Brown had lost sight of Nail in the tear gas and turmoil of gunfire and men coughing and hacking and running about in near-blind panic. Although his gun appeared in his hand, he found it impossible to discern friend from foe in the smoke and gas. All but blinded, he located the doorway by chance and dived through it with others into fresh air, his great bulk knocking over a couple of raiders in gas masks attempting to enter. He whirled to fight, but Defenders and attackers were so mixed he hesitated to fire for fear of killing his own people. It was against his nature to run, but he saw no alternative except to offer himself as a target to men not handicapped by loss of vision. He bolted for the nearby line of elms, threw himself to the ground in a thicket and waited for his eyesight to return.

Shooting ceased almost as abruptly as it began. Noxious gasoline fumes filled the air. Windows in the schoolhouse glowed. Flames began lapping, as though seeking oxygen to breathe. Heated eerie light drove darkness into the trees. Armed men in black still wearing gas masks ran about shouting at each other as they broke for their vehicles parked down the road. One attacker was so excited he thrust his automatic rifle at the moon and released a burst. Another man cursed him.

As far as Big C could tell, most of the Defenders had escaped into the woods. The aggressors were after bigger game. He spotted Sharon, dazed and with her hands cuffed, being hustled off by a squad of goons.

Not far behind rushed another squad with Nail in its midst. He was struggling but appeared hampered by cuffed hands and the effects of tear gas.

Big C swore underneath his breath as he chose caution over valor and held his fire. As far as he knew, he was the only armed man among the Defenders and was thus heavily outgunned. A one-sided firefight likely ended in the deaths of Defenders and perhaps even Sharon's and Nail's.

He sprang to his feet. Crouched over and using the trees as cover, he headed at a fast dogtrot toward the invaders' vehicles, hoping to reach them before they sped off with his friends. He would let circumstances there dictate actions.

He encountered other militiamen lying low in the darkness. In his haste he did not bother to stop for explanations. He had almost reached parked cars north of the schoolhouse, out of the firelight, when the vehicles started peeling out, slinging gravel. Too late. He broke into a full run.

Only a heavily-armed rearguard of four attackers remained when Big C reached the site. These men were backing toward a four-wheel-drive Ford Ranger, the only vehicle left, weapons ready in case their victims rallied. Big C spotted a lone straggler hurrying along the road in the moonlight. Apparently, the others hadn't missed him yet. Big C crouched in ambush as the guy approached a curve in the road that hid him from view of his comrades clambering into the Ford's open bed.

He smelled the man's sweat mixed with the odor of gasoline and smoke from the burning school.

His quarry was a small man, not much more than a kid. Big C sprang from hiding. In a single practiced movement, he disarmed his prey, ripped off the guy's gas mask, clamped a big hand over his mouth, and snatched him back into the darkness of the trees. He threw him on the ground and straddled his body as he heard the attackers' remaining vehicle peel out. The kid was so terrified he was sputtering into the baseball mitt-sized hand that covered most of his face. Big C tapped the muzzle of his Glock against his captive's forehead.

"Nod you understand what this is," the cop hissed.

The kid nodded, kept nodding.

"Nod some more you understand you do anything except keep your mouth shut until I say otherwise I put a bullet through your pointy little peckerwood head. Got it?"

Continued nodding.

"You can stop now. We in agreement."

Big C relaxed his grip. The kid whimpered. Nearby came some rustling through the undergrowth. Still astraddle his prisoner, Big C swept his weapon toward the sound. Two shadows emerged.

"Identify yourself or you dead," Big C challenged.

"That you, Brown? It's us."

Big C recognized the voice. "All right."

They were a couple of Defenders named Cantrell and Beaver, the latter a full-blood Cherokee Indian. They squatted next to Big C and his captive.

"What you got?" Beaver asked.

Instead of answering, Big C shot back a question of his own. "Have you see Colonel Mosby?"

Suspicion was taking root in Big C's mind.

"Last I seen him," Beaver said, "he was in the woods out back. Him and Shorty Smith. Man, we didn't stand a chance tonight. They was all over us."

"Any casualties you know of?" the TPD officer asked.

"I seen somebody fall in the grass. I couldn't tell who it was. Them bastards ran off with Miss Lowenthal though. I think that's who they was after."

The prisoner's choked sobbing drew Big C's attention. Another tap on his forehead with the Glock made sure the cop had his undivided attention.

"You all by yourself now, man," Big C informed him. "Ain't nobody come to help you. I ask you some questions. You lie to me, I will kill you. Do you believe that?"

The kid *believed.*

"Good. You come here to kidnap a man and a woman. Where you taking them?"

Two Defenders died in the attack, gunned down in front of the schoolhouse. Colonel Mosby conducted a headcount to ascertain that no one was missing other than James Nail and Sharon Lowenthal. Fire quickly gutted the old school and collapsed much of the exterior natural rock walls. Militiamen, now armed, stood somberly around the fallen bodies of their comrades as the flames receded. One of the dead was a farmer named Calhoun, the other Luther Hawkins, the man Big C suspected, along with Tom Fullbright, of being an informant for the Homies.

"Them sons of bitches will pay for this," Fullbright muttered as he stared down at his dead friend. Some of the others glared balefully at Big C's prisoner lying in the grass with his hands and feet tied with pieces of electrical cord.

Colonel Mosby, who stood next to Big C, looked paler than normal and stood with his lean frame hunched at the shoulders. His head looked small and his nose huge in the light from the schoolhouse embers.

"The sheriff's department will have to be notified," he decided. "What about him?"

He indicated Big C's prisoner.

"Leave him here tied up for deputies to find."

Big C stood looking at the dead bodies of his fellow militiamen.

"Not a pretty sight, is it, Colonel?" he said.

Mosby seemed to choke on words lodged unspoken in his throat.

"How's Alice and the kids?" Big C inquired softly. "They getting over Ol' Ranger dying?"

"They'll be all right," Mosby finally replied in a small voice.

"You a cold liar, Colonel."

There was no reaction from the militia leader.

"Walk over here with me," Big C ordered.

Mosby followed dutifully, anguish written all over his narrow face. They stopped out of earshot of the others.

"*They* shot Ol' Ranger, didn't they?" Big C said, his dark eyes boring into the commander's. "It was a warning the same could happen to your wife and kids."

Mosby almost passed out on his feet. He licked his dry lips.

"I—"

"It wasn't Tom Fullbright or Luther Hawkins set the trap," Big C said, his voice low so that nearby militia wouldn't overhear. If they knew the situation with Mosby, they would likely execute their own leader. "You the one played us, Colonel. You the only one know I bringing James and Sharon to the meeting."

Mosby still couldn't find his voice. Big C lowered his own voice to a threatening growl.

"Colonel, you the one also set up Ron Sparks. You and I are going to have a little back to Jesus session."

Mosby stared at Hawkins' and Calhoun's corpses lying obscenely in the firelight, blood drenching Hawkins' shirt and part of Calhoun's skull blown away.

"He promised," Mosby blurted out suddenly. "He promised nobody'd get hurt. He just wanted to arrest that rogue cop and the girl. That's all, I swear."

Big C likewise looked at the corpses. "Kimbrell? I see he kept his word as usual."

"I had to do it," Mosby wailed in a thin, wavering voice. "You seen how Alice and the kids were. They're scared to death. Hell, man, *I'm* scared to death. These people are serious."

Big C took the Colonel's arm and guided him away from the fire-lit clearing toward the darkness of the elm groves.

"Now, Colonel, you going to tell me all about it..."

# Chapter Thirty-Three

## Ozark Mountains, Arkansas

Coming face to face with his daughter's killer so unexpectedly stunned Nail that he neglected to resist when the young AmeriCorps men pulled Sharon and him out the back of the van and dropped them on the ground. Sharon cried out and gasped to catch her breath.

"Put this on your lying show, bitch," someone taunted.

Nail's eyes fixed on the Green Shirt with the tattoo. The hate and fury he felt was enough to peel paint off a new barn. Only through arrogance or incompetence would the man have allowed his dragon to show from the helicopter when he and his still-unknown accomplice opened fire at ORU.

He seemed to know who Nail was. He kicked the cop in the ribs with a steel-toed combat boot. "Wha' the fuck you staring at, asshole?"

Pain shot through Nail's body, but he refused to give his tormenter any satisfaction by reacting to the kick. He suffered through. His eyes bored into the killer's. *My time will come,* was their unspoken message.

"That's enough, Forbis," crackled the voice of a squat, bulldog-shaped man who pushed his way through the gathered Green Shirts. He was an older man with ruthless eyes set deep into a broad face. He stared at Nail on the ground, then looked at Forbis in disgust.

"You're the real asshole, Forbis," he growled. "He knows who you are. You might as well have been wearing neon on that fucking tattoo."

Forbis stiffened, but held his tongue. The bulldog seemed to be his superior.

"Get these prisoners out of here," he barked.

"Where do you want them?" Forbis asked with open resentment.

Bulldog bristled. "Forbis, I don't care who you think you are, you ain't shit to me. Separate 'em. Throw one in the stockade and put the other in the CQ building until I get word from Tulsa about what they want done. Did we lose anybody?"

A man who seemed to be the commander of the raid stepped forward hesitatingly. "We can't account for Carlisle."

Bulldog glared. "Fuck!" he said.

That these people were not attempting to conceal their identities or their participation in the ORU massacre reinforced in Nail's mind the inescapable conclusion that Sharon and he were not meant to leave here alive. Bulldog stalked away. Several young men, not much out of their teens if at all, freed the prisoners' legs and lifted them to their feet while Forbis watched.

"You're going to die, Forbis," Nail promised. "Then I'll kill your partner."

It was an old cop's ruse intended to trick a suspect into thinking the cop knew it all. It worked. Forbis reflexively exchanged looks with another Green Shirt, this one thinner and likewise in his thirties, with eyes as cold and inexpressive as a snake's.

"What's your name?" Nail asked him. "I want to know who I'm killing."

This individual returned Nail's hard gaze with one of his own. "Henshaw," he scoffed. "I want *you* to know who puts the bullet through *your* head."

Forbis and Henshaw remained behind while some of the younger Green Shirts hustled the prisoners toward a military-style cantonment area. Nail took in his surroundings for future references. The van had dropped them off at an unpaved parking lot where a number of other vehicles were parked. Vans, SUVs, off-road four-wheel-drive Broncos and Safaris, a couple of military-style Humvees, all painted black with the AmeriCorp logo of crossed shovels on their doors.

The sun was rising red and inflamed as they crossed a manicured parade field where platoons of Green Shirts armed with the latest version of the M16 main battle rifle were already conducting close order drill. Other formations sweating at PT double-timed among the spread of long, low buildings as they chanted revised Jodie calls:

*I wanna be a Green Shirt Ranger.*

*I wanna live a life of danger.*

*One-two-three-four...*

*Sing it some more.*

*Anastos! Anastos! Anastos!*

This was a paramilitary boot camp, pure and simple, and heavily armed. It occurred to Nail that government was about to turn a corner—or had already turned the corner—into a chilling new realm that would have been unimaginable only a few years earlier. Sharon shuddered and looked at Nail. They were being escorted side by side.

"Are you all right?" Nail asked her.

"It's according to how you define *all right*," she whispered bravely.

"Sharon, I'm sorry I got you into this," he apologized. "I should have sent you back to New York."

"It wouldn't have mattered where I was. Do you see what's going on here? We've got to somehow get the word out."

Two of the five guards in the escort meandered off toward what was obviously a chow hall, judging from the odors of coffee, bacon and eggs that wafted from it. The three remaining were equipped with holstered sidearms. Sharon lowered her voice.

"You recognized the tattoo?"

"Forbis and Henshaw. Don't forget those names." What he meant was, *Don't forget them in case I don't make it and you do.*

Their guards were watching activities on the parade field as they walked rather than paying strict attention to their duties.

"In police work," Nail whispered, "we say it's important to know who fired the bullet, but it's more important to know who paid for the bullet."

"Kimbrell?"

"He's part of the chain, but I'm not sure he paid for the bullet."

It gave Nail a headache trying to picture the complicated monster behind all the grasping tentacles that seemed to reach out from everywhere. There was nothing either of them could do as long as they were prisoners.

"Where's your ball cap?" Nail noticed. She was squinting against the bright rising sun.

"I suppose I lost it at the school."

"The first thing I give you—and you lose it."

She gave him a wan smile. "It wasn't the first thing."

"And that would be—?"

"I'll let you figure that out."

She was one plucky lady.

"That's enough talking," a guard commanded in a surprisingly boyish voice.

They approached a one-story green-painted building that reminded Nail of a company HQ at Fort Polk or Fort Benning. A sign over the door read *Stockade*. The sun felt warm on Nail's face. He didn't want to go inside. He thought he might never see another sunrise. Even more agonizing was knowing that what happened to him likewise happened to Sharon. One of the guards rapped on the door.

"You do realize what they're going to do to us?" Sharon asked him.

The boyish Green Shirt refused to make eye contact. He looked over her head. His face drained of color.

"You will be an accessory to murder," Sharon reminded him bluntly.

He licked his lips and looked at his partners when he replied, "Ma'am, it's necessary that some obstructionists be eliminated in order to build a society that is equitable and just for all."

Like he was reciting it by rote.

"You could let us escape," Sharon suggested.

"Ma'am, I'm sorry. I have my orders."

The door opened and the prisoners were marched into an office occupied by three other Green Shirt cadets. Two of them escorted Nail down a narrow hallway to a barred cell furnished only with a toilet bucket in the corner. Nail stopped and looked back. The hall door into the office was still open. He saw Sharon being dragged off. He tried to break past his guards to get to her, but he was no match for them with his hands tied behind his back. The Green Shirts shoved him stumbling into the cell and slammed the heavy door. He heard it lock.

"James, I'll be waiting!" Sharon shouted, and then she was gone.

## Government Revises School Breakfast

***(Minneapolis)***—*Thanks to the intervention of the First Lady and President Anastos' Council on Fitness, Sports and Nutrition, students like Mickey Rodriguez no longer have to go without breakfast because of late buses or overslept alarm clocks.*

*Starting this week, high schools will serve free breakfast in the classrooms. Teachers say this will ensure student do not miss breakfast...*

*"I was always missing breakfast because I have to get up really early and I didn't get here in time for me to eat in the cafeteria," said Rodriguez, a senior.*

*Every student, regardless of family income, is welcome to eat free breakfast through the program, funded by the federal government. Currently, 88.4 percent of students receive free lunches and breakfasts. That percentage is expected to grow...*

# Chapter Thirty-Four

## Washington D. C.

It was Sunday and normally Dennis Trout's day off. He and Judy had just flown back from New York on the seven a.m. shuttle when his cell rang. Wiedersham asked him to stop by the office on a couple of matters. Trout supposed overtime went with his new status.

Everything was good between Judy and him again. They had had a nice dinner in Times Square—*not* The Pig Out Café—and attended *Phantom of The Opera*. They had remained in their hotel room all day Saturday. Judy was bubbling again. Or *babbling*. Whatever. His announcement that Wiedersham wanted him to work Sunday instead of touring the Smithsonian as they originally planned failed to dampen her revived spirits.

"I'm seeing you tonight?" she asked with a suggestive smile.

"Marilyn has plans," he apologized.

If anything put the damper on her, that would. She shrugged. Puzzled, Trout reflected on how well both his women seemed to be taking disappointment. When he walked into Wiedersham's office, the Majority Leader handed him a memo distributed on State Department letterhead. It began with the Subject line: *International Small Arms Destruction Day.*

*The United States is joining the UN effort to curtail ownership of and trade in small arms and light weapons...*

President Anastos was asking Congress to allocate one hundred thirty million dollars to buy back an estimated million-and-a-half guns off American streets and destroy them. Every cokehead in the nation's ghettos, barrios and cracker neighborhoods would be bringing in their stolen Saturday Night Specials and, no questions asked, selling them to the government in order to use the cash to buy other, better weapons off the streets. With enough dough left over for a good hit of crack or crystal meth. It was insane, but Trout kept his mouth shut.

"Get with Gubbins and prepare a press announcement before Zenergy gets all over it with their Second Amendment bullshit," he instructed. "You know what to say."

Trout could spin with the best of them. "That it'll make America safe...?"

"*Safer*," the Leader corrected. As was his habit, he changed topics abruptly. "So how did your meeting go yesterday in New York?"

Trout thought of John's comment about chaos and about how rioting and violence in the streets were a necessary ingredient to "fundamentally transform the United States." He remarked on how the protests against financial institutions going on in New York seemed made to order as part of the expanding chaos.

Wiedersham gave his barking laugh at Trout's naïve observation. "What makes you think made to order?"

Trout blinked in surprise. "You mean they weren't *our* people—?"

"Even chaos has to be organized or it never begins. You're in the big leagues now, Trout."

Trout swallowed any second thoughts he may have entertained. "I'd rather be on the wave of history than bucking it."

"Pragmatic," Wiedersham said. "I like pragmatic. You can trust that over ideology."

There was a small pause while the Leader regarded his chief of staff. Trout guiltily concluded Wiedersham must know about Judy since he had provided two Broadway tickets and reservations for two at the Hilton in New York—and had known Marilyn was staying home. To Trout's relief, however, Wiedersham avoided broaching the topic. Instead, he snatched a sheaf of documents from his *IN* box and thrust them at Trout.

"This came in last night while you were in New York," he snapped. "Fuckheads. Do they really think they can get away with this shit?"

He savagely punched numbers into his phone. "Jackman, get your ass over here... I know it's Sunday. Don't give me any of your fucking lame lip. I want to talk to you and Hillard. If you can't control your state legislators, we'll get somebody who can."

Jackman and Hillard were U.S. Senators from New Hampshire and not likely to challenge Wiedersham's authority. Not only was Wiedersham Senate Majority Leader, he was also a member of the President's circle of anointed insiders.

Trout understood his brother-in-law's choler after he scanned the documents thrust at him. The New Hampshire State Legislature had passed a "nullification" resolution declaring "certain actions of the federal government totally void." It seemed there were still a few politicians around who had a set of balls. Something in Trout admired their defiance.

The proclamation reminded Congress and the U.S. President, in much the same language as that issued by a band of colonials in Philadelphia two centuries ago, that:

*Any act by the Congress of the United States or Executive Order by the Judicatories of the United States of America which assumes a power not delegated to the government by the Constitution and which serves to diminish the liberty of the any of the several States or their citizens shall constitute a nullification of the Constitution by the government of the United States of America...*

*That, therefore, all acts of Congress of the United States which do abridge the freedom of religion, freedom of speech, freedom of the press, are not law, but are altogether void, and of no force...*

*Acts which could cause a nullification include, but are not limited to:*

*I. Establishing martial law or a state of emergency within one of the States without the consent of the legislature of that State;*

*II. Requiring involuntary servitude, or governmental service other than a draft during a declared war;*

*III. Surrendering any power delegated or not delegated to any corporation or foreign government;*

*IV. Any act regarding religion, further limitations on freedom of political speech, or further limitation on freedom of the press;*

*V. Further infringements on the right to keep and bear arms...*

*Any future government of the United States of America shall require ratification of three quarters of the States seeking to form a government of the United States of America and shall not be binding upon any State not seeking to form such a government...*

That things in the country had sunk to this level left Trout stupefied. Nullification was paramount to a state of revolt against the federal government. If allowed to stand, it could inspire other disgruntled states to follow suit. Wasn't that how the Civil War started?

Wiedersham hung up the phone in refueled rage. Apparently, he had been working himself up all weekend over this.

"Who's the Regional Homeland Security Director in New Hampshire?" he demanded of Trout. "Find out and get him on the line. It's time these cocksuckers understand where the power is. Knock a few of them in the dirt and they'll come around. They'll know better than to fuck with me next time."

# Chapter Thirty-Five

## Ozark Mountains

As soon as the cell door clanged behind him, Nail limped to the single barred window that looked out upon the parade field to see if he could tell where these people were taking Sharon. She and her escort were crossing the field toward buildings on the other side. Sharon walked with her head held high in defiance, as though she knew Nail watched and was sending a message that she believed in him. She soon disappeared behind a long, green barracks. There were three or four other structures beyond, one of which was likely the CQ where Sharon was to be confined.

Nail allowed himself a moment of despair. What made Sharon think he could save her when he hadn't even been able to save his own daughter? He was no shining knight on a white horse out to slay dragons and rescue maidens. He was just an ordinary cop starting to comprehend that he may be involved in something way over his head.

But he was stubborn. Connie used to say he had a head as hard as an anvil.

He inspected his cell from wall to wall, corner to corner, limping from the old bullet wound. The walls were rough-hewn pine two-by-eights solidly attached to what he assumed to be standard two-by-four studs. The ceiling was likewise constructed. The floor was a concrete slab. There was one steel door, solid except for the barred window at the top and a small opening at the bottom for sliding in food and water. Inside, opposite the door, was the steel-barred window. The slops bucket offered the only prospect of a weapon. It was soft plastic.

Nail returned to the window and looked out through the bars. He watched Forbis and Henshaw cross the parade ground with several other Green Shirts and enter the long, green barracks. Revenge was not a laudable quality, as he had realized from investigating homicides. Yet, thoughts of revenge consumed him.

"Everything will be solved peacefully through God if you stand where you're supposed to stand," Sharon liked to preach, contending that everything went up for grabs when people resorted to violence and picked up guns.

Maybe God needed a little help sometimes. Those responsible for the deaths of Jamie, Jerry Baer and the others at ORU that fateful day were never going to be brought to justice in the traditional sense.

Sharon would have to realize that. They seemed to be protected from high up the political chain. Cops liked to say that at times justice came only from the barrel of a cop's gun.

Nail didn't have a gun. He was locked in an escape-proof cell with his hands bound behind his back. Unless he found a way to escape, today would likely be the last he or Sharon ever saw.

# Chapter Thirty-Six

## Ozark Mountains

The problem with doing nothing was not knowing when you were done. Nail paced his cell and counted his paces: four one way, eight the other. He stared out the window toward the green barracks across the parade field where he last saw Forbis and Henshaw. Beyond were the smaller buildings where Sharon's guards had taken her. He listened with his ear next to the steel door and heard a murmur of conversation and laughter coming from the stockade's guard room.

To test the guards' response, he called out to them through the tiny window in the door. "Hey, up there! I need a drink of water."

Feedback was about what he expected from this bunch of young cutthroats. "Drink piss, pig!"

A half-hour passed. Then somebody slipped a tin cup of water through the slot at the bottom of the door. Nail peeped out the window in time to recognize the boyish Green Shirt whom Sharon had engaged about letting them escape. Apparently, he possessed a seed of conscience somewhere inside all that brainwashing.

"How am I going to drink with my hands tied?"

"Sorry. You'll have to do the best you can. I'll be back for the cup in a minute. Don't let on to the others that I brought it."

He walked away. Since his hands were tied behind his back, Nail lay belly down on the floor and used his chin and lips to tip the water into his mouth. He *was* thirsty. The sharp edge of the thin-rimmed cup nicked his lip. Quickly, he poured what was left of the water on the floor and turned around to pick up the cup with his hands.

Scrambling to his feet, he fumbled the cup and dropped it. It clanged on the cement floor. Nail froze, fearing he may have alerted his guards. His young benefactor had obviously gone against the others in bringing him water. He needed the kid to return for the cup rather than the others.

Loud laughter came from up front. The guards sounded too immersed in smoking and joking to pay much attention to a prisoner who, after all, was trussed up and safely locked in his cell.

Retrieving the cup, he backed up to a loose nail in the wall he had noticed earlier. The head of the nail barely protruded. It took him only a few minutes of feeling with his hands to insert the thin lip of the cup behind the nail head and pry it from the wall to a length of about an inch. Another few minutes of sawing the plastic tie-strip across the nail head and his hands broke free. Thank God for plastics.

He was unlikely to get another chance—if merely freeing his hands in a jail cell could be considered a chance—so he had better make this one good.

He placed the cup on the floor two paces inside where it could be seen by anyone looking through the door window. Then, pretending he was still bound, he sprawled with his back against the wall, closed his eyes, and feigned sleeping. Hey, it always worked for Humphrey Bogart and Clint Eastwood. He hoped Sharon had at least one more wish from the falling star in her bag.

"Psst! Hey! Wake up in there. I need the cup back."

Nail snored deeply.

"Mister? Wake up."

Nail snored. He heard the boy turn and walk away.

It hadn't worked.

He was about to give up when he heard the rattle of a key in the door. The boy must have gone to retrieve it. The door opened. Through slitted eyelids, Nail watched the kid hesitate in the doorway as he glanced back toward the guardroom, then back at the tin cup only two steps away.

*Damn!* The kid appeared unarmed. Nail needed a gun, but he had to play out the hand dealt him.

*Come on in, said the spider to the fly.*

The boy did. He bent over to pick up the cup. In that instant, while his attention was diverted, Nail sprang to his feet like a cat. The old bullet wound had never handicapped him. In a single bound he was on the Green Shirt, one hand muffling his mouth, the other arm around his neck to choke off his breathing. He shoved the door closed with his foot and frog-marched the kid to the far corner of the room to establish ground rules. Too bad there wasn't a fence post available.

The Green Shirt was so damned skinny that Nail almost felt sorry for him as he applied pressure with his neck hold to stop the kid from fighting back. Lucky the kid wasn't the size of Man Mountain Dean or that murdering piece of shit Forbis.

"I don't want to kill you," Nail said. "You might live if you do what I say."

The boy relaxed, accepting the terms.

"How many guards up front? Use your fingers."

The kid held up five fingers. Nail cut off his wind. "How many?"

Two fingers.

"That's better. They armed? One finger for yes, two for no."

One finger.

"How come you're not packing? Never mind."

Nail swept his captive's feet out from underneath him and dropped him to a sitting position. The Green Shirt's eyes wallowed about in terror. He seemed to understand that this hard, Indian-looking man would snap his neck like a twig if he had to.

With one hand, the other keeping his prisoner muzzled, Nail ripped off the boy's AmeriCorps T-shirt and tore it into thick strips, using his knee and free hand. Soon, the boy was gagged and tied hand and foot with strips of his own T-shirt and his boot laces and belt.

The key was still in the door. Nail bent over the kid. "I expect you to wait here for me," he quipped.

He locked the cell door behind him, pocketed the key, and slipped down the hallway toward the other door, a plan already formed in his mind. He listened with his ear close to the door. He heard the voices of two men.

The old trick of faking sleep had worked once. Why wouldn't another old trick work just as well?

He flattened himself against the wall so that when the door opened inwardly he would be behind it. Turning his head away to project his voice down the hallway, he let out a low moan. Everything went quiet in the guardroom.

"Smitty?"

Nail waited a couple of heartbeats and groaned again.

"Stop fucking around, Smitty!"

A chair scraped across the floor. Footsteps approached. The door opened. A Green Shirt stepped tentatively into the hallway. Bigger and stronger-looking than Smitty, with his head shaved. He wore a Glock in a holster. Maybe Smitty was unarmed because they didn't trust him to carry.

"What the fuck you doing, Smitty?"

He started down the hallway. Nail hesitated a moment to make sure the second guard wasn't following. He pushed the door closed with his knee and pounced. The Green Shirt yelped in surprise. Nail threw him to the floor and ripped the pistol from its holster.

A chair in the other room crashed to the floor. Nail tapped his victim on the head with the butt of the gun. Well, maybe a bit more than a tap. Blood sprayed.

Nail snapped upright and pivoted toward the door, his thumb instinctively switching the Glock to safety *Off.* The door banged open.

The other Green Shirt filled the doorway. Seeing Nail, his hand snaked toward the gun at his belt.

The sound of gunplay would bring others running. It had to be avoided. Nail greeted the Green Shirt with a cold grin, his gun leveled, steady and pointed at mid-mass.

"One of us is going to die," he promised in a low growl.

Hand still on the butt of his gun, the Green Shirt's gaze reflexively shifted toward his bleeding buddy on the floor. This guy was holding his head with both hands, blood spurting between his fingers while he tried to push himself into the wall to escape from the mad Indian standing above him.

"The surest way to get your heads blown off is to have them up your asses," Nail warned.

# Chapter Thirty-Seven

## Ozark Mountains

Green Shirt training seemed to have been suspended as the heat index pegged around one-ten, all activity moving indoors out of the sun. Nail was armed and dangerous with the pair of Glock 19s he relieved from the two guards, who, along with the kid Smitty, were now tied hand and foot in his former cell with plastic tie-strip handcuffs he located in a closet in the guard room. The only sounds they made were muffled complaints through their gags.

The shaved-head guy was still bleeding pretty good from where Nail tapped him on the head, but he wasn't seriously injured. Nail had stripped the other of his black jeans, bill cap, green T-shirt and holster and donned them himself. His new apparel fit a bit snug, but it would have to do. The shaved-head man was more Nail's size, but he had blood all over his uniform.

Disguised in the AmeriCorps outfit, Nail hoped to locate and reach Sharon before he was discovered. He would deal with Forbis and Henshaw later—pass jail, skip trial and go directly to the morgue. But Sharon came first.

The groomed parade field that lay between the stockade and the long green barracks was about one football field across. The only way to reach the CQ where Sharon was apparently being held was to cross it in the open.

Nail jerked the bill of his purloined uniform cap lower over his eyes to hide his features. He was about to turn from the office windows to head for the door when he spotted two Green Shirts exiting the green barracks. The larger of the two resembled Forbis until he removed his cap to swipe sweat from his brow, revealing a full thatch of short black hair.

They headed toward the stockade. At this rate, Nail was going to have his old cell filled with Green Shirts. Somebody was bound to get suspicious. Nail had learned in the army that the best battle plan rarely survived first contact with the enemy.

The kid Smitty gave him an idea. He hurried to the locked cell, untied the kid's feet and escorted him to the guard room. The two Green Shirts were halfway across the parade field and still coming.

"Do exactly what I say and you and those two assholes coming out here will live," Nail informed him. "I'll strangle you if you make an attempt to warn them."

The cop untied his hands and removed his gag.

"Sit at the desk," he instructed. "Don't get up for any reason. Get rid of those guys if they come in here. If anything goes wrong—"

Nail let him take a long believer's look down the barrel of his Glock.

"P-Please. I'm supposed to get married next month—"

"Congratulations. We don't want to make her a widow before she's a bride. Act natural. I'll be in the hall behind the door watching every move you make."

"Y-Y-yessir," Smitty stammered.

Nail placed both hands on Smitty's shoulders and leaned over face to face with him.

"Calm down. Your life depends on it."

He was taking a big chance on the kid, but it seemed his best option. He limped to the hallway door and closed it behind him, leaving the door cracked enough that he could see most of the room. Smitty flinched but remained seated when the two Green Shirts sauntered in. Neither was armed. Nail figured they had been sent over from CQ to check on the guards.

"Damn, Smitty, you're sweating like a hog," the black-haired one observed. The other was a redhead. "Turn up the air."

"It's set on eighty," Smitty managed with some degree of normality. "That's regulation."

"Dude, you look like shit," the redhead noted.

"Uh..."

"What's the matter with you, man?" the dark one demanded.

"I'm...uh...not feeling well. I've been vomiting all day."

"Why don't you rack out? We don't need three guards to watch one asshole. Speaking of assholes, how's he doing?"

"He's in his cell."

"CQ says make sure not to open his door for nothing. He's a cop and they say he's a mean son of a bitch. Where's Crabb and Pee Wee?"

"They, uh, went to the mess hall to get some iced tea," Smitty lied with growing confidence. "They'll be right back."

"There'll be a fecal storm if the Commander finds out they left their post without reporting in."

"You won't tell?" Smitty whined. "They'll be back real quick."

The Green Shirt visitors laughed. "Dude, you are such a pussy."

"I'm not a pussy."

"Then you're the next thing to it."

"H-How long we gonna be on watch?"

The dark-haired Green Shirt shrugged. “I guess until they tell us. We’re outa here, pussy. Tell Crabb and Pee Wee they’re pushing it, taking off like they did.”

They laughed and shut the door behind them as they left. Smitty slumped at the desk, looking spent. Nail came out and checked on the departing Green Shirts through one of the windows. They were going back the same way they came. The somnolent hum of a hot summer’s day remained otherwise undisturbed.

“I-I did what you said,” Smitty hazarded.

“You did good, kid.”

“W-What are you going to do with me?”

“That depends. Which one of those buildings is the CQ?”

“It’s the lower white one behind the green barracks.”

Nail thought about it. Somebody was bound to notice one man out in the heat and question his purpose. He wondered if he could hole up until evening when activity started to pick up again. He sank onto the spare chair at the desk where he could watch Smitty and at the same time keep his eyes peeled out the window. Smitty shifted nervously.

“Is it true you was a police officer?” he asked to break the stale air. He sounded calmer.

“What else have you heard?”

“They said you was with the terrorists who hung the federal worker in the cemetery.”

“Do you believe that?”

“I—” Smitty hung his head.

“How did you get involved with this bunch? You don’t seem the type.”

“They’re like my family—”

“That’s not what I asked.”

Smitty looked up inquiringly, as though to gauge the cop’s interest. Nail encouraged him with a flick of his hand.

“I guess it was Michael Moore,” he said hesitatingly. “You know, the fat guy who makes movies? I seen him, like, on *Oprah* or something. He was saying like how young people have to face the truth. We ain’t never going to be rich. The system is rigged in favor of the few fat cats and we aren’t one of them. Not now. Not never. I couldn’t find a job, so when I heard about AmeriCorps, I went and signed up.”

He suffered himself a tremulous half-grin, as in apology.

“Were you at the old schoolhouse last night with the others?” Nail asked.

Smitty actually blushed. He was probably no older than eighteen or nineteen, one of the little hill boys like Nail had been growing up. Sharon said kids like him were being indoctrinated in "social justice" and "liberation theology" through the public education system.

"There used to be shows on TV like *Father Knows Best, My Three Sons,* and *Leave It To Beaver* in which fathers were strong role models," Sharon had pointed out during their stay at the Safe House. "Today, father figures on the boob tube are a bunch of dolts and fools. It's part of the Progressive culture to break down the family. Families fall apart, kids leave home, creating a vacuum for government to fill. If I had children of my own, they'd never step one foot into a public school."

She was opening Nail's eyes bit by bit.

Movement outside caught his attention. He stood to get a better look through the window as a party of four Green Shirts appeared from around one end of the Green Barracks and headed west toward the rise of forested hills nearby. Sharon's red T-shirt stood out in the field of green.

Smitty's face bleached to corpse pale. "Mr. Nail," he said in a choked voice, "they'll be coming for you next."

# Chapter Thirty-Eight

## Ozark Mountains

Smitty acknowledged what he said nearly everyone in camp already knew—that Sharon and Nail were going to be made *disappeared* in order to avert any kind of controversy over their deaths. The tattoo on Forbis' arm was visible even from a distance.

"I don't want nothing to do with this," Smitty said.

"Prove it."

Changing plans, Nail hurriedly stripped off the guard's uniform he had just put on and returned to his jeans, T-shirt and ball cap. He gave the guard's holster and one of the Glocks, unloaded, to Smitty. The other pistol, loaded, he stuck in his belt underneath his T-shirt in the small of his back where it would be easy to reach with his hands loosely tie-stripped behind to give the appearance that he was cuffed.

"If anybody stops us," he told Smitty, "you're escorting me to the woods."

A back door down the hallway led out onto the parade ground. In Nail's former cell, the shaved-headed man, Crabb, was still issuing complaints through his bloody gag. Pee Wee huddled in a corner with his legs pulled up to his chin.

Nail exited and walked at a fast pace along the edge of a single line of widely-spaced cedars, Smitty a step behind in his role as appointed guard. Sharon and her escort were ahead of them by a considerable lead and were approaching a wooded hill.

The sun bore down. Nail's shirt soaked up perspiration from heat and anxiety. Sharon and the Green Shirts with her entered the trees out of sight. Nail increased his stride without breaking into a jog that might arouse the suspicion of observers. His limp was nothing more than an inconvenience.

Smitty glanced back and uttered a warning. "Oh, God! They've found Crabb and Pee Wee tied up. They're heading this way."

Nail looked and saw five or six Green Shirts racing after them. It wouldn't take them long to catch up. Nail thought he recognized the figure leading the pack. Henshaw, the other gunman from the helicopter. Nail ripped his hands free.

"Smitty, you're on your own," he snapped as he broke into a full run toward where he last saw Sharon entering the woods. He experienced a flash of déjà vu—of his desperate and ultimately unsuccessful attempt to reach Jamie in time. He mustn't fail again.

Could fate be so cruel?

To his astonishment, Smitty remained at his heels when he reached the forest shadows.

"They'll think I helped you escape," he panted. "They'll kill me too. There's a clearing straight ahead."

Nail ducked and dodged through the trees and, sure enough, quickly approached the edge of a clearing. Sunshine washed it in bright summer radiance. Across its center burbled a stream from out of the mountains. Nail heard the howling of their pursuers behind him.

Ahead, Sharon knelt on her knees by the brook with four Green Shirts surrounding her. She was looking up directly into Forbis' eyes, defiant to the end. Nail had never met a woman with that kind of courage. Forbis pressed his pistol against her forehead. One of the cadets, perhaps more squeamish than the others, walked off with his back to the developing scene.

She had seconds left to live.

Nail dropped to one knee to use his uplifted leg as a brace. It was a long shot, even for an expert marksman. For Sharon's sake, his first shot had better be good.

He squeezed the trigger. The Glock bucked in his fist.

Forbis jerked as the bullet slashed through his brain. His weapon discharged at the same instant and appeared to blast a plume of flame directly into Sharon's skull. Her body plunged out of sight into tall grass next to the stream. Forbis toppled the other way, dead before he hit the ground.

"*Sharon!*" Nail bellowed.

Too late. Just like before.

Rage and grief drove him headlong toward where Sharon went down. Heedless of his own safety, his gun spitting fire in all directions, he charged directly through the three surviving Green Shirts. Caught by surprise, in shock at witnessing the annihilation of their leader, they lost their nerve and scattered without so much as drawing their weapons.

At the same time, armed men exploded from the underbrush on the other side of the brook, splashing through the water in full cavalry mode. Nail attempted to take a shot, but his gun was empty. Somewhere within the fog of combat that enveloped his brain, he heard a familiar voice shouting.

"James, no! It's us, bro'!"

With a muffled sob, Nail dropped to his knees in the grass next to Sharon. He crushed her limp body into his arms, against his chest. He heard a gasp, felt her move.

"*Sharon?*"

"What? *What?* I can't hear anything. Everything's a roar."

Nail's bullet had smashed into Forbis' brain just in time. The boom of the Green Shirt's gun next to her head had deafened her.

"I knew God would bring you in time," she managed.

With Sharon safe in his arms, Nail became once more cognizant of his surroundings. Forbis lay unmoving nearby, his skull ripped open and brain matter spilling out into the grass. Smitty was on his knees next to Nail, vomiting up breakfast. Several men Nail recognized from the Defenders' meeting at the schoolhouse took up a perimeter around them. A black Incredible Hulk fell on both knees to embrace Sharon and Nail together.

"You two all right? God, when I thought... We almost not make it in time."

"How did you find us?" Nail began.

"No time explain, bro'. Got to get the hell out. They be coming like cockroaches."

Nail helped Sharon to her feet.

"What are you saying?" she shouted, still deaf from the gun shot.

Big C had a 30.06 Winchester with scope slung over one massive shoulder. Nail's eyes hardened when he looked back toward where he last saw Henshaw and his squad. The job wasn't finished yet.

"Give me the rifle," he requested of Big C. "This'll only take a minute."

## Militia Attacks AmeriCorps Youth

***(Little Rock, Arkansas)****—A militia-instigated burst of violence in Arkansas this afternoon left two youth service workers dead. The attack occurred at approximately one p.m. at an isolated AmeriCorps forestry camp in northern Arkansas. Witnesses said a group of youth assigned to the region to construct hiking trails and monitor conservation efforts was ambushed by an unknown number of men wielding automatic weapons. None of the AmeriCorps members was armed. The dead are identified as Orville Forbis, 32, and Earl Henshaw, 28.*

*The attackers are believed to be militiamen from Oklahoma. Known as the Defenders, they have been particularly active in recent weeks. The Defenders are believed responsible for hanging undercover Homeland Security agent Ron Sparks in an Oklahoma cemetery and for the attack at the ORU Center in Tulsa that left conservative TV talk show guru Jerry Baer and seven others dead.*

*Two members of the Defenders were slain the night before the Arkansas attack near Bunch, Oklahoma, in what authorities are describing as a clash between rival militias over policy and tactics...*

*White House spokesman Dewey Gubbins said the administration is considering declaring a national state of emergency and imposing martial law in several states if the violence continues to escalate...*

# Chapter Thirty-Nine

## Keystone Lake, Oklahoma

The moon was high by the time Nail and Sharon pulled his old green Chevy pickup through the wire fence gate and followed the long ruts across the field and through the trees to the concealed cabin on Cottonwood Creek. So much had happened within the past forty eight hours that it seemed they had been away for days.

Sharon emitted a weary sigh. "Home sweet home, be it ever so humble..."

"You'll soon be barefooted and smoking a corn cob pipe."

Her ears were still ringing and she didn't hear him. "Do you suppose they'll come looking for us here?" she worried.

"Big C put the deed and utilities for the cabin under an assumed name and address that'll be hard to trace back. Thank God for paranoia."

Nail unlocked the cabin door and turned on the lights. He stood in the doorway looking out.

"There's a thunder boomer coming," he predicted.

"What?"

He faced her so she could read his lips. "A thunderstorm."

Lightning slashed across the black sky, illuminating the overgrown drive to the cabin and the pickup parked out front. Big C should be arriving shortly.

"We got us a war now," one of the Defenders said before the militia split up to find its individual way back to Oklahoma. "They are going to be on us like chickens on corn."

"Best ya'all lay low then," Big C told them. "I be in touch."

"I wager it won't be long until they 'find' evidence at the scene of the crime and issue an APB for me and some big, black, bald dude," Nail said.

Big C grinned tightly. "Big, black, bald, handsome, charming..."

They raced through the back part of the woods to where their vehicles were parked on a logging road.

"Best we split up too, James," Big C said. "You take your truck. I got a ride back to mine. Catch you at Safe House later."

Smitty was still pale and terror-stricken when Nail and Sharon dropped him off in Muldrow where he could phone his dad to come get him. He said he was through with AmeriCorps and was willing to go public on TV as to what really happened at the camp should Sharon require it. Nail thought of what had befallen Greg Morris and Joshua Logan.

"You go home and keep your mouth shut, Smitty. Understand?" he said.

"I'm sorry for what we done to you," Smitty apologized, tears of regret running down his thin cheeks. "It was wrong."

"It was wrong," Nail agreed. "But you made up for it when it really counted."

Sharon sat as close to Nail as she could get for the rest of the drive to the lake, her hand gripping his knee as though to reassure herself that he was there with her and that they were, miraculously, still alive. Nail couldn't even look at her without shuddering at how close he came to losing her. Neither of them was yet willing to talk about what had transpired. Their nerves were shot; they mostly rode in silence, keeping their eyes peeled for the "Black Mollies" the Homies drove. Nail figured it would take some time, several hours at least, before the manhunt began in earnest. They should be able to hide out at the Safe House until some of the heat blew over.

Cool-headed again, Sharon suggested they stock up on supplies on their way to the Safe House, as it might be days before they dared venture out. Nail stopped at a travel plaza where Sharon could scrub Forbis' blood off her face without being noticed. Afterwards, they purchased fresh vegetables, fruits, meats, cereals and dried goods like beans, flour and rice at a Wal-Mart in Sallisaw. No pork 'n beans.

Thinking ahead, Sharon selected a laptop computer, printer, scanner and a video camera with which to tape programs in exile for *The Jerry Baer Show*. Nail threw into the cart two pay-as-you-go cell phones and phone cards that would take the Feds awhile to locate and trace. That accomplished, they passed a book store where Sharon insisted they stop.

"They took the reading list you made for me," he apologized.

"We won't need it."

The book store had one copy of *Atlas Shrugged* by Ayn Rand. Sharon bought it, along with *1984* by George Orwell and *Going Bonkers: The Wacky World of Cultural Madness*.

"We won't be restocking these titles," the clerk said. "We received a government directive listing books that will be out of print from now on."

Now, as the storm approached the cabin, lighting up the windows strobe-like, Sharon began preparing dinner at the propane stove.

Neither of them had eaten since the previous evening in Stillwell. Nail's mouth soon watered with the aroma of meat frying and bread baking. While he waited, he called Lieutenant Jack Ross on one of the throw-away phones to catch up on any news.

"Kimbrell is snooping around," Ross relayed. "He said he has evidence that you and Corey Brown led the ambush against the AmeriCorps workers in Arkansas. It's all over the news. You and big C had better take to the mattresses. There are federal interstate murder warrants issued for both of you."

It hadn't taken long for Kimbrell to identify Big C. After all, how many black Incredible Hulks were associated with Nail?

"James, I'm opening an ATM account for you under the name Roger Carroll," Ross offered. "I'll keep money in it and get the cards to you somehow."

"Jack...?"

"Is the girl from Jerry Baer still with you?"

"Sharon."

"She's good people, James. And you're a good cop." He hesitated. He voice turned wistful. "Good luck, James. To the three of you."

Nail hung up and told Sharon about the murder warrants. She turned from the stove with spatula in hand and a towel wrapped around her waist as an apron. She had showered and changed clothes. Nail wondered if she could ever scrub the stain of this day off her soul.

"I suppose that makes us *real* fugitives now," she said.

"Bonnie and Clyde."

"That ended well."

He walked up and put his arms around her from behind while she cooked. There was nothing left to say.

Big C arrived in time for dinner, ushered in by the crack of a bolt of lightning that bounced down the creek like St. Elmo's fire. He slammed the door against the weather and shuddered.

"Starting to rain," he announced. "Gonna be real toad strangler. Umm, something smell good."

"I was hoping you'd get here," Sharon said.

"You can hear again!"

"What?"

They all laughed.

"I want you both to know that not one can opener was employed in preparation of this meal," she said.

"My kind of woman," effused Big C.

She laughed at him. "I thought you preferred blondes."

"Now, tell us how you found us at the camp?" Nail asked Big C when they sat down for the late dinner. It was almost midnight by now.

"Let's have a nice meal first," Sharon suggested with a tired smile. "We have a lot to thank God for."

That was the cue to bow their heads.

"Lord God, thank You for providing our needs, and for delivering us from the shadows of this day. Lord, we would like to pray for the souls of those who departed this world at our hand. Forgive us for what we had to do. Bless this food we are about to receive, and be with us, Lord, in the perilous days ahead. Amen."

There was no further discussion of Nail's killing the Green Shirts. He would deal with it his own way. He recalled how horrified Connie had been when he shot the man that time to save Big C's life. "You mean, you can kill a man and it doesn't even bother you?"

*She* had never had a cocked gun pressed against *her* forehead.

After they ate and cleared the table, they sat over coffee in the living room while Big C told them everything he had found out. How he captured one of the attackers at the schoolhouse, who revealed the location of the AmeriCorps camp. The Defenders had arrived just in time.

"Colonel Mosby was snitch inside the militia," Big C explained, sipping coffee. "He set it up for Homies to kidnap you two and get rid you. Kimbrell behind it all. He terrorized Mosby's wife and kids. He even shot Ol' Ranger, the kids' dog."

Big C explained further how Ron Sparks had heard from his contact in Washington that "people" might be plotting to assassinate Jerry Baer when he made his public appearance in Tulsa. Sparks passed the information to Colonel Mosby, who he assumed would contact Tulsa Police and Jerry Baer's security. Sparks couldn't do it himself without blowing his cover. Instead, Mosby went to Kimbrell.

"And so Kimbrell had Sparks hung and blamed it on the Defenders," Nail said.

"Kimbrell organized it all. Everything from your daughter's boyfriend bringing out PEIU and ACOA demonstrators to the stolen chopper and the shooters."

"Motive?"

"Jerry Baer getting too close to the truth and people starting to listen. Everything else just to shift blame or cover up. My guess is he got marching orders from someplace higher up."

"My guess is with yours," Nail agreed. "How did Logan and Morris fit in?"

"Greg Morris call me that morning the Homies kill him," Big C said. "He meeting Logan at McDonald's because he saw something prove who really hung Ron Sparks. I suppose to meet Greg too, but the Homies beat me there."

"Morris saw the hanging," Nail surmised. "Kimbrell had to get rid of him. From the jailhouse note Logan left me, Morris must have told him something about it over the phone."

"Sharon suppose to be killed along with Baer," Big C went on, speculating. "James, you got in middle because of Jamie, started nosing around and—"

"—here we are. And we still don't have all the marbles."

"Nor do we know who they are or how many," Big C added.

Nail and Sharon were on the sofa, she nodding off with her head on his shoulder.

"I told you at the beginning that this went deeper than you'd ever believe," she reminded Nail.

Nail took the coffee from her hand before she spilled it. None of them had slept much for more than forty eight hours. They were out on their feet.

"What did you do to Mosby?" Nail asked.

Big C looked at him. "Man got a good family. I expect him and them are in Arizona by now."

Nail nodded approval.

"Bro'," said the black cop. "Look like it three of us against the entire U.S. Government—and I don't know can we win or not."

"Three Musketeers," Sharon mumbled.

Big C's lips curled slightly in a grim smile. "One for all, all for one."

Nail said, "That's better than Bonnie and Clyde."

A bright flicker of lightning and the instant crashing of thunder rattled the cabin's windows. Rain drummed on the cedar shake roof.

"A storm's coming," Nail said. "It's coming all right."

# PART II

*"Each generation of Americans is conditioned to accept less freedom than the generation before."* — Donna Sue Sasser

# Chapter Forty

## Washington, D.C.

Dennis Trout heard Judy finish her shower and turn off the water. He waited for her in her cramped living room, watching TV. She kept the apartment clean and neat, he gave her that, even though the cheap furniture she insisted on was more suitable for a room at Motel 6. You could take the girl out of Bugfuck, but you couldn't take Bugfuck out of the girl.

"I'm getting dressed now, honey," Judy sang out.

He was taking her out to *The Fountains* for dinner, which meant he didn't have to dress. She kept a spare wardrobe for him in her apartment. He had changed from "work clothes" to fresh slacks and an open-collar sports shirt. Marilyn thought he was working late again.

The TV networks were full of some twit actress named Lindsey and her third or fourth drug bust. Talking heads gravely deliberated over whether or not she deserved to go to jail, and, if so, for how long. Trout flipped channels in disgust. *This* was what passed as hard news? Cakes and circuses to keep the sheep busy until the wolves got around to eating them.

CNN was airing something about Michael Jackson the pop star. Wasn't he dead or something?

CBS played a live shot of President Anastos giving a news conference of sorts in the Rose Garden. The late sun reddened against his long face. His head automatically began its teleprompter wag when he started to speak.

"Uh, change has not come fast enough for too many Americans," he baritoned. "I know that. It hasn't come fast enough for me either. I, uh, know it hasn't been fast enough for many of you who fought so hard during the election for, uh, hope and change. The fact is, uh, it took you to get where we are now and it'll take time to get the change we want."

Judy stuck her bleached head out from the bedroom. "Just another minute, honey. I want to look pretty as a pea for you tonight."

She seemed as happy as a hog in slop, as they might say in Bugfuck. What she perceived as "pretty as a pea" usually meant something tight with plenty of sparkle and cleavage. Sometimes, he questioned his taste in women.

"Honey...?"

"I heard you, sweet dumpling," he replied, mimicking her down-home corn pone Okie tawk.

She giggled. "Whatcha watching?"

"Lies and hog wash."

"Oh. Politics." Still giggling, she popped out of sight. He heard her singing happily to herself. He wondered if it was Michael Jackson.

He flipped the remote to Zenergy News. The crawl across the bottom of the screen caught and froze his attention: *State Senator Morgan Lance of New Hampshire has been killed in a tragic one-car accident on Highway 93 near Manchester. Lance was the primary author of a state proclamation that threatened to nullify federal authority...*

Blood drained from his cheeks as he stared at the screen. "They'll know better than to fuck with me," Wiedersham had threatened. The federal judge who struck down President Anastos' ban on oil drilling in the Gulf had also died tragically and suddenly, of an accidental drug overdose. "Judge Fielding won't be a problem," Wiedersham had promised.

Was it mere coincidence that people who "fucked with" Wiedersham and Associates ended up dead? "*Make* an incident," Wiedersham raged when the Tea Party marched on the Capitol—and three were gunned down. Coincidence that the administration's number one nemesis, Jerry Baer, ended up assassinated in Tulsa?

"Dennis?" Judy stood in the doorway looking at him. "Dennis, what's wrong? You look like you've seen a ghost."

Trout shook himself out of the trance into which he had lapsed. He knew what he was getting into when he signed his pact with the devil.

*I'll give you wealth and power,* promised the Evil One.

*Goody! Where do I sign up?*

He continued to stare at the TV screen. A shot of State Senator Lance's mangled BMW flashed on the screen, accompanied by a voiceover explaining how the State of New Hampshire was withdrawing Lance's nullification proclamation from consideration.

Trout had to get hold of himself. Everything he wanted, *everything*, was within reach. All he had to do was hold his nose and go forward. After all, didn't the ends justify the means?

"The test of true leadership," Wiedersham liked to say, "is when you can make those tough decisions that you know are best for the common good."

Judy bent over Trout to get his attention. The gold-plated locket he gave her dangled between her cleavage. She wore more rings than she had fingers.

"Dennis...?"

"Do you have any Maalox?"

"There's a convenience store on the corner. I'll run get some?"

He was still staring at the TV screen when the apartment door closed behind her. Wasn't he as guilty as Wiedersham if he knew about all this and continued to go along silently just to get his ticket punched?

This morning, Wiedersham had taken him to a "Next Step" conference, saying he, Trout, should begin making appearances where he could be seen among Progressive supporters. The campaign for the Illinois 9th District seat was already down to its last heat while Trout hadn't even left the starting gate. Not to worry, Wiedersham reassured him. Things had been "arranged."

Trout declined to consider himself a political radical, not in any true sense. He was pragmatic, like his brother-in-law. However, most of those at the Next Step *were* true radicals, prominent among them three ageing hippies from the late 1960s and 1970s: Bob Carter and the Ackharts, man and wife. All had been members of the Weathermen and, more recently, founders of The Renewed Weather openly advocating "the destruction of U.S. imperialism and the achievement of a classless world under The New World Order."

Bob Carter, a small, bespectacled, inoffensive-looking man in his late fifties, was head of the George Zuniga-funded World Alliance. Congress had not written the twenty-five-hundred page Health Care Bill that nationalized health care in the U.S. and placed one sixth of the nation's economy under government control. Carter and his allies had, with the guidance, no doubt, of Mr. Zuniga. Carter, along with Bill Ackhart and Ackhart's wife, Bernadine Samson-Ackhart, had also drafted much of the President's Economic Stimulus package.

Bill and Bernadine Ackhart were professors at the University of Chicago who had worked with President Anastos and ACOA during Anastos' "community organizer" years and were later Anastos' neighbors in Chicago. The couple had been on the FBI's Most Wanted list in the early 1970s for a series of bombings against the police and uncooperative politicians. Ironically enough, the City of Chicago awarded them its Citizens of The Year Award in 2006, followed by the same award for Patrick Wayne Anastos the following year.

Present and prepared to take the "next step" were a number of others whose faces Trout recognized but until now had not met personally. Wiedersham made a point of introducing him around. As chief of staff, Trout previously stayed in the background and had not attended these meetings.

Duane Smith—White House Environmental Czar, former Black Panther member, union organizer, President of PEIU, board member of SIGA, and avowed communist—called Trout "brother." Speaker of the House Barbara Teague merely stared at him with her blank Botox expression. Homeland Security Director Vladimir Gonzalez looked like he might fit in well with Nazi Germany's diminutive-brained Gestapo or Stalin's KGB.

Ira Romero, the President's chief of staff, and Press Secretary Dewey Gubbins represented the White House, along with Regulatory Czar Sam Shrader. George Zuniga was not personally present, but he was well represented. What surprised Trout most was the number of mainstream media people present. Famous faces from the networks and current events magazines, obviously insiders who took no notes or video. There were also CEOs from major corporations that had recently been bailed out of their economic woes by the President's Stimulus Package and subsequently nationalized. Five or six other stern-looking men spoke little or no English. Interpreters accompanied them.

Zenergy News, Trout noted puckishly, was not represented.

The conference goal, as best Trout understood it, having arrived in the middle of what was apparently an ongoing discussion over many months, was directed toward bringing about "change" in the U.S. Government. "Revolution" was bandied about as cavalierly as gossip at a PTA meeting.

"In my opinion," remonstrated a well-known TV anchor, "we must do all we can to destroy Zenergy News and the idiocy it foments. This isn't about defending Anastos. This is about how the Rightwing media kills any chance of discourse that actually serves the people. Common interest, as Walter Lippman said, eludes public opinion entirely. It can be managed only by a specialized class since the public are mentally children and barbarians. In order to have a semblance of control, we need a tougher legal framework that will be provided by The Fairness of Airwaves Doctrine..."

Wiedersham and Barbara Teague reassured him that FAD was coming.

"The average American is trained to be passive," Majority Leader Wiedersham pointed out to the assembly. "The average American is ready to say 'I give up.' We have to count on that. The coming mid-term elections are critical in putting our people in place and our movement in control. The Immigration Reform Bill now in the House will legitimize twelve million undocumented immigrants and allow them to vote for us. Not that we necessarily need them, but it will give the appearance of legitimacy..."

It wasn't who cast the votes but who *counted* the votes.

"The masses will fight for socialism when they understand that the fight for material conditions cannot be won under imperialism," declared the former Black Panther Duane Smith. "Holiday Inn, American Airlines, all of Hertz's automobiles, your TV set, you car and your wardrobe already belong to a large degree to peoples in the rest of the world, particularly to peoples of color..."

Trout stared. What the hell did *that* mean?

There seemed to be some disagreement in the conference over when the "Next Step" should be taken.

"We find ourselves in a situation where the movement that we built for hope and change is on the bubble," interjected the President's chief of staff, Ira Romero. "There is great danger in delay. We must strike *now...*"

Everyone finally conceded that it was up to Mr. Zuniga, the President, and the International Board for Social Justice to make the call on when the United States and the globe was ripe. It was quite obvious to Trout that Progressives considered themselves *good people* come to save America and the world.

Trout's head was spinning by the time it was over. On the way out, Wiedersham barked his strange laugh and said, "In six months, it'll be done. Dennis, you and I will be two of the richest and most influential men in the universe."

Thinking about that now in Judy's apartment put Trout's head back on straight. The end game made everything in between worthwhile. He turned off the TV and was feeling much better by the time Judy returned with his Maalox.

"I don't need it now," he decided. "Put it in the medicine cabinet for later. I'm hungry."

## Universities Employ "Facilitators"

***(Harvard)***—*Universities and colleges are employing student "facilitators" to monitor hate speech on campuses nationwide. Should students be engaged in incorrect, harmful or anti-government speech, facilitators will step in to correct the offenders. Second and third offenses could lead to fines and incarceration. Duane Smith, President of PEIU (Public Employees International Union), which represents most school teachers and university employees, explained that such intervention will help create an atmosphere of inclusivity...*

# Chapter Forty-One

## Keystone Lake, Oklahoma

Recent events coupled with Nail's inability to attend his daughter's funeral left him empty and restless. Burning at the back of his mind was the conviction that the nightmare wasn't over yet, might never be over. Green Shirts Forbis and Henshaw pulled the triggers, but someone else bought the bullets. Someone else had Jamie's blood on his hands, someone else higher than Kimbrell. Lust for revenge raged deep in Nail's soul.

Things at the Safe House between Nail and Sharon after Arkansas were reserved, almost formal. They took no time for fishing, leisurely coffee over the breakfast table, or long talks by the creek underneath the stars. Part of it was because every Fed in the nation, as well as state and local police, was hunting for them. The hideout couldn't hold forever. They would soon have to split up, move on, and keep moving.

The other part of it, Nail suspected, was that Sharon saw a side of him at the AmeriCorps camp that she didn't realize existed. A hard, violent side that had caused Connie to divorce him.

Sharon was also changed. Getting splattered with the brain blood of a man seconds away from killing you was enough to give even the toughest cop or soldier PTSD. She had witnessed *reality* as few others had.

"None of us will have a private life again," she said. "We must activate the American people. When I go to bed and say my prayers, I ask God what else can I do to wake up America before it's too late."

She kept herself occupied writing pieces for *Truth* and preparing in exile the next *Jerry Baer Show,* now being billed as *The Jerry Baer Show w/Sharon Lowenthal.* The show, she learned through internet conversation with Zenergy executive Carl Patton, was being cut from five evenings a week to one night until lawyers could clear up the mess in Oklahoma and get her back to New York. The laptop she bought in Sallisaw provided her the means to stay in contact with the show's twenty or so loyal reporters and investigators not yet scared off by threats and the increasingly dangerous atmosphere coming out of Washington. This week's would be her first production as star of the show since Baer's slaying; she wanted to get it right.

In the meantime, Big C painted his red Ford pickup black to disguise it; he intended to lift new plates from some junkyard the next time he dared venture out. He played with the idea of linking up the Defenders with militias in other states to declare war against the United States *Government*. Nail had not yet reached that point, although, like John Wayne said, there came a time when a man had to fight back.

Sharon argued with Big C. "Don't you understand that that's what they want us to do? They *want* turmoil in the streets. It doesn't make any difference if it comes from the Right or the Left, it will allow them to act to restore order. And they will abolish the Constitution and the Bill of Rights in the process."

The nation had been brought to its economic, cultural and political knees while Nail was too busy living life to realize it. Time at the Safe House provided him the opportunity to catch up on history and current events that he had neglected since *Desert Storm*. He read *1984* and *Going Bonkers*, sitting outside on the big log by the creek with a pencil to underline key passages. *Atlas Shrugged* was such a door stopper that he was saving it for later.

In *Bonkers*, he underlined:

*If we remain intimidated by the insanity infecting our culture and stoically accept the madness of our Brave New World, we essentially concede away the final remains of liberty. It isn't civility to remain silent; it's cowardice. If I go down, I prefer to go down firing from the bulwarks rather than with a whimper in the shadows of madness and tyranny.*

Passages from *1984* seemed even more pertinent. He highlighted one phrase in particular and read it over several times, then closed the book and sat for a long time thinking about it.

*Do you begin to see, then, what kind of world we are creating? It is the exact opposite of the stupid hedonistic Utopias that the old reformers imagined. A world of fear and treachery and torment, a world of trampling and being trampled upon, a world which will grow not less but more merciless as it refines itself. Progress in our world will be progress toward more pain.*

James Nail was beginning to see.

Supported by the internet which, so far, was still ungoverned from Washington, Sharon and Big C spent their evenings together introducing Nail to the major players in Anastos' government.

"It is no conspiracy anymore," Big C proclaimed. "These people doing all this in the open now. They think they got us cowed down."

Sol Alinsky, Cloward and Pivens, Students for a Democratic Society, ACOA, George Zuniga, Duane Smith, PEIU, the New Weathermen, dozens of other individuals and groups whose radical agendas seemed to be playing out in Washington… These were the players. Avowed Marxists surrounded The One in the White House. Health czars, green czars, auto czars, financial czars, media czars... Over forty "czars" at last count, a kind of U.S. politburo that was not elected or approved or vetted by Congress. Anastos merely appointed them with the authority to regulate and control virtually every aspect of American commerce. A caucus led by House Speaker Barbara Teague was initiating a movement to repeal the 22nd Amendment to the Constitution in the event of a national crisis. If successfully repealed through the states, the amendment would allow a president to serve more than two terms in office. Say, President-for-Life Patrick Wayne Anastos.

Big C said, "This is the same stuff thugs did in Italy and Germany in 1930s."

"Scary stuff," Nail agreed.

Sharon downloaded a copy of Sol Alinsky's *Rules for Radicals* from the internet, along with *The Weatherman Manifesto* written by, among others, Bill Ackart and Bernadine Samson-Ackart, who were involved in bombing police stations and the Pentagon in the 1970s and were now personal friends and associate "community organizers" of the President of The United States. The publications laid out philosophy and tactics for fomenting a Marxist revolution to seize power.

Nail had to read the dedication page in *Rules for Radicals* twice.

*Lest we forget at least one over the shoulder acknowledgment to the very first radical, from all our legends, mythology, and history (and who is to know where mythology leaves off and history begins, or which is which) the first radical known to man who rebelled against the establishment and did it so effectively that he at least won his own kingdom—Lucifer.*

Big C was fixing himself a sandwich in the kitchen. Sharon sat at the table working on her laptop. She looked up at Nail, who was reading on the sofa by the window's light, and saw him shaking his head over the Alinsky title page. She got up and walked over to him.

"His tribute to Lucifer should erase all doubts that what we are confronting is raw evil," she commented.

"How do we stop it if it's gone this far?"

"Our weapon is truth," she replied bravely. "The days are over when we got out of bed with the New York *Times* and had dinner with Dan Rather—and kept quiet in between because our elite betters told us what to think. The flame of truth is hard to put out once it's kindled."

"And if nobody believes you?"

"Then we're doomed to repeat history."

Big C sank down on the other end of the sofa with his sandwich. "Peanut butter and bananas," he announced. "Me and Elvis."

"It's the oldest story of mankind," Sharon continued. "If we go down this poisoned path, all knees will bend and all heads bow."

The way she looked at him. There was something she wasn't telling him. Nail had thought so all day from the way she avoided him. She sighed a sad note and walked to Nail's window to block the light. Looking out, she said, "Our attorneys at Zenergy have gotten the material witness warrants against me lifted. I received the e-mail this morning."

Here it came.

"It won't be safe for the two of you to be with me after my first show airs Friday," she went on, with her back still to Nail and Big C. "I'll have to be able to use the phones and computers. Homeland Security can trace them."

Nail got up and stood beside her at the window, looking out.

"I'm returning to the studio in New York beginning with next week's show," she announced.

"Have you forgotten what happened in Arkansas?" Nail demanded. One kiss under the stars gave him no claim on her. "They don't care about a warrant. Going back to New York is what they want you to do."

Big C sided with his friend. The low-tone disagreement went back and forth, with Sharon contending that she would have around-the-clock bodyguards. Besides, she was too high profile for anything to happen to her.

"And Jerry Baer wasn't?" Nail argued in frustration.

"They hold off maybe few weeks," Big C pointed out. "Then they be coming, sis. Won't be nobody there love you like James and me."

She turned from the window to face them. She took one of their hands in each of hers and squeezed.

"This is bigger than us," she insisted. "It's about saving the country. How can I ever justify myself if I quit?"

"You can justify it if you're dead?" Nail retorted. "I'm going with you."

"James, no. They'll be looking for that."

After dinner on Thursday, Sharon loaded the program DVD of *The Jerry Baer Show w/Sharon Lowenthal* into the player so they could review it in its entirety before she dispatched it electronically to Carl

Patton in New York. It would air tomorrow at five p.m. Eastern Time. Nail and Big C had acted as cameramen for her portion while she spliced in clips received via internet from Jerry Baer reporters and investigators. Big C pulled up the ratty easy chair to watch while Sharon sat on the sofa with Nail and took his hand. Big C smiled his approval.

As in real life, Sharon projected a straightforward and sincere presence on the screen. People *had* to believe what she said. The show began with a video clip of President Anastos addressing the auto workers union in Detroit. Government had just bailed out another economically collapsing motor company and took control of it.

"How's this capitalism working for you?" the President smirked. "Did it give you a job? *We* gave you your jobs back."

Union members cheered. Pre-prepared signs bobbed. The camera's eye zoomed in on **Workers of the World Unite**.

Sharon came on in a close frame. She spoke gravely while looking directly into the eyes of her audience. "Folks, as most of you know, this is our first show since Jerry was assassinated. Before he died, he promised that the only way he would shut up was if—" She choked up and took a moment to recover. "Someone shot him. I, Sharon Lowenthal, renew the pledge."

Somewhere outside the cabin a whippoorwill called to its mate and a pack of coyotes yapped.

"I'm speaking to you tonight only because of a remarkable police homicide detective who has so far saved my life twice. But for him I would have died with Jerry. His daughter was killed that dreadful day. He saved my life a second time at an Arkansas AmeriCorps camp where the training is not construction and road building but instead weapons and military drill. I was kidnapped and would have been executed except for him and another brave Tulsa police officer, both of whom are fugitives with federal government warrants issued for their arrest. They will not receive a fair trial. Chances are they will not receive a trial at all if they are apprehended."

She chronicled the ordeal that began with the raid at the Bunch schoolhouse and concluded with their escape from Arkansas. Government agents, she said, hung Ron Sparks in the cemetery and gunned down two witnesses who knew the truth, the same way federal agents attempted to execute her.

A Jerry Baer clip from a previous show appeared. "Since President Anastos' election," he said, "I have had views confided to me privately by some of the most prominent men in the field of commerce and manufacturing. They are afraid. They know there is a power being organized that is so subtle, so watchful, so interlocked, so complete, and so pervasive that they had better not speak above their breaths when they speak in condemnation of it."

Bill Ackart's image flashed onto the screen, saying, "We have an urgent responsibility to destroy capitalism from within in order to help free the world and ourselves from its grasp. We will use all weapons available to us."

Sharon came back on with the cabin's fireplace shown in her backdrop.

"The infrastructure of our new rulers is in place," she said. "A 'shadow government' waiting for the right time to collapse the U.S. Republic and take over. The time of freedom is drawing short. The Senate and the House are being packed with corrupt politicians and ideological Progressives-Marxists. It has been going on for years. They have automatically rubber-stamped every socialist program to come along without even bothering to read bills that are designed to bankrupt and destroy the nation."

A congressman from Michigan, in office for over forty years, had been caught by Zenergy News unintentionally admitting as much over the Healthcare Bill: "Read the bill? What good is reading the bill if it's a thousand pages and you don't have two days and two lawyers to understand it?"

For most of the hour, Sharon explored what was about to transpire, interspersed by clips of politicians, "community organizers," and other radicals declaring their intentions "in their own words," as she and Jerry Baer before her were fond of saying. She delivered a chilling summary at the end.

"Folks, as I explained earlier in this program, I know from horrible personal experience that President Anastos is establishing a KGB-like security force to help impose a Marxist dictatorship on the United States of America. We are just one incident away from martial law, be it declared because of an Islamic terrorist attack, a major financial blowout, a widespread natural disaster, or civil unrest. It's becoming clearer every day that the groundwork is being laid for a seamless transition into totalitarianism. The Constitution and Bill of Rights will be suspended and what government officials believe and do, no matter how arbitrary, will become law. You can be sure that all this is about to happen—and it will happen very quickly."

Sharon paused and gazed soberly out at her audience. “Folks,” she said, “we are one catastrophic event away from the total transformation of the United States of America.”

The DVD went off, the TV screen turned blank, the mournful yapping of coyotes echoed in the silence.

# Chapter Forty-Two

## Chicago

There were 360 Starbucks locations in the Chicago area serving "the finest Arabica" coffee. According to a Zogby poll, people who patronized Starbucks differed mightily from those who swigged at Dunkin Donuts. Liberals and Progressives were twice as likely to be found at Starbucks while men who knew how to change their own spark plugs went to Dunkin's and would rather be chained to the soap aisle in *Bed, Bath and Beyond* than have to utter bastardized Starbucks Latin to order a lousy cup of Joe.

Senate Majority Leader Joe Wiedersham and his chief of staff Dennis Trout entered the Starbucks on LaSalle Street. Trout's fine brown hair looked thinner than usual, although he had taken great pains with conditioner to fill it out to a younger look. As for the haggard look on his face, no amount of Speaker of the House Botox could have helped it. The little coffee house hostess took a second look at them. She appeared about eighteen, still with that clueless look of a teenager.

"Are you *them*?" she inquired, awed.

Wiedersham smiled. Politicians liked being recognized by the little people.

"I just seen you on TV," the girl gushed to Trout, gesturing toward the Plasma flat-screens located at various sites around a room filled with some of Chicago's coolest people. "You're going to be the next politician. I liked what you said about people needing help from our government."

She took their orders and left. The Majority Leader was in jovial form, at least by his standards, even though there had been a glitch in the press conference/town hall meeting at which Wiedersham introduced his young protégé and Trout announced that he was filing for the 9$^{th}$ Congressional race. Before the arranged event, Wiedersham had summoned Trout to his hotel suite, paid for compliments of the American taxpayer. The Leader wore a Jack Victor original suit with a power tie by some wop whose name Trout couldn't recall; he still looked as though he had slept in it.

"We're getting into the race late because it took more persuasion than we expected to get that idiot Spencer to drop out and let you have the candidacy," Wiedersham said. "Your Republican opponent will campaign hard up until a week before the election, at which time he will retire for personal reasons."

Trout went deer-in-the-headlights as he recalled the New Orleans oil spill judge who "overdosed" and the fatal car crash after the New Hampshire nullification proclamation.

"Don't look so slammed," Wiedersham said with a bark of laughter. "Spencer accepted a position on the President's economic recovery team. We're going to campaign hard, like it really makes a difference on the outcome. It'll all be over in a few months. *We* will be in charge."

Trout was going to be rich and powerful.

"There is one little matter, however, that we need to discuss," Wiedersham added.

*Uh oh!*

"President Clinton's staff called it the 'bimbo eruption.' We're vulnerable because Zenergy and the Rightwing talk gurus are just waiting for a slip."

Trout's face reddened. Wiedersham must have known about Judy all along. Did he also know that she was Ron Sparks' cousin?

"Dennis, you can fuck who you want and God knows I would if I had to be married to my sister. But do it discreetly. I don't want to wake up some morning and see a John Edwards bastard child or a Bill Clinton blue dress on Zenergy. That little trailer trash whore is the only thing that can do you in."

Trout's temper flared in Judy's defense, but he reined it in immediately, relieved that neither his brother-in-law nor George Zuniga's "John" had apparently made the connection between Judy and her Oklahoma cousin in the cemetery. Perhaps they considered her too simple to have her properly investigated.

Besides, he had to remember what was at stake. *Congressman* Trout—and the several million dollars he stood to garner from Petrobras investment dividends through his brother-in-law and Zuniga.

Trout wondered if he had packed his Maalox.

"Marilyn will campaign with you part of the time," Wiedersham continued. "The Homers respond to all that happy family stuff."

Sure enough, Marilyn had shown up in time for the press conference/town hall meeting. She flew in early and took a limo to the courthouse to be present at the photo op. It took place in a reserve conference room. Select local and national media had been invited, along with about fifty "ordinary" citizens chosen by the Chicago Democratic Party. Chicago's mayor and the Illinois governor were present, flashing their predatory political smiles and looking superior because of the insider knowledge they possessed that could deliver for the proper candidate. Trout recognized a sacrilegious thought for what it was, but he couldn't help it: *Why do the worst people rise to the top, based on promises that normal people would never make?*

Trout wondered if getting into this campaign made him a "worst" person.

Marilyn pasted herself to Trout's side at the filing conference, with her arm hooked through her husband's, wearing a phony adoring smile whenever she looked at him. The only thing missing in the warm little political scene was Reggie the pink poodle taking a leak on Trout's leg.

"Dennis Trout is a thinking man's candidate," was how Wiedersham introduced him. "I expect him to do well among voters with IQs in triple digits."

Trout rose to polite applause. Someone, he didn't know who, had prepared a speech for him. It sounded stilted and ideological, the same old populist bombast, but Trout bravely waded into it.

"A strong and durable economy requires some countries not to have the advantage," he recited. "I think that we all have the same interests and that in the U.S. we can compete with anybody as long as we have an even playing field."

To Trout's ears, it sounded like recycled Anastos campaign rhetoric. Which it probably was.

"I think, ultimately, the rate of growth of material consumption is going to have to come down and there's going to be a degree of wealth redistribution in terms of energy and natural resources in order to leave room for people who are poor to become more prosperous..."

A redneck wearing a baseball cap stood up during the short question and answer session that followed. Trout failed to see the sandbag coming.

"What makes politicians in Washington think they can fix anything in light of failures like Medicare and Social Security?" the Homer asked.

"With qualified people in power," Trout responded off the cuff, "the Federal Government can 'fix' most anything in this country."

The redneck wasn't through.

"What is an economic stimulus payment?" he asked.

Trout started to get uncomfortable. "It is money that the Federal Government will send to taxpayers to help stimulate the economy."

Trout overheard Wiedersham's angry hiss as he leaned over to Chicago's corpulent mayor. "How did that asshole get in here?"

The burly redneck refused to sit down and hush. "Where does government get the money?" he demanded.

"From taxpayers." *Uh oh.* Trout felt suddenly boxed in.

"So government is giving me back my own money?"

Trout's eyes desperately searched the room for an out. "Next question?" he pleaded.

"You, sir," accused the redneck, "and people like you are destroying the nation."

"Well, I'm sure glad you're here to save it," Trout snapped.

The guy was too stupid to know what was best for him.

It took two cups of Starbucks coffee for Trout himself to swallow all the crap he was dishing out.

## President Pitches Cheap Credit

***(Washington)***—*With mid-term elections approaching, President Anastos broadened the appeal of his administration by promising to help Americans suffering from inflation caused by international capitalism. His new program will provide disadvantaged Americans and immigrants with a special, no-interest government credit card that can be used to shop at state-run stores opening in major cities nationwide. It is known as the "Good Life Card."*

*He called it evidence that he is committed to making the good life in the United States accessible and affordable for all, not just the rich.*

*"I'm going to sell you some tremendous refrigerators—very cheap. Among the best in the world," he touted during a televised event. "Gas stoves at half price, water heaters, washers, television sets, air conditioners—on your Good Life Card with no down payment..."*

# Chapter Forty-Three

## Keystone Lake, Oklahoma

The mainstream media went ape the morning after *The Jerry Baer Show w/Sharon Lowenthal* aired. Pundits from government-supported news outlets called Sharon a liar who consorted with killers and terrorists of the tinfoil hat variety, a "seriously disturbed Jewish woman...divisive...misinformed..." *Modern People* implied a sex scandal involving Baer and her, which may have led to his murder. *American Post* called for increased government intervention to control "hate media." Cable TV talk shows were all over her...

James Nail finally had enough of it. He got up from the sofa in front of the TV and walked out the back door without a word. He stood on the banks of Cottonwood Creek looking down the brown stream where it twisted through sycamores and cottonwoods toward Keystone Lake. He had become even more distant after Sharon announced she would be returning to New York to video her next show. It was only a matter of a few days at most before Nail and Big C would have to likewise abandon the Safe House.

Big C sipped ice tea while looking out the kitchen window at Nail by the creek. Nothing like a frosty glass of it on a Saturday afternoon after mowing the grass. No use leaving the place all grown up in weeds when everyone left.

"The man got it bad for you, sis," he said.

Sharon's eyes hadn't left the back door through which Nail had disappeared. Big C smiled. "Girl, I know James for over twenty years. Connie the love of the poor sucker's life. After she kick him out, there been no other female in his sorry life 'cept for Jamie."

"What about you, Corey? Are there any females in your life?"

"I what you might call a serial monogamist."

She changed the subject. "So what are James and you going to do? You can't go back to the police department."

Big C thought about it before answering.

"This thing done stuck in James' craw," he said. "He never going to rest until he get it out."

"I'm afraid for him," Sharon said.

"He afraid for you too, sis."

She rose from the sofa and put on another ball cap Nail found for her in the closet after she lost the first one during the raid at the schoolhouse.

"You'll look out for him, Corey?"

"Sis, we been watching over each other long time."

She went out the back door, closing it behind her. Big C continued looking out the window. Nail still stood solitary in the summer sunshine by the big fishing log. Sharon walked up behind him. She stopped with her shoulder touching his arm. Neither spoke. Both looked down the creek. Their hands sought out each other's and they stood silently holding hands.

Big C turned away. Previously, Nail and he had had a real purpose in life: *To Serve and Defend.* Now, they were fugitives on the other side of the law. Big C didn't like the feeling. As an active militia member, however, he must have known this day would come.

He sank onto the sofa and flipped the cable back to Zenergy. It blurred in front of his eyes. He couldn't get the *Lady Clairol* blonde from the cemetery out of his mind. Something about Judy Sparks-Taylor's innocence, her vulnerability, triggered something in his protective nature. She might not be bright and worldly by Washington standards, but she was *real.* A country girl was as out of place among the politicians in D.C. as a chick hatched by a mama duck and asked to learn how to swim. What happened to her if they discovered *she* had been Ron Sparks' source of information?

Restless, Big C got up and returned to the kitchen window with his tea. He still sweated, so he stripped off his T-shirt. Nail and Sharon remained standing on the creek bank. Standing there like that for their last little time together. *That* was the saddest thing he had ever seen, sadder than a pair of ex-cops who didn't know where the hell they were going or what they were going to do.

After a minute or so, he made up his mind. He punched Judy's cell number into one of the Wal-Mart throwaway phones. She answered on the first ring, like she was waiting for a call.

"Corey? I thought you was Dennis. I'm still glad to hear from you. This ol' girl has been feeling powerful neglected."

"You all right?"

"You got no idea what politics is like. Dennis left to go campaigning in Illinois. He promised me all those things he and me is going to do when he's rich and gets rid of his wife—then he goes and takes Marilyn with him and tells me I got to keep quiet and hide under the bed until he's ready for me. Him and Marilyn is on all the news, all lovey-dovey and acting the perfect little family, right down to their pink poodle."

"Sound like he going to the dogs, poodle-wise," Big C commiserated, trying to make a joke to lift her spirits.

Judy emitted a hopeless little giggle. Her mood seemed to improve as the conversation continued in a light bantering tone. She suddenly turned serious again.

"Corey, they're showing your picture on the news. You and that other cop that slugged you at Ron's funeral—"

"I explain all that next time I see you."

"The news is saying you killed some people and might be accompanied by that woman from *Jerry Baer—"*

"Judy, look—"

"Don't worry, Corey. I seen her show last night when she told what really happened. You and me, we don't really know one another, but you seemed like a nice guy that wouldn't do nothing like that without a reason."

"I am a nice guy."

She tittered.

"I can prove it."

"How are you going to do that from all the way in Oklahoma?"

"What I show up on your doorstep and ask to go for another walk?"

"I suppose I'd just have to go. I ain't had no Sno Cone since. Way Dennis acting, he don't give a darn for nothing except his career anyhow."

"So you think Sharon Lowenthal telling the truth?" he probed carefully.

"I was watching her show when Dennis telephoned last night. He got mad when I told him what I was watching and ordered me to turn the channel. Dennis said she won't ride so high and mighty when Mr. Wiedersham gets her back to New York."

"What you reckon he mean by that?"

"I don't know. He just told me to change channels."

"Did you?"

She giggled. 'I ain't as blond and obeying as he thinks I am."

"I didn't think you blond from the beginning."

"I sure could use me another Sno Cone."

Big C returned to the window after he hung up. Nail and Sharon were sitting on the log, still holding hands.

# Chapter Forty-Four

## Skokie, Illinois

Dennis Trout swigged Maalox like a man dying of thirst coming upon an oasis in the Sahara. He was pissed, which was why he was out driving aimlessly; he needed some time alone away from advisors and aides and all the other assholes who surrounded him on the campaign trail. Marilyn, thankfully, had chosen to stay at the hotel in North Chicago with Reggie. She was pissed too about something or other—a chronic condition with her, it seemed—and calling him by his last name. "Trout, you are so fucked up." He telephoned Judy because he needed to talk, but she was also on the rag about something. The cunt told him—*him*—that she couldn't talk now. Probably dying her hair or watching *As The Stomach Turns* on soap TV.

A red light caught his rental Prius on Madison Street that ran west in Skokie to U.S. 41. Wiedersham had selected the car for him, as he seemed to select almost everything else in Trout's life. His campaign-wise brother-in-law thought it proper that Trout demonstrate his support for President Anastos' environmental initiative by driving a "green" car rather than the Buick Trout preferred.

He took the opportunity at the red light to nip from the pink stuff while he waited. His fingers drummed impatiently on the steering wheel. He turned the radio up so loud it vibrated the little roller skate car. *Pink* doing *Dear Mr. President*, an attack on former President Bush.

His thin hair stuck up like bristles on a hairless Chihuahua. A restive hand raking across his scalp returned with a glob of whipped cream.

"Fu-uck!"

He had about had it up to *here.*

The whipped cream came compliments of some bitch where he was addressing a meet arranged by the Illinois National Education Association. Normally the NEA, like most unions, sucked up to Progressive candidates. Everything was going along fine until some clown who said he was a student stood up to ask a question at the end. Instead of asking a question, he read a statement to the effect that he wanted the U.S.to investigate Israel's war crimes against the Palestinians.

As the student finished reading his statement, the bitch rushed up out of nowhere and smashed a whipped cream pie in Trout's face. Security hauled the guy and the twit out in handcuffs, both of them shouting, "*Allahu Akbar! Death to the Great Satan!*" Trout was so furious he didn't give a damn if Homeland Security took them out in the woods and shot them in the head after making them dig their own graves.

Wiedersham downplayed the incident when he reached Trout by cell phone. "It was a Tea Bagger plant trying to make us look bad. They were really Jews. That's how we'll spin it to the press. They can't touch us, Dennis. We're riding high."

Trout didn't feel like he was riding high. Cream pie in his hair and all sticky on his shirt, coat and tie. He turned *Pink* up even louder to dilute his anger. His fingers stuck to the volume knob. He licked them. Coconut cream. He hated fucking coconut.

A Dodge SUV in the lane next to him honked. The driver motioned for Trout to roll down his window.

"So you're listening to rock, huh?"

"You think?"

"Maybe you should listen to Rush Limbaugh instead so you can learn how Anastos is screwing up the country."

*That* observation, Trout suspected, came compliments of the *Anastos/Trout* bumper sticker on the Prius. Another Wiedersham idea.

The gray-haired old man in the SUV waved and went on through with the green light. Trout's lane was slow enough to allow his rage to build. This was one fucking sick world with everybody in it seemingly mad at something or somebody. It would be a much better world when the assholes were all gone.

Trout had his eye on the SUV several cars ahead of him. Stepping on the gas, the tiny tires on the Prius screeching like a piss ant, he whipped into the other lane and got right on the old man's bumper. Cars honked. Trout ignored them.

He swerved up beside the SUV at the next red light. The old man glanced over. Trout shot him the finger. He had an urge to jump out, pull the guy out of his car, rip off his head and piss down his throat. There was something to be said for road rage.

The SUV ducked into the next residential street while Trout gave chase, hoping the old fart would get nervous, then scared, then terrified, then have a massive MI and slam into a parked car.

There were stop signs at every intersection. Trout stared balefully into the old man's rearview mirror, trying to catch his eye. The SUV started making rolling stops, then no stops at all.

These little fucking people really thought their opinions mattered.

The SUV got stuck behind a hockey mom, or whatever they were calling themselves these days. Trout accelerated into the opposing lane and stopped next to his victim and turned his radio up loud again. The elderly asshole glanced in Trout's direction; he looked terrified. Trout leaned over so the senior troglodyte could get a good look at his face and remember who he had fucked with when Trout won the election.

Then Trout let him go. He pulled over to the curb and gulped a mouthful of Maalox. He felt better after he got out and used his key to scrape the *Anastos/Trout* sticker off his bumper.

## Circuit Court Overturns Voter ID

***(Phoenix)***—*Chaos erupted at the Maricopa County Courthouse in downtown Phoenix today after a three-judge panel from the Circuit Court of Appeals decided that people need not show proof of citizenship in order to register to vote. The crowd chanted, waved Mexican flags and bore signs charging racial discrimination against undocumented aliens.*

*The Appeals judges called the Arizona requirement for proof of citizenship inconsistent with the National Voter Registration Act, further stating that having to prove one is an American citizen in order to vote is an undue burden on minorities and immigrants...*

# Chapter Forty-Five

## Keystone Lake, Oklahoma

Before Sharon left the Safe House to return to New York, she, Big C and Nail met Lieutenant Jack Ross before daybreak on an open-all-night Wal-Mart parking lot in Sand Springs, a Tulsa suburb. Ross would transport her to the airport since it was unwise for either Nail or Big C to take the chance.

"Most of the TPD cops won't be looking too hard for you," Ross said, "but some are already kissing up to the Feds. Kimbrell's Homies have the airport covered like stink on you-know-what. Kimbrell's a real piece of work. It appears the Feds might appoint him our new police chief once the police are nationalized."

Ross handed Nail and Big C each an ATM card under assumed names.

"A number of secret patriotic donors have deposited money in the accounts to keep you going for awhile," he said.

Nail and Big C protested against accepting charity.

Ross said, "It's not charity. These people understand what's going on and they're not happy about it. Look at it that you're fighting for them."

It wasn't much of a farewell event in the parking lot. Sharon suggested they offer a prayer.

"We must continue to pray as if everything depends on God while we behave as if everything depends on us. We must never forget that we're on a holy mission. Where politics wishes to do the work of God, it becomes not divine but demonic. God can overcome evil if we but depend on Him."

They joined hands behind Big C's pickup and Sharon asked for God's guidance in the terrible days ahead. Afterwards, she hugged Big C and kissed him on the cheek. She lingered in Nail's embrace. Big C saw tears trickling off her chin.

"Wishes on a falling star come in threes, don't they?" she whispered. "I still have one more wish coming."

Then she was gone. Big C and Nail returned to the cabin, each quiet and contemplative and keeping to himself. Nail brooded most of the day while sitting on the fishing log. In a way neither man could define, Sharon had managed to convey to them the enormity of events that were history in the making. Big C wondered how the Founding

Fathers might have felt when they signed the Declaration of Independence.

That evening, he joked about their seven-course meal—a bucket of leftover Kentucky Fried chicken and a six pack. They watched the Zenergy Channel while they ate. President Anastos and his teleprompter were doing a live telecast from the White House Rose Garden.

"During this Recovery Summer, we have, uh, fought back from the worst of the recession, but we still have a lot of work to do," he said, head wagging from side to side. "Let me be very clear, individual salvation is not going to, uh, come about without collective salvation..."

A mouse appeared suddenly on the screen out of nowhere and scurried across in front of the President's lectern, as though mocking him. A female among the press corps emitted a shriek. Big C jumped to his feet and let out a whoop of laughter.

"It's a sign!"

Nail remained silent, glaring at the TV.

The picture switched to an Atlanta, Georgia, suburb where thirty thousand people thronged a Federal Building to put their names on a list for the government to subsidize their rent and house payments. In Boston, high school students and their teachers demanded students be issued free condoms, along with no interest Good Life credit cards. In Pittsburg, protestors angry over high unemployment rates rioted. A flash mob of more than one hundred descended upon a Walgreen's in St. Louis and stripped it like a swarm of locusts. A bunch of antiwar demonstrators in Washington ran amuck. Homies arrived to keep order, but not to fire on them as they had the Tea Partiers. No one interfered with Cindy Sizemore when she climbed on top of a parked car with a bullhorn.

"You get America out of Afghanistan and Israel out of Palestine and you'll stop the terrorism," she raged. "Just what is the noble cause Americans are dying for? Freedom and democracy? Bullshit! They're dying for oil to make oil companies richer. They're dying to expand American imperialism in the Middle East. America has been killing people since we first stepped on this continent. We are the ones responsible for death and destruction. Our only hope is a One World Government. I'm going all over the country telling people their country is not worth dying for..."

Egypt, Syria, Turkey, Algeria, Saudi Arabia and most of the rest of the Middle East was in revolt as the Muslim Brotherhood and communists worked together to overthrow governments and implement "change." In Cairo, one hundred thousand demonstrators roared in unison, "Kill the Jews!"

A pretty black reporter named Arthell in Chicago interspersed a lighter note in all the chaos and mayhem when she showed a clip of a congressional candidate named Dennis Trout getting smacked with a pie in the face. So this was the wimp with whom Judy was having her affair—balding, pale-skinned, haggard-looking? Big C almost fell out of his chair laughing. He hoped Judy saw it.

Then it was right back to the same old turmoil, turbulence and deceit, mostly from Washington. There was a shot of Senate Majority Leader Joe Wiedersham fork-tonguing about the new Health Care Bill and what socialized medicine meant for "the people."

"We're going to get public option," he promised. 'It's just a matter of when. ACOA and PEIU have been a major factor in helping us develop and execute the strategy that makes great progress on our goals and in motivating the public to support them."

Big C recognized that as politicalese for, "We've rammed this down your throats and now you're going to pay for it whether you like it or not."

Nail got up and took the Winchester 30.06 from a corner of the room. He spent the rest of the day cleaning the rifle before he retired to Sharon's bed. Big C understood. It was like sleeping in her bed brought him closer to her.

Nail was gone the next morning in his old pickup when Big C awoke. He had left a note on the table by the coffee pot where Big C would find it.

*Had some business to take care of. Back later.*

The scoped 30.06 was also gone.

## Oklahoma Homeland Director Slain

***(Tulsa)***—*The Regional Director of Homeland Security based in Tulsa, Oklahoma, was slain early this morning as he emerged from his home to drive to work. Witnesses in the upscale neighborhood where Anthony R. Kimbrell, 45, resided in South Tulsa said they heard a single rifle shot at approximately 7:20 a.m. Kimbrell died instantly from a high-powered rifle bullet through the head...*

*Kimbrell's assistant director, Gary Philby, told reporters that a sniper killed the Director. He named former Detective James Nail as a person of interest...*

*"Nail is a rogue cop who should be considered armed and extremely dangerous," Philby said. "He is a former sniper for the Tulsa Police SWAT team and was trained at Quantico by the FBI..."*

# Chapter Forty-Six

## Keystone Lake, Oklahoma

There was no discussion between Nail and Big C about the bullet through Kimbrell's skull. However, both understood that it was more urgent than ever that they flee the state. And soon. According to TV news, Homeland Security and AmeriCorps were sending in task forces to hunt down the two fugitives. "Sources" further related how Sharon Lowenthal had already been questioned in New York but provided authorities no helpful information.

Nail thought they should stick together; Big C pointed out that it was best they split up and assume aliases. "They looking for a redneck Indian and a nigger traveling together."

"What will you do, C?"

Big C shrugged massive shoulders difficult to disguise on the run. The two men sat together on the fishing log by the creek.

"I think to get the Defenders back together," he decided.

"It's come to armed rebellion?"

"Bro', I love Sharon like my own sister, but she can talk peace and God-love till the cows come home and Jesus break the eastern sky and it not going to make a bit of difference. Things done gone too far. What about you? Where you going?"

"Maybe it's better if we don't know where each other's at?" Nail suggested.

"It's no good plan to go to New York."

Nail nodded without comment. Both men watched the brown water rushing by after the recent rains. Big C broke the silence presently to tell a story from when he was a kid coming up in the Oklahoma Panhandle, where blacks and some Indians still share-cropped.

"We so poor poverty was a step up," he began. "But we proud and don't take handouts from nobody. It embarrassing to take welfare in them days. They seven of us living in a three room shack west of Guymon. One year the crops fail and we have no choice except starve. Pop sent me to county barn to pick up what he call 'gimpy groceries.' Government surplus commodities. Sign your name and they fill your tow sack with cheese and rice and beans and powder milk. I only twelve, but I was a scrapper. Fight at the drop of a hat, even if my own hat—"

Nail grinned tightly. "I can't believe that about you."

"I not always the peaceable sort like I am today. Anyhow, I'm in line and this man work for the government push me or something. I'm ready to fight. What he say make a bigger impression on me than anything else in my life. He say, 'Boy, if the government feed you, it will do what it damn well please.' From that day on, I never took nothing from nobody I didn't earn. Tolstoy right when he say, 'The more is given, the less people will work for themselves, and the less they work the more they poverty will increase.'"

Big C sometimes surprised people with how well read and knowledgeable he was when all they judged him by was his fractured grammar, which Nail suspected he affected to some degree to keep him tied to his roots.

"What happened to us?" Nail wondered dourly. "To us as Americans?"

"Government feeds us," Big C responded. "One in six owe his living in some form or other to government. We become slaves, more so than my old great-great-grandpappy ever was on the plantation. It make no difference what color your skin is. We got the entitlement culture. We think we entitled to what somebody else got, no matter if we earn it or not. Once you become a slave, you sign up to do massa's bidding."

He glanced over to see if Nail was following him. Nail sat with his hands clasped across his knees and his head down, listening.

"Massa going to take care all us chil'ren 'cause we too stupid to do it ourself. Massa going to tell us how much money we can make, what we can eat, where we allow to live, where we work... We so stupid government put warning labels on lawn mowers: 'Don't stick your hand in the blades.' You can't escape. On your mattress—*on your mattress!*—it say; 'It's a violation of federal law to remove this label.'"

Nothing got Big C hotter than talking about government intrusion.

"We was once independent-minded folks who take care of ourself and our own people. We expect nothing from government except to be left alone. Now, we demand government give us Social Security, unemployment insurance, Medicare, Medicaid, student loans, food stamps, welfare, a college education... On and on. What Sharon and Rush Limbaugh and Zenergy News doing is trying to educate people. But it never going to work until we build back a independent culture that allow for the Constitution. That is not going to happen. It's done too late for talk. They nothing left except action for the few of us left who still values freedom."

Nail realized from his experience as a cop that people had a general propensity for obeying authority. Blind obedience certainly followed "if the government feeds you." It was all too big, too overwhelming for him to believe he could have any impact on turning the country back from the direction it was headed. Especially since his own life from here on meant surviving on the run, living underground like a chased rat.

Out off the Creek Turnpike in Tulsa he had seen a billboard that he suspected expressed the future of mankind.

**There Is No God**
**Rational Atheism is the Answer**

Was that truly what man had to look forward to? Belief in *nothing?*

# PART III

*"If we understand the mechanism of the group mind, it is now possible to control and regiment the masses according to our will without their knowing it."* — Edward Barnays, *Propaganda*

# Chapter Forty-Seven

## Chicago

"*Rich* people will be there. The best kind," Majority Leader Joe Wiedersham said, followed by that bark that served as laughter. "They'll cheerfully cough up their dough for the cause."

"For hope 'n change," Trout muttered and hurriedly smiled to mask his growing cynicism.

Wiedersham hailed the black limo waiting for them in the roundabout of the Hyatt-Regency. Justin Cobb, 34, Wiedersham's new chief of staff and Trout's replacement, was already waiting in the car. Cobb had been a campaign gofer during Anastos' run for the presidency. He was younger and thinner than Trout and wore an Al Capone hat that lent him a cold, sinister look. The look didn't change when he doffed his hat in deference to Wiedersham. Trout doubted the guy ever woke up in a cold sweat at night over *anything* Wiedersham might ask him to do.

The political event to which they were bound was being held at the McCormick Place Convention Center, on the outdoor terrace overlooking Lake Michigan by moonlight. Part fund-raiser, part testimonial to the late leftwing Professor Howard Rhine, it was being attended by the glitterati of Hollywood, the media, and other sympathetic Marxist-leaning reformers. George Zuniga was coming. President Anastos opted out, since Zenergy News was certain to be lurking in the shadows in ambush. Soon, Wiedersham predicted, they wouldn't have to worry about Zenergy News, Rush Limbaugh, Sharon Lowenthal....They wouldn't have to worry about elections.

Out of curiosity, since Trout had never heard of Howard Rhine, he had conducted a web search beforehand. Although government was constantly scrubbing the web for detrimental or offensive references to government, Trout found enough to learn that Rhine had been a member of the Communist Party USA and a professor at the University of Chicago with Anastos buddies Bill Ackart and Bernadine Samson-Ackart, the 1970s activists-bombers. He was a lifetime member of The Institute for Open Societies, a pro-Marxist think tank founded by George Zuniga, and he had authored the revisionist textbook, *A People's History of the United States*, that was being force fed to college students in at least thirty states so far. The American Progress Center, also founded by Zuniga, conceded that Rhine's text "basically offered nothing in terms of ways to think about solutions to the problems of the world—but most of the best people have read it and that's a pretty impressive achievement."

Trout scoffed at the reference to "best people." *He* had never read it.

Rhine's New York *Times* obituary described him as "an activist, a socialist, a pacifist, an anti-racist who never strayed from his conviction that humanity was capable of making this a better world."

Trout doubted Wiedersham knew squat about the man they were honoring and probably cared less. What was important was the fundraising and making an appearance among people who counted. Hold your nose and go for it. For the good of the nation. For the good of the world. For your own good. Better to be a shepherd than a sheep.

Wiedersham and Cobb began their intrigue before the limousine had gone a block from the Hyatt-Regency. Wiedersham settled in the rear seat with Trout while Cobb faced them in the other seat. Although a soundproof glass between them and the driver permitted normal private conversation, Cobb leaned toward the Majority Leader like Reggie did when he thought Marilyn was going to pet him. If he'd had a tail, it would have been wagging like crazy. The guy's ass kissing was pathetic.

Wiedersham crossed one leg over the other. He glanced at his watch. His shoes were Italian Gravitas, his watch a Rolex Oyster. On his lap lay an open copy of *Wall Street Journal* bearing the headline **Jerry Baer's Warriors Turn to Sharon Lowenthal**. Wiedersham and Cobb seemed to be in agreement that the cunt had to be derailed before her train picked up speed.

Judging from her first rabble-rousing show, she might easily surpass Baer in influence and popularity among America's Homers. Although Trout didn't know it for a fact, he suspected Wiedersham was behind lifting the warrant for her arrest in order to clear the way for her return to New York where she would be more accessible.

"Boss, how does this sound?" Cobb asked, snicking on the overhead lamp in order to read a statement. "'I hereby offer to negotiate a one-hundred-thousand-dollar payday to the person or persons who will come forward with a sex tape or phone record or anything else that succeeds in discrediting Sharon Lowenthal and removing her from the public eye—?'"

Wiedersham frowned and flicked his fingers. The pleased-with-himself look disappeared from Cobb's face.

"Boss, they won't be able to trace it to us—"

"Where do you propose releasing it?"

"Radio Air America?"

"Too obvious. Let me think about it."

Trout turned his head away and looked out the window as the limo picked up speed on South Lake Shore Drive. Headlights were already coming on.

"Don't look so stressed, Dennis," Wiedersham admonished, barking more quick laughter. "There won't be any coconut cream pies tonight."

Cobb sniggered. Trout glared at him. Wiedersham's foot crossed over the opposite knee and began to jiggle.

"What about the Tulsa cop that shot Kimbrell?" Wiedersham asked Cobb. "Is he fucking the Lowenthal bitch when he's not shooting people? We might explore that possibility."

"Apparently, his daughter was killed when—"

"I know all that. Kimbrell was a fool for not taking care of business when he had the opportunity. From what I gather, this Nail is a loose cannon. Mr. Zuniga doesn't like loose cannons. They make people nervous."

Wiedersham's foot jiggled harder.

"He got his revenge," Cobb said reassuringly. "That's probably the last we'll hear from him until he's in jail."

"I'm not so sure," Wiedersham pondered. "Anything on the black cop with him?"

"Homeland Security promises they'll soon catch both of them."

Wiedersham sneered. "Vladimir Gonzalez couldn't catch his ass with both hands."

*We are charming bastards, aren't we?* Trout thought. The Saul Alinsky method of persuasion in action. You ridiculed the worthy, attacked the courageous, bribed the weak—*like me*—and intimidated the cowardly and ignorant, until no one remained to question your power and you were secure and ready to implement real change. In the name of the people, of course.

The limo slowed and pulled into the Convention Center, terminating further conversation. Other limos and chauffeur-driven cars ahead were releasing their beautiful people. An attractive blonde in a low-cut gown smiled and wiggled her fingers at Wiedersham when he got out on the sidewalk with Cobb and Trout. Trout recognized her as the upcoming new starlet in *Forever Sundown*. He wondered who was buttering her toast.

Someone popped up in front of him with a video feed.

"Get that thing out of my face," he snarled, "or I'll shove it up your ass and call you a popsicle."

## First Lady Targets Childhood Obesity

***(Washington)***—*First Lady Cynthia Anastos unveiled more of the President's Fitness, Sports and Nutrition Program at a D.C. middle school today in the administration's ongoing crusade against childhood obesity. She said the President will sign an executive order requiring school teachers to monitor the weight of all children and issue a "body mass index" on report cards. The idea is to "encourage parents of overweight children to seek help for their kids—and themselves." Parents who fail to heed body mass index reports are subject to child abuse action from the Department of Human Services and may face criminal or civil charges...*

*"This will make the American people healthier and happier," President Anastos said. "If they won't do it for themselves, then we'll make sure they do it..."*

# Chapter Forty-Eight

## New York

What appeared to be an elderly man with a limp shuffled past Rockefeller Center. A hole in the right shoe of his old sneakers exposed a bare big toe. His hair was gray but thick. Likewise the mustache. He wore horn-rimmed glasses mended with a paper clip through one of the arm hinges. Ratty jeans and a too-big flannel shirt with an oil stain on the back, as though from crawling in and out from underneath a car, completed James Nail's disguise. He carried a Missouri driver's license and a Social Security card in the name of Jonathan Harker. Even Big C would probably not have recognized him.

The worst part of living with the homeless guise was sleeping outdoors and in Dipsy Dumpsters in alleys. Last night he crashed in Central Park, pushing himself in underneath bushes near The Pond where police weren't apt to find him. He had lost weight too, picking up only one meal a day at a mission or Salvation Army soup kitchen. On the positive side, the human wreckage that wandered the streets of New York was all but invisible to most people. The homeless had almost doubled in recent months, what with the collapsing economy, providing Nail even greater concealment.

This was the best way he knew to keep a protective eye on Sharon without the police or Homies slapping a collar on him. TV sets in display windows sometimes ran photos of Big C and him. They were described as "domestic terrorists...armed and extremely dangerous." *Enemies of the State.*

Nail's weary, limping gait brought him to Avenue of the Americas and the Zenergy News Building where Sharon's studio was located. The constant din of traffic and the throbbing buzz of people trapped in the canyons of Manhattan's skyscrapers jangled his nerve endings. New York reminded him of the frenzied, mindless energy of an ant colony that had been poisoned. People rushing about all jammed together in each other's armpits and bad breath.

It did provide a certain anonymity, however.

Down the block from Zenergy a stand of suffocated maples within a wall pretended to give the city a splotch of greenery and perhaps remind inhabitants that there *might* be life elsewhere. It was still early light, the morning rush beginning, when Nail posted himself against the wall, sitting clumped up with his back against it, waiting for Sharon to arrive accompanied by her two private bodyguards. Nail had little faith in her security. Bodyguards hadn't done Jerry Baer any good.

Normally, since Sharon lived only a few blocks away, she and her escort walked to and from work; Nail usually followed at a discreet distance. This morning, however, a car picked her up, either because she had other things to do on the way to work or because the sky threatened rain. Nail was watching from an alley across from Sharon's *Hampton Arms* apartment when the car arrived. That, not Central Park, was where he spent most nights in order to be nearby in the event of danger. He was prepared to keep up his vigil, no matter how long, since he knew in his gut *they* would come after her again sooner or later.

She was late arriving at the studio this morning. It made him uneasy when she was out of his sight or varied her routine. Maybe she stopped in to visit Jerry Baer's widow and kids on her way to work, as she sometimes did.

To kill time and give the impression that he was doing something, he removed a worn paperback from inside his shirt, tucked into the waistband of his loose-fitting jeans next to the .38-caliber S&W Featherweight Big C had given him before they split up. Ayn Rand's classic *Atlas Shrugged.* Sharon said the novel ranked near the top of a *Subversive Literature* list secretly published by the government. Reading, he went over the same passage two or three times; he kept glancing up to let his eyes sweep the street and sidewalks for signs of Sharon or of trouble.

He had become a familiar figure on Avenue of The Americas for those who deigned to notice. Most pedestrians stepped over his outstretched legs without so much as glancing at him. Police mostly ignored the homeless, but occasionally some beat cop would come along, kick his foot and order him to move on. He would get up and walk around the block and come back.

Finally, Sharon's company car stopped in front of Zenergy and let her and her bodyguards out on the sidewalk. One bodyguard was dark with shoulders like a linebacker's, the other fair with a shirt collar larger than his hat size. Good enough to ward off the errant street mugger or average masher, not good enough to protect the hope of the nation's freedom from what must surely be coming her way.

Nail sprang to his feet, startling passersby, in order to watch for threat as well as to catch a glimpse of Sharon's black hair and saucy walk through the throngs of foot traffic before she disappeared inside. Each day he had to suppress the almost overwhelming urge to rush to her. Except for her existence, his days would have seemed so much bleaker.

Sometimes, like this morning, she hesitated at the door to the Zenergy Building to look around, as if she felt someone watching her. Her eyes swept the street, brushing past the now-familiar sight of the old homeless man next to the maples without recognizing him.

As with every other morning, Nail slid down the wall when she disappeared inside and settled on the sidewalk to wait for her to come out again. He had picked up occasional indications that *they* might have her under surveillance waiting for him to show up. His making contact with her would likely be fatal to both of them.

The rage that consumed him following Jamie's murder had since subsided to a seething anger. His only remaining role was to protect Sharon from harm while she went about saving the nation. He read his novel as pedestrians rushed by as though they did not see him. Thunder rumbled overhead, barely audible above the noise of the city. Rain was coming and the temperature was beginning to fall.

Rain started falling at noon. Nail placed *Atlas Shrugged* into a plastic baggie and stuck it into his waistband beneath his shirt. He got up and looked around and moved underneath a nearby awning protecting the door to an investment firm. He sat against the wall, partly protected from the rain, pulled his knees up to his chin and wrapped his arms around them to help conserve body heat. It never occurred to him to abandon Sharon. He was on-station for most of twenty four hours a day, taking time to sleep and eat only when she seemed safe or when she was out of his reach on business.

He shivered. A man in an expensive raincoat and hat carrying an umbrella ducked in underneath the awning and out of the downpour. He stopped in front of the door and collapsed his umbrella. He glared at Nail.

"Hey, slick. You can't sleep here. Beat it."

Nail looked up. Piercing blue eyes staggered the man back on his heels; he fled through the doorway without another word. Nail dozed off in spite of being wet and cold.

It was still raining hard at quitting time. Sharon wearing a see-through raincoat and rain hat came out with Shoulders and Big Neck. A company car pulled up for them. Traffic was heavy and the driver had to wait for an opening. Nail spotted a man in a trench coat standing down the block from the Zenergy Building with water streaming off his hat brim. The way he watched Sharon was more than casual. A cab with its engine running waited nearby at curbside.

As soon as Sharon's car slid into traffic, the man in the trench coat dashed to the waiting cab and jumped in. Rubber hissed on wet pavement. The cab almost caused a four-car pileup before it straightened out several cars behind Sharon's ride, following it.

Ignoring his limp, Nail took off in a desperate run toward Sharon's apartment building six blocks away, splashing through puddles, weaving recklessly in and out among raincoats and umbrellas, creating mini-chaos and eliciting various insults.

# Chapter Forty-Nine

## New York

A half-crazed street bum charging through the rain-soaked streets of New York cleared a path of all but the most obtuse and belligerent. Volleys of curses followed in James Nail's wake. *They* knew where Sharon lived; to locate her residence wasn't why the trench coat was tailing her. The guy had something more sinister in mind.

Nail rushed past both vehicles when they got caught in one of the city's ubiquitous traffic jams. He slowed to a fast walk in order not to look conspicuous. He chanced a good look at the perp in the trench coat. Through the cab's rain-swept side window he saw a man of about thirty five or so with a little Fu Manchu encircling thinly-compressed lips. The guy was leaning forward from the backseat to keep an eye on Sharon's car a few places ahead.

The sky dumped another bucketful of water on the city. Old Styrofoam cups, tatters of paper, food scraps, dead pigeons and other debris gurgled down the gutters. Nail reached Sharon's apartment building well ahead of the cars. It was a tall, stately red stone set back on a side street lined with scraggly Boston pear trees. Nail ducked into the alley halfway down the block and hunkered next to a dumpster that belonged to an Italian restaurant where he commanded a good view of the front of the *Hampton Arms*. Gray sheets of rain and the cloudy twilight of approaching evening camouflaged his presence.

He recovered an old square of plywood he had used before and held it over his head like an umbrella. Rain falling straight down into the concrete canyon drummed on it deafeningly while he waited. He tried not to think of the consequences if Sharon were headed elsewhere instead of coming home.

Nail had worked many gang crimes during his years with the TPD. Everything from drive-by shootings in wars over drugs and territory to Mafia-type networks that corrupted businesses and politicians through vice and greed. Until now, however, he would never have believed that the federal government could have developed into one massive ideological criminal enterprise run by real-life commies who would do *anything* to accumulate power and achieve their goals. The only difference between it and some Don in Chicago or Miami trying to control the dope or whore trade was the much-longer reach of government's arm.

He was shivering again from exposure by the time Sharon's company car pulled up and stopped at the apartment complex. She and

Shoulders jumped from the back seat in their rain gear and ducked through the rain to the building's protected entrance. Sharon tapped in a code, the door opened and both disappeared inside. The car left with Big Neck still in the backseat. Nail knew the routine; Big Neck would relieve Shoulders at midnight. Obviously, neither had detected the tail.

Down the block, the cab turned the corner into the side street and slowed until the way was clear. It crept past the apartment building. The Fu Manchu character was clearly casing the place and up to no good. The cab went on and turned at the next intersection.

Nail waited while evening began earlier than usual because of rain and lowering clouds. Worker ants hurrying home to their nooks and crannies thinned out as rush hour ended. Nail stepped clear of the alley to take a look and almost collided with a big man walking past wearing an ankle-length black raincoat. The guy shoved Nail out of the way, muttering, "Fucking vagrants."

Nail repressed a response and slunk back into the alley.

Full night fell. Street lamps glowed weakly in the watery air, casting strange wavering shadows. Nail had about decided nothing was going to happen tonight when Fu Manchu from the cab suddenly appeared on foot, as though washed up out of the shadows. He glanced furtively into the mouth of the alley, but Nail hugged the wall out of sight in the darkness.

Fu Manchu trotted across the street to the entryway of *Hampton Arms*, into the light washing out through the glass doors. Nail watched him peep inside. Then he looked up and down the street before turning back and taking a dimly-lighted walkway that led alongside the building toward the rear courtyard. Even though no one was apt to be out this late in this weather on this side street, no real pro would have taken such a chance at being seen and later recognized. A real pro certainly wouldn't have taken a cab to the scene—unless the cab *wasn't* a cab.

As soon as the prowler was out of sight, Nail ducked across the street after him, Big C's little .38 Featherweight in hand. It was darker around back of the building, but there was still security lighting. He caught up to Fu Manchu peering around the next corner into the fenced courtyard that contained the swimming pool. Nail approached cautiously, puzzled by the guy's behavior. Sharon lived on the third floor. Was this guy a cat burglar—or was he merely reconnoitering for some future action, getting the lay of the land? The best way to find out was to ask.

He was two paces away when Fu Manchu apparently sensed his approach and whirled around. Nail stuck the .38 in his face. The intruder slowly lifted his arms. Rain hissed on his hat.

"My wallet's in my inside pocket. There's no need for this to get messy."

"It's already messy."

Nail snatched the guy and slammed him against the wall. "Assume the position."

The guy spread 'em, leaning against the wall like he had done it before. Nail relieved him of a Beretta 9mm from underneath his trench coat. He stuck it in his belt. He pressed the cold, wet steel of his .38 against the base of the man's skull.

"Whether or not you walk out of here depends on your answers," he offered.

"I'm Homeland Security," the man blurted out, sounding almost unglued. "I have ID. I'm working on a case."

"Is that a fact? Who's the name?"

"Walter. Walter Roland."

"Not yours. The case?"

"I... It's federal business."

"Careful now." Nail pressed the muzzle harder against the agent's neck. "Sharon Lowenthal? Am I right?"

The agent said nothing. Nail felt him trembling.

"Who gave you your orders?"

"I—Everything comes down the chain."

"What were you supposed to do?"

"Nothing. I swear. Just look."

"Didn't your mama teach you not to swear?"

It was at that moment he caught a whisper of movement to his rear. Feeling like an idiot himself, an amateur to have been caught off guard, he wheeled around to find a gun pointed at him, center of mass. Behind the gun was a clean-shaved face and the black raincoat of the asshole who had shoved him earlier. He should have figured on Fu Manchu's cover.

This one meant business. A gut feeling and the guy's eyes told Nail he was a trigger pull away from death.

Nail bounced back and away from Fu Manchu. Crouching, he swept his .38 on target and fired. His opponent's gun blossomed flame at the same instant. The bullet slapped his rib cage like a sledgehammer, knocking him flat on his back. Everything blurred before his eyes. He felt himself blacking out like when he was shot at the ORU Center.

# Chapter Fifty

## Washington, D.C.

At almost the same time that James Nail was shot in New York, Dennis Trout's "Bimbo Eruption," as Wiedersham referred to Judy, was in the bathroom putting on too much makeup and touching up her Lady Clairol. Trout had dropped in on her unexpectedly after having been *summoned* by his wife back to Washington for a function at the White House. He had needed his ashes hauled in the worst way before going home to face Marilyn and her pink poodle.

"Damn you, Trout," Marilyn said when she issued the summons. That was her way of letting him know not to fuck with her. "Don't let your attitude screw things up. The *President* invited us to attend a state dinner for the Chinese premier. Everyone who's *anyone* will be there."

*Congressman* Trout. He had to keep reminding himself.

One of these hallelujah days he was going to dump his bitch of a wife. When he had the balls. And the money. But—listening to Judy in the bathroom—not for any Bugfuck, Oklahoma. He could do better than that. In the meantime, Judy threw a wicked Lewinsky and kept her mouth shut otherwise. She knew who buttered her toast as well as he did.

He was unwinding by writing in his notebook and watching TV after a quickie roll in the sack to relieve campaign pressure. Judy had been watching reruns of *The Bachelor* and Trout didn't bother changing the channel. He was only half paying attention when a Public Service Announcement came on, paid for by federal stimulus funds. The ad showed a morgue scene with a background of somber music. A fat man lay on a gurney with one exposed hand death-gripping a half-eaten Big Mac. His wife sobbed uncontrollably.

"High blood pressure, high cholesterol, heart attack," droned a voiceover. "Tonight, make it vegetarian."

The shot closed with a shot of the villain—the Golden Arches of McDonald's.

The ad made Trout uncomfortable. As an "insider," he understood what lay behind it. Regulatory czar Sam Shrader's job was to "fundamentally transform" the lives of ordinary Americans through rules and regulations. That meant everything from their diets to their medications to the way they interacted with each other. The ads were a "nudge." If they didn't work, next came taxes—and if *that* didn't work, punishment. One way or another, people were going to behave the way their government wanted them to.

He shoved such thoughts from his mind when Judy peeked out through the bedroom doorway. She giggled coyly. "Do you want to use the powder room after we've—? Well, you know."

"I'm fresh enough. What I need is a drink before I have to go." He had changed into khaki slacks, Dockers and a blue short-sleeve shirt she kept for him in *his* closet.

"There's some Scotch in—"

He cut her off. "You're out of it."

"Heavens to Betsy! I clean forgot to buy some more."

She came out brushing her hair and looking as cheap as ever in half-exposed boobs, between which dangled the gold locket he gave her. She bent over to peck him on the lips. Her breath smelled like tobacco.

"Is that your little insurance notebook?" she asked him.

"It's private."

"Like a diary?"

"What am I—a school girl?"

"You sound like you could use some Maalox."

"Judy, what I can *use* is to go out for a drink and forget about Illinois."

Unperturbed, she continued to brush her hair. She glanced at the TV.

"I seen it when that nasty bitch hit you square dab in the face with the pie. You looked so awful I almost cried."

"Judy, if you're ready, let's go."

She paused with brush in hand to study him. "Dennis, you've changed like day to night since you started running for Congress."

"Politics is nasty business."

"I seen you on TV and your wife—"

"Let's not do this again," he interrupted. "I've told you, it's all show for the campaign."

"You don't never let me finish what I got to say. I see ya'all on TV and she's all giggly and hanging on your arm. But you look miserable. I hope you ain't looking like that when you and me gets together."

"Stop it, Judy. Just stop it."

He stood up abruptly, stuffing his pen into his shirt pocket. On their way out, he absently-mindedly left his notebook on the dinette table. They locked the door. Then he unlocked it again and returned for his notebook. He didn't want to forget it there. He trusted Judy no more than he did Marilyn not to open it. They were both women, weren't they?

# Chapter Fifty-One

## New York

Nail knew it was the end if he let himself black out. He bounced up from the ground on nothing but raw grit, still gripping the .38 in his fist. Fu Manchu took his little Fu Manchu and hauled ass. The other Fed was down for the count, his legs twitching in death spasms.

Nail's only thought was to put distance between himself and the "crime scene." He stumbled off in the blinding downpour. Police in Manhattan were quicker to respond to gunfire than were cops in Harlem or the Bronx where they heard it every night.

He dropped Fu Manchu's Beretta in the first trash receptacle he came across and shambled on, hunched over his wound and attempting to hold himself together with his hands and arms. Cold rain soaked him to the skin, but his ribs felt wet and warm. He didn't know how hard he was hit, but he was bleeding pretty badly and getting short of breath. At least he wasn't stretched out like the other guy waiting to be slabbed and tagged.

His intentions had been to scare the piss out of the Fu Manchu guy; let his bosses know Sharon was protected, not kill him. It hadn't worked out exactly that way. The black raincoat guy was the fourth man he had killed since all this had started—more gunplay than during *Desert Storm* and his years on the TPD put together. No regrets, just making note of it. Connie would have been horrified.

He had to keep going. It was all over for Sharon if the Homies captured him—or he died. The predators were circling. They weren't about to let up until they destroyed her as they had Jerry Baer.

He dared not seek medical help. Doctors were required to report bullet wounds. He mustn't let the Feds make the connection between the dead man and Sharon and bring all this down on her. The Homies were looking for a reason to arrest her.

Out of breath, panting from pain and loss of blood, he leaned against a wall in the drenched shadows and looked back. Lights were flashing on all over the apartment complex. He opened his shirt and gingerly examined his wounds, discovering with his fingers a puncture entrance on his right side and a ragged exit in the meaty part of his back. Pressing against his ribs produced crackling, grating sounds of shattered ribs, accompanied by piercing pain. He feared he might be hemorrhaging internally and that shock was imminent.

Scattered traffic passed in the dark rain with headlights diminished and driver vision restricted. He moved on in his awkward, limping side-to-side gait. Sirens wailed in the distance. He headed for Central Park and managed another block before flashing blue lights telegraphed the approach of a police car. He ducked for the nearest alley as a prowl car squalled around the corner of the intersection ahead. Its headlights washed across him briefly before he blended into alley shadows. Emergency lights slapped buildings on either side of the street as the cruiser slowed and stopped.

There were always Dipsy Dumpsters in alleys. Nail clambered painfully into the nearest one and pulled the heavy lid down. He was somewhat relieved to find himself waist deep in plain household-type trash, probably apartment house wastes, rather than garbage from some restaurant or grocery store.

Peering through the crack between the lid and the receptacle, he saw the shadow of the cop stretched long in his direction by the headlights of his parked cruiser. A Kell flashlight probed the rain-swept alley, flaring against the dumpster. Nail cringed away from it, holding his breath and trying not to give himself away in his suffering.

Rain howled against the metal lid above Nail's head. Water dribbled down his back. For what seemed an eternity, the patrolman's flashlight beam searched and picked at the dark. He must have left his car door open or his window partially down, for Nail heard a continuous stream of police calls crackling from the cop's radio.

The cop was entering the alley for a closer inspection. Nail left his gun stuffed in the waistband of his trousers. He could never take another street cop's life. This was just an average Joe, not a Homie. A flatfoot fighting crime and evil with little or nothing to do with the vast federal apparatus that was on its way to taking over the nation.

He wondered if Sharon's God would listen to him if he prayed.

His vision blurred and split into various sight patterns, like that of a spider. The cop morphed into four or five images, all of whom were headed directly for him. He realized he was losing consciousness. He'd probably wake up in a jail cell or, as his granny used to say, he'd wake up to find himself dead.

The officer walked past the dumpster and shined his light behind it. He hesitated as though uncertain whether he had seen anything after all. Maybe he had had enough of the rain, perhaps he heard himself being paged over the radio. Whatever the reason, he gave up and returned to his car. Blue lights still flashing, it left in a hurry toward the scene of the shooting. Darkness returned to the alley.

Nail toppled backward into the trash. Shock was setting in. He fumbled for the TracPhone in his front pocket. He couldn't recall Big

C's number. Then he remembered it had been programmed in. He felt for the dial button and pressed.

## Homeland Agent Ambushed

***(New York)****—A Homeland Security agent was shot to death tonight in an upscale apartment complex where Rightwing talk show hostess Sharon Lowenthal is believed living. Authorities identified the agent as Roth Bennett, 37.*

*A second agent, Walter Roland, witnessed the murder. He said he was working a case in the Hampton Arms Apartments when a man with a gun confronted him and questioned him about Lowenthal. When Agent Bennett came to Roland's assistance, he was gunned down in cold blood. Bennett had not drawn his weapon...*

*The assailant's description, plus other details surrounding the crime, lead police to believe the assailant may have been former Oklahoma Police Detective James Nail...*

## Chapter Fifty-Two

### Birmingham, Alabama

Big Corey Brown sat in *Ruby's Ribs* at a Formica table with two other crew who had lost their previous jobs and were now doing road construction under a Federal Stimulus Plan. One was "Skinny Jim" Jefferson, the other "Squeaky" Talbot, both as dark as Big C but rougher looking in a southern country boy sort of way.

Big C's TracPhone buzzed, but there was no one on the other end when he answered it. The callback said "unidentified caller."

"That you ol' woman, Vernon?" Squeaky teased.

Skinny Jim guffawed. "Keepin' tabs on his black ass, wonderin' why he ain't home. I bet she six-foot-fourteen and with an ass broad enough to last till sundown next year."

"Vernon" was Big C's cover name. Vernon Smith. He figured his best bet of blending into the population until things cooled off—or heated up, whichever came first—was to find a big southern city full of African-Americans. First day in Birmingham, "Vernon" hooked a job working on a mostly-black crew for a minority construction company with a federal contract. The crew, it seemed, survived on barbeque, fried chicken and beer. KFCs and B-B-Q joints down south also served collard greens and fried okra. The only thing missing was watermelon. Posing as Vernon, Big C felt like he was living the stereotype.

He got up from the table, which was littered with soiled paper towels, *Ruby's Ribs* boxes, bones and beer cans. "Gotta go make this call," he excused himself.

"Oh, yea-a-ah," Skinny Jim cackled good-naturedly, rolling his eyes. "He gotta check in, what he gotta do."

"You got me," Big C said over his shoulder as he hurried toward the door. "She one bodacious woman."

He plopped down in a wooden rocker on one end of the rustic front porch where darkness concealed him. A constant stream of traffic headlights going past on I-65 reflected the concern on his face as he dialed Nail's TracPhone and heard the vibrating sound it made. They had agreed to contact each other only in an emergency. He waited, but there was no answer. Cold seeped into the pit of his stomach.

He dialed again a few minutes later. Still no answer. He returned inside and made excuses that he had to get home right away.

"You pussy-whipped," Squeaky decided, feeling his beers.

"I wear the pants. She just tell me which pair to wear," Big C quipped back.

He was staying in an upstairs rented room on Crestwood. More stereotype. A rooming house with peeling white paint and police breaking up the family squabble next door every Saturday night. He locked his door when he got home to keep Bertha the live-in landlady from busting in on him unannounced; she had a thing for him. He settled on the bed with its rusted iron bedstead and squeaking springs and tossed his work cap in the corner. He had let his hair grow out to a length Pop would have called "nappy." It changed his facial appearance, but there was little he could do about his size.

He began dialing Nail's number every few minutes until he had to plug in his phone charger to keep the routine going. His distress grew as minutes turned into hours. There was nothing Big C could do this time to ride to his old friend's rescue. For all he knew, James might be dead by now.

Although he couldn't be certain, he suspected Nail had gone to New York to be near Sharon. He thought about phoning her, but dismissed the impulse. A call would only worry her and prompt her to do something reckless.

He kept dialing.

He turned the portable TV to a local newscast, as the rooming house had neither cable nor satellite. About one a.m., a streamer across the bottom of the screen announced that a Homeland Security agent in Manhattan had been gunned down by a terrorist.

By four a.m., he was ready to conclude James was either dead or in custody. He lowered his head into his big hands and sat there on the bed for a long time while he remembered the times Nail and he had had together. Other cops sometimes referred to them as "Salt and Pepper."

He decided to make one last try before he gave up. He punched in the numbers slowly and deliberately, as if concentration might make the difference in getting through. He heard the vibrating sound. He started to press *End Call* when a feeble voice rose on the other end.

"C...I...I... It's up to you to protect her... I'm dying..."

# Chapter Fifty-Three

## New York

Daylight like dirty gray dishwater seeped through the crack between the dumpster and its lid. James Nail stirred and painfully opened his eyes to discover, with some surprise, that he was still alive, although buried up to his neck in trash. He felt stiff and weak when he tried to move, but at least his wounds had stopped bleeding.

Rain no longer drummed on the lid; he was still cold and damp. He shivered and tried to stand, succeeding only in burying himself deeper in the dumpster's contents. He finally gave up. Without the strength to get out of the damned thing, he figured his only choice was to lie right where he was like so much discarded spoiled meat until the trucks came and hauled him off with the rest of the garbage to be ground up and recycled.

He would rest some and try again.

His heart raced with apprehension when he thought about Sharon. Last night was further proof that *they* intended to shut her up. He still found it near impossible to comprehend how the U.S. Government had sunk to this. Dissidents in the old Soviet Union must have experienced the same disbelief at the knock on their door in the middle of the night.

Brisk footfalls approached in the alley. Nail reached for his S&W .38. It must have slipped from his belt during the night. He dared not rustle around for it. He lay perfectly still. The lid cracked open. Bags of trash and garbage sailed in on top of him. The lid slammed and the footfalls receded.

With an effort, he pushed the heavy bags to one side and caught his breath. He heard morning traffic picking up out on Avenue of The Americas, a cacophony of blaring horns and racing engines. The city was awaking, like an enormous monster stretching and coming to life.

He made another attempt to escape from the dumpster, but soon fell back exhausted. He rested, breathing hard, then sweating as the risen sun glared down the length of the alley and heated up his steel prison like an oven. He extracted his cell phone from his pocket with fumbling fingers. He was dialing by feel in the dark dumpster when the instrument vibrated, startling him.

"C?" he said into it.

"James, how you doing?"

"Like what the bear leaves when he goes in the woods."

"I'm on the road to New York now. I got somebody closer help you, man, until I get there."

Nail coughed and had to wait for a spasm of pain to pass. "Not Sharon!" he croaked. "Too dangerous."

"Bleach blonde from the cemetery. Remember her? Judy Taylor," Big C said. "I talk to her and she driving to New York now. She need to know exactly where you at."

Nail told him.

"Say what? A trash can?"

"We all get dumped one time or another."

"You wait right there, understand? It good to hear—"

Nail's phone went dead.

He drifted in and out of consciousness, sleeping some, only half-awake at other times. His lips were parched and his throat so dry he could hardly swallow. He felt around for a bottle of water or soft drink with some left in it. After sorting through soiled diapers, potato peelings and some old clothing, the best he came up with was a half-rotted orange. He peeled it, a laborious process in his condition. Never had he tasted anything in his life quite so delicious.

He searched for another orange and found an apple core. He ate it and immediately fell asleep.

It must have been hours later when the rusty squeaking of the lid being raised startled him awake. His eyes adjusted to daylight to discover a blond head poked over the side of the dumpster and curious brown eyes regarding him.

"Detective Nail?"

"Jonathan Harker," he automatically corrected her.

"Maybe I got the wrong trash can—"

"If you're looking for Oscar—"

"Corey sent me. Big C."

Nail recognized her then.

"Are you too bad off?" she asked.

"It's according to the definition of 'too.'"

"Can you get out of that thing?"

"If you'll help me."

She glanced around. "Hurry while there ain't nobody looking."

He took her hands and she pulled. He sank into his bedding, but his feet found bottom. Pain in a dizzy rush almost caused him to pass out.

"You gotta hang on," Judy encouraged. "You don't look near so dangerous as when you socked poor Corey in the jaw at the cemetery."

Finally, with much straining and more agony, he toppled over the lip of the container and landed on Judy, her body cushioning his fall. She hastened up and helped him to his feet.

"You smell something awful," she decided. "I seen on TV this morning what happened."

While he waited to catch his breath, he heard chanting and shouting and marching feet instead of normal traffic noises. He scowled. There was something disconcerting about the sound of feet tromping through a city. He looked around for Judy's vehicle.

"I couldn't get my car downtown," she explained, reading his thought. "There's some kind of big hoop-dee-doo protest against the mosque the Muslims are building next door to where they blew up the Twin Towers. I guess we got to walk out to where I parked my car."

He looked at her in disbelief. "Every cop and Homie in the state is looking for a Skid Row bum with blood all over him."

"I thought of that," she responded. "Can you walk if you lean on me?"

"I saw the movie, but... Never mind."

He noticed the big paper bag she brought with her. She delved into it and produced an assortment of materials, including bandages and tape, poster board, colored markers, a flute, an Uncle Sam hat made of paper, an American flag...

"So we're doing show 'n tell? Lady, in case you haven't noticed, I've been shot and if I don't make it out of here soon you'll have to carry me—which I'm pretty sure you can't do."

Patiently, Judy explained. "When I see what was going on, I bought all this stuff at a store when I parked my car. The woman said they were selling lots of flags and Uncle Sam hats for the event. That's what she called it—an event. I figure I'm going to be Uncle Sam, you a survivor of Nine-Eleven. Now hush up your yapping. We got to get you out of here."

The girl was smarter than she appeared.

Concealing themselves in the shadows behind the dumpster, Judy first bandaged Nail's wounds. Her face turned ashen at their sight, but she bravely continued. She wrapped his head in gauze to heighten the effect of his disguise. His shirt and jeans were crusted with real blood. Then she donned her Uncle Sam costume and pondered over the poster board.

"What do you think it should say?"

"'Don't tread on me?'"

"I'll draw the snake too."

She attached a thin-slatted handle to the protest sign and helped Nail to his feet. He felt pale and out of breath.

"I can walk on my own," he protested.

"You wouldn't make it out of the alley," she scolded. "Do like I say before I get a peach tree switch after you."

With his arm over her shoulders and hers around his waist, they managed to work their way back to Sharon's street, which was only a block off Avenue of The Americas. Nail hadn't gone far after being shot last night. Ahead at the intersection, a noisy, colorful river of humanity flowed past carrying signs and waving American flags. Nail wondered about Sharon when they passed her apartment building. He hoped she was right about God looking over her since Nail hadn't done a very good job of it.

They joined the protesters, melding in. Thousands of angry-sounding people packed the wide avenue and seemed to stretch out of sight. Lee Greenwood's *God Bless the U.S.A.* blasted from portable loudspeakers. Signs stabbed the air. One said **Sharia** in dripping blood-red letters. Another asked, **President Anastos, Whose Side are You On?** Two men dressed as Colonial Americans marched by pulling a mock missile ridden by mannequins in Islamic terrorist garb. Police and Homies armed with automatic rifles lined the route, but did not interfere. The mood of the crowds, Nail sensed, was volatile.

He wasn't the only one limping and hobbling along as a Nine-Eleven survivor. "You are great!" someone applauded him. "Mister, you look like you really *are* injured."

"I'm an out-of-work Broadway actor," Nail replied.

Judy had no more than assured him they hadn't much farther to go when a Homie in full riot control mode, all in black, broke away from the sidelines and started briskly toward them. Nail spotted several other armed Feds rushing in his direction. Judy stiffened and began trembling.

Nail had no right to take her down with him. There was no way he could escape, badly wounded as he was. He started to push her away and order her to run when, unexpectedly, the Homies stormed past them and descended upon another victim. More Homeland Security and NYPD materialized. A roar of protest echoed with rippling effect down the avenue. The march bogged down and came to a halt. Tear gas grenades began popping like fireworks. Toxic mist clouded the street, sending protesters into panicked retreat, tramping each other as they scattered. A phalanx of police armed with shotguns and riot batons cleared a pathway through the march, their clubs thudding against bones and flesh.

"Judy, how far's your car?" Nail hissed.

Too frightened to answer, she pointed in a general direction that, fortunately, was the direction in which many of the marchers were attempting to escape. Carried along in the stampede, Nail and Judy managed to break free into a side street where her eight-year-old Honda sat parked against the curb. They piled into it. Nail collapsed in the back seat, breathing heavily and suffering from excruciating pain.

Judy recovered her senses and maneuvered the Honda through packed streets over which police and the feds had not yet taken control. They fled Manhattan via the Lincoln Tunnel just before authorities sealed it.

"You did good," Nail complimented her, after which he became only vaguely aware of what was going on, his recent exertions having taken their toll on his ravaged body.

## SEC Chairman: Finance Bill Not Public

***(Washington)***—*Under President Anastos' Finance Reform Bill, action by the Securities Exchange Commission headed by SEC Chair Ben Robbins will not be open to public scrutiny. The Freedom of Information Act does not apply whenever government is compelled by an economic crisis to move against any financial institution, business enterprise or individual, Robbins said, adding that the public does not have a right to know what transpires between government and private enterprise.*

*"You know, sometimes these pundits, they can't figure me out," the President said. "They say, 'Well, why is he doing that? That doesn't poll well.' I know it doesn't poll well, but it's the right thing to do for America."*

*President Anastos is doing what he said he would do when he ran for office. He has used government as an instrument to narrow the gap between the haves and the have-nots; he injected $900 billion in tax dollars to stimulate the economy and prevent a depression, he has provided health coverage to thirty-five million uninsured citizens; he has made America safe from domestic terrorism; and, now, he has reordered the relationship between government and investors and consumers...*

# Chapter Fifty-Four

## Washington, D.C.

The State Dinner for the Chinks at the White House had been more of the same old bullshit, everybody kissing everybody else's ass and pretending to all get along. The only thing missing was a bunch of LGBTs holding hands and singing *Kumbiya.* It was enough to make Trout throw up in his won ton soup. Marilyn scowled at him all during dinner and hissed warnings in his ear, each proceeded by, "Trout, you bastard."

After a word from Marilyn, Wiedersham had taken him aside. "I'm beginning to have doubts about your loyalty as a team player, Trout."

The next morning, Saturday, Trout made an excuse to get out of the house and keep a tryst with Judy. At least that congenital dimwit didn't call him by his last name. Since Marilyn expected him back within an hour or so to attend another of her screwy society functions, he had little time to pound off last night's taint from the White House. As he was leaving Judy's apartment, she received a ring on her cell. Usually she took her phone calls in front of him. This time she looked surprised when she answered and slipped into the bedroom to take it in private.

"Who is it?" Trout demanded.

"A girlfriend."

She hung up after asking the girlfriend to call her back in a few minutes. She wore a guilty look when she returned to see Trout off. He was in too much of a hurry to press the issue.

"I'll have some time off tomorrow," he promised.

She nodded, looking distracted. And then she had phoned him Sunday morning saying she couldn't see him today after all. The bitch! He paid for her fucking apartment and kept her in a style of luxury to which she had never aspired to previously. What made her think she could put *him* off?

It had not been a *hell of a weekend.* It had been a totally *fucked-up weekend,* Trout conceded peevishly on Monday as he made his way to the den with coffee and his notebook to catch the beginning-of-the week news cycle. He had already called a cab to pick him up at nine a.m. to drop him off at Wiedersham's office for the usual bullshit session before he continued on to the airport and the campaign trail in Illinois.

He paused at the bottom of the stairs with his coffee to listen for Marilyn or Reggie. Satisfied that they weren't stirring yet, that he had at least a few minutes of peace to himself, he hurried to his recliner in the den and sat with notebook on his lap, coffee on the little end table, and began channel-surfing the news channels. It was one of his few indulgences. That and Maalox.

President Anastos was all over the nets and cables. The Nobel Committee was awarding him this year's Peace Prize. Trout could see no accomplishment that warranted it. More likely, he suspected, the award had something to do with George Zuniga and One World Government.

"We will move forward together as a united world during this, uh, time of economic and social change," the President declared on one channel, "or we will perish separately."

Chaos seemed to be consuming the globe. The Middle East was in flames, despots and dictators toppling like dominos, being replaced by even more despots and dictators. Egypt, Syria, Libya, Turkey, Saudi Arabia, Algeria, Morocco...Scenes of cities burning flashed on the TV screen. Rioters thronging the streets. Soldiers firing machineguns. Dead bodies. Protest signs featuring the hammer and sickle of the International Workers Unions.

**Social Justice!**

**Kill the Jews!**

**Throw off the yoke of Capitalist Imperialism!**

The hammer and sickle also appeared at union picketing in Wisconsin, Indiana, Pennsylvania, Ohio, Illinois... A red-faced commentator on CNN was screaming and shouting, raving, "Progressives in Congress are fighting like hell for a jobs bill to create more jobs. This is an ideological war. I say it on camera tonight. I will fight those bastards trying to take down President Anastos. I will fight those bastards because I know what they want to do. They want to take down our President and our American workers. They want to destroy the American dream, control minorities and concentrate the wealth at the top..."

Members of the New Black Panther Party accused of voter intimidation in Ohio appeared on another channel, foaming at the mouth.

"I hate crackers, every iota of every cracker! You call yourself a black man, then you have to start killing white crackers. We kill the men, we kill the women, we kill the babies..."

A 9-1-1 recording played: "There's a white guy getting beat up by about one hundred black people. It's like a freaking riot out there. My mom just got attacked by a mob… She's bleeding a lot."

It was like that on all the channels. One good thing, Trout thought: all the turmoil in the Middle East and the interruption of the oil supply was going to drive Petrobras oil investments through the roof and make him a very wealthy man.

Justin Cobb, Wiedersham's chief of staff, was present when Trout arrived at Wiedersham's office. He wore Kenneth Cole shoes that matched his boss's. Trout's lip curled at sight of the mustache Cobb was growing. It would never be much to look at; he kept it rubbed off kissing Wiedersham's ass.

When Trout walked in past Liz, Wiedersham and Cobb were speculating about the murder of the Homeland agent in New York. Both seemed to think the killer had to be the Okie cop who had already killed Kimbrell in Tulsa and the AmeriCorps kids in Arkansas. Rumor going around had him a trained sniper seeking revenge for the death of his daughter.

"Gonzalez thinks the Homeland agent wounded his shooter before he died," Wiedersham pointed out. "If that's true, he must still be in New York. Gonzalez needs to catch the son of a bitch before he does real damage."

"Maybe we can tie that cunt Lowenthal into a conspiracy with the cop," Cobb suggested.

"Uh," Wiedersham grunted. He motioned Trout to have a seat.

He looked harried, his eyes red-rimmed and his heavy jowls sagging. He rose from his magnificent desk and strode over to the wide window that overlooked Constitution Avenue and the Washington Mall, the same window through which Trout had watched Homeland Security gun down Tea Party protesters only a few weeks ago. When he turned back again, he seemed revitalized.

"Fuck the cop," he said. "What is occurring around the world is bigger than him, bigger than all of us. Politicians are cheap. They come and go and are useful for making things happen—"

It was a statement Trout couldn't deny. He *had* been bought. So had Wiedersham, for that matter. So had Anastos. Wiedersham had referred to Judy as a whore. Was he—was any of them—so much different or better?

"But *we*," Wiedersham amended, the emphasis excluding himself from both categories of *politician* and *whore,* "are here forever in the shadows, working and waiting. Once the United States falls, the new global government will eliminate wars and poverty and disease..."

That didn't sound like Senate Majority Leader Joe Wiedersham. "Do you really believe that?" Trout challenged.

Wiedersham shrugged, the old pragmatic politician returning. "What difference does it make? We'll be a part of it. The next months leading up to mid-term elections are the most critical period in our history. Candidates like you, Dennis, will pack Congress prepared to carry The Plan forward. From now until the elections, insiders will be attending a series of seminars and summits to prepare us to take over and govern the United States as part of a coalition with the rest of the world. We all must make tough decisions and act decisively in the days and weeks ahead."

This was sounding more and more like the plot from a James Bond movie.

Wiedersham paused. His narrow, dark eyes bore into Trout's. "Dennis, certain people are beginning to have doubts about you. We have to know we can depend on you."

# Chapter Fifty-Five

## New York

James Nail opened his eyes to the view of a muddy-colored ceiling with a cobweb in the nearest corner and a housefly trapped in it. His ribs were wrapped so tightly he could barely breathe. A faded green bedspread was pulled up to his chin. An IV on a stand fed nutrients into his arm. He struggled to throw off the spread and sit up.

"He's awake," a voice said.

Pain wracked his ribs. A gentle hand on his chest forced him back onto his pillow. A small hand touched his face. He looked up into dark eyes soft with concern and compassion.

"Sh—Sharon?"

"I'm here, darling."

"It's not safe."

Wherever *here* was.

"You almost lost your life for me—again," she said. Tears streaked her lovely cheeks. She gripped his hand in both of hers. "James, I should have known. Sometimes I could almost feel you nearby. You don't have to keep getting shot to attract my attention."

She bent over and kissed him tenderly on the mouth. It was the best medicine he could have received. He couldn't take his eyes off her. She wore a dark green turtleneck sweater, black jeans and a red ribbon to hold her ponytail.

"Where am I?" he asked.

"You're safe—at least for now," she assured him. "I prayed every night that God would look over you. He answered my prayers through Judy Taylor. She brought you here."

Big C stood behind Sharon with a bright grin that seemed to consume his dark face. He looked different with all that kinky hair he had grown since Oklahoma. The big man knelt at bedside and crushed Nail's other hand in his.

Judy Sparks-Taylor leaned toward the bed from a cheap "Naugahyde" chair on the opposite side of the bed. Gone was the Uncle Sam costume she wore the last time he saw her, in its place faded fishermen's jeans, cowboy boots, a low-cut blouse with lace around the neck and at the cuffs, and a gold locket chain around her neck. Nail smiled at her.

"Thank you, Uncle Sam," he whispered.

"Are you hungry?" Sharon asked.

Surprisingly, he was. He took that as a good sign.

"I get it," Big C offered.

"You'd better start with chicken soup," Sharon proposed.

Big C opened a can, poured the contents into a bowl and put the bowl in a microwave.

"We cooking again, bro'," Big C said, grinning, referring to the recent can opening days of their bachelorhood.

While the soup warmed, he opened a slit in the window blinds to take a look outside, letting in some of the night diluted by the flashing red and green sign outside: *MOTEL.* Sharon explained they were in a cheap motel room off I-95 where, Nail suspected, rooms went for the day or night or *part* of either, no questions asked. The door displayed various pry bar marks around the lock, mute testimony to the type of neighborhood it was.

In answering his other unspoken questions, Sharon explained that it was Monday evening and that he had been sleeping for the past two days. An emergency room doctor she knew who would keep his mouth shut had come and gone. Nail had lost a lot of blood but he would survive with rest and nourishment.

Nail's mouth watered from the aroma of the heated soup when Big C removed it from the microwave. Although the IV had kept him fed and hydrated, it wasn't the same as real food. Big C brought the bowl and a cup of steaming coffee to bedside. Sharon fed him with a spoon since he was too weak to do it for himself. While he ate, savoring the renewed strength forging through his body, Sharon coyly revealed that she had bathed him. He blushed.

"Shaving was kind of tricky," she said. "I kind of liked the mustache, so I left it."

Big C pulled up another chair and sat next to Judy to share his coffee with her. She took a pack of *Winstons* from her purse, but returned them. None of the others smoked.

Nail's wallet lay open on the lamp table. Sharon glanced at his fake driver's license and smiled. *"Jonathan Harker?"*

The others laughed with her.

"Why would you choose the name of Dracula's nemesis?"

"Isn't that who we are?" Nail replied. "Vampire hunters?"

"Do I recall," Big C said, "they were four friends like us went hunting Dracula. In the end, only one survives."

## White House Announces Suppression Program

***(Washington)***—*White House spokesman Dewey Gubbins announced today that President Patrick Anastos is rescinding the long-standing prohibition against targeting for assassination foreign heads of state. President Ronald Reagan initiated the executive order against such actions over thirty years ago.*

*The new Anastos Doctrine also allows targeting persons either on the battlefield or off the battlefield, including U.S. citizens at home or abroad, if they are considered terrorists or are involved in terrorist activities.*

*Speaker of the House Barbara Teague and Senate Majority Leader Joe Wiedersham held a press conference following the President's signing of the executive order.*

*"There are dozens of persons who are U.S. citizens that are very disconcerting to us," Speaker Teague said. "This option allows government to better secure the safety of citizens in a world growing increasingly dangerous..."*

# Chapter Fifty-Six

## New York

Nail suspected "evidence" would soon surface to establish Sharon's involvement in crimes attributed to Big C and him. Already, headlines on government-influenced newspapers and tabloids strewn at the foot of his bed were screaming the connection:

**Jerry Baer Paramour Takes Murderous Lover**

**Militia Terrorist Ties to Sharon Lowenthal**

**Killer of Homeland Agent Linked to Rightwing Talk Hostess**

Judging from the headlines, someone was trying awfully hard to collect the one hundred grand offered by an anonymous underwriter to anyone who provided scandal to discredit Sharon. Was this how government worked "for the people" in these dangerous times?

The gravity of the situation settled around the four people isolated in the seedy motel room. Rather than vampire hunters, they had become the intended prey of a goliath Dracula who threatened to gobble them up in one bite and the free world in the next. Still, they had little choice but to fight on—until they either slew Dracula or Dracula repopulated the world with bloodsuckers.

Nail basked in Sharon's presence and attention, although he accepted that it was temporary and that he would soon have to send her away for her own good. After all that had transpired, Nail suspected their names had been promptly added to a secret "hit list" in the bureaucracy. Once again, they would all have to move on to more secure locations. Being constantly on the move was the nature of people running from the law.

In the meantime, feeling like the conspirators they indeed were, they gathered around Nail's bed in order to fill each other in on what had transpired since they were last together. Sharon still didn't completely trust Judy, even though the blonde had apparently funneled inside information to her cousin and put her skin on the line to save Nail. She was nonetheless linked through Dennis Trout to big time globalist political players like Senate Majority Leader Wiedersham.

"I'm grateful for what she did for James," Sharon had conceded to Nail and Big C when Judy walked to a nearby convenience store for cigarettes. "It's just that I'm concerned that she may be too naïve to maintain security."

Nail took Big C's side. "I don't think we can be certain of *anything* anymore," he said. "I know one thing: I might not be here if it weren't for her."

Sharon sighed. "Our lives seem to be inextricably entangled one with the other."

One of the little group's major concerns was rightly the President's Suppression Program in which the feds apparently targeted suspected terrorists for assassination. Nail and Big C were being painted as domestic terrorists.

"Zenergy tried to look into it through the Freedom of Information Act," Sharon explained. "I'm naïve enough to believe the Constitution still means something. Homeland Security responded to our FOI by saying their records system wasn't configured in a way that allowed them to perform a search. Therefore, they declined the request."

"Who would have thunk it?" Big C said sarcastically.

"Two of our investigators involved in the FOI resigned after receiving threats," Sharon went on. "They were literally frightened of their lives and immediately left the state. I've been doing some research on my own. What I've discovered is a series of suspicious deaths. People who go against the administration end up dead—the Louisiana judge who ruled against Anastos on the oil drilling ban; the New Hampshire legislator who had the gall to try to limit federal authority over his state; Jerry Baer... Only God knows how many others."

"Josh Logan, Greg Morris...," Big C said. "Ron Sparks..."

Judy blanched and stared at her new friends as if they had all gone insane.

Sharon said, "It seems even petty bureaucrats may have the authority to order assassinations. Kimbrell in Tulsa likely ordered Ron Sparks killed."

"He was the go-between for what happened at ORU," Nail speculated grimly. "All this is reason enough that we get you somewhere safe."

"'All that is required for evil to prevail is that good men do nothing,'" Sharon quoted, paraphrasing. "None of us will ever be safe again if we run. Only the truth will set us free. It's in God's hands."

"We got to help the Big Man," C said. "They coming hard after the militias. Confiscating guns and putting pressure on local radio and TV that don't go along. We been hearing rumors of concentration camps."

"Something is coming down," Nail agreed.

"And soon," Sharon added. "Weekend after next, the *One Nation* rally is bringing a million radicals to the National Mall in D.C., the intent being to intimidate and overwhelm the American public with the power and scope of Anastos' 'hope 'n change.' They want to make the rest of us feel alone and discouraged and therefore more submissive.

"Look at the sponsors and you know what it is. Communists, National Socialists, radical Islamists... *The Communist Party of the United States; La Raza; PEIU; Center for Community Change;* George Zuniga's *World Alliance* and *The Institute for Open Societies; American Progressive Center; Democratic Socialists of America...* Card-carrying, diehard, I-love-Stalin Marxist communists. They don't even try to hide it anymore. President Anastos is endorsing the rally. It's on the White House website. They're busing people in, paying union workers and members of more than thirty radical organizations to appear. I keep appealing to the President on the air: 'Mr. President, denounce these Marxists and socialists who have contributed ultimately to one thing—mass graves.'"

"Sure and he listening to you," Big C said, even more sarcastically. "You won't see Homies enforcing the No Protest law against *them*."

Judy sat glued to her chair, eyes wide and mouth open in astonishment. "I feel like something done walked over my grave," she murmured.

"A shadow has fallen across the nation's grave," Sharon said. "This is the beginning of the end of the United States of America if these people have their way. There are powerful forces in the world coordinating to take America down and destroy the Western way of life, planned and deliberately instigated—border problems, a sieve that is overwhelming our culture with illegal immigrants who have no motivation to become part of the melting pot, some of whom are terrorists biding their time; a national debt that cannot ever be repaid and which will soon destroy our economy; wide distrust of government and each other; energy problems that can be solved internally by drilling offshore and in our own coal and oil resources but won't be; wars on two fronts; terrorist threats; political correctness; Islam extremism growing within our own country; a collapsing financial system, causing recession and unemployment; and, increasingly, enemies within. We could weather any of these things alone, but not all of them coming on us at the same time. The collapse of the dollar is the end game if the goal is to destroy America. Jerry Baer tried to warn people what was happening."

"And people didn't believe him—and they won't believe you," Nail said, grunting with pain as he shifted in bed. At least the IV had been removed.

Sharon touched his shoulder. "They don't *want* to believe that a president of the United States would, *could*, do such a thing."

Big C stood up in exasperation.

"Do any of us *want* to believe it?" Nail said.

Big C sat back down. Sharon resumed where she left off as though rehearsing for her next show.

"For the last several weeks," she said, "Zenergy researchers, producers and I have been following up on reports of a series of secret international meetings and summits being held inside the United States. Socialists and Marxists from all around the world are attending to discuss the topic of how to bring about the final conversion of the United States to a Marxist nation. George Zuniga, we hear, is the major player behind the gatherings. People will have to wake up and believe if we can discover where these summits are being held and somehow get inside one of them to expose it."

Nail reacted sharply. "It's too dangerous."

"It may be our last chance to stop them," Sharon shot back.

The exchange left a long, strained silence in the cheap room, punctuated by a barely-audible gasp from Judy. Nail finally broke the hush. "Too bad we all couldn't go John Galt."

Sharon managed the ghost of a tired smile. "You *have* been reading."

"I lost my *Atlas Shrugged* when I got shot. I didn't finish it."

"We'll get you another copy. There's nothing I'd like better than to find a John Galt sanctuary to disappear to and live a normal life. But there's nowhere to go. Individual liberty will disappear off the face of the earth if we lose this fight. It'll be the dark ages of *1984* forever. Big Brother will triumph."

## Food Prices Spark Riots

***(Miami)***—*Continuing high unemployment and a spike in food prices triggered deadly rioting overnight in Miami, Seattle, Kansas City, and other cities across the nation. Angry young people rampaged through Miami's Liberty City district, throwing stones, looting shops and drawing police gunfire that killed at least nine people...*

# Chapter Fifty-Seven

## Washington, D.C.

Senate Majority Leader Joe Wiedersham summoned his protégé, Dennis Trout, off the campaign trail to attend what he referred to as one of a crucial series of conferences and summits crafted to help prepare selected U.S. leaders for global governance. Trout felt flattered even while he had to double his intake of Maalox to quell the roil of his rebellious stomach. His father, were he still alive, would not be proud of him; his father *believed* in the special character of the American people, the Republic, and the Constitution.

His father had been old-fashioned and idealistic. Times for men like him had passed. It was a New World and anyone who didn't want to end up in the slag piles had better compromise and latch onto the comet that was sweeping the world.

Dennis Trout tried to think about his father as little as possible.

Wiedersham instructed Trout to report to the Kellogg Conference Center at 9:00 a.m. on Monday. Trout took off from Chicago on Saturday to spend a night with Judy while informing Marilyn that he wouldn't be home until late Sunday. The only thing Marilyn wanted out of him anyhow was a free ride to the top. Let her sleep with Reggie the pink poodle.

Judy told him nothing about why she had been in New York most of the past week other than that she was looking after a sick cousin. How many cousins did this bitch have? He supposed everyone from Bugfuck, Oklahoma, was cousins to everyone else—some of whom ended up hung in cemeteries.

She seemed more ditzy than before, not quite as puppy-wagging-the-tail as usual. She wasn't even *that* enthusiastic in bed, which put him in a sour mood and set him to pondering the state of their rather odd relationship.

In Washington, it was accepted that Senators and Congressmen have their little pieces of tail discreetly stashed somewhere in cubby holes they paid for. Although Wiedersham was often critical of the custom on practical rather than moral grounds, Trout suspected his brother-in-law was as disturbed by his *choice* of Bimbos as by a "Bimbo Eruption" per se. Bimbos were more acceptable in Washington society these days after the Clinton Bimbo-on-her-knees-in-the-John era. Providing the Bimbo wasn't a dimwit hillbilly who probably hadn't worn shoes until she started school, if she even went to school.

The way things were going—his meteoric rise into the elite governing classes—Trout expected he was going to have to dump his goofy piece of trailer trash sooner rather than later. But not yet.

While he took a hot shower in her grubby little bathroom, drawing it out as long as possible to delay another meeting this morning with Wiedersham, after which he would have to go home to Marilyn, he heard Judy watching a soap or some infantile women's gab show on TV. He finally forced himself to get out of the water and dry off. He put on a fresh suit, button down pale blue shirt that accented his eyes, a red power tie, and a new pair of Kenneth Cole shoes like the latest fashion display by Wiedersham and his new kiss-ass chief of staff, Justin Cobb. It did no harm to play up a little to his brother-in-law whose coattails he was riding to wealth and power.

Judy looked up from the sofa and smiled when he came out dressed and ready to go. "Don't you look nice, Dennis."

She was still in her nightie, a sheer little thing through which was visible the black triangle that had proved throughout the ages to be the bondage of many a man. He felt himself aroused. She had a body that more than made up for her lack of brain.

No time. He turned away and spotted his notebook open on the dinette table next to his briefcase. He had been making a few notes over coffee, but he was certain he shut the book on his way to the shower. He glanced at Judy. She seemed absorbed in her inane program. He noted the passages on open display in his bold, scrawled handwriting before he closed the notebook and stuffed it into his molded leather briefcase.

*What I know is that Wiedersham is a ruthless son of a bitch and it pays to watch your back. He sees himself as a king of the world—or at least a prince underneath whoever the king is going to be when this all plays out. I'm not sure from where he receives his orders. I think they come from somebody like that creepy character George Zuniga who has more money and power than God. Joe says even President Anastos gets his orders from higher up.*

*Things are happening real fast. Joe says the summits will prepare all of us to govern when the time comes...*

Judy smiled at him and stretched like a cat, one boob struggling to escape. He shrugged off his suspicions; he must have left the notebook open himself. She hadn't any more inclination to treachery or deceit than a cow or a sheep. She even lacked normal curiosity.

## Marxists Look To Future

***(New York)***—*Revolutionaries and radicals gather daily at the Brecht Forum Community Center on West Street to pontificate and plan for a future free of capitalism. Activists, agitators and community organizers join together for classes on "Josef Stalin: The Vision;" "The Principles of Mao;" and "Freedom after Capitalism is Gone." On game nights, regulars put aside their copies of Marx and play a Marxist version of Monopoly called "Class Struggle." In a nation grown increasingly cynical, the New York Times reports, the Brecht Community Center is a "surprisingly open and idealistic place..."*

# Chapter Fifty-Eight

## Washington, D.C.

Armed AmeriCorps guards manned all entrances to the large Kellogg Center where The International Summit on Social Justice was being held. Flags of socialist and Marxist governments blazed on the stage, as well as the flags of nations bent on going that direction. China, Russia, North Korea, Cuba, Venezuela, Iran... Greece, Nicaragua, Jordan, Britain, the United States... Delegates arrived solemn and reserved and spoke in low tones in various languages, as though to prevent being overheard by spies. Interpreters at banks of microphones to one side of the stage stood ready to translate conference speakers.

An AmeriCorps officer properly vetted for inside duty ushered Majority Leader Joe Wiedersham and future Congressman Dennis Trout to front row seats reserved for international spokesmen, organizers and other VIPs, an indication of Wiedersham's status. Wiedersham had been selected to open the summit and introduce President Anastos, who would speak via remote from the White House. It was considered too risky for him to appear in person and chance being linked to the gathering by Zenergy News or some crafty rightwing blogger. The U.S. flag flying next to those of China and North Korea seemed to Trout to be a *fait accompli* that America was next to fall in line.

As the two politicians took their seats, Wiedersham said, "My sister called this morning. She said you left before she was awake."

*Fuck Marilyn.*

The guy knew how to irritate Trout's ass off. That fucked-up little bark that served as laughter but was not quite laughter. His expensive duds that always looked as though he had slept in them. The narrow, mocking eyes and blubbery jowls... Part of Trout's irritation today rose from Wiedersham's refusal to tell him in advance what the summits were about, other than in general terms of "preparing to govern." Everything about the conferences was classified *Top Secret:* who attended them, where they were held, even that they *were* being held, topics discussed... If word leaked out prematurely, Wiedersham said, it could be explosive enough to set back the movement for months.

Trout looked around for the spooky dude with the spooky East European accent and located him sitting on-stage in the center of a mixed-nation delegation. Even though George Zuniga was backing

Trout's campaign, the guy still gave him the creeps. Zuniga was the man known for having broke the Bank of England and, Wiedersham said, would do the same to the U.S. Federal Reserve to open the way for the collapse of the United States and the ascent of a New World Order. Like so many of the Progressives Trout had met through his well-connected brother-in-law, Zuniga was a narcissistic sonofabitch who pretended to know better than God how the world should be run. Trout recalled a Zuniga quote from a Progressive publication:

"It is sort of a disease when you consider yourself some kind of a god, the creator of everything, but I feel comfortable about it now since I began to live it out."

Wiedersham rose and stepped to the podium on-stage and lifted both hands as though to part the waters.

"We are in a fight for the minds of men," he was saying when Trout's wandering mind finally focused, "for the conquest of their convictions and hearts, to open the eyes of the intelligent few to the possibilities of regimenting the public mind that all the planet may be able to thrive. In order to get things like universal health care and free education and decent standards of living for people in Bangladesh as well as in the United States, we are going to have to redistribute the pie so that everyone can have social justice..."

Trout doubted Wiedersham gave a flying fuck about "social justice" unless it was defined in terms of political power. Wiedersham continued.

"The governing classes must rise to lead and make the tough decisions that can save the world from disaster and that will lead to peace and prosperity for those most deserving. Global governance is the answer to the social, climate, economic and population challenges this generation faces. An international order is within our reach for the first time in the history of mankind..."

Trout had to admit that his brother-in-law was a gifted orator. One could almost overlook his rumpled appearance and abrasive character.

"It is therefore with great honor that I introduce Patrick Wayne Anastos, President of the United States. President Anastos can do more than speak the truth. President Anastos knows how to *be* the truth. He is an evolved leader who will bring evolved leadership to the United States and to the world..."

The President's image flashed onto a huge screen in a bigger-than-life telecast from the White House. The familiar Presidential Seal on his podium had been replaced with Anastos' campaign shield featuring its iconic "A" logo emblazoned against a field of stars and stripes, under which appeared: *Vero Possumus.*

*Yes we can.*

Wiedersham retook his front row seat next to Trout as Anastos began his teleprompter wag.

"Fucking dickhead," he sniped, glaring at the screen.

"The need for de-development, uh, presents the world with a major challenge," the President began. "It is up to us to design a stable, low-corruption economy in which there is a more equitable redistribution of worldwide wealth. Redistribution of wealth within and among nations, uh, as well as among a necessarily smaller and more manageable population, is absolutely essential if a decent life is to be provided to every sustainable human being..."

What the hell did he mean by *sustainable?* Trout's stomach was already starting to sour.

While the President's opening remarks may have been purposefully vague, his words carefully chosen to permit damage control if necessary, there was nothing equivocal about what followed. The program began with a film in which historical Progressives from the late 19th Century to the present extolled the virtues, indeed the *necessity*, for worldwide population control if the human race and the planet it inhabited were to survive. It featured George Bernard Shaw, Nobel Prize-winning playwright and one of the founders of England's Fabian socialist movement a century ago. Typical intellectual with a beard, high-foreheaded and high-handed.

"I think it would be a good thing," lectured the dead man preserved in film, "to make everybody come before a properly appointed board just as he might come before the income tax administer and, say every five years or every seven years, and just put them there and say, 'Sir or madam, will you be kind enough to justify your existence...?' A great many people will have to be put out of existence simply because it wastes other people's time to look after them."

He was followed by shots of professors, environmentalists, scientists, politicians, and other prominent people, all saying essentially the same thing—that it was necessary to eliminate undesirable populations for the greater good of the collective. To Trout, there was something surreal about the intellectual and social elites of the world getting together in secret to focus on one of the primary objectives of One World Government—population control.

"The simplest answer is that the world's population should be about two billion, and we've got six billion now..."

“”If I were an animal, I would like to return as a deadly virus in order to contribute something to solve overpopulation...”

“We are the riders of the Pale Horse and we have the means to eliminate uneducated masses...”

“Childbearing should be a punishable crime against society, unless the parents hold a government license...”

“In order to stabilize the world population, we must eliminate three hundred and fifty thousand people per day. It is a horrible thing to say, but it’s just as bad not to say it...”

“The Earth can only be saved if ninety percent of the human beings alive today are purged from the planet...”

“Society has no business to permit degenerates to reproduce their kind... We have no business to perpetuate citizens of the wrong type...”

“Adding a sterilant to drinking water or staple foods is a suggestion...”

“The state must interfere on behalf of the really fittest...”

“Universal Healthcare must include the provision, based on objective judgment, that care will be rendered on the basis of individual merit and level of productivity...”

“There’s nothing wrong with killing things that are replaceable...”

Trout was sweating and feeling sick to his stomach by the end of the film, Nevertheless, he stood with the rest of the auditorium and applauded wildly. The elites obviously agreed upon the principle of eugenics, the necessity to reduce the global population by weeding out undesirables. *How* it was to be done was the challenge. The congregation broke up into smaller workshops to discuss specifics.

## President Seeks Increased Power

***(Washington)***—*President Anastos today asked Congress to grant him special powers to issue executive orders in order to quash growing disturbances across the nation. Congress immediately granted his request. The temporary measure will allow the President to bypass Congress for a period of one year. The unusual petition followed thousands of demonstrators marching down Pennsylvania Avenue in protest over alleged voter irregularities in the upcoming mid-term elections. Dewey Gubbins, White House spokesman, described the rioters as "tea-bagger revolutionaries." They were driven back and beaten by police and Homeland Security...*

*Two marchers were killed...*

# PART IV

*"Freedom is a fragile thing and is never more than one generation away from extinction."* — President Ronald Reagan

# Chapter Fifty-Nine

## Scranton, Pennsylvania

The candle in its globe on the table in an intimate corner of *The Eclectic Diner* diffused soft shimmers of light into the faces of James Nail and Sharon Lowenthal. They chose the restaurant because it had enough atmosphere to make it a night out but was remote enough that no one was apt to recognize either Sharon or Nail through their minimal disguises. They held hands across the table, their drinks almost untouched.

"Is this a real date?" Nail asked.

"Feels like a date."

"I want to kiss you."

"In public?"

They leaned toward each other across the small table and kissed briefly but tenderly. Both appeared more sober and reflective when they withdrew. Nail entertained no illusion that their time together was not coming to an end. In this Brave New World, there was no such thing as Happily Ever After.

They glanced as in common accord toward the restaurant windows and the violence that seemed to lurk against them in the darkness beyond. Only Big C's presence out there watching over them on this special night held it in abeyance.

Sharon had wanted Nail to recuperate in North Dakota or Wyoming, somewhere far away, but he insisted on remaining near her. They compromised. After Judy returned to D.C., Sharon and Big C had moved Nail out of the seedy motel in New York to a pay-by-the-month apartment she found across the Pennsylvania line in Scranton, far enough from New York that Homies wouldn't likely be out in force searching for Nail.

"I'm a fast recuperator," Nail had promised. Hair had almost grown back on his head to cover the scar from ORU.

He seemed to be coming along. Fortunately, the Homie's bullet had made a clean in-and-out hole, striking no vital organs.

This being their first real date, they agreed to discuss nothing beyond the moment—like any other normal couple going out for dinner.

The waitress at *The Eclectic Diner* was small and dark black with a pretty face and a name tag that introduced her as *Chloe*. She refilled their drinks and displayed gleaming teeth in a friendly smile.

"It's wonderful seeing happy folks like ya'all," she said. "People ain't so happy no more."

Sharon took Chloe's hand and squeezed it, smiling. "It's our anniversary," she said.

Chloe beamed. "How many, folks?"

Sharon laughed delightedly. "Eight weeks."

It occurred to Nail that if this was the anniversary of their having met, it was also the anniversary of the deaths of the people they loved.

"Newlyweds, huh?" Chloe said. "God bless you folks."

"God bless *you*," Sharon responded. "You're a Christian?"

"They ain't took that away from us yet. Ma'am, you sure do look familiar, like I seen you before."

"We just moved here," Sharon said.

Chloe moved on to another table and Nail lifted a brow. "Newlyweds?"

"Tonight is what we have," she said, and left it at that.

"It seems like I've always known you."

"Yes," she said. Then, a little wistfully, "I miss the Safe House."

TV sets were hooked to the walls in the restaurant, as in most public places these days; it seemed people couldn't even go out to eat without being accompanied by their boxes. Nail and Sharon had an unavoidable view of the nearest one. It was tuned to CNN, which Big C referred to as the *Communist News Network*. A commentator was busy lauding the big *One Nation* rally at the Lincoln Memorial in D.C., extolling it as the greatest gathering since the Civil War era. He had a PEIU representative cornered at the bottom of the steps leading up to Lincoln.

"Have these workers shown up because they're being paid or because they want to?" he asked.

"Union members are doing this for both reasons. They're being paid, which is only fair, and they want to stop the un-Americanism and lies of the Tea Parties, talk radio, Sharon Lowenthal and Zenergy News. We're ready for a fight."

CNN and the networks had edited tight in order to show only the more innocuous elements and placards.

**Full and Fair Employment**

**Silence Tea Party Lies**

**Educate Every Child**

Zenergy News, on the other hand, as Nail saw at the apartment before they left for dinner, aired it all. Chanting fanatics wearing red Mao and Che Guevara Tees and waving signs revealed the true color of *One Nation.*

**Capitalism is Failing**
**Socialism is the Answer**

**Capitalism Sucks**

**Make the Rich Pay**

**Vote for Hope, Not Hate**
**Communist Party USA**

Jerry Baer had tried for the past two years to expose what was happening. People weren't listening, or if they were listening they weren't doing enough to stop it. The Anastos juggernaut's takeover of the nation proceeded unchecked.

Nail shook his head in disgust. "We can't escape them even for a little while," he groused.

"Are you ready to blow this joint, Jonathan Harker?"

They walked outside. The street was almost deserted. Only a single streetlight struggled valiantly against the darkness a block away. The ten-year-old tan Toyota Sharon bought for Nail at a used car lot, paying cash under an assumed name, sat parked in a customers' lot with four or five other vehicles. He had abandoned the old pickup he drove from Oklahoma; it was likely stripped down to its frame by this time on the mean streets of New York.

He looked around. He didn't see Big C's clunker, but he knew his faithful friend was somewhere nearby, watching over them. A man could go an entire lifetime without a friend like that.

They had intended seeing a movie on their first date night. Sharon moved close to him once they were in the car and pulling out of the lot. He stopped the car so they could kiss. The kiss turned passionate. She broke first. Her eyes were dark, moist and demanding in the light from the dashboard panel.

"Let's go home instead," she said.

Like a typical cop, he attempted to cover with a flippant remark the flood of emotion that made his voice crack. "Your place or mine?"

"*Ours*," she said.

There was pain in his side from the unhealed bullet wound, but Nail barely noticed it when he opened his eyes. Last night was so incredible that it took him a moment or so to orient. He felt the length of Sharon's warm body snuggled close in his arms, one of her bare legs between his, her arm across his chest and her tousled hair dark in the nest between his shoulder and neck. He lingered in his contentment. He needed this moment of awaking to last forever, even though there was no such thing as forever. Not in this life.

Not since before his wife left him had he experienced serenity to settle his unsettled soul. There had been other women from time to time over the years. Mostly one night stands, sweaty trysts in some woman's house or apartment. A three-month thing with a female detective had been his longest-running relationship. Connie was always between him and any other woman. Until now.

Nail was a one-woman man; anything less would have been an affront to Connie, even though she no longer wanted him. And to Jamie.

At some point last night Sharon and he decided to get married. Marriage would make the night okay from her moral Christian perspective, if not exactly right. They came to the decision together.

There was only one hitch. They could never marry like ordinary people, not under their true names. The tabloids would be all over it, followed by Homies and the FBI.

"My groom would be 'Jonathan Harker' on our marriage license?" Sharon exclaimed, laughing with him. "Maybe I could change my name to Mary Shelley, you think?"

Under whatever names, they would never be able to hold back indefinitely the maelstrom of events into which they had been cast.

"When we marry, I want it to be under our true names," she decided. "Maybe a Jewish wedding even though I'm a Christian convert."

"I'd marry you in a Buddhist temple, in a Creek Indian wigwam, in the middle of Transylvania..."

"Would you really?"

"Try me."

She giggled naughtily. "I already have."

Now, with daylight breaking through the bedroom window, Nail was forced to accept reality. Last night and *now*, these few hours, were all they had.

Her dark lashes fluttered. She must have felt him awake. Her eyes opened. She smiled. She lifted her head and kissed him.

"I love you, Jonathan Harker."

"Morning breath and all?"

"Bullet holes and everything."

It had been a long time since a woman told him she loved him. Not since the early days with Connie—and look how well that turned out.

"I—" he began.

"Don't say it unless you mean it."

"I love you."

"When did you know," she asked, teasing. "After you got me in bed?"

"I think I must have known when I woke up in the hospital in Tulsa and you were there."

"We just needed each other."

"Are you all right?" he asked her. "I mean, about last night?"

"I think God will understand. These are unusual times. Sort of like people during World War Two."

They lay together in each other's arms for a long time, eyes closed, luxuriating in the warmth of their conjugal bed, as though trying to will more minutes into the *now*. Nail could almost hear the cosmic minutes ticking away.

"I'll cook breakfast," he offered.

"Let me," she countered with a giggle. "Once we're married, you must promise never to open another can of beans. Wake Corey. I'm sure the dear man must be famished while we lie here in our selfish indulgences."

# CHAPTER SIXTY

## Chicago

"They spent a fucking fortune getting Anastos elected president—three hundred sixty million, to be precise—and they intend to get their money's worth out of the goofy bastard," Senate Majority Leader Joe Wiedersham said as the entourage of three limos, escorted fore and aft by siren-screaming motorcycle cops, raced toward Chicago's O'Hare Airport to meet Air Force One when it arrived.

Congressional candidate Dennis Trout rode the lead vehicle with his brother-in-law, along with Wiedersham's chief of staff Justin Cobb and Chicago's Mayor Deagan, whose bulk reminded Trout of Boss Hogg. Wiedersham was wearing a new suit. Trout had stopped trying to guess the labels; they all looked the same on him anyhow.

Trout had discarded his Kenneth Cole shoes for a pair less ostentatious and as different from Wiedersham's as he could find. That meant a pair of cheap Oxfords from Wal-Mart. Cobb, on the other hand, still wore his Coles and a suit of the same cut as Wiedersham's. Trying to get *his* toast buttered.

*Talk about goofy bastards!*

A warren of political advisors and handlers, security people and lawyers occupied the two trail cars—along with Marilyn and her pink poodle Reggie. She had intended to go home until she learned President Anastos was coming to Chicago to stump for her husband during a brief stopover at the airport. After that, you couldn't have driven the ladder-climbing bitch off with bullwhips.

"People need to see *us* with the President," she rationalized. "Everyone will know we have arrived. Trout, don't fuck it up."

"You have a filthy mouth, Marilyn, you know that?"

"Just don't fuck up things, Trout."

"Or you won't speak to me anymore?"

"Or you'll find your skinny ass back out on the streets working for minimum wages where I found you."

Trout had had his *own* dreams back then. He wanted to be a novelist. Now look at him. A man could be diverted by the prospect of wealth and power to the point that he would wear Kenneth Cole's and tolerate living with a pink poodle.

It was hard to see the point of all this anyhow if the election was already in the bag, as Wiedersham claimed. Pressing the flesh; kissing babies and asses; breathing the stench of "the People's" bad breath; getting insulted and hit in the face with pies. Wiedersham said it was because they had to keep up the outward appearance of legitimacy until the time was right. The Homers mustn't know what was planned for them until it was too late. Two weeks from now, the Sustainable World Conference would lay out the plan and the final timeline for, as Anastos often said, "the complete transformation of the United States of America."

Out of chaos came order.

Trout sucked another draught from his Whiskey Sour as the caravan of limos and cops screamed toward O'Hare, stopping other traffic on the streets. Cobb glared at him with disapproval. Trout glared back.

Wiedersham settled it. "Dennis, you've had enough."

It was better than swigging Maalox on the rocks. Nonetheless, Trout dutifully sunk his glass in a cup holder to show he could take it or leave it. He put on his happy face.

Satisfied, Wiedersham resumed the campaign briefing with which he began haranguing Trout as soon as the caravan left the hotel. Taking advantage of the ride to lay out position shifts Trout was to take on key issues, stressing campaign talking points.

"We don't call it a stimulus bill anymore," Wiedersham was saying. "Message experts say we're to call it 'the Recovery Plan.' That plays with the Homer Simpsons. More positive."

*Yessuh, massa.*

"There's also revised messaging in the Healthcare Law. Instead of saying the law will reduce costs and national deficits, emphasize how, with a little tweaking, universal healthcare is an entitlement that will cover every little Who in Whoville from cradle until the sonofabitch dies."

Don't mention the eighteen-*trillion*-dollar national debt, the forty million people on food stamps, double-digit unemployment, the growing poverty rate, government's control of financial institutions, business and energy... Keep on the happy face. Tell the Homers that "hope and change" will save them from the "destructive policies" of the Tea Parties and other obstructionists.

The underlying message that must never be spoken was that voters were stupid and must be forced to do what was best for them.

Trout thought these briefings unnecessary and boring. After all, advisors and handlers under Wiedersham's tutelage scripted Trout's speeches for him. Almost nothing that issued from his lips in public was his own. He was like a puppet enslaved to his ventriloquist master.

"The Tea Party philosophy is that every man is for himself and owes no responsibility to his neighbor," Trout informed a campaign rally at a basketball arena in Skokie, following President Anastos practice of using teleprompters to keep him on track. "The Far Right in this country believes that there should be no more taxes, no more government, no more safety nets for the poor and disadvantaged and elderly, no more anything. You know who these people are. They're mean-spirited and selfish. It has led to concentration of wealth in the hands of the richest Americans while everyone else suffers. It's only fair and just that wealth be taken from those who hoard it and redistributed to those who need it..."

On an Evanston football field, he delivered this gem of wisdom: "The Rich Right through its PACs and anonymous organizations dominated by rich fat cats is trying to flip Americans into a white heat. Disinformation campaigns appeal to people's baser instincts rather than to their more caring social rationale. Honest to God, half of these Tea Baggers are rabid and need psychiatric help. Nobody can be that angry that long and it be healthy for you."

He had the people with him. He could feel it. It felt good. No pies in the face or anything.

"People who hate immigrants, gays, African-Americans, women and other minorities are trying to make the election a referendum rooted in anger and apathy and amnesia. This is a bare knuckle fight for the future of this country and for the world. It's a struggle between the Far Right that would return to the failed policies of the past and those who want to move American forward into peace, prosperity and social justice for all..."

He started to add "amen," but caught himself in time.

Wiedersham suggested Trout make the contrast between the despised Far Right and the forward-looking Progressives even plainer. At an indoor convention center in Niles, Trout's teleprompters guided him through, "Is anyone starting to see parallels here between the Tea Baggers and their tactics and the rise of the Brown Shirts in Nazi Germany? Violence instigated by Tea Parties reminds me of how Hitler took over Germany by yelling and marching and shouting down meetings. Is that what we want in this country? A Nazi America?"

It was all spin, much of it outright lies to cover up the real truth, the rest of it so distorted that anyone who believed such crap had to be an idiot or an ideologue. A fly landed on Trout's lip while he was speaking in Niles. Another buzzed around his head. He half-expected a plague of them, like from *The Amityville Horror*. His left eye began to spasm, a nervous tic that started a week ago and made him look as though he were winking at people as if to say, *Hey, it's all bullshit, but we're in this together, right?*

Air Force One was just landing at O'Hare when the Wiedersham caravan arrived and sirened on through to where a small crowd of people waited excitedly on the tarmac. Most were local, state and national media, the rest "common people" vetted and allowed past security as window dressing for the President's "pit stop," one of several he was making today on behalf of chosen candidates. He seemed to be everywhere during this crazy season leading up to mid-term elections. How many millions of dollars, Trout wondered cynically, were American taxpayers shelling out so this clown could caper around the country stumping for Progressive politicians?

It gave Trout little solace in assuming that President Anastos had his own ventriloquist—George Zuniga?—to pull his strings and that advisors and handlers likewise kept him in line and wrote his speeches. The difference between Trout's camp of cynical pragmatists and Anastos' was that the President's camp consisted of true Marxist believers. Every time Trout happened to run into one of the White House czars through Wiedersham, the czar was saying something like, "This generation's children belong to us because we control education. Their parents will pass on. Their descendants, however, now stand in our camp. In a short time they will know nothing else but this new community."

Regulatory czar Sam Shrader was being prepped to take over Chicago as mayor. One time he dropped by Trout's campaign headquarters and laughed like a maniac and his eyes bugged out when the discussion turned to how that babe on Zenergy New Channel, Sharon Lowenthal, might die of a heart attack.

"I never knew I had this much hate in me," he confessed. "But she deserves it."

Air Force One taxied up to the roped-off tarmac. A Marine Corps band struck up a march to be followed by *Hail to the Chief* when the door opened and the President stepped out onto the flag-draped platform. A bunch of grade school kids chanted, "Ummm Ummm Ummm, Patrick Wayne Anastos..." Another bunch of kids wearing green Junior AmeriCorps Tees delivered the Pledge of Allegiance, but in the new vein of the times. *I pledge allegiance to the Earth and all the life it supports, one planet in our care with sustenance, respect and social justice for all...*

A presidential aide ushered Wiedersham and Trout to the platform to stand and be photographed with the President while he delivered his standard spiel about how America needed dedicated young public servants like—reading his teleprompter to see who he was endorsing—"the next congressman from Illinois, Dennis, uh, Trout!" Trout noticed Anastos was back to wearing an American flag lapel pin. Kissing up to the Homers after having first declared, "I decided I won't wear that pin on my chest. Instead, I'm going to tell the American people what I believe, what will make this country great..."

When the National Anthem played, Anastos gave his customary "crotch salute," standing there with his hands clasped in front of his groin while everyone else stood at attention, hands over their hearts.

Trout's eye tic'd. Back during Anastos' campaign for the presidency, a retired Air Force general on *Meet the Press* asked the candidate why he didn't follow protocol when the National Anthem played.

"As I've said about the flag pin," Anastos said, "I don't want to be perceived as taking sides. There are a lot of people in the world to whom the American flag, uh, is a symbol of oppression. The Anthem itself conveys a war-like message. You know, uh, the bombs bursting in air and all that sort of thing. If the National Anthem should be swapped for something, uh, less parochial and less bellicose then I, uh, might salute it. As President of the United States, I will, uh, use my power to bring change to this nation and offer a new path..."

*What were we thinking?* Trout raged to himself. *What the hell have we elected President of the United States?*

## President on Campaign Tour

***(Chicago)***—*President Patrick Anastos is dashing across the country to help his party retain power in the November mid-term elections.*

*"Don't give in to fear," he encouraged supporters Thursday at a whistle stop in Chicago for Congressional candidate Dennis Trout.*

*He is covering more than 12,000 miles in one week. In addition to Trout, he will be raising money for Senator Patty Murphy of Washington, Governor Ted Striker of Ohio, Senate candidate Harry Reems of Indiana...*

*"If you believe we need to fundamentally restructure our economy and re-establish popular control over the private corporations which have distorted our economy and hijacked our government," he said in Chicago, "then you must vote for Dennis Trout."*

*Thousands of well-wishers chanting "The One! The One!" met him at O'Hare when Air Force One landed. A huge sign greeted him. It said: "Chicago believes anyone who has passed healthcare reform, signed economic stimulus bills, tackled global warming, moved to restore economic and social fairness, recast America's global image, commands war zones in Iraq, Afghanistan and Libya, won the Nobel Peace Prize, nominated two Supreme Court Justices, solved the AP oil spill crisis, and overhauled financial regulations deserves our gratitude. Thank you, Mr. President."*

# Chapter Sixty-One

## Scranton, Pennsylvania

Events had caught up with them, as Nail knew they must, and now Sharon's and his *now* was over. She wept openly but silently before she returned to New York. She was on a mission from God and needed to be there.

"I still have one wish remaining on our star," she said. "I'll save it until we really need it."

Many of the real stars were burned out and dead a million years before their light finally reached Earth.

Sharon argued that the enemy wouldn't try against her again, not after the last incident at her apartment had been hammered by Zenergy and talk radio. It would be too conspicuous if something happened to her now. Besides, Zenergy was going to double her security.

"These people not attack open-like," Big C predicted gloomily. "They make it like an accident."

"Paul Revere never wavered," Sharon returned. "I'm afraid we don't have much time left."

Nail, still weak from his wound, promised to remain in Scranton until he recovered. Sharon's doctor friend warned that too much activity would likely reopen the bullet holes and invite infection. Nail also posed more of a hindrance to her in New York than an asset, as Homeland Security would be sticking to her tighter than shingles on a roof, looking for him.

Left unspoken was the vow he took: *I couldn't save Jamie—but I'll kill every commie in Washington all the way up to the White House if that's what it takes to save Sharon.*

She led them in a final prayer, asking God to keep them safe in the trying days ahead. Neither of them mentioned marriage; that would have to wait until this was all over and they had lives again. And then she was gone alone on the drive to New York. Bodyguards would rendezvous with her en route.

Big C departed the following morning after a cryptic cell phone call from Lieutenant Jack Ross' wife in Tulsa. Big C turned on the speaker mode to allow Nail to listen in on the conversation. Marsha's voice sounded thin and distressed.

"Thank God I found you, Corey. I tried to get James. It was on the news that he was shot."

“I’m right here, Marsha,” Nail said. “I lost my phone. What’s the matter?”

She sobbed openly. “They’ve... They’ve taken my husband.”

“Marsha, who took him?” Big C cried.

“I didn’t know where to turn except to James and you.”

“Who took him, Marsha? Where did they take him?”

“He disappeared. That’s all I know, Corey. I haven’t heard from him in a week.”

She was crying now, big, wet sobs of desperation. “I—I think they’re listening in on my phone calls.”

“We better hang up,” Big C agreed. “Don’t do nothing till you hear from me.”

“Corey—”

“We get him back. I promise.”

Big C clicked off and he and Nail sat looking at each other, the same thoughts going through their minds: *It could be a trap.*

Nonetheless, Big C threw his things together. Nail walked him to the junker the big man had picked up in Alabama. They had agreed that Nail, who was in no condition to travel, should remain near Sharon in case she needed him.

“I pick up a new pay-go phone and call you the number,” Big C promised. “I keep you informed.”

He looked at Nail and nodded, as though to himself. Before he drove off, he advised, “Lift up the back seat of your car.”

Nail discovered the 30.06 Winchester rifle and sniper scope underneath the seat of his Toyota. He stared at the weapon for a long minute, recalling Sharon’s admonition that there had been enough killing. Killing, she said, ultimately destroyed the soul.

“I do only what I have to do,” he had replied. “For everything there is a season... A time to kill, and a time to heal.” A paraphrase from the King James Bible, which was among the books she purchased for him.

Nail checked the Winchester to see if it was loaded. Next to it was a full box of ammo.

# Chapter Sixty-Two

## Washington, D.C.

Judy Sparks-Taylor's apartment was set in a fashionably rundown neighborhood occupied mainly by students and grad instructors a couple of blocks from George Washington University. Pizza huts, sandwich shops, a McDonald's, used text book shops and used furniture stores, apartments *For Rent* tucked back into alleys and above dry cleaners or Laundromats. Instead of Big C's picking Judy up at her apartment, which could be dangerous, she packed a bag to meet him in front of Quizno's.

"I never know when Dennis might show up," she explained.

Big C spotted the slim, bleached-blond figure in jeans and sneakers on the street in the bustle of the lunch crowd. He parked down the street and watched for signs that it might be a setup. He had no reason to distrust her, especially not after she had stuck out her neck for James. Still, she *was* a crooked politician's babe and... Well, politicians were parasites, as they continued to demonstrate, and capable of any damned thing.

After watching for ten minutes and seeing nothing to trigger his cop's radar, he got out of his car and merged into the flow of pedestrian traffic as best his six-six frame permitted. He carried a Beretta 9mm stuffed underneath his shirt in the small of his back where he could get to it. Judy hurried to meet him. She took his hand and drew him round the corner.

"I'm afraid," she confessed.

"Do he know?"

"Dennis has been pecking around like an old barnyard rooster. Asking a lot of questions about my cousins."

"Maybe you better change cousins to uncles."

She gave him a stern look. "Corey, I ain't kidding. The people Dennis is with are mean enough to shoot neighbors' dogs. He come over last night after you called on the phone. He knows I was fibbing when I told him I was going to Oklahoma for a few days 'cause my mama needs me. I thought he was going to hit me. He goes, 'Nobody from Bugfuck, Oklahoma, leaves Congressman Dennis Trout until *I* say I'm through.'"

Anger welled in Big C's chest, but he resisted the impulse to suggest she walk away from that cheap dump Trout rented for her and keep going. The idea of Trout touching her again disgusted him. Still, where would she go? It was risky enough for her to be with him for the next several days, and selfish of him to have asked her. He was already starting to regret it.

"Looky here..." he began.

She clasped her small hand across his mouth, as though anticipating his objection. "Corey, you're the only man in a long time that don't treat me like I'm some kind of Dust Bowl trash. Wait right here. I left my bag in Quizno's for safe keeping. Don't worry. He's in Illinois. If he wants me, he'll call me on my cell. We got a whole week, Corey. Just me and you. A couple of Okies going back home."

It would have been faster to take a flight, but airport security all over the nation would be on the alert. The clunker Big C purchased in Montgomery under his assumed name of Vernon Smith was a 2000-model Chevrolet Impala, color green, a reliable working class car. There was a time when a black man and a white woman traveling together would have attracted unfriendly attention, especially from small town cops. Times had changed some since then.

Although Big C wasn't overly concerned about being recognized, he nonetheless remained in the car when they stopped for fuel or takeout and let Judy handle it. No use pressing their luck. They took I-95 south from Washington, then I-40 west, traveling hard to reach Oklahoma as quickly as possible. Exhausted, they stayed part of one night in a Motel 6.

C took his shower first at her insistence. Then she showered and came out wearing a brief black nightie to climb into the same bed with him, although there was another bed available. He thought he had never seen a more lovely vision. He felt an overwhelming desire to draw her into his powerful arms, but he was almost afraid he would crush her like a delicate flower.

"You sure?" he asked her.

"No," she admitted—and moved against him. "I forgot to turn out the light."

They made love slow and languorously. Afterwards, Judy sat up in bed and wept. Big C held her against his broad chest. His heart went out to this country mouse who had gone to the big city and ended up mistreated and tossed about by one abuser or another.

"What can I do?" he asked gently.

She sobbed in great heaves. "Don't ever stop being you, Corey. Promise?"

"We get to Tulsa, we walk across the River Bridge again and buy Sno Cones."

"Somebody might recognize you."

Things were never going to be normal again. Not for them, not for the rest of America.

It was a good trip mostly, in spite of Big C's rush to get to Tulsa and find out what lay behind Marsha Ross's call. To Big C's continuing delight, he found his buxom travel companion quick and agile, uneducated but not at all intellectually slow.

She had had to quit school in the ninth grade, she explained, because her dad ran off with a barmaid from the Dew Drop Inn in Vian, leaving her mom with five kids to raise. As the elder sibling, she lied about her age to waitress in cafes. Later, she worked bars and clubs until her brothers and sisters were out on their own.

"I always wanted to get my GED and go on to college," she said wistfully. "I never did seem to get around to it. Dennis told me I didn't have the mind for education."

She drew food stamps and went on welfare for a spell before she discovered big boobs, blond hair and a well-shaped behind were assets better than a gold mine in Washington, D.C. Trout was her second sugar-daddy politician. The first had been a fat, bald senator with a wife and three kids back in Ohio. He dumped Judy and ran for cover to avoid a scandal after his wife learned he wasn't spending all his time debating on the Senate floor.

"I guess you can say Fancy is my name. That's a Dolly Parton song. 'Be nice to the gentlemen, Fancy, and they'll be nice to you.' Does that make you think bad of me, Corey?"

"Girl, I see your heart and find it noble."

"I always told myself I was going to be a swan someday."

"I doubt you ever a ugly duckling."

She laughed. "You wouldn't say that if you seen me at fifteen slopping the hogs."

"Lucky hogs."

When it was her turn behind the wheel, Big C waved a copy of a slim publication on the cover of which was a likeness of Thomas Jefferson and the title *The Constitution of The United States*. Judy had never read it, not even in school.

"Listen to the disclaimer they put on it."

He read it to her:

*This book is a product of its time and does not reflect the same values as it would if it were written today. Parents might want to discuss with their children how values of race, gender, sexuality, ethnicity and interpersonal relationships have changed since this was written before allowing them to read this classic work.*

"Does that mean it's x-rated?" Judy asked innocently.

"What it mean, girl, is we losing freedom. My great, great granddaddy was brought over from Africa on a slave ship. Socialism the same thing where a small bunch of slave masters tell the rest of us how to live. We all going to be slaves again, no matter we black, brown, white, red or purple."

## FCC To Hold Hearings On Offensive Speech

***(Washington)***—*Speaker of the House Barbara Teague, members of the National Action Network, and the Federal Communications Commission met Tuesday to discuss "standards of decency" when referring to elected officials and other public servants. In the meeting, Speaker Teague called on the FCC to regulate radio and TV personalities.*

*"What Rush Limbaugh, Sharon Lowenthal and others have done, I believe, pushes the envelope beyond free speech," Teague said. "We intend to follow that up with public hearings and bring to task some of them to explain how they justify the use of federally regulated airways to justify offending people with whom they disagree..."*

# Chapter Sixty-Three

## Oklahoma City

It could almost be a law that tall, lanky men like Lieutenant Jack Ross have short, plump, happy wives. When Big C and Judy entered the Pizza Hut located off I-44 in Oklahoma City, the first thing he noticed from across the room was that Marsha Ross' eyes were swollen from crying and she appeared years older than the last time he saw her. She occupied a booth against a plate glass window that provided a view of the capitol dome in the distance. They had agreed to meet here rather than in Tulsa where he was more apt to be recognized.

A stylish brunette in her thirties occupied the booth with Marsha. Big C stopped at the door. Like all hunted men, he was skittish of strangers. After a moment he escorted Judy through the dinner-hour crowd and past two boys playing a video shoot-'em-up game. He smiled at Marsha when she looked up. It was the first time he could remember that she didn't laugh with delight at seeing him and jump up to give him a hug. The brunette solemnly moved over to Marsha's side of the table to leave room for Big C and Judy on the other side. Her name was Carolyn Moulton.

Marsha reached across the table to Big C. His massive hands devoured hers. She batted back tears.

"I always thought Judy was a pretty name," she said to Judy.

They ordered a large pizza with everything. Judy asked for a Coke and Big C a Mountain Dew. When the waitress left to fill their orders, Marsha said, "I did like you told me to make sure I wasn't followed out of Tulsa."

"How about you, Carolyn?"

"I'm staying in Oklahoma City. No one knows I'm here, not even my husband."

While they waited for pizza, Big C explained about Nail and how he was shot saving Sharon from another probable assassination. "They trying to shut her up," he said.

"Jack was afraid that would happen. He left two numbers he said I should call if I needed help. Your's and James'. He said the numbers couldn't be easily traced. James didn't answer."

"I'll give you his new number. Marsha, what happened?"

Her head lowered as she fought for control. There was more gray in her hair than Big C remembered. After a minute, she looked at him again.

"I-I never really thought this could happen in America."

"Germans didn't think it happen there either."

"That sounds like what Jack would say."

She took a sip from her glass and continued, "You know about the Oath Keepers...?"

Peace officers and military who took a vow not to act beyond the reach of the Constitution even if the government ordered it.

"Jack and I took the vow together before all this started," Big C said.

Marsha nodded. "About two weeks ago, my husband and several other lieutenants and sergeants on the PD were ordered to attend special in-service training in Wichita, Kansas. I've since learned they were all Oath Keepers. Jack was uncomfortable about it because he was told they would have to turn in their guns when they arrived."

"But Jack went to Kansas anyhow?"

"Corey, I asked him not to. We have an FBI agent living next door to us—"

"Bob Nelson," Big C recalled. "He was also an Oath Keeper."

"A month ago, Bob parked his car in his drive and we haven't seen him or his family since. Someone comes to mow the lawn and pick up the mail, but the Nelsons have disappeared. There's a new Regional Homeland Security Director named Gary Philby who took Kimbrell's place. I heard Jack and Bob talking one time about how Philby considers Oath Keepers unreliable should the government have to declare martial law."

*They weeding out the troublemakers,* Big C thought.

"Always before, Jack called me every night when he was away," Marsha resumed, her voice strained from worry. "I haven't heard a word from him this time since he left. I went to the police station to inquire. The new Police Chief—Earnest Bruton. You remember him, Corey?"

"Bruton the Crouton from Internal Security. Kiss-ass."

"He *is* a kiss-ass," Marsha agreed. "Jack said he was put in that position for when they federalize the police."

People like Bruton easily became KGB or Gestapo running roughshod over people.

"Bruton told me it was none of my business where Jack was," Marsha continued. "He told me to go home and keep my mouth shut.

Corey, I've been hiding out in a motel since then. I'm afraid the same thing will happen to me as it did to Misty Nelson after they took Bob away."

"You need find somewhere else safe to hide," Big C suggested. "Probably another state."

Marsha choked up. "I can't leave without Jack." She looked to her companion. "Carolyn, you want to take over from here?"

"My husband is an optical surgeon," the grim brunette began. "About a year ago, he accepted a position in a mental health facility in the Colorado Rockies near an isolated little ski village called South Fork. The money was good, so we agreed we should separate for a year and build up a nest egg. We live in New Mexico. Cass comes home on weekends. I began to notice he seemed extremely stressed out. He has nightmares. Finally, even though the doctors there are sworn to secrecy, he told me what was going on. He said they would kill him, and me, if they found out he was talking."

She took a deep breath to calm her nerves.

"This place," she said, "is as bad as anything that might have come out from behind the Iron Curtain in the 1930s. Electrified fences surround it. Armed guards patrol the perimeter. Cass was assigned to the hospital to remove corneas from patients. Apparently, they are political prisoners deemed dangerous to the government. Cass thinks there may be dozens of other facilities like it hidden all over the United States. People are... People are..."

It was like she found it so beyond belief that she couldn't say it. Finally, she did.

"It's something out of a SciFi horror movie. People are being executed as needed and their organs harvested for distribution to hospitals. What's left of the bodies are incinerated. One hundred percent of those sent there will never leave that place. There's a big turnover. More buses come every day filled with new prisoners."

Tears ran freely down Marsha Ross's cheeks. Judy turned pale, her mouth agape. Big C expected almost anything from Washington, anything but *this*. Incarcerating people who opposed government social policies started with World War I and President Woodrow Wilson, who tossed thousands of citizens in jail for no greater crime than speaking out. Until now, however, the U.S. Government had never resorted to political genocide.

"There was a boy in one of the cells named Smitty," Carolyn went on. "He had been an AmeriCorps volunteer. Something had gone wrong and he was arrested and sent to South Fork. Cass felt sorry for him, but there was nothing he could do.

"About two weeks ago, Smitty's cellmate was taken away for surgery. They moved a new guy in with Smitty, a Tulsa policeman named Ross. Smitty begged my husband to get in touch with Sharon Lowenthal from the TV show. He told my husband she would remember him from something that happened in Arkansas. She and you, Corey, and Detective Nail must have made some impression on him."

Big C waited for her to go on.

"Cass forbade me to contact Sharon Lowenthal because he said she was likely next on the hit list and would end up in a place like South Fork, along with anyone associated with her. That could be dangerous for him. I just couldn't do *nothing*, understand? I started trying to find Jack Ross' wife and finally located Marsha hiding in a motel, scared nearly to death."

"Trusted friends of ours on the police department put me in touch with her," Marsha explained.

"I don't blame her for being scared," Carolyn said. "So, Marsha called you, Corey. That's about it. I don't know what you can do about it. That place is like Fort Knox or something."

Big C had to ask it. "Carolyn, you know if Jack's still alive?"

Marsha hung her head.

Carolyn said, "As of day before yesterday he was."

"My God in Heaven," Judy wailed. "Does things just keep getting crazier?"

Big C took her hand and squeezed.

"We may still have time," he said to Marsha. "Carolyn, I going to need some information. I need the location the concentration camp, layout, guards, anything else your husband might have told you."

## United Nations to Patrol New York

***(New York)***—*Due to a series of events which has caused wide international notice, such as the anti-illegal immigration law enacted by the State of Arizona, the United Nations has announced that its nation members will begin patrolling the New York City borough of Staten Island to safeguard Mexican and Arab Muslim immigrants...*

# Chapter Sixty-four

## Chicago

Dennis Trout had no one. Judy bailed out on him when he needed her most, making an excuse that she had to go to her mother's in Bugfuck, Oklahoma, for a few days. Ever since she left, she kept sluffing him off when he cell-phoned her.

"Dennis, my mama and me is at the hospital. Can I call you back later?"

"Dennis, I'm cooking 'cause the whole family's coming over for fried chicken and mashed taters."

He lashed out at her in anger and frustration. "Are you fucking somebody else, Judy?"

She hung up on him. *The cunt hung up on him.*

He called her back after he cooled down. "I'm sorry, Judy. I've been under a great deal of stress. This was a bad time for you to leave town."

"Can we talk when I get back to Washington, Dennis?"

*Can we talk?* was always a bad sign.

"You *are* coming back?"

"Where else would I go?"

She didn't say she loved him.

The nervous tic in his left eye got worse. Wiedersham suggested he see a doctor. Marilyn said it made him look ridiculous.

What he needed was to escape this sham campaign for awhile. People around him ate, slept and lived politics twenty-four hours a day, even when they went to the john.

After delivering one of his canned speeches at a baseball field, he looked up to see a small private airplane flying over bearing a two-word message emblazoned on the underside of its wings: **Stop Anastos**. A "Freedom Rally" was being held on a soccer field at the same sports' complex. Out of impulse and curiosity, he donned dark glasses and a hat so he wouldn't be recognized and slipped away to take a look for himself. A first-generation Vietnamese man was starting to speak.

"Nearly forty years ago," he said, "I left South Vietnam for political asylum in the United States. I still remember vividly the communist tanks rolling into Saigon, although I was only six years old. Trust me, such images can never be erased. My family was among the first one hundred thousand Vietnamese refugees allowed to come to America. It was a miracle from God.

"I am telling you right now that this is the greatest country on earth. Freedom and opportunity to succeed put me here today. This person standing in front of you could not exist in a socialist communist environment. But what I see now is that old nightmare of communist tanks rolling into Saigon starting to replay in America. If you don't know it, if you think socialism is a people's movement, I can tell you from experience that the only difference between socialism and communism is the caliber of the rifle aimed at your head..."

Trout felt sick. He fled to his hotel room and swigged from a bottle of Maalox, followed by a chaser of Jack Daniels. His eye twitched like crazy.

# Chapter Sixty-Five

## Scranton, Pennsylvania

*The Jerry Baer Show w/Sharon Lowenthal* aired *live* from New York. James Nail was waiting for it so he would know she was all right so far. She appeared on the screen, beautiful and as high octane as ever with her curly black hair and dark eyes, wearing a blue-gray pants suit and a blue ribbon in her hair.

*If anything ever happened to her...*

Alone in his tiny hideout in Scranton, waiting to heal from his wounds, Nail rushed from the frig with a Coke and a bologna sandwich and plopped into an overstuffed chair that was no longer *that* overstuffed. Sometimes he thought the world might have been better off if TV had gone kaput fifty years ago for all it and its video game progeny had dumbed down and savaged the culture. Tonight, however, it allowed him to at least see Sharon.

She gave a cherry "Good evening, America!" She looked tired, stressed. With deliberate irony, *The Communist Internationale* played in the background:

*'Tis the final conflict,*
*Let each stand in his place.*
*The international working class*
*Shall be the human race...*

An old video of Ronald Reagan filled the screen: "Those who have known freedom and lost it will never know it again."

Sharon reappeared, perched on the edge of a table stacked with books. Behind her stood the well-used blackboards made famous by Jerry Baer.

"All over the world," she began, looking directly into the watching eyes of America, "socialists and communists are coming out of the woodwork. Americans are being pitted against each other by those who seek complete power. When the United States was still on its way to becoming the freest, most productive nation in the world, Alexis de Tocqueville concluded that the rich and the powerful would somehow find a way to kick the door of freedom closed. America, that door is closing."

She was energetic and persuasive, but Nail was starting to doubt that anything could wake up a people gone asleep over the years. Big C liked to quote his old grandpappy.

"Give to a pig when it grunts and to a child when it cries, and you'll have a fine pig and a bad child."

Americans had become "bad children."

Sharon peppered the show as usual with clips of the powerful and influential caught openly revealing their socialist mindsets and declaring their intentions, President Anastos had recently begun referring to himself as a "citizen of the earth."

"International order is one we must achieve," he said.

Former Black Panther Duane Smith, now current White House environmental czar and PEIU president, delivered his own prognostication. "Free enterprise has failed, never to be revived. America needs 21st Century State Capitalism—like the Chinese."

"The Constitution really doesn't prohibit the government from doing virtually anything," said Senate Majority Leader Joe Wiedersham, a rumpled, obese man in a thousand-dollar suit. "Theoretically, nothing prevents the government from taking one hundred percent of your income."

A prominent guest on a late night talk show was berating the rise of the Tea Party Movement. "The nice thing is that people who are too dumb or lazy or uninformed to cast a ballot aren't compelled to vote; they can join a Tea Party. Far too many people are voting as it is. We're going to have to drag the ignorant hillbilly half of this country into the next century, which in their case means the 19th Century. They're too stupid. They are like dogs. They can understand inflection, they can understand fear, they can understand dominance. They don't understand issues..."

Sharon lowered her head, as though in prayer. Nail felt her anguish. She looked up into the camera.

"America, if there's one thing these good, tolerant, open-minded Progressives cannot stand, it's Middle America. Your old-fashioned decency rubs a lot of lefties the wrong way. They look with suspicion on hayseeds in the heartland who fly the flag on the Fourth of July. They snicker at ordinary folks who like to go bowling or who pray or stand for the Pledge of Allegiance at a high school football game. They don't understand why anyone would *want* to eat at Golden Corral or Red Lobster or shop at Wal-Mart...

"Government wants to tell you hayseeds what to eat, how much air to put in your tires, where to live, how high to set your thermostats, how much money you can make....Government takes away our personal sense of responsibility. While we were asleep, government through handouts taught people not to believe in themselves anymore—to depend on government instead. Progressives want us to believe in a Nirvana Utopia. They sell the idea by using envy and government checks like candy from their pockets, taking power in exchange for promises of 'hope and change' they can't possibly keep. This is not fairness. This is lust for power, the face of tyranny in disguise."

She referred to a passage from Cloward and Pivens on how to destroy capitalism and replace it with socialism:

*Gradually expand government spending until the country nears fiscal collapse. At that point, a public accustomed to its entitlements will presumably turn on its capitalists masters when they propose cutbacks to restore fiscal balance...and turn the nation's fiscal crisis in a socialist direction.*

Sharon returned. "The ideas of Karl Marx have killed one hundred million people," she said. "It's starting all over again—*here in America.* Through high powered satellites, drones and massive databases, government can track and control us by using our cell phones, cars, credit cards, driver's licenses, and passports. Government agents can secretly open the mail of American citizens, read our e-mails, listen in on our phone calls and serve search warrants without authorization of a judge. Local police are being federalized; AmeriCorps is building a private army. The Constitution is being shredded before our very eyes."

A man identified as a former FBI agent came on to stare boldly into the camera as he related how he went undercover to infiltrate a radical organization led by President Anastos' confidantes Bill Ackart and Bernadine Samson-Ackart. At one of their meetings, he said, the conversation turned to the subject of how to best counter obstructionists by building "reeducation camps" and "mental health facilities" in the American Southwest. Those who were too hardcore to the right to be reeducated would have to be eliminated.

"There I was," the agent said, "sitting in a room with thirty other people with graduate degrees, powerful people in government, listening to them figure out how to eliminate twenty-five million people—and they were dead serious."

The agent had been killed in a mysterious hunting accident afterwards.

Sharon displayed an official-looking document.

"This is a copy of the Presidential Directive that establishes presidential continuity of government provisions, or ECG—*Enduring Constitutional Government,*" she explained. "During an emergency, the President of the United States may declare ECG and maintain it until *he* decides the coast is clear. It involves emergency action that can be implemented in the event of a national crisis, such action including the arrest and detention of 'traitors,' 'insurrectionists,' 'criminals' and other malcontents by military commanders appointed to run state and local governments."

Nail realized he was sitting on the edge of his chair and hadn't taken a single bite from his sandwich. He couldn't help sensing death trains or their equivalent being marshaled in rail yards across the nation. Long chains of cattle cars filled with human cargo to be hauled to mass graves. Unexpectedly, he thought of Lieutenant Jack Ross and the enigmatic phone call from Ross' wife: "They've taken my husband!"

"There are four conditions that must be present for Marxists to make their move to power grab the government," Sharon continued. "They are: a bad economy; high unemployment; high dependency on government; uncertainty and fear among the population. Doesn't it sound like everything might already be in place waiting for a crisis to set it in motion?"

George Zuniga appeared on the screen. A large-headed, ageing man whose East European accent completed his villainous appearance. "Zee main obstacle to a stable and just world order is zee United States," he said.

Sharon pointed out that Zuniga had been influencing elections for years. "Expanding his influence," she said, "through groups such as ACOA, World Alliance, and the Institute for Open Societies." Zuniga, she continued, was the primary source of funding for scores of organizations promoting Progressive agendas. *Time* magazine reported that "not another single outside group has had so much sway over the government as The Institute for Open Societies." An "open society" meant Marxist.

"I don't think it's going too far to compare him to the evil emperor from *Star Wars*," Sharon continued. "President Anastos carries a Blackberry around in case Zuniga calls. What Zuniga wants, Anastos gives him. Zuniga supplies the talking points and makes policy in virtually everything."

His Open Societies was donating millions to buy up journalists and media outlets, most recently National Public Radio. Sharon played a clip of a mainstream news interview with the "Spooky Dude."

"In view of recent evidence suggesting that zee incendiary rhetoric of Zenergy News' hosts such as Sharon Lowenthal may incite violence," he maintained, "I have now decided to support organizations that will hold Zenergy News accountable for the false and misleading information they so often broadcast. I am supporting NPR and other media in an effort to more widely publicize zee challenge Zenergy poses to civil and informed discourse in our democracy."

Immediately after this pronouncement, the "drive-by media" had taken up the howl. Sharon demonstrated with clips.

"We can't just dismiss Lowenthal," a popular CNN anchor expostulated. "There is a good reason why we have exemption of free speech. We need to regulate and protect people from irrational, uncomfortable or offensive speech through passage of Senator Wiedersham's FAD bill."

Speaker of the House Barbara Teague came on, staring out from her expressionless Botox surgeries. "I looked up the definition of sedition, which is 'conduct or language inciting rebellion against the authority of the state.' A lot of these statements coming from the likes of Sharon Lowenthal rub right up close to being seditious."

"We need to do whatever we can to regulate and control capitalist speech, eliminate it if possible," chimed in President Anastos' Regulatory czar, Sam Shrader, on another clip.

A shiver ran up Nail's spine at Sharon's summary: "The mainstream media has fallen into Zuniga's toilet and are splashing around in it like it's holy water. They have got to take out Zenergy News in order to move forward in the shadows. They have got to take me out."

Jerry Baer had already been *taken out.*

Sharon was standing up now, moving about on the TV set at Zenergy. She stopped. The camera closed in. She looked directly into it. Her boldness, her raw courage surprised and delighted Nail. At the same time, it made him nervous and unsettled about her safety.

"Dietrich Bonhoeffer was a minister in Germany when Hitler rose to power," she said. "He tried to get other ministers to join him in opposition. 'Silence in the face of evil is itself evil,' he preached. 'God will not hold us guiltless.' America, freedom is being crushed today in countries around the world. If America goes into decline, the light of liberty will start to flicker everywhere in the world. No other country is going to ride in to save us. Americans are all alone on a hostile planet. Speaking out is becoming harder and riskier because we didn't speak out at the beginning. America, you are going to have to stand up against some of the most powerful people and institutions on the planet."

She let that sink in before a quote from *The Coming Insurrection* popped up on her display screen. That and Alinsky's *Rules for Radicals* were the playbooks for American Progressives campaigning to "fundamentally transform the United States of America."

*Visibility must be avoided. But a force that gathers in the shadows can't avoid it forever. Our appearance as a form must be reserved for the opportune moment. The longer we avoid visibility, the stronger we'll be when it catches up with us. And once we become visible our days will be numbered. Either we will get in a position to break its hold in short order, or we'll be crushed...*

"America, the masks are starting to come off, but they're not visible yet. We must make them visible and watch them scurry. What you see and hear on this program during the next few weeks will shake you like never before as we run down these cockroaches and show them to you in the full light of their intentions..."

Nail sprang to his feet in sudden comprehension, his sandwich and Coke forgotten. Before Sharon returned to New York, she had been talking about secret international meetings and summits the "Shadow Government" was holding to discuss the final transformation of the United States to a socialist nation. If someone could discover where these summits were being held, she pointed out, and sneak inside to expose them...

## Students Demand More Funding

***(Washington)**—Tens of thousands of students staged marches in cities across the nation today to demand more public funding for higher education. The unexpectedly large protests were backed by faculty, the National Education Association and the Public Employees International Union (PEIU). ACOA, American Progress Center, The Institute for Open Societies, and Students for A Democratic Society (SDS) were also represented...*

*There were reports of windows broken and fires set in several locations. Homeland Security Director Vladimir Gonzalez warned that violence is being initiated by Rightwing counter groups bent on discrediting peaceful student demonstrations...*

# Chapter Sixty-Six

## Green Country, Oklahoma

Militia cells across the breadth of the United States were organizing and arming themselves, creating intelligence networks and communications' links, training for revolution against their government. It was nutcake to think a few farmers and good ole boys armed with pistols and rifles could take on the power of a United States corrupted by One World commies. Hitler, Lenin, Stalin, Karl Marx and the other socialist crusaders of evil who made the 20th Century the bloodiest in the entire history of mankind were sniggering in their moldering graves.

In Big C Brown's opinion, it was already too late to peacefully wean the country from Big Brother's teat. Polls showed that forty percent of Americans in general—seventy percent of those under the age of twenty five who had attended public schools—openly approved of socialism.

"Even if we do stop Marxism this time," Sharon Lowenthal often warned, "it'll be only a matter of time until it reemerges—and the next time it will take over if we go back to sleep. These people will never give up their crusade to stomp the boot of communism on our necks."

Once violence started, it was unpredictable where it would end. Still, there came a point when a free man had no choice but to fight if he intended to remain free.

"What are we going to do, Corey?" Judy pleaded.

She felt so small and vulnerable in his big arms. "Judy, we must be soldiers."

"I can't go back to him," she protested. "Not after *us*."

"You have a mission," he reminded her. "If Trout's notebook contain information like you say, we need get it to Sharon."

He felt like a pimp asking her to do it. All he needed was a pink Cadillac, a Super Fly hat and baggy pants wiping out his tracks. He would miss her country girl innocence not yet jaded by the big city, in spite of all she had gone through, but for her to stay with him was too dangerous.

Big C put out feelers to the Defenders after his meeting with Marsha Ross and Carolyn. Tom Fullbright was the new commander of the Defenders, having assumed leadership after Big C cleared him by exposing Colonel Mosby as the snitch behind Ron Sparks' hanging. He was a wiry Cherokee of about thirty and, like many of the Indians from the hills of eastern Oklahoma, a man of few words.

Gary Philby, the District Homeland Security Director who took Kimbrell's place, was putting pressure on the militias in his area. He was organizing groups like the New American Protective Society and the Homeland Security League to develop informants and spy on disloyal neighbors. To avoid being noticed, Big C met with Fullbright and some of the other Defenders in an old abandoned store in the secure little community of Hanson near Sallisaw while Judy waited for him in a Sallisaw motel room. There was no electricity in the meeting place. Someone produced a kerosene lantern and placed it on an upturned vegetable crate in the center of the room where it illuminated about a dozen tense faces. The militiamen were a rough-hewn bunch, not particularly well-educated by Progressive standards, most of whom were living on the edge of poverty after having lost their jobs due to the tanking economy or because of pressure from Homeland Security. Big C kept to himself any reservations he entertained about the Defenders' ability to take on a heavily-armed contingent such as that guarding the "mental health facility" in Colorado.

"We might be able to recruit the Colorado Sons of Liberty," Fullbright suggested. "They'll almost double our force. They have a .50-caliber Browning machinegun."

Having lost two men to the AmeriCorps raid on the Bunch schoolhouse, the Defenders were eager to take the fight to the enemy. Big C recalled how, once before in America, a few farmers got together to fight for liberty—and won.

Big C stood up in the yellow light from the lantern and explained how it was the militia's duty to rescue Lieutenant Jack Ross and as many others as possible from a secret extermination camp and bring them to the American people as irrefutable proof of what the Anastos' administration planned for the nation. For security reasons, he withheld the location of the camp. He couldn't afford loose lips.

In that humble, isolated shack built in a previous century, Big C concluded with a short speech in the strong, simple language that ordinary men of the soil understood. Sharon would have declared it worthy of John Adams.

"That watchman Paul Revere who made the most famous ride in history of the world is riding again," he began in a ringing voice. "We must likewise have balls to muster with the free and the brave, else we be judged cowards unworthy to live free. We are drawing a line in the sand to tell a repressive government *No!* No more commies in the

White House, no more laws, rules and regulations that oppress people. Not one inch more will we yield. The time is arrive! Rebellion is at hand!"

These good, common men from the hills sprang to their feet and thrust their weapons at the wind-rattled roof of the old store and cheered. They had followed this big black ex-cop to Arkansas for that little fight, such as it was, and trusted his judgment and generalship. Little Tump Kinsey shoved a fist at the ceiling. He was almost seventy.

"We Vietnam vets can still fight!" Tump shouted.

"I know you can and you will. None of us who has been in combat is fond of it, but we do what must be done."

They were ready. Mad as hell and they weren't going to take it anymore. Big C ended with the famous quote from John Stuart Mill: "War is an ugly thing, but not the ugliest of things. The decayed and degraded state of moral and patriotic feeling which thinks nothing is worth a war is worse. A man who has nothing which he cares more about than he does his personal safety is a miserable creature who has no chance of being free, unless made and kept so by better men than himself."

He paused and, after a long moment, added, "You are those better men."

## President Signs Education Transformation Bill

***(Washington)****—Flanked by public school teachers from across the nation, President Anastos signed into law the Education Transformation Bill that proponents say will streamline American education and make it more relevant to the challenges faced by a modern society. Speaker of the House Barbara Teague called passage of the bill "a great vote for our children."*

*"If Congress hadn't passed this bill," the President said, "education would have sunk into a crisis we may not have been able to reverse. For every day we drag our feet on key issues like this, more of our citizens will lose their jobs and their dreams."*

*Due to the flagging economy, the bill calls for saving money by the elimination of certain niche programs that are no longer necessary for a good public education. Among those programs being dropped are U.S. history, civics, economics, and academies on the U.S. Constitution and Bill of Rights...*

# Chapter Sixty-Seven

## New York

Executive Producer Carl Patton of the Zenergy News Cable Station received a phone call from a man who identified himself as "John."

"I work for Mr. Zuniga," John said. "I think we should meet for lunch."

"Why would I want to do that?"

"To hash out some critical issues that affect your TV station, the nation, and particularly Miss Sharon Lowenthal."

They met at a little out-of-the-way eatery on Broadway. John was about fifty, nondescript, but with an air of authority that came from associating with powerful men. It didn't take him long to get to the point. They were still waiting to be seated when John began.

"Sharon Lowenthal is corroding the foundation of America and instigating violence," he said.

They were shown to a table before Patton came up with a response. As soon as they were seated, John continued with an accusatory diatribe against the "Rightwing conspiracy" led by Zenergy News and Sharon Lowenthal against George Zuniga.

"Why is she focused on Mr. Zuniga?" John demanded. "Why does Zenergy allow it?"

"Can it be because Zuniga's name and his various Open Society projects keep popping up wherever there are failed economies and failed nations?" Patton shot back. "Zuniga has spent the past quarter-century recruiting, training, indoctrinating and installing Marxist operatives in countries around the world to establish a One World socialist government. Now he's targeting the U.S."

"His influence is overhyped," John insisted.

"Is that a fact? Let me revisit his *modus operandi*. He moves in, forms a shadow party which leads to a shadow government built on bribery and corruption. He takes control of the airwaves, destabilizes the nation's economy through massive state overspending and corporate bailouts, provokes or exploits a national crisis, after which his shadow government takes power in order to quell massive unrest initiated by various leftwing organizations and so-called community organizers. Feel free to stop me at any time—John, is it?—when you think I've gone wrong."

"These are not normal times," John replied, unperturbed. "Mr. Zuniga does not accept rules imposed by others. If he did, he would not be alive today. One needs to adjust one's action to changing circumstances."

"I read somewhere that he considers himself a god, sort of like the world's conscience."

"The world needs a conscience."

"Some people think he may be the Antichrist."

John scoffed at the suggestion. "I don't think you understand me, Mr. Patton. If people like Sharon Lowenthal—and you—don't recognize that the world is changing, they will be left behind. She is hurting Mr. Zuniga and his business."

The meeting and the lunch ended right after the salad arrived. With a slow, sinister smile, John rose to his feet. Before he walked out, leaving Patton with the check, he handed Patton a DVD of an old movie—*A Face in the Crowd* starring Andy Griffith as Larry "Lonesome" Rhodes, a drunkard and petty criminal who becomes a powerful radio personality before being corrupted by the system. The movie ends with him posed to commit suicide by jumping off a building.

"Give this to Ms. Lowenthal with Mr. Zuniga's compliments," John said.

The news media had compared Jerry Baer to Lonesome Rhodes just before he was gunned down in Tulsa at the ORU Convention Center.

# Chapter Sixty-Eight

## Chicago

Strategy meetings were breaking out somewhere every week. Something was about to happen. Majority Leader Wiedersham expected Trout to attend them. *When* he became the junior congressman from Illinois, his loyalty to the cause must be well-tempered by the growing fires of the coming workers' revolution.

Today's summit was being held in the meeting hall of a Chicago AF of L/CIO, a dingy, depressing place out near the old stockyards. About thirty people showed up. Trout recognized some of them as, like himself, Illinois candidates for office, no doubt placed in position by George Zuniga and his friends. Others were key leaders in the labor movement—teachers, state employees, airport air controllers, most of whom represented the Public Employees International Union, PEIU. The topic tonight, as Trout soon learned, was a frank one on what labor and community organizers could do to help collapse the American economy, a prerequisite for a Marxist takeover.

The keynote speaker was Duane Smith, White House Environmental Czar and current head of PEIU. Trout had encountered him before, during conferences on the AP oil spill, the "Next Step" Conference, and at several other insider meetings. He was no doubt a major player. Behind the podium as he took the stage hung a large red and yellow bunting inscribed with Karl Marx' war cry: **Workers of the World Unite**.

The continuing objective of these summits, Smith explained, was to "create conditions of ungovernability" as explicated by Francis Fox Pivens.

"What the folks in charge want—you know, the big banks and everything—what they want is stability," he said. "There are extraordinary things we can do to destabilize the folks that are in power. For example, a quarter of the people who own a home are underwater. They are paying more for their homes than it is worth. Ten percent of these people are now in strategic default, meaning they are refusing to pay but they are staying in their homes. They figure out it takes a year to kick me out of my home because foreclosure is all backed up. I'm going to say I won't pay. It's a good business decision. What would happen if we organize these homeowners in mass to do a mortgage strike. Just say if we got half-a-million people to agree we won't pay our mortgages. It would literally cause a new financial crisis for the banks, but not for us. We would be doing quite well, thank you, because we wouldn't be paying."

A prattle of laughter rippled through the small audience. Trout did not laugh.

"The folks that control this country care about one thing—how the stock market does, how the bond market does. I think we need a very simple strategy. How do we bring the stock market down? How do we interfere with their ability to be rich, which means we have to politically isolate them, economically isolate them, and disrupt them."

Trout squirmed in his seat. What if his father was still alive and knew he was mixed up in all this?

"A bunch of us around the country think about who would be a really good company to hate. We decided that would be J.P. Morgan Chase based in New York. So we're going to roll out over the next couple of weeks, as soon as we can get enough people together. A week of action in New York with the goal of—I don't want to give away the details because I don't know which police agents are in the room."

More conspiratorial laughter.

"Labor can lead. We do have money, we have millions of members who are furious. We also need coalitions of community groups if we really believe that we are in a transformative stage of what's happening in the decline of capitalism. We need to confront this in a serious way and develop a real ability to put a boot in the wheel. We have to think about how, together, labor and community alliances are building something that really has the capacity to disrupt how the system operates..."

Trout's practical side kept telling his uncomfortable side that what he was doing was securing his future. Buttering his toast. He was sweating and his left eye twitched.

"I assume some of you have been invited to the Sustainable World Conference on Lake Ontario two weeks from today," Smith concluded. "It is there that we will propose and debate final solutions. Until then, everybody, you know, must continue to work to produce chaos in his region to allow us to at long last implement social and economic justice. Truly, we are at that point. Workers of the world unite!"

Trout's eye began tic'ing. Since linking his fate with his brother-in-law's, he had seen enough to know that once someone was *in* there was no safe way to get *out*.

# Chapter Sixty-Nine

## South Fork, Colorado

The crude map Carolyn sketched for Big C in Oklahoma City showed the "mental health facility" situated west of the Great Divide in the San Juan Mountains, at the end of a narrow road blocked off and guarded against intruders. Big C couldn't be sure how accurate the map was, since Carolyn drew it from memory off directions supplied by her husband. He and Tom Fullbright set out for Colorado to scout the camp while the rest of the Defenders stayed behind near Alamosa to link up with Colorado's Sons of Liberty in the mountains and wait for the call to action. Judy decided to spend a day or so with relatives in Oklahoma before returning to Washington.

Fretting that they might be too late to help Lieutenant Ross, Big C and Fullbright rushed on through South Fork to reach their destination at a pair of remote trout lakes in the mountains north of State 160 and east of Wolf Creek Pass. It was already getting late in the valleys and hollows when they arrived in Big C's rattletrap Impala. The early arrival of fall put enough bite in the air to encourage rutting elk to bugle and discourage most hikers and backpackers. Elk hunting season was still a few weeks away.

"We got a hour or two daylight to burn," Big C commented as he and Fullbright stuffed their backpacks with enough supplies to last several days. Once they studied the detention facility and devised a tentative assault plan, Fullbright would hike back out to guide in the militia while Big C maintained surveillance on the target.

They left a note on the Impala's windshield in case a Ranger happened by. The note said they were backpacking and would return in a few days. The vehicle shouldn't arouse suspicion since its registration checked to Vernon Smith, the alias Big C used in Alabama. The two militiamen hoisted packs and followed the trail that led around the little lakes and climbed through big timber toward the summit of the Divide. They wore roughout hiking boots, jeans and light jackets, with heavier coats in their packs to be used against high mountain weather. Big C carried a Glock stuffed in his backpack, Fullbright a .45 in a belt holster. Big C calculated they should reach the facility by tomorrow evening.

Shadows in the lowlands turned from murky gray to deep purple. Scarlet streaked the skies beyond the westernmost mountain peaks. A bull elk bugled, a high whistle that ended in a series of coughs, answered by the lonely cry of a loon on the lake.

They camped in the timber when night made hiking hazardous. Tucked into sleeping bags, they listened to the mournful inquiry of a nearby owl. Fullbright said Indians believed owls were harbingers of death.

## FCC To Regulate Internet

***(Washington)***—*Requirements mandated by Congress in its Economic Stimulus Bill direct private cable and communications companies to provide the Federal Communications Commission (FCC) with all internet data about individual homes, including what speeds they have, the kind of services a person uses, and their IP (internet protocol) addresses. Additional regulations being planned through the Wiedersham-Teague Fairness in Airwaves Doctrine (FAD) will enable federal government websites to combat foreign and domestic terrorism by tracking private citizens who visit certain websites... Government has already seized more than 1,000 domain names and shut down 1,000 websites—sites apparently engaged in illegal slander against the government...*

*Citizens may report the e-mail addresses of suspicious persons to Whitehouse.gov...*

# Chapter Seventy

## Washington, D.C.

*Out!* That was what Trout kept thinking on the short flight from Chicago to Washington. He rented a car at the airport and drove to the Russell Building. Senate Majority Leader Wiedersham appeared to be in prime Godfather mode in his new Italian suit that was already rumpled across his ample belly. Justin Cobb propped himself against the doorframe of Wiedersham's office as Trout showed himself in, past Liz' reception desk. Wiedersham calmly looked him over.

"You've been drinking again." An assessment, not a question.

"One on the flight." His anger rose. He stuffed it back down. He felt his left eye tic.

"I've warned you, Dennis. Booze and bimbos are the two things that will be your undoing in this business."

"You forgot the third—conscience," Trout muttered.

Wiedersham leaned forward and propped his elbows on his desk to regard Trout from beneath shaggy eyebrows. Like a lab scientist scrutinizing a new species of bacteria through a microscope.

"I warned Marilyn about marrying you," he said.

"You should have warned me instead."

This was no way to get his toast buttered.

"Trout, you can be replaced." In a low, threatening growl, "You are on your way to Congress. A prince with wealth and power in a New World Order—"

"In exchange for which I am willing to give up my soul."

"In exchange for which you were to give up that foolish blue-collar sense of self-righteousness. We serve for the improvement and betterment of mankind—"

"You serve for the improvement and betterment of Joe Wiedersham."

Justin Cobb bounced off the doorframe and moved toward Trout. Trout thrust a finger at him, like a sword. "Don't even think it, ass-wipe."

Wiedersham slowly rose to his feet. Trout backed away, his eyes darting suspiciously, palms extended in defense, thin hair tousled over his forehead, the cuff of one trouser leg stuffed into the top of an argyle sock.

"Dennis, go home and sober up. You're not thinking clearly."

"I'm thinking clearly for the first time. Joe, we're in bed with communists who want to destroy the country. A rat's nest of them all the way to the White House. We're dupes. Worse than dupes. A dupe is gullible and naïve and stupid. We *know* what we're doing, which makes it evil. It disgusts me, sickens me to my stomach to think how I went along because of selfishness and your nagging ladder-climbing sister. I should have married a fucking snake instead. A snake's family has more principle—"

"Get out of here!" Wiedersham shouted in sudden fury.

Alarmed, Liz appeared in the doorway behind Cobb. She ducked back out of sight.

"You're finished, Trout. Through!" Wiedersham raged. "I tried to give you a chance for Marilyn's sake. I should have known you didn't have the balls for it."

Maybe it was the liquor. Whatever, Trout felt better than he had in ages. He parted his lips and expelled a loud, insulting burp that eased the pain in his gut like Maalox never could.

"So what now, brother-in-law?" he jeered. "Are you going to have me hung in a cemetery? Shot? OD'd? Killed in a car crash? Do you remember the advice you gave me on how to survive in politics? 'Everybody has something to hide,' you said. 'Find out what it is and you have 'em by the short hairs.' Joe, I took your advice. Fuck with me and Zenergy News will know everything. You and this piece of shit—" He jerked a thumb at Cobb—"can go suck air. Fuck both of you."

He felt good. Even though his eye was tic'ing like mad. He turned his back on Wiedersham—that felt good too—and without another word marched *out.* Liz at the front desk looked pale and frightened. He did not notice Cobb follow him out of the building.

# Chapter Seventy-One

## Washington, D.C.

Brandi was working the lunch shift at *The Fountains*, Judy's favorite low-class bar/restaurant tucked appropriately back behind the bail bondsman office. Dennis Trout took a stool at the far end of the bar down from a bleached blonde wearing tight everything who reminded him of Judy and therefore acerbated his foul mood. Brandi served him his usual.

"Another tough day screwing the voters?" she sniped. Judy must have told her about his campaign, or else she had seen him on TV.

He flipped her off with a middle finger. "Screw them."

"See if I vote for you."

"You have to be able to read the ballot first. Keep the drinks coming and keep your mouth shut."

Brandi kept them coming, as icy to him as the drinks she served. His quarrelsome posture warned off anyone else who might think to occupy the stool next to him. Sitting there with his blood pressure pumping the top limits, stewing over dupes and dupery. His old dad had warned him: "There are more commies in Washington than I saw all the time I was in Vietnam."

His father had served with the 101st Airborne. He returned, married, and built a successful real estate business in Illinois before he turned, briefly, to politics. He did two terms in Congress before he fled, declaring, "They ought to have listened to Joe McCarthy."

Trout personally knew at least one hundred members of the House and Senate who had come out of the closet and were now self-proclaimed Marxists, Maoists, communists or socialist sympathizers. All working toward a Utopian society, no matter how many Homers had to be sacrificed to achieve it.

Brooding, he sucked the dregs from his drink and crushed the ice between his teeth before he knuckled the bar for another refill. Until this morning in Wiedersham's office, he had so successfully repressed his conscience that he wasn't sure he still possessed one. He had come so close to getting what he thought he wanted. What had spurred his downward spiral? Booze and bimbos, as Wiedersham asserted?

It had to be the notebook. Writing everything down encouraged personal analysis and self-awareness. Not good traits for politicians who bowed at the altar of self-deception. Now, the drunker he got, the more clearly he saw things. These people—Wiedersham's people, President Anastos' people, Zuniga's people—spoke with tongues as forked as the roads that led to Washington, D.C. Through the magic of their political dupery and a compliant press, Stalinists were being alchemized into civil libertarians, Marxists into defenders of "the working man," murderers like Mao and Lenin and Castro into peace activists. Expropriation of private property became land reform. Tyranny, theft and seizure of personal wealth were "social justice."

People used to laugh at Pop for warning against Marxists taking over colleges and high schools, the news media, politics and other American institutions.

Trout missed his dad. Sitting alone at the bar, he had never felt so isolated or vulnerable in his life. Marilyn had always cared more about her pink poodle than she did him. Judy abandoned him to go home to Bugfuck. Spasms in his eye blurred his vision. His belly ached and he thought about the Maalox in his briefcase. He placed his foot on the briefcase to make sure it was safe. He carried the notebook in it wherever he went.

He took out his Blackberry and dialed Judy's cell. There was no answer. *Slut!* She was probably still in Bugfuck screwing her cousins. She was no different than that trailer trash intern who sucked Clinton's knob in the White House toilet.

On second thought, it was *he* who was fucked. He should have known it the moment he turned his back on Wiedersham and walked out of the office. It had been a foolish act of defiance, blurting out about his "insurance" and threatening to release it to Zenergy News. Brother-in-law or not, Wiedersham wasn't likely to give him a pass. He was lucky if he didn't end up dead like so many others who stood in the way of progress.

Brandi delivered a fresh Whiskey Sour. It sloshed over onto the bar. Scowling with fury, Trout recoiled to keep from getting splashed. When he looked up, he glimpsed a familiar figure near the door foyer. His tongue froze against the roof of his mouth. He caught only a glance before the figure disappeared out the door, but it was enough for Trout to be sure. Justin Cobb, Wiedersham's Chief-of-Staff and chief lackey, must have followed him.

"Sorry about that," Brandi apologized sincerely, wiping up the spill.

Trout kept staring at the front door, barely aware of her. Something cold and clammy stirred inside the liquor fumes that befogged his poor brain. He went in an instant from don't-give-a-shit inebriation to mere muddled drunkenness.

"Look, I'm sorry about—" Brandi tried to apologize again.

The muscles in Trout's eye were twitching insanely. Brandi stared.

"Are you all right?"

"Bring me coffee. Black."

The coffee was hot and as bitter as his life. He slugged it down, only half-aware of the TV behind the bar turned to CNN. What the hell was he going to do now? He had made his bed, as Judy would have put it, and now he had to lie in it.

In a moment of weakness, of regret, and of cold fear that sobered him even more than coffee, it occurred to him that perhaps all wasn't lost after all. He still might be able to retrieve his life, make amends. Marilyn was right. Without her and Wiedersham, he was just another minimum-wage slob out in the streets with the other Homers.

Impulsively, his heart racing, he dialed his home number, prepared to take Marilyn out to *Komi's* for dinner, send her roses, kiss her ass and her brother's ass and Reggie's too, if that was what it took. He would even give up Judy.

Marilyn picked up on the first ring. "Trout, you dirty sonofabitch!"

"Wha—?"

She hung up on him.

He sat there in a funk staring sightlessly at the TV screen behind the bar. He pushed back his coffee cup and ordered another Whiskey Sour. Brandi looked at him, but brought it anyhow.

The more he thought about what happened, the more furious he became. He'd had it up to *here* by the time he gulped down still another drink. He called home again. The answering machine picked it up. Marilyn had changed the message on it.

"*Trout,*" it taunted, "*you and your slutty tramp can both go to hell.*"

Wiedersham must have told her. Fuck them both very much, thank you. He didn't need either of them. He dialed again. This time he left a message of his own.

"We'll meet you there in hell, bitch."

He glared at the TV. To his surprise, a photo of Judy and him appeared on TV. He recognized the setting—from the time he took Judy to New York when he met "John." Apparently, someone had followed them there to collect "insurance" for Wiedersham. A voiceover from behind the photo narrated in a smarmy tone:

"Leading Illinois congressional candidate Dennis Trout involved in steamy love nest with former hooker. She is identified as Judy Sparks-Taylor, cousin of Homeland Security Agent Ron Sparks, who was found hung by militia members in an Oklahoma cemetery..."

Pop always said people ate their own when their own stepped out of line.

Had he been sober and therefore more aware of himself when he left *The Fountains*, he might have noticed how his left foot dragged slightly. His eye also tic'd, like the shutter of a digital camera gone ape. Bile rose in his throat and he felt it surging through his veins. Numbness set it on the left side of his face. His toast had been buttered all right—with rancid fat.

A beginning rain turned the late afternoon as gray and gloomy as his inner weather. Naturally. God was going to piss on him too. He hunched his neck into his shoulders and trudged to the parking lot across the street where he left the BMW he rented at the airport. He was soaked by the time he reached it, chilled to the bone already, with water streaming from off his head and making his balding look more pronounced.

He tossed his briefcase into the passenger's seat and looked around before sliding underneath the steering wheel. There was a dark four-door sedan parked across the lot from him. Rain made it difficult to be sure, but he thought he saw two figures occupying it. He flipped them off with savage fury, jumped into the BMW, and fishtailed off the lot onto 6th Street. The dark sedan followed.

A half-hour's drive later, he carried his briefcase into Judy's apartment, letting himself in with his key, bolting and chain-locking the door behind him. He walked through the silent kitchenette-living room and into the bedroom. Missing her and angry with her at the same time, muttering deep in his throat where resentment and anger formed.

On Judy's dresser he discovered the gold locket he gave her, which she always wore between her cleavage. He picked it up, glared at it, then wrapped the delicate chain around his knuckles and ripped it to pieces. He ground the locket beneath his heel when it fell to the floor.

He found what he was looking for in the drawer of the nightstand next to her bed. Homers believed in God, guns and NASCAR. He checked to make sure it was loaded, then stuffed the .357 S&W revolver into the waistband of his suit pants.

The notebook was no longer inside his briefcase when he exited the apartment building. He carried the gun in his other hand against his thigh. Rain fell harder than before. Through its skeins he saw the ominous dark sedan that had followed him from *The Fountains*. It was parked down the block. Exhaust emitted into the cold, wet air told him its engine was running.

Both front doors suddenly popped open. Two men in raingear and hats pulled low jumped out and hurried toward him, walking in a way that let him know they meant business. Trout made a break for his BMW, dragging his left foot. The two men ran to cut him off, their footsteps pounding on concrete and splashing through puddles.

Realizing he couldn't reach his car ahead of them, he whipped up the .357 and fired. Two quick shots that, for all he knew, sent slugs ricocheting all the way across the city; it was the first time he had fired a gun since he was a kid at home with Pop.

The two men were near enough for Trout to see the shock that swept Justin Cobb's face underneath his hat. He and the other character did a nervous little jig in the rain, like puppets, before they ducked for the cover of a line of Boston pears and their hands fumbled to draw weapons from underneath their raincoats. Obviously, they had expected Trout to be the puss he had always been or they would have approached more cautiously.

Trout winged another shot in their direction for good measure. It sent both attackers flopping belly down into the rain-swollen gutter. He was laughing wildly, maniacally, as he roared off in the BMW and turned toward Takoma Park and home.

## Illinois Congressional Candidate/Wife Found Dead

***(Takoma Park, Maryland)****—Late this afternoon, police responded to a neighbor's call for help to find Illinois congressional candidate Dennis Trout and his wife Marilyn dead in their fashionable eastside residence. Police described the bloody scene as an apparent murder-suicide.*

*"It appears Trout murdered his wife Marilyn, then turned the gun on himself," said a Homeland Security detective. The couple's poodle was also shot to death.*

*Marilyn's brother, Senate Majority Leader Joe Wiedersham, said Trout may have "gone off the deep end" after the news media exposed his extramarital relationship with a Washington, D.C. prostitute...*

*"Dennis was a dedicated public servant," Wiedersham said. "He was leading the polls to become the next congressman from Illinois' Ninth District. The people lost a great man who would have fought on their behalf. I have lost my only sister and, until he let the pressure destroy him, a loyal friend..."*

# Chapter Seventy-Two

## Scranton, Pennsylvania

Limping on his bad leg, James Nail paced his one room digs, glowering at his watch and aimlessly stopping to look out through the window at the sunrise over Scranton. He felt weak and nauseous, having suffered a relapse after Sharon left. The doctor no longer visited, but he had left a supply of antibiotics. They seemed to help, but his injuries were still suppurating yellow exude.

He returned to the sagging sofa and the stack of books on the end table that Sharon left for him to read before she returned to New York. He hadn't realized how woefully ignorant he had been. He and—presumably, most other Americans—until Sharon took it upon herself to oversee his education on the major issues of these troubled times. He picked up the copy of *Bloodland's Europe: Between Hitler and Stalin* and turned to a dog-eared page. He tried to read to keep his mind occupied and off Sharon and what she might be up to concerning the secret international meetings and her determination to infiltrate and expose them.

He thought of Jamie and how he had failed her. She took after her mother Connie, who had been a Progressive rabble rouser in college. Jamie and her goofy boyfriend Rupert with their Che Guevara and Mao T-shirts rabble-roused a new generation through ACOA, PEIU, Open Societies and other Leftwing networks. The most enthusiastic supporters and enforcers of Josef Stalin's destructive policies in the old USSR were the younger people who had been "educated" in the Soviet schools and believed in the promise of the new system.

Socialism had failed wherever it was attempted, commonly in the deaths of millions. Karl Marx predicted that free enterprise and the ruling middle class would be overthrown into a classless society in which all means of production would be publicly owned. There would be no need for government in such a perfect society. Everyone would be "equal." There would be "social justice."

Only, government under socialism never seemed to wither away; it only grew stronger and more oppressive. The results of socialism in the United States, if the nation continued down this path, were as predictable as they should have been in the old Soviet Union or in Hitler's Germany. Stalin and Hitler were directly culpable in thirteen million deaths.

"Socialism in general has a record of failure so blatant that only an intellectual could ignore or evade it," economist Thomas Sowell wrote.

Between 1931 and 1933, Nail read in *Bloodlands*, the Soviets created famine when the Communist government seized food from farmers to feed city industrial workers. The famine, along with deportations to gulags and mass murder of hundreds of thousands of resisters, almost wiped out the country's food producers. A similar series of events might be playing out in the United States. There were already warnings of impending food shortages due to inflation and Federal regulations against farmers. According to this morning's Zenergy News, more than three thousand people were lining up in Washington, D.C. waiting for food handouts.

*Bloodlands* painted a grim picture of America's likely future under Marxist control.

*As the state police, the OGPU, found itself obliged to record, in Soviet Ukraine "families kill their weakest members, usually children, and use the meat for eating..." One mother cooked her son for herself and her daughter. One six-year-old girl, saved by other relatives, last saw her father when he was sharpening his knife to slaughter her...*

*The good people died first. Those who refused to steal or prostitute themselves died. Those who gave food to others died. Those who refused to eat corpses died. Those who refused to kill their fellow men died. Parents who resisted cannibalism died before their children... The boys and girls lay about on sheets and blankets, eating their own excrement, waiting for death...*

*Several women...formed "something like an orphanage... The children had bulging stomachs; they were covered in wounds, in scabs; their bodies were bursting. We took them outside, we put them on sheets, and they moaned. One day the children suddenly fell silent, we turned around to see what was happening, and they were eating the smallest child, little Petrus. They were tearing strips from him and eating them. And Petrus was doing the same, he was tearing strips from himself and eating them, he ate as much as he could. The other children put their lips to his wounds and drank his blood. We took the child away from the hungry mouths and we cried..."*

*A black market arose in human flesh; human meat may even have entered the official economy... In the villages smoke coming from a cottage chimney was a suspicious sign, since it tended to mean that cannibals were eating a kill or that families were roasting one of their members... More than one Ukrainian child had to tell a brother or sister: "Mother says that we should eat her if she dies..."*

Fellow-traveling Progressives in the United States had aided and abetted Stalin. Walter Duranty, the New York Times correspondent in Moscow, covered up the Great Famine and Stalin's effort to "socialize" the country. He maintained that the mass deaths through hunger served a higher purpose.

"You can't make an omelet without breaking eggs," he was famously quoted as saying.

"To such people and their counterparts today," Sharon liked to point out, "the ends justify all means."

Restless as a caged rat, Nail rose from the sofa and paced to the room's single window, slipping the curtain aside to let in a thin bar of morning sunlight. He tried raising Sharon again on his new TracPhone. She hadn't called him last night as she usually did to let him know she was okay.

He reached her voice mail. He dialed the studio and learned she was "on assignment."

He tuned the TV to Zenergy, hoping he might learn something. Someone with a British accent was explaining how the Federal Reserve was monetizing the national debt by printing and distributing another nine hundred *billion* dollars in "job stimulus funds," making gigantic inflation as certain in the U.S. as monetizing had in Weimar Germany three quarters of a century previously.

"By the end of the year," the Brit predicted, "one quarter of Americans will not be able to afford food. A loaf of bread will cost twenty-three dollars, a small can of Folgers coffee seventy-five dollars. Orange juice will be going for forty -five dollars, Domino sugar for sixty-two the pound, a chocolate candy bar for fifteen dollars..."

Time was running out. For the nation. And for Sharon. At least three times she had survived attempts against her life because, as she put it, God and James Nail were looking out for her. Opposition media had strived to dig up dirt to smear her reputation. That wasn't working fast enough. She was still on the air shining the light on cockroaches.

Sharon needed him. Nail had not felt this helpless since the helicopter gunmen opened fire on the crowd at ORU and he couldn't reach Jamie in time to save her. He should never have let Sharon return to New York alone. Like a wounded fugitive ex-cop could do anything to help her when he barely had the strength to cross a parking lot or a street.

Nail returned to the sofa. On the battered coffee table in front of him lay two snapshots side by side—one a publicity photo of Sharon, the other of his daughter Jamie. Nail rubbed his eyes. Suddenly prompted by the chilling thought that the proximity of the photos to each other might in some way foretell a common tragedy, he separated them by the length of the table.

He had never cried for his lost daughter. Cops didn't cry, *couldn't* cry. Now he did, all alone, wounded and feverish, hiding out in a rented room. Sobbing into his hands, his body wracked with the effort, ashamed for his weakness, yet unable to help himself. What had happened to him and to all the other Americans that they could allow this to be happening *here?*

After awhile, he stopped weeping for Jamie, for all those long-dead Russian children, for himself, for his country. He lifted his wet face from the palms of his hands. His blue eyes hardened as they settled on the 30.06 Winchester leaning in a corner of the room.

*My God, what fools people were.*

## Impending Food Crisis Predicted

**(Washington)—***"Is the Earth running out of food? That's what sociologists warn if world leaders don't act now and negotiate food security policies at this week's Climate Change talks in Cancun."* Time magazine.

*Scarce food, like oil and energy, could shape global politics over the next decades. That's the warning coming from Washington as global food demands collide with strained supply sources. High prices or shortages could destabilize not only poor countries but richer ones as well. The present food price surge is the highest in 38 years. It has already triggered food riots in about two dozen countries around the world and prompted demonstrations and protests in American cities...*

*"Americans have no Constitutional right to produce, obtain and consume the foods of their choice," said Sam Shrader, head of the President's Office of Information and Regulatory Affairs. "There is no deeply rooted historical tradition of unfettered access to food of all kinds..."*

*In a statement today, President Anastos promises to recruit unemployed workers, using conscription if necessary, and truck them to rural areas to work on communal farms for the American people...*

# Chapter Seventy-Three

## Colorado Rockies

Big C and Tom Fullbright broke camp and were up and on the march as soon as dawn provided enough light to illuminate the trail. They munched energy bars and sipped water from canteens for breakfast. They emerged into open elk pastures and rocky outcroppings above the tree line and continued climbing heavily to bare ridges spotted with old snow that made Big C think of Sno Cones.

He took out binoculars to glass the opposite ridge. According to Carolyn, the detention camp should lie about fifteen miles further, in a valley between two lesser mountain ranges. He still had difficulty wrapping his mind around the idea of death camps in America.

Detecting nothing so far except more timber and hills and a herd of elk in a clearing, he and his sidekick dropped down from the Divide and worked their way west through rugged, boulder-strewn forest. It took little imagination to see why these were the *Rocky* Mountains.

At mid-afternoon, they climbed out of a steep canyon to the crest of a low mountain range. While they took a break and gnawed on strips of high-protein beef jerky, Big C scanned for the camp with binoculars, finally locating some kind of new construction all but concealed in conifer trees. The largest building, as best he could tell at this distance, was five or six floors tall. Possibly a hospital nestled among long, two-story barracks freshly painted in camouflage green. High razor wire-topped fences with guard towers enclosed the compound.

He handed the binocs to Fullbright, who took a look.

"We need get closer," C said.

They worked their way to the next ridgeline, reaching it an hour or so before nightfall. The new position provided a better view of the installation. The two men lay side by side bellies down on a boulder-strewn outcropping.

Big C estimated one hundred acres or so of fenced compound with at least a dozen buildings, including the hospital and a large round structure made of brick and concrete that resembled a power plant. A stubby industrial chimney protruded from it. Big C saw no signs of "patients," although Carolyn had said six thousand people might be incarcerated here. The only people moving about were armed Green Shirts in combat garb. Big C counted nearly two hundred engaged in various military and security activities, plus others manning six guard towers on stilts overlooking the cantonment area. "Fields of fire" had been cleared on all approaches. Patrols in Humvees with mounted machineguns roved the perimeter.

A black-and-white camp robber bird making strange little sounds from a nearby thorn bush caught Big C's attention. It seemed to be warning them.

While they continued to watch, two buses trailing each other arrived on the narrow unpaved road from State 160 and stopped at the security gate. Guards armed with M2s mounted the buses to walk through and apparently check passengers. The setting sun was in Big C's eyes, preventing him from making out details of the passenger loads other than that both vehicles appeared packed.

Big C pointed out a thick electrical cable that ran from a kind of utility building near the guard shack to the fence. Fullbright nodded grimly. A raven soared in and landed on the top strand of wire. There was a flash, a puff of smoke and fire. The raven vanished.

"Damn!" Fullbright exclaimed.

After being admitted into the compound, the buses drove to a tunnel beneath the hospital, into which they disappeared. Big C took a closer look through the binocs at the power plant and its chimney. Shocking how much it resembled a more modern version of the furnaces he had seen in photos of Auschwitz or Dachau.

The bus drivers and accompanying security apparently intended to spend the night, as they did not reemerge from the tunnel. As evening's purple began to spread across the valley, a column of oily smoke issued into the clear Colorado air from the power plant, turning anvil-topped as winds aloft across the Divide caught it. Big C put down his binoculars but continued to stare at the camp as the reality of what was happening down there slowly sank in. He turned to look at Fullbright.

"Tom, you need to leave at first light to bring in our men," he said. "If there must be war, there no better place than this for it to begin."

# Chapter Seventy-Four

## Scranton, Pennsylvania

The early afternoon sky over New York City was overcast and threatening when Nail pulled his old Toyota onto the parking lot of *Hampton Arms*. He sat behind the wheel looking over the stately Redstone complex. The swimming pool and rear courtyard were unoccupied. The old saying about a criminal returning to the scene of his crime was largely unproven, yet he was back to where he shot and killed the Homie who menaced Sharon's life.

Feeling as exposed as a streaker in the Super Dome, he got out of his car and limped painfully toward the apartment building's rear doors, alert for anything out of place or potentially threatening. He was unarmed, having lost his sidearm in the alley dumpster the night he was shot. Carrying the 30.06 into a New York building would have been too conspicuous.

Sharon's apartment was the most logical place to begin his search. He didn't know what he expected to find. His face edged sharp dread as he took the elevator to the third floor. He smiled at a young couple who got on the elevator with him. They ignored him. He was grateful for the New Yorkers' proclivity to mind their own business.

He stopped at Sharon's door to take a long, ragged breath. He didn't smell anything; a corpse didn't start to smell for about forty eight hours or so. He let himself in with the key Sharon had given him.

The telephone was ringing. He waited inside the door until Sharon's answering machine picked it up and he heard her recorded voice inviting the caller to leave a message. The caller hung up.

Nail swept the apartment, looking for a body, although he didn't want to think of it that way. There was a bedroom, a study, a living room, a kitchen/dining room, and a bath with a Jacuzzi tub. The only thing he found out of place was the desk light shining in the study. At the end of his search, he leaned on the kitchen bar to catch his breath, unaware that he had been holding it the entire time out of trepidation for what he might discover.

He didn't know whether to feel relieved or not.

He went through the apartment a second time, this time looking for some clue that might indicate where she had gone. Her haunting fragrance lingered in the bedroom. He crushed her pillow to his face and drew in her scent until it seemed to fill his entire being. They were engaged to be married, yet this was his first time in the place she lived.

The prospect of her having vanished as a result of hostile intent drove him to near panic.

A cop had to keep his head.

Her answering machine was full of messages. He listened to them. There were several from various people at the Zenergy studios, several more from the security service that provided bodyguards, the content implying that she had given her security the slip, others from a "Rose Marie" and a "Lakisha," several from Jerry Baer's widow, and at least a half-dozen from Carl Patton, her executive producer.

*"Sharon, this is Carl. Pick up if you can hear me..."*

It troubled Nail that her landline automatically transferred unanswered calls from her home phone to her cell and apparently she wasn't answering her cell either. Nail had been dialing that number all day.

He checked the closets for empty hangers and missing luggage. Whenever Connie packed for a trip, she left discarded items in her wake to be picked up on her return. She claimed all women were like that. Everything in Sharon's closets seemed to be in order.

Carl Patton had provided two callback numbers on the answering machine. Sharon had said that Patton would always know where she was. "You can trust him," she said. "If you have to call him, identify yourself as 'Mr. Harker.' He'll know who you are."

Nail tried the office number first and was advised Patton was on assignment. He dialed the other number. Just as he was about to give up, Patton picked up in a breathless voice. From the background noise, he could have been in the middle of a riot or some natural disaster.

"This is Harker," Nail said. "I promised to call if I came to New York."

There was a pause on the other end, as if Patton was trying to remember. Then he said, "Oh! Mr. Harker! Good to hear from you. We need the extra sound system you promised. I'll meet you in Central Park." He forced a laugh. "You'll recognize me. I'm the skinny dude in front of the Zenergy News camera."

Obviously, Patton was wary of his cell being tapped.

"I probably won't see you in the crowd," Patton added, "so you'll have to look for me. I'm up to my butt in alligators."

## Congress Approves Strict Handgun Law

***(Washington)***—*In response to waves of Rightwing violence, Congress approved what lawmakers say is the strictest gun law ever passed in the United States. The new law bans sale of all firearms for a period of one year. It also prohibits current gun owners from stepping outside their house with a weapon, even onto their porches or into their garages.*

*The law furthermore mandates that police departments register every gun owner and every weapon he possesses. Guns not registered will be confiscated...*

*"There's just too much potential for violence by Right-wingers such as the Tea Parties and the militias who have declared their hostility against government," said Speaker of the House Barbara Teague. "We need protection for the people..."*

# Chapter Seventy-Five

## New York

Nail left his Toyota parked in a *Guest* spot at *The Hampton Arms* where it probably wouldn't be noticed and walked to Central Park. He heard clamor coming from the park when he was three blocks away. He took a breather against a lamp post before he entered off East 59$^{th}$, past two New York cops in riot gear. Several thousand people were gathered in raucous disarray around a hastily-constructed stage at the Duck Pond where speakers were apparently taking turns haranguing/entertaining them.

Radicals in beads, ragged jeans, red bandanas, face tats and piercings dominated the turnout, reminiscent of the 1960s *Days of Rage.* Protesters wearing hammers and sickles on their Tees chanted and thrust at the overcast sky various placards proclaiming the inevitable ascendency of **Social Justice** and **A Workers' Paradise**. Acrid clouds of marijuana smoke made Nail cough. A banner stretched above the stage proclaimed **National Socialist Forum: Transforming The USA**. Apparently, the law against demonstrations still applied only to Tea Parties and conservatives.

In order to blend in, Nail picked up a discarded sign that read **Yes We Can**. It made him cringe, but he waved it enthusiastically as he headed toward the stage, where he expected to find Patton and his Zenergy camera crew. Provided they hadn't already been mugged by this bunch or thrown out of the park by Homies and Green Shirts.

The guy currently addressing the crowd from the stage looked like some crackhead throwback with a gray ponytail, earrings and beard.

"We want to thank, like, the AF of L/CIO and PEIU for working hand in hand with CPUSA to make this event a happening. They helped organize buses from schools and passed out antiwar, antiracist, anti-capitalist literature...

"We must realize that, like, the Tea Party Movement and its auxiliaries is a white supremacist mob. And this mob is coming for you. We all want to raise people's consciousness, but, like, we also want to fight these people. Right? So I think it's like both things. We want to fight people who are on the other side of the barricade who are fighting us. We have to fight them. This is, like, we're a militant organization when it comes to the fight against gay bigotry, the fight against racism and sexism. The labor movement has this old saying—like, if you can't open their minds, open their heads..."

These people made Nail's skin crawl. He had caught glimpses of the future they pledged through the AmeriCorps in the Ozarks and the assassinations of Jerry Baer, Joshua Logan, Ron Sparks... Only the Lord knew how many others may have gotten in their way.

Sharon was in their way.

Nail pushed on through the raucous throng as he anxiously scanned for Patton and the Zenergy News' crew. He kept his head lowered to avoid any chance recognition, although these people seemed too whipped up to pay attention to anything except their inane chanted slogans. A great claw of lightning crashed through the darkening overcast, followed by a rumble of thunder that sounded like an angry crowd above shouting back at the angry crowd below in a lost language.

The crowd parted up front long enough to reveal the Zenergy logo on a shoulder camera. Nail recognized Carl Patton from his self-description: "Skinny dude in front of the camera." Nail made his way toward him. Patton was attempting to interview a Rupert look-alike carrying an **Execute War Criminals** sign.

"Sir, what war crimes are you protesting today?" Patton asked his victim, who looked as though he had been caught stealing watermelons.

"Racist fucking... You know. Like... *racists!"*

"Sir, sir. What *war* crimes are you protesting today?"

"You know. Like, war crimes. *All* war crimes... The Jews..."

"Do you know who organized this event today and who gave you that sign?"

"Ummm... I don't know..."

A second man slapped the microphone away from the watermelon thief's face.

"I did," he snapped.

"You did? What organization are you with?"

"We have no interest in talking with you."

"Moveon.org? The Institute for Open Societies? PEIU? Communist Party of the USA...?"

"We have no interest in talking with Rightwing media."

"Why did you give this man a sign to stand out here and protest today and he doesn't even know what he's protesting? He's not able to answer."

"We have no interest—"

"He's not able to answer for himself?"

"We—"

"He's holding a sign at a protest..."

Nail caught Patton's eye. Immediately, Patton gave up his non-interview and shuffled toward Nail with his cameraman in tow. He glanced at Nail's sign, smiled wryly, and thrust his microphone in Nail's face, as though to interview him.

"Nice touch," he said. "Mr. Harker, I presume? I recognize you from your picture on the news."

Nail looked at the microphone.

"It's turned off," Patton said. He was about thirty-five with sandy hair, sunken cheeks and a haggard brow.

Nail got right to the point. "Where's Sharon?"

Two armed youth in AmeriCorps combat regalia swaggered toward them. Patton shifted tones, saying, "Keep the mike to your lips, sir, while you're being interviewed. Sir, what are you protesting?"

The Green Shirts glared at Patton but barely noticed Nail. They moved on.

"These are some spooky people," Patton said.

"You have no idea."

When all was clear again, Patton said, "Sharon left the studio yesterday with her bodyguards to follow up a lead for her next program. She ditched her bodyguards, however, telling them she had to do this alone—"

"Did the lead have something to do with George Zuniga?" Nail demanded.

"She was working on a secret international summit called The Sustainable World Conference. George Zuniga is behind it. She was trying to get inside and obtain video to expose what these people are up to."

"She knows where it's being held?"

"I can't be sure."

"She hasn't checked in?"

"Not a word."

Nail was about to explode. "That's all you know? How could you let her do this?"

"I'm sorry—but you know how stubborn she can be."

Nail knew that well enough. He took a deep breath. The pain in his side ricocheted up through his chest and head.

"Are you all right?" Patton asked.

"Yeh." Nail had to move fast, but in which direction?

"Another thing you ought to know," Patton recalled. He briefly recapped his "Lonesome Rhodes" visit with Zuniga's henchman, John. "From the way he talked, Sharon may be on the President's Suppression list. No doubt you are too."

"Any idea how we can get hold of 'John?'" Nail asked, grasping for straws.

Patton shook his head. He thought a minute, frowning. "There was something else. A woman named Judy called the studio early yesterday morning asking for Sharon. A secretary took the message. When Sharon came off the set, she took a look at the message and hightailed it out. An hour later, Mitch and Roger—her security—came back in saying she had ditched them—"

The look on Nail's face stopped him. "Do you know Judy?" he asked.

"What did the phone message say?" Nail asked. He hadn't found anything from Judy on Sharon's answering machine. Sharon didn't trust her enough to give out those numbers.

"Pretty cryptic," Patton replied. "Something about chickens coming home to roost and she knew where they were roosting."

Nail cast aside his sign, wheeled and bolted toward the park exit, leaving Patton standing befuddled with his microphone and cameraman. The abruptness and ferocity of the downpour that caught Nail before he escaped Central Park, that drenched the socialist masses and sent them fleeing for cover, possessed the urgent quality of a perilous storm in a dream, unleashing terror from heaven that could not be tamed.

## Banker Pay to be Cut

***(Washington)***—*As police clashed with protesters in the streets of Europe and America, UN world leaders preparing for the forthcoming G-20 meeting closed ranks to limit pay for bankers worldwide and to initiate action to bring world banks under UN control. Risky behavior by banks has contributed to the global financial meltdown...*

# Chapter Seventy-Six

## Washington, D.C.

It was after midnight when Nail arrived at Judy Sparks-Taylor's apartment near George Washington University. The air smelled freshly scrubbed in D.C. and there were puddles of water on the streets. Nail was taking a chance showing up at Judy's apartment; there was no way to determine how much the Feds might know about her connections to Sharon, Big C and him. Still, it was a risk he had to take. Time might be running out for Sharon.

He circled the block twice while he looked for suspicious parked cars or other signs that hostile eyes might be watching her apartment. The neighborhood was mainly a college residential area, with stately old homes gone to seed and turned into apartments for let. The second floor light in the window of the address Judy supplied him on the phone was burning. He parked at the curb down the block and walked to the common door for the four or so apartments in the old house. It was unlocked; Judy said it would be. He stepped into the foyer and waited a few minutes to make sure he wasn't observed before he climbed the stairs to Judy's apartment.

She had sounded bad when he telephoned her before driving from New York. "I come back as soon as I heard about Dennis on the news," she explained. "I found somebody done broke in my apartment and trashed the place like they turned a sow loose in it."

"Stay put where you are, Judy, until you hear from me," he commanded.

Before leaving the Big Apple, he tossed his TracPhone into the bed of a wrecker stopped to haul away what was left of a car crash. Let the feds follow *that.* He had used the throwaway enough by this time that the NSA might have latched onto his signal.

He knuckled Judy's door and stood to one side out of the line of fire. She opened almost immediately; she must have been waiting up for him. She wore a long cotton robe and no makeup. Her Lady Clairol blond hair hung in wilted strings down to her shoulders. She looked as though she hadn't slept. She pulled him inside and bolted the door.

"It's all my fault Dennis got hisself kilt," she wailed. "If I hadn't gone gallivanting off to Oklahoma with Corey..."

It was news to Nail that Big C had taken her with him, but he didn't inquire into it. There were more pressing matters.

"Whatever happened to Dennis, it wasn't your fault, Judy. He brought it on himself."

Judy led him to the sofa. The cushions looked to have been knifed. "Whoever broke in did it," she explained, sitting on one end of the couch and rubbing her face wearily with both hands. "They pulled up the carpet and threw stuff out of the closet all over the floor. I ain't got it all cleaned up even yet."

"Any idea what they were looking for?" Nail asked her.

"It's been all over TV about me and Dennis," she snuffled. "Calling me a whore and all. It wasn't like that. They said Dennis shot his wife and then shot hisself. I don't believe none of it, James. *They* kilt him. As sure as God made little green apples, *they* did it. Listen to the message he left on my answering machine. I saved it."

She got up and turned it on to release a thin voice sounding highly stressed or drunk, possibly both: *"Judy, this is Dennis. I took your pistol. They're going to kill me."*

"Did you call the police?" Nail asked.

She nodded. "Neighbors told me there was an OK Corral out front. Somebody was shooting. It had to be Dennis."

She opened her hand to display a broken necklace and gold locket.

"The burglars didn't break in to steal," she said, staring at the locket with clouded eyes. "This is all I own worth much. Dennis gave it to me."

"You made a call to Sharon's studio," Nail reminded her. "What did you mean about the chickens coming home to roost?"

"You remember I told ya'all about Dennis' notebook? He wrote down stuff in it about them secret meetings she was talking about."

"They were looking for the notebook?"

"Some of these old houses has got secret places in the walls. Dennis knew about it. I guess he hid his notebook in it for safekeeping when he took my pistol. That's where I found it."

She got up and started toward the dinette table. Nail followed, struggling to rise from the sofa. He felt leakage from his wounds. Judy looked back.

"You're still hurting, James."

"A little stiff." A thick spiral notebook lay on the table. It looked well-used. "Is this it?"

He sat down at the table.

"This is the page about the secret meeting," Judy said, turning the pages for him toward the end of the notebook.

*Joe thinks I'm drinking too much. He's becoming a bigger nag than his sister. My stomach is upset all the time and I chunk up from stress when I get up in the morning. That's what's wrong with my eye too. I could say I had no idea what I was doing when I let brother-in-law draw me into all this, but I'd be lying to myself. I made a pact with Satan and now Satan demands his pound of flesh.*

*These people are as serious as a dead baby. Millions of people will be killed before this is all over. Next Monday, Joe and others like him are gathering with George Zuniga at Lake Ontario for The Sustainable World Conference to "establish new rules of international law and to rearrange the entire financial order." They're making plans to collapse the U.S. economy and implement martial law to install Anastos as the puppet in a communist regime...*

Trout had been conscientious in dating his entries. "Next Monday" was two days away.

"Did Sharon call you back?" Nail asked.

"She got all excited when I read the part in the notebook about Lake Ontario. Like she knew exactly where it was. I tried to warn her, what with Dennis being murdered and all. I don't think she was listening, James. That girl is done about to become a chicken in a house full of coyotes."

## Rage From The Right: A Report

***(Washington)****—A report issued by the "Countering Violent Extremism Working Group" warned that so-called "patriot cartels" like the Tea Party Movement that see the Federal Government as part of a plot to impose one-world government on America have come roaring back after years out of the limelight. The report defines Rightwing extremists as "divided into those groups, movements and adherents that are primarily hate-oriented (based on hatred of particular religions, racial or ethnic groups) and those that are mainly anti-government, rejecting federal authority in favor of state or local authority, or rejecting government authority entirely."*

*"The Tea Parties and other such groups are shot through with veins of radical ideas, conspiracy theories and racism," said Senate Majority Leader Joe Wiedersham (D-Ill).*

*"They caught fire after the election of President Anastos," said Speaker of the House Barbara Teague (D-CA). "There is little difference between them and mass murderer Timothy McVeigh who bombed the Murrah Building in Oklahoma City. They are all terrorists or potential terrorists one match away from lighting the fuse..."*

*The report suggests worsening economic woes, potential new international restrictions on firearms, and the recruiting and radicalizing of returning military veterans are leading to the emergence of terrorist groups with violent potential. The report also warns law enforcement agencies and citizens to watch out for and report anything suspicious, such as: vehicles with anti-government bumper stickers; large secret meetings; Constitutionalists; individuals with radical ideologies based on Christian views; and individuals who oppose illegal immigration, increased federal powers, restrictions on firearms, abortion, taxes, and who express conspiracy theories about the loss of U.S. sovereignty...*

# Chapter Seventy-Seven

## Colorado

An Apache gunship flew over on two separate occasions while Big C maintained surveillance on the detention camp and waited for Tom Fullbright to return with the militias. He rooted into dense brush not yet denuded by approaching autumn to hide while the chopper patrolled the surrounding mountains and forests before it returned north toward the Air Force base at Colorado Springs. Big C guessed he would have no more than an hour tops to pull off an operation against the hospital before air cover responded with missiles and Gatling guns.

Militiamen were going to die here in Colorado. The "mental health facility" was so well-armed and well-defended that a bunch of common Americans could never hope to overcome it by direct force. Victory depended on stealth and cunning. Even so, the inevitable price the militia must pay was worth it if enough prisoners could be liberated so that Americans saw what was happening and began to react.

*If* the country hadn't become so cowed-down that it was incapable of acting. *Newsweek* and others in the mainstream media were already declaring the U.S. a socialist state. *Now, aren't you much better off for it?*

More than a quarter of all Americans didn't know from whom the United States gained its independence; eighty percent couldn't name more than one of the Bill of Rights; most had never read the Constitution or the Declaration of Independence; ninety percent of college grads couldn't pick out Iraq on a map, even though the nation had been at war there since 2003...

So, take the average American conditioned to look to government to supply his needs and take care of him. He lost his job. The dollar bottomed out, his kids were hungry, he was afraid and angry, there was rioting and chaos everywhere... And, then, there *he* came, riding up on a white horse. *The One*. Promising, "I can restore order. All you have to do is give up freedom, which at best is messy and nasty."

Did Average Joe Six-Pack ask about the Constitution?

The death camp in Colorado was one in a long tradition of such camps established to eliminate dissidents and dangerous reactionaries throughout socialism's dark history.

Big C's cynicism failed to improve when Tom Fullbright returned, arriving like a shadow out of morning mist to inform the ex-cop that only thirty-six Defenders and fifteen from Colorado's Sons of Liberty volunteered for the mission. These few were waiting a mile back at the end of a narrow box canyon, crowded underneath a ledge to avoid detection from the air. Fifty-three men total, counting Fullbright and Big C, to take on an armed, electrified fortress defended by machinegun-equipped Humvees, armed troops and helicopters.

"I guess most didn't mind a fight," Fullbright alibied with a shrug. "But they consider this suicide. So they went home."

Big C thought of the raven who torched itself on the electrified fence.

Most of the militiamen who accompanied Fullbright were in their late twenties and thirties. One or two, like old Tump Kinsey from Hanson, were Vietnam vets. A few were Iraq veterans. Sad, Big C thought, that none of them were of the under twenty-five, dumbed-down, entitlement-brainwashed generation.

The army, if such a shabby lot could be dignified with the title, sprawled about underneath the ledge, rested against their backpacks, or stood leaning against the rock wall sipping from canteens. They wore turkey-hunting camouflage or scraps of army uniforms and were armed with everything from hunting rifles and shotguns to pistols of various calibers. Tump Kinsey carried a Chicom AK-47 he brought back from Vietnam. One of the Sons of Liberty thought to set up security at the mouth of the box canyon with a .50-caliber Browning machinegun. A weapon worth its weight in gold.

"Good job," Big C complimented the gunner, a Chicano named Campione.

"I brung two cans of armor-piercing ammo," the man said. "You think this won't stick a crick in their asses?"

After introductions all around, Big C squatted with a stick to sketch in the dirt while the men formed a grim circle around him. The briefing turned even more somber as the big commander detailed in frank terms what they were apt to encounter and his concept of the operation.

"This the road coming in to camp," he explained, sketching with the stick. "Two transport buses arrive every day packed with patients. The road twist and turn between a creek and the mountains, which mean they have to drive slow. That's good. Buses drive through the gate—*here*—and go to this tunnel underneath the hospital, where they stay overnight. Corpses are burned after nightfall to cover smoke coming from the furnace stack."

Some of the men paled. Others looked angry.

Big C continued his briefing. The militia force would break down into three elements. Big C and one element would hijack the buses on the road coming in and use them as Trojan horses to get past the gate guard and into the compound. Once inside, they would eliminate the gate guards and deactivate the electrified fence to allow Tom Fullbright and his component to break through on the north and create a diversion while Big C's men released and rescued prisoners.

"We can't take out all the prisoners on two buses," one of the men pointed out.

"Unfortunate," Big C acknowledged. "But we still let everybody loose. Tear a hole in the fence so those we can't get on buses can make a run for it. That a better chance than they got in there. What important is that we rescue as many as we can so they tell the country what is going on here."

If at all possible—and if he was still alive—Lieutenant Ross had to be among those on the buses. Big C owed that to Jack's wife.

Campione would lead the third, smaller element consisting of the .50-cal machinegun and marksmen armed with hunting rifles.

"You set up on this ridge—*here*," Big C instructed, pointing with his stick to the crude map in the dirt. "Success depend on you knocking out the roving Humvees so they don't get through the gate at us. They going to have Apache gunships in the air if we not out of there in less than one hour. Remember that, everybody, and keep the timing going."

Big C paused and looked around the circle of tense faces.

"Once the mission done," he said, "haul ass when you see the buses exit the gate. We will set the buses in defensive posture three hundred meters down the road and wait until everybody aboard or accounted for. There should be enough confusion to give us some time."

Withdrawing, the loaded buses would return to State 160 and haul over Wolf Creek Pass to the small lakes where the militiamen had concealed their private vehicles down a barely-passable dead-end road. If all went well, Big C's army, along with those they rescued, would be scattered and in hiding while the Feds were still trying to sort through the chaos left behind at the detention compound. Several thousand escapees running all over the hills should keep Green Shirts and Homies occupied for days. With more luck, Zenergy News and Sharon Lowenthal would be on the story within hours after things erupted.

"Everything must be ready tomorrow evening," Big C concluded. "Questions?"

What followed was more a mixture of nervous comments and doubts than questions. A tall, raw-boned man from the Colorado contingent seemed to be having the most second thoughts.

"We're going to be shooting other *Americans?*" he protested nervously.

Big C understood the man's reservations; he had read about the Civil War and brother against brother.

"We all got to deal with it in our heart and conscience," he said. "In the Ozarks, The Defenders saw Green Shirts preparing execute innocent Americans with bullets through they skulls. What we got to understand is we fighting evil. They are murdering people down there inside that electric fence and harvesting they organs. There are other facilities being built like it all over this nation. Gulags like Solzhenitsyn wrote about. Are we to stand by like helpless children and *watch?* Or will we stand up like men?"

He stopped in front of the squeamish Coloradan. "What's your name, soldier?"

"Potter, Fred."

Big C turned to the Colorado commander and ordered him to disarm Potter and assign someone to watch him. No one must be allowed to leave because of doubts and possibly betray the operation.

"Anybody else have a problem?" Big C asked.

The rest of the force expressed solidarity; this was something that *had* to be done.

"Good," Big C approved. "If a bunch of World War Two Jews armed with pistols in Warsaw ghetto could stop the Wehrmacht in its tracks, then we should be able bust out a few prisoners."

A Baptist preacher from Mazie, Oklahoma, suggested they ask for God's guidance in these perilous times. Rough men from the hills and mountains and plains of Oklahoma and Colorado, tough men of the soil, independent, resilient men, many of whom were military veterans, men of character and strength and courage, men like those who had served at Valley Forge, all bowed their heads.

## FAD Bill Passes: Zenergy News To Be Indicted

***(Washington)***—*Speaker of the House Barbara Teague (D-CA) kept the House in late session tonight in order to pass the Fairness of Airwaves Doctrine (FAD). President Anastos declared it an emergency measure to stem the tide of treasonous anti-government rhetoric that poisons the nation's airwaves, a vital step in restoring order to the nation. Senate Majority Leader Joe Wiedersham (D-Ill), one of the bill's original supporters, said FAD will go a long way in restoring "civil and inclusive dialogue" in radio and TV.*

*White House spokesman Dewey Gubbins said the Justice Department's first step would be to indict Zenergy News for conspiracy against the government. Zenergy has spearheaded a wave of hate directed against the President and his administration...*

# Chapter Seventy-Eight

## Washington, D.C.

Majority Leader Joe Wiedersham liked to boast that his second residence in Washington, D.C.—his first being in Chicago, both of them on the taxpayer's tab—was only a block away from the Georgetown redbrick where John F. Kennedy lived when he was nominated for the presidency in 1960. Georgetown was one of the most affluent and exclusive communities in the nation's capital, occupied by politicians, lobbyists and luminaries like Senator John Kerry, Former Secretary of State Madeleine Albright, and Watergate reporter Bob Woodward. *The Exorcist* had been filmed on 36th Street NW. Too bad, James Nail thought, that the entire town couldn't have also been exorcised.

He and Judy were en route in his Toyota to Wiedersham's residence. Judy knew the way. Dennis Trout had been showing off one day and drove her past JFK's house, in the process pointing out Wiedersham's mansion on N Street.

"These politicians got their gumption to live like this and call other people fat cats," she remarked. She had asked Trout how politicians get so rich.

"Connections," Trout replied. "We're going to live here after I win the election."

She hadn't asked him if by *we* he meant her—or him and Marilyn and Reggie.

Today's run on the Wiedersham estate was a recon to check out the lay of the land for tomorrow morning. According to the notebook, Wiedersham expected Trout to ride the limo with him on Monday—tomorrow—to the meeting site on Lake Ontario. Nail figured *he*, and Judy, would take Trout's place.

"Lake Ontario" seemed to have triggered something in Sharon when Judy read the passage from Trout's notebook to her over the phone. She must have somehow connected all the dots. Nail was convinced they would find Sharon at the secret summit meeting—if he could *persuade* Wiedersham to take them there.

While Nail drove, Judy filled him in on the meeting Big C and she had had with Marsha Ross and Carolyn at the Pizza Hut in Oklahoma City. The last she saw of Big C, he was rounding up the militia to rescue Lieutenant Ross from a secret detention center in Colorado.

"Corey treated me better than any man ever, like I'm a real person. I'm afraid I ain't never going to see him again either..."

Big C could take care of himself. Sharon, on the other hand, although resourceful and resilient, was on her way to a Devil's den from which even God might not be able to save her.

Judy had learned through Trout that his brother-in-law was so preoccupied with schedule that he even brushed his teeth and went to the toilet by the clock. He had a limo driver fired once for being five minutes late picking him up at his mansion to drive him to the office. Trout was counting on Wiedersham's obsession with punctuality to make what he had to do easier.

It was now quarter till seven. Trout told Judy that Wiedersham liked to be picked up at precisely seven.

Clouds hanging in the northern and eastern skies were translucent with diffused sunrise. There was a spray of rain in the air. Nail parked at the curb beneath the overhang of a giant spruce down the block from Wiedersham's place. He and Judy in the rusty old Toyota looked as out of place in this neighborhood as two whores in church. To cover their asses against nosy neighbors and even nosier cops and Homies, Nail had lifted a couple of magnetic signs off a parked truck and slapped them on either door of the Toyota: *Hughes' Landscaping Service.*

"Dennis wasn't no bad man at heart," Judy said while they waited. She stared at the broken locket and chain clutched in her hand.

Nail opened *The Notebook*, curious about what else he might discover in it. Entries in the thick steno pad went back for nearly a year, apparently to when Trout began struggling with his conscience. It was dynamite stuff alluding to conspiracies, betrayals, crimes, and suspected crimes...

*Joe was talking on the phone with that Homeland prick Vladimir when Tea Baggers were marching on the Capitol. I overheard him say, "Fuck them. Create an incident." After that, I heard the shooting...*

*It tears me apart not to tell Judy about her cousin. They were close; she talks about him quite a bit. I'm not sure what all this is about, how Joe can be involved in so much shit. This is mafia stuff, having Judy's cousin hanged. And in a cemetery...!*

*Nobody fucks with Joe. He's the go-to guy to get things done without anyone knowing. He talks to George Zuniga, to the President... Then strange things happen. Jerry Baer is gone, that judge from*

*Louisiana ODs, congressmen from New Hampshire have car crashes... You don't cross these people...*

*I think Joe is afraid of what that cop from Oklahoma will do. It seems the cop is out for revenge and if he finds out Joe was behind the helicopters... Well, he's already killed the shooters, but that might not be enough...*

Nail had to take a deep breath over that entry before he continued.

*These people are starting to scare me. All the Global Government talk. They're building detention camps, private armies, plotting euthanasia... Sometimes I feel like I'm living through the Stalin era...*

*Marilyn thinks I should be grateful to Joe for all he's doing for us. I'm beginning to question if having my toast buttered is worth it. They'll get rid of me too as soon as I'm no further use. Joe says President Anastos is a useful idiot and can be killed just the same as anyone else if he gets in the way or fails to live up to expectations...*

*Jerry Baer was a threat to what Joe calls "the Shadow Government." Then that Lowenthal babe takes over and she has to go...*

Judy nudged him. "There's a limo coming."

Black and long of the type contracted by the government from private companies to chauffeur around important politicians. It entered the opposite end of the street, eased slowly down the block in the misting rain, and pulled into Weidersham's drive. Two men occupied it. It was precisely one minute until seven.

A lean man wearing a trench coat and gangster hat got out of the passenger's side and walked to the front door, leaving the driver waiting with the limo engine running.

"I think that there's Justin Cobb," Judy said. "He took Dennis' place when Dennis started running for Congress. Dennis said he carries a gun. Dennis never did own one. I guess that's why he took mine."

In spite of the hat and trench coat, the guy looked more like a pencil dick with a calculator than a gangster packing heat. Still, Smith & Wesson could turn a wimp into Machinegun Kelly.

A fat man in a rumpled but obviously expensive raincoat came out of the house and hurried with Cobb to the limo. Cobb opened the back door to allow him to slide onto the back seat. Nail's eyes narrowed. He thought of the 30.06 in the trunk of his Toyota.

But for now, this corrupt piece of shit was more valuable alive than dead.

## Center Warns Against "Patriots"

***(New York)***—*A report this week issued by The Center for American Justice (CAJ) profiled "40 individuals at the heart of the resurgent patriot movement." The Federal Government considers CAJ its primary source for information regarding domestic terrorists from Rightwing militias, conservative and libertarian extremists. Here are the 40 names in order of perceived threat:*

*1. Sharon Lowenthal, host of Zenergy News' anti-government The Jerry Baer Show w/Sharon Lowenthal;*

*2. Rush Limbaugh, conservative radio talk show host;*

*3. Joe Bannister, former IRS special agent, tax protester and Tea Party leader;*

*4. Chuck Baldwin, pastor, syndicated columnist, Constitution Party presidential nominee;*

*5. Robert Crooks, Iraq war veteran, anti-illegal immigration proponent;*

*6. Larry Pratt, Tea Party leader, militia member, executive director of Gun Owners of America;*

*7. Stewart Rhodes, army veteran, Yale Law graduate, founding member of Oath Keepers;*

*8. Michele Bachman, U.S. Representative from Minnesota;*

*9. Ron Paul, U.S. Air Force veteran, medical doctor, U.S. Representative from Texas, former Republican candidate for President...*

# Chapter Seventy-Nine

## Colorado

From the tiny barred window of his cell, Lieutenant Jack Ross of the Tulsa Police Department had watched the buses arrive every day. As usual, one followed the other across the compound and disappeared beneath the "hospital" where he was being held. The windows of the buses were tinted opaque. Ross assumed the incoming "patients" were drugged, as he had been when he arrived by the same manner two weeks ago. When he revived, his abduction in Wichita and transportation here—wherever *here* was—seemed like the hazy memory of some bad dream. He was lying on a narrow military-style cot in a cold, bare room.

He opened his eyes and blinked twice at a burning light bulb on the ceiling. The ceiling and walls were painted in hospital beige. A voice asked, "What did you do?"

"Huh?"

He swung his legs gingerly to the floor and caught his head in both hands. He rubbed his face to restore awareness. Someone had stripped off his police uniform and replaced it with green hospital scrubs. His shoes and socks were gone. He looked up through his fingers after a moment. A skinny kid who appeared to be about eighteen or so sat on the other cot. He also wore scrubs.

"Where am I?" Ross murmured through his grogginess.

The kid shrugged. "Rocky Mountains, I think. We're mushrooms—kept in the dark and fed bullshit."

He got up and padded to the barred window. The pane was tinted red from the setting sun. He had to stand on tiptoes to look out.

"Buses come almost every night," he said, looking back at Ross. "They unload and go back the next morning for another load. People who come in here never go out again."

He walked back to his cot and sat down. "I'm Michael Smith. You can call me Smitty. What did you do?"

Ross looked around. Two cots, sink in one corner, toilet stool in the other. A framed slogan on the wall: **Social Justice Through Social Awareness**. What the hell was this—*1984?*

What *had* he done?

"What is this place?"

"They call it a mental health facility." Smitty swallowed hard, his Adam's apple bobbing. "It's an extermination camp."

Ross looked up sharply. Smitty continued in a hollow voice, "People are being murdered for organ transplants."

Ross struggled to his feet. "That can't be right, Smitty."

"I been here two weeks and you're my third roommate. Patients come in, none of them ever leave, but the hospital never gets full."

A quote from one of Sharon Lowenthal's programs flashed through Ross's mind. From Stalin: "*We will mercilessly destroy anyone who, by his deeds and his thoughts—yes, his thoughts!—threatens the unity of the socialist state.*"

Ross recalled the Department of Homeland Security Terrorist Watch List circulated to all police departments. It contained the names of over two million Americans considered "unreliable" or who posed a "threat" to the U.S. Government—a list that was growing by twenty thousand a month. Your name got on it if you had purchased and registered a firearm, spoke out against government policy, belonged to a Tea Party, became an Oath Keeper...

"Your name came up in the James Nail case," the new piece-of-shit TPD Police Chief, Bruton the Crouton, had warned Ross a few days before assigning him to in-service training in Wichita. "That's dangerous. A word to the wise. You're on The List."

Neither Ross nor Smitty was allowed to leave the cell, not even for exercise or a shower. They watched time pass and the buses arrive from through their one tiny window. One day, three stout "nurses" came in and strait-jacketed Ross, placed him on a gurney, and delivered him to an examination room for a thorough physical checkup that centered on his heart and eyes. On the way, he was pushed through halls lined with locked cells which he assumed to be filled with unfortunates like himself who had angered the government in ways they may not even have been aware of. Medical personnel dressed like normal doctors and nurses looked the other way as he was trunneled through. As though he didn't exist. Or that he was less than human. Or already dead.

"That's what they do," Smitty commented when Ross was returned to their cell. "You get one more exam before it's your turn and I get a new roommate."

Through the window, Ross could see a high barbed-and-electrified fence and a gate through which roving Humvees were constantly coming and going. Armed AmeriCorps Green Shirts ranged the compound. Occasional Apache helicopters thumped overhead. Almost every evening he saw covered gurneys being pushed toward the menacing concrete building to which a squat smokestack was attached. Smoke emitted from it almost every night, all night.

At least these people were practical. They harvested useful organs first.

Ross discovered that he and Smitty had common acquaintances—James Nail and Sharon Lowenthal. Smitty told him about his role in Nail's and Sharon's escape from the AmeriCorps camp in the Ozarks.

"They were going to shoot her in the head! I couldn't be a part of all that anymore. Detective Nail told me to go home to Chickasha and not say nothing to nobody. But they said I was seditious and came anyhow. They took my fiancée too. I don't know what's happened to her."

Ross wondered about his own wife.

Guards and nurses came for Smitty one afternoon. "It's my second exam!" he wailed. He had to be sedated and Ross had to be restrained in order for the aides to trundle the kid out of the cell. When they returned him an hour later, he was too frightened to stand. He lay on his cot, weeping.

"They want my eyes," he speculated. "That's what they were looking at. It's my turn. This is the way it happens. They'll take me tomorrow."

Smitty remained inconsolable and unable to sleep. Ross pounded on the steel door with his fists—but no one responded. As dawn approached, Smitty said, "Doctor Moulton works here. He's not like the others, but he's afraid. I asked him to call Miss Lowenthal or Detective Nail and tell them what's happened. People need to know."

They came for Smitty and took him away. It did no good to resist; the two prisoners were quickly overpowered. Ross's new roommate was an elderly former state representative from Arizona, whose offense, apparently, was his support of an Arizona anti-illegal immigration bill—a racist hate crime. He lay on his cot staring at the ceiling.

"This can't be," he anguished. "This simply cannot be happening. Not in America."

## Anastos Calls for "True Revolutionaries"

***(Washington)—****As he leaves for secret high-level economic meetings Monday with other world leaders, President Patrick Wayne Anastos vows to accelerate his drive to bring "hope and change" to the United States. He urged supporters to become "true revolutionaries" as they prepare for crucial political battles ahead.*

*"Radicalize the revolution," he exhorted, calling on allies to "create truly revolutionary groups, the vanguard of the people..."*

# Chapter Eighty

## Washington, D.C.

Neither Nail nor Judy slept well, she in the bed, he on the lumpy sofa in a cheap roach motel they rented under assumed names out on Route 29. Judy kept trying to call Big C's cell, but there was no answer, which further distressed her. Nail's concern for Sharon increased his own anxiety. Desperation seemed to contaminate the air they breathed.

"We're a doozy pair of vampire hunters," Judy commented dourly.

Morning arrived at long last with increased cloud cover that promised to produce more rain. They left the motel and breakfasted in the Toyota on coffee in paper cups and packaged donuts while they waited on the street down from the *Congressional Limousine Service,* the chauffeuring firm that provided service for Wiedersham and other important politicians.

At 6:00 a.m., Nail called the limo service on Judy's cell. While he waited for an answer, he looked out the Toyota's window to where the Washington Monument speared the low, dark clouds. More clouds obscured the dome of the Capitol Building at the other end of The Mall. The scene no longer inspired Nail; he had learned too much about the ruling classes in recent weeks.

"Congressional Limousine," a professional voice announced.

"This is Justin Cobb, Majority Leader Wiedersham's Chief of Staff," Nail said with feigned annoyance. "I'm calling to confirm that you have Senator Wiedersham down for the day and overnight."

"Just a moment, please, sir."

Nail heard papers rustling.

"Sir, we have you listed as point of contact."

"I am just reconfirming. Overnight to New York, correct?"

"Watertown, sir?"

"Good man. Second point. You're already late. You didn't remember that he needed it an hour earlier this morning?"

"It says the usual time here."

"An hour earlier," Nail snapped. "Good thing I *did* call to reconfirm."

"Yes, sir. Bill will leave right away to pick you up first as usual, Mr. Cobb."

"Is Bill our regular?"

It was doubtful whether either Cobb or Wiedersham bothered to learn the names of their chauffeurs.

"Sometimes we have to switch out drivers to cover sick days and the like," the dispatcher said. "Robert is your regular."

"I'll be waiting." Nail hung up, satisfied that their targets wouldn't smell a rat when a "substitute" driver showed up. Especially if the driver was female.

True to the dispatcher's promise, "Bill" pulled out of the parking garage minutes later in a black limo, tinted windows and all. Judy, now at the wheel of the Toyota, followed it for a couple of blocks before a red light caught it. She pulled abreast of it in the inside lane. Traffic was light this early in the morning near the university. The limo driver was not as wary as he might have been in a more dangerous part of the city where pizza delivery guys hesitated to go after dark. Bill therefore immediately powered down his window when Nail flashed his Tulsa detective's badge out the Toyota's window and pointed at the limo's rear tire, as though to indicate a problem with it.

Bill was an older guy, about fifty, wearing a black chauffeur's jacket and a military-type bill cap with the company's emblem on the peak. Smiling, Nail stepped out of the Toyota, stuck a pistol through the open window and pressed its muzzle against Bill's temple. *Toys 'R Us* marketed surprisingly realistic-looking toy guns.

"Dude, I don't carry no cash," the driver blurted out immediately.

Nail reached in and snatched the keys. "Move over."

Cold blue eyes, swarthy skin and the determined set of the jaw convinced Bill. Trembling, he scrambled across the seat to the passenger's side. Nail shot a quick look around to make sure there were no witnesses before he slipped under the wheel, restarted the engine and turned at the next red light. Judy followed in the Toyota until Nail parked and left the limo on a side street while they transferred Bill to the Toyota for transport to the roach motel. A few minutes later, they had him bound, gagged and relieved of his uniform on the floor of the cheap room, for which Nail had paid three days in advance. Judy donned Bill's coat and hat.

"I'll bring you more company," Nail promised Bill before they left him. "You'll be safe here. I'll call up in a day or so and have the police rescue you."

The guy's eyes walled about like balls on a pool table. Nail patted him reassuringly on the shoulder, locked the door and placed a *Do Not Disturb* on the knob. They returned to the parked limo on the side street and left the Toyota parked in its place after Nail retrieved the 30.06 Winchester from its trunk.

"You're not bleeding again?" Judy asked him when they were on the road again.

"I'm fine."

All the activity had reopened his wounds. The bandages felt wet against his ribs. He checked to make sure he wasn't leaking through his shirt.

Wearing Bill's uniform, Judy drove up to the door of Cobb's apartment on 16th. Nail lay concealed on the wide back floorboard behind the passenger's seat. The tinted windows prevented Cobb from seeing him until it was too late.

Cobb rushed out wearing his trench coat, gangster hat and a scowl. Judy jumped out to open the front passenger's door for him. Cobb stopped in surprise. She kept Bill's cap pulled low over her eyes and tilted her head low just in case Cobb had seen a photo of her somewhere. The only thing he seemed to notice was how well she filled out her jeans.

"You're early," he protested mildly.

"The Majority Leader called for an earlier pickup," Judy said with her most dazzling smile. She was playing her part to the hilt.

Cobb's frown vanished. He didn't bother asking why Wiedersham bothered making his *own* phone call. He was too busy hitting on Judy.

"Where have they kept *you* hid?" he asked with a wink.

"The limo service figures you ol' boys need the best," Judy bubbled. She stuck out her chest so the jacket parted to display cleavage. She bent over to offer more distraction while she helped him take his seat and buckle in.

"I've seen you somewhere before," Cobb said.

"I bet you say that to all the blondes."

Cobb hesitated for a moment to study her. He shook his head. *Couldn't be.* His eyes were still on the scenery down Judy's blouse when a pistol muzzle pressed against the back of his head. An edged voice warned, "I'd just as soon waste you as not."

Like most bullies, Cobb was a coward at heart when the chips were down. Nail reached across and relieved him of the 9mm Beretta he carried in a shoulder holster. Now he had a *real* gun.

In short order, Wiedersham's chief of staff found himself gagged and trussed head and foot in the motel room with the limo's chauffeur. Nail glanced at his watch. They would have to push it to arrive at

Wiedersham's house before he started trying to call Cobb to complain of tardiness.

"Mustn't keep the Majority Leader of the Senate waiting," Nail said.

# 22nd Amendment May Be Repealed

***(Washington)***—*The U.S. Congress has voted to begin proceedings to repeal the 22nd Amendment to the Constitution. The 22nd Amendment limits a president from serving more than two terms in office. President Anastos said additional terms will give him time to initiate reforms toward keeping his promises to ensure human happiness and well-being for everyone, rich or poor...*

# Chapter Eight-One

## Washington, D.C.

Two years ago, Zenergy executive producer Carl Patton had been leery about unleashing Jerry Baer into what some colleagues feared would become a new chapter of McCarthyism. Commies underneath every bed and all that. Except for Baer's assassination and now Sharon's disappearance, however, he regretted not one minute of Zenergy's campaign against tyranny.

There *were* commies underneath every bed, including the bed at the White House and others slept in by politicians like that evil son of a bitch Wiedersham. So many of them in D.C. all whispering "social justice" into the President's ear—Barbara Teague, Ira Romera, Duane Smith, George Zuniga, Bill and Bernadine Ackart....Working to foment unrest in the streets at the bottom while waiting like predators at the top to pounce on the right crisis to impose order to what they themselves were sponsoring. Jerry Baer and then Sharon after him referred to the approach as the "downside up, upside down" theory, with the American people caught in the middle of the trap like mice.

Little by little over the decades, Americans had compromised away their God-given liberties in the name of what they perceived to be security. *Vote for me and I'll give you—everything!* A government with the power to take from some to give to others had the power to take everything from everyone. It was now takeaway time.

Most of the media had already succumbed to government pressure to conform. Like court eunuchs in the Ottoman Empire. Only Zenergy News Cable and a small segment of talk radio and the internet survived to spread the truth. Their days were numbered. Passage of the FAD bill would see to that.

"While we can't say what Sharon Lowenthal or Rush Limbaugh can or cannot say," Speaker Barbara Teague declared ingeniously after the final vote on FAD, "I feel the FCC does have the right to regulate and say the public has the right not to be offended."

"Access to the internet and the airways," added Senate Majority Leader Wiedersham at the same news conference, "is a civil rights issue. Each radio and TV station and each internet site will be required to pass a Public Values' Test. If they don't pass it, their license will be stripped from them and assigned to someone who will use it appropriately in the public interest. Parasites like Lowenthal,

Limbaugh, Hannity and the Zenergy fat cats should be called out for what they really are. They're useless eaters, they're nasty, they're evil, they're liars, thieves and cheaters against the American people."

Gone were the days when the media were watchdogs against political corruption and misdeeds. Patton guessed that by the end of next week the government would have closed the doors to Zenergy and any other outlet it considered hostile. Independent news and commentary were becoming relics of past liberties.

Until that happened, Patton intended to keep the pressure on that bunch of Marxist coyotes in Washington. He consulted his watch. Ten until seven a.m. He didn't think the limo would be late. The driver wouldn't *dare*. He leaned forward over his steering wheel and peered at Majority Leader Wiedersham's Georgetown mansion down the street, staking out the place. He and Alfred his cameraman prepared to play ambush journalism as soon as Wiedersham came out to get in the limo.

Alfred was a middle-aged man with an old-fashioned crew cut. Normally as cool and implacable as Alfred the Butler in *Batman*, today he was scared and tinkered with the video feed on his camera in order to keep his hands and mind busy. Patton was sweating too. He was none too confident that his surprise ambush would elicit much of value from the politician, but he had to try for Sharon's sake.

It was general knowledge in upper circles of power that the President, along with most of the White House czars and the Congressional leadership, would not be available for the next several days; they would be attending an "economic summit," according to White House spokesman Dewey Gubbins. It was Patton's goal to goad Wiedersham into providing some clue as to where the top secret Summit was being held.

"If we can get an admission on camera that the summit is being held," Patton fretted, his thin face hollow in the cheeks, "they won't dare do anything to Sharon for fear the public will know."

"I don't think they give a rat's ass anymore what the public thinks," Alfred said.

The two newsmen initially discussed and then discarded the idea of attempting to tail the limo to its destination. They weren't professional gumshoes. What they needed was the Okie cop. The poor bastard was in love with Sharon. But Patton had no idea how to contact him, hadn't heard from him since he took off from Central Park like a scalded ape.

Patton nudged Alfred when a black limousine turned onto the street from the other end of the block. Alfred snapped the covers shut on his camera. They had to be ready to get in, slam their questions at

Wiedersham, then get out again quickly enough to avoid security and the cops. Today's little ploy was enough to draw both of them some "reeducation" time at "facilities" the government was supposedly constructing in the West.

The limo eased down the tree-lined street. Although the side windows were tinted, the angle of approach allowed Patton a view through the clear windshield. He recognized the gangster hat worn by the front seat passenger—that obsequious, ass-kissing little weasel, Justin Cobb.

The long, black car pulled into Wiedersham's driveway. Patton kicked over his engine and sat idling while he waited for Cobb to get out to escort his boss from the house to the vehicle. Instead, Cobb remained seated.

After several minutes, Wiedersham's stout figure burst out the front door and stomped toward the limo, his posture and bearing telegraphing the ass-chewing he was obviously prepared to deliver for Cobb's having violated protocol. He carried a thick briefcase and his own luggage. W*ould the indignities never cease?* Definitely on his way out of town.

Patton slammed in his gas feed and whipped his Hyundai in behind the stopped limo to block its retreat. Alfred and he bailed out and cut off Wiedersham before he reached safety. The Majority Leader stopped, scowling. The camera was already rolling.

"Senator!" Patton snapped. "Will you explain for our Zenergy News audience the purpose of the Sustainable World Conference you will be attending starting tonight?"

"You're trespassing!" Wiedersham lashed back. "Get the fuck off my property."

The newsmen held their ground. Wiedersham flapped an angry hand for Cobb to come to his aid.

"Senator, is it true that the purpose of this summit is to plan the final economic de-stabilization of the United States…?"

He heard a car door open, the rush of feet approaching. Expecting Cobb, he wheeled about to fend off an attack. It took him an instant to recognize the man wearing Cobb's hat.

James Nail stormed past the reporters. To nosy neighbors, it might appear the Majority Leader was being rescued from the pesky news media. Only Patton and Alfred saw the handgun Nail jabbed into Wiedersham's ribs.

"You want to get that piece of junk car of yours out of the way so we can get out of here?" Nail growled at Patton as he shoved the shaken politician toward the limo's back door, held open by a blond woman wearing a chauffeur's costume.

# Chapter Eighty-Two

## Washington, D.C.

The unexpected arrival of Carl Patton and his cameraman couldn't have been more perfect had it been planned as a cover for Wiedersham's "rescue." The Majority Leader sat frozen in stunned silence on his side of the wide executive-style back seat of the limousine as it sped away. The Indian-looking gunman on the other end of the seat regarded him from eyes that resembled blue slivers of ice.

Part of the job description for a homicide detective was to make perps sweat. Wiedersham's expensive business suit already looked damp and slept-in. Dark eyes sunk into the pasty jowls of the malevolent Pillsbury Doughboy shifted nervously. A cold half-smile touched Nail's lips. He could almost read Wiedersham's fears: So completely did the tinted windows isolate him from the outside world that no one was apt to hear him scream.

Wiedersham wet his thick lips with the tip of his tongue. "Where's Cobb?" he demanded in his best authoritarian tone. He was a man accustomed to power. "Do you have any idea who you're fucking with?"

A man less self-assured would have gone to pieces.

"Who the hell are you?" the politician asked in a dreadful whisper when he received no response.

Nail's eyes continued to bore into Wiedersham's. The fat face folded into pale, moist lasagna the instant he recognized Nail.

"You're the cop!" Hands trembled lying in his lap. "I can get you money—"

"I'm not a politician. I can't be bribed."

Judy took a left to shortcut through Georgetown University. All the usual suspects—teachers unions, student organizations, PEIU, ACOA, One Worlders—were already out organizing the day's protests against "imperialism," "hate," "racism," "sexism," "lack of equality" and the other inequities of capitalism that seemed to bring geeks out of their parents' basements.

Nail grunted with distaste. As far as he was concerned, these assholes could starve if the only thing they knew to do was latch onto a bunch of politicians who promised to take from the *greedy rich* so that nobody would have to work in the coming Socialist Utopia.

And after the Fat Cats were all used up?

Judy made her way across campus and headed the limo north on U.S. 81.

"My people will be looking for me," Wiedersham warned. "Where are you taking me, Nail?"

"You're taking *me* to The Sustainable World Conference at Lake Ontario."

He watched Wiedersham struggle to hide his surprise. "Do you have any idea what security will be like there?"

"I'm sure you'll find a way, with the right incentive."

"You're too late, Nail. Nothing can stop us now. The countdown is starting."

As a politician, the man had used words as weapons most of his life; he couldn't seem to stop now.

"This country is collapsing, Nail," he insisted. "The Homer Simpsons of the world are too stupid to rule themselves. It's up to their betters to drive them to a better place."

"You have it all figured out," Nail said.

"You don't have to be one of the Homers, Detective," Wiedersham offered slyly. "There's a place for you if you're smart."

The hard lines in Nail's face remained. He tipped his gun so that Wiedersham was staring into its barrel.

"I'll want Sharon Lowenthal released when we get to the lake."

"Be realistic, man. Besides, what makes you think we have her?"

"The only way you and I are leaving there without her is if you and I are in body bags," Nail warned.

## Banks Closing Adds To Pressure

***(Washington)****—More than 40 banks, including some of the largest in Washington, New York, Los Angeles, Chicago, Philadelphia and Miami, have shut down operations one after the other this week, with others closing their doors almost hourly. CitiBank announced it was closing all its branches. Panicked people across the nation gathered in lines desperately seeking to withdraw their savings out of fear of cash shortages...*

# Chapter Eighty-Three

## Watertown, New York

Nail recalled reading somewhere that the small city of Watertown on the Black River about twenty miles south of the tip of Lake Ontario had more millionaires per capita than any other city in the nation. He doubted any of its residents realized the irony of a bunch of the wealthiest redistribute-the-wealth Marxists in the world gathering there. He let Wiedersham sweat during most of the limo drive from Washington to Watertown. Police detectives whose job entailed penetrating the seedy minds and black souls of assorted perverts, torturers and murderers were good practical psychologists.

The general public failed to realize that most perps actually *wanted* to talk in order to justify or excuse or explain their guilt and their behavior. The secret to interrogation lay in encouraging them in a way commiserate with their personalities. People like Wiedersham who considered themselves superior to the general population were actually more easily manipulated than run-of-the-mill variety thieves and crooks. Wiedersham was a blusterer who *knew* he was right and everyone else was wrong. A man like that found it all but impossible to resist showing off. Nearly everyone in official Washington seemed to be narcissistic to one degree or another, from the President down to the Congressional mail clerk.

Nail sat silently in the moving limo waiting for the pressure to build. Every time the pol opened his mouth, Nail withered it shut again with a hard look. Wiedersham seemed about to explode from tension. Only the purr of the big limo's engine and the periodic swipe of windshield wipers against a misting rain marred the silence.

About a half-hour short of Watertown, Nail tapped the barrel of his gun on the glass shield that separated the driver from the passenger compartment. Judy glanced at him through the rearview mirror and nodded that she understood; it was time to implement the rest of the plan.

The Majority Leader's confusion turned to mild alarm when Judy whipped the limo off the main road onto a side road. His alarm became palpable fear as she slowed several times to permit Nail to survey even smaller, more isolated roads. Finally, she stopped and backed up to the entrance of a narrow, muddy logging lane that led downhill into new growth red pine. Nail tapped the glass shield again and she turned into the ruts, jouncing the passengers, stopping in the pines out of sight of infrequent passing traffic.

Wiedersham cried out in near-panic when the engine cut off and the door clicked unlocked. He seemed ready to forsake all caution and make a run for it. Nail shrugged.

"Make my day," he said in his best *Dirty Harry* manner.

Casually, and therefore all the more disturbing to the politician, Nail got out, strode to the other door and yanked Wiedersham out onto the wet grass by the collar of his expensive suit coat. On his knees, he stared up at Nail's gun. It was probably the first time in his life that his tongue failed him. He shivered from terror as much as from the chill. Judy remained in the car, looking straight ahead. The sky hung low and gray, spitting rain, promising much worse as the day wore on.

Nail pressed the muzzle of Cobb's pistol an inch into the fat at the back of the politician's neck. Although the Beretta could be fired double-action on the first shot, Nail clicked back the hammer for effect. Wiedersham winced.

"Do you know what happened to Kimbrell in Tulsa?" Nail asked.

Wiedersham nodded spastically.

"And the two goons who shot Jerry Baer at ORU and killed my daughter?"

Another spastic nod.

"I'm sure you also recall the Homie you sent to murder Sharon Lowenthal in New York?"

Light rain collected like blisters on Wiedersham's pale face.

"A maggot like you surely understands that I have nothing to lose by killing you. I'm going to ask you some questions. Think them over. A lie will come back to bite you in the butt."

Nail almost heard the man's brain working as it calculated risks and options, weighed in on hope and change.

Wiedersham finally found his voice. "Don't be stupid," he protested. "Secret Service and Homeland have that place sealed up tighter than a nun's pussy."

"Where is it?"

Wiedersham hesitated as he thought over his options, which must have seemed limited under the circumstances.

"It won't do you any good even if I tell you," he protested.

"Where?" Nail sunk the muzzle of the Beretta another inch into the politician's fat. Wiedersham's entire body shuddered, like he could almost see the bottom of the abyss.

Nail deflected the muzzle of his gun and squeezed the trigger. The bullet seared the skin on Wiedersham's neck and gouged a plume of sod out of the earth directly between his knees. The fat man pitched forward, screaming and writhing on the wet grass and grabbing at his neck. Judy popped out of the limo but stopped at the front fender.

Nail waited until the Majority Leader regained some control before he crouched over him.

"I'll ask the question one more time," he threatened.

"You've busted my eardrums!" Wiedersham shouted

Nail cocked the Beretta. Wiedersham heard *that.*

"The Butterfield Mansion," he muttered, beaten. He was a coward, like most such men, and a pragmatist who had to realize that his only chance of survival was to cooperate.

Nail left him moaning in the wet grass while he spoke to Judy. She looked pale and shaken, but she agreed to take a look at the Butterfield Mansion for him, paying particular attention to security measures, cover and concealment, and avenues of approach and egress. He didn't think police would have found Bill and Cobb yet and therefore would not have alerted Homeland Security.

"Don't take unnecessary chances," he cautioned. "Pick me up here in two hours."

Judy indicated the much-humbled fat man in the soggy suit. "Does he know where Sharon is?"

"I'm sure he'll have told me by the time you return."

She started the limo and disappeared up the logging road on her way to Watertown. From Wiedersham's expression, Nail couldn't tell whether he considered her departure a good sign or not.

As soon as the limo disappeared from sight, Nail jerked the frightened politician to his feet and marched him to a thick fallen log a few yards deeper into timber. Wiedersham seemed appalled that Nail had shot him and then made him suffer the further indignity of sitting astraddle one end of the log.

"Do you know how much this suit costs?" he demanded indignantly.

Nail switched on the hidden voice recorder in the pocket of his windbreaker before taking a seat on the other end of the log facing Wiedersham. A "confession," along with Trout's notebook, would go a long way in convincing the American people of the peril they faced. If there were still enough people left out there who gave a damned.

Nail winced. He recognized the putrid stench emanating from his wound. Iraqi *Desert Storm* prisoners who suffered from untreated trauma smelled like that. Septicemia. But before God called in his warranty, he was determined to free the woman he loved and strike a blow for American liberty. A big-time order for a small-time cop.

"I know who she is," Wiedersham finally ventured, glancing toward the lane from which Judy had disappeared in the limo. "She's the piece of slit-tail my former brother-in-law shot himself over. He was a weakling. I would never have taken in the cowardly bastard if it hadn't been for my sister. He ended up killing her, too."

"And the dog," Nail reminded him.

"*I'd* have shot the dog," Wiedersham admitted with nervous laughter, his palm pressed against his scorched neck. It was not bleeding, but it had to be painful.

Wiedersham couldn't seem to stop talking once he started, whether from nervousness or because it was his stock in trade. Whereas in the limo Nail had kept Wiedersham's tensions deliberately bottled, he now encouraged him either by short general questions or by silences Wiedersham seemed compelled to fill.

"You must understand, Detective," Wiedersham said, feeling his way, "that what you're witnessing is the inevitable tide of history to which you either adjust or perish." He paused and studied his opponent. "I truly doubt you're capable of understanding what I'm talking about."

"Try me. We have time."

"The tide of history killed your daughter, Detective. It will inevitably neutralize obstructionists who stand in the way of ultimate peace and justice for all peoples around the planet."

Nail stuffed his rage back down. He had a feeling this piece of shit didn't believe a word he was saying.

"You don't impress me as a hope 'n change kind of guy, Wiedersham," Nail said conversationally.

Wiedersham seemed pleased with Nail's insight.

"Pardon me for saying so, Detective, but you Tea Bagger types are so fucking naïve. Detective, a man has a choice to either take the winning side of history, or the losing side. I choose to be on the winning side."

The more he talked, the more his self-assurance seemed to build. All his life he had used intimidation and his golden tongue to get him by.

"Do you realize that hard-cores like yourself, Detective, are a minority? Not a lot of Homer Simpsons believe in freedom and capitalism. Your average Homer is not capable of running his pathetic little life. Do you realize that nearly half of American households receive government benefits of some sort? One in six are on full subsistence. It's called social conditioning through education and handouts. The Homers will vote for whoever promises to give them the most that they don't have to work for. The biggest argument you can make against democracy is a five-minute conversation with your average voter."

"I thought we were done with the commies when the Soviet Union fell."

Wiedersham chuckled grandly, getting into it now that he thought the burn on his neck was the worst he might expect.

"Don't blame people like me for what's happened," he said. "Blame yourself. Blame your willingness to give up everything in order to be cared for like children. For nearly a century, politicians have merely been agents doing precisely what we have elected them to do—using the power of office to take what belongs to one American and redistribute it to other Americans, or to confer special privileges on some that are denied others. Socialism is such an easy sell because it preys on greed and envy."

A stab of pain shot through Nail's chest. He bent forward against it.

"You have blood poisoning, Detective. I can smell it," Wiedersham observed. "It won't kill you, however. You know why? Because *they* are going to kill you first."

Nail flicked his gun barrel to remind the politician to keep on track. Wiedersham seemed pleased to have an audience who appreciated his cleverness.

"We're days away from a global socialist government," Wiedersham boasted. "The United States is the last major holdout and it'll soon be gone, a victim of the doctrine of the inevitability of gradualism. The radicals of the 1960s failed at open revolution—so what they did was go underground, scrub themselves clean so they wouldn't look like radicals, and reemerge as *Progressives.* While the Homers took their liberty for granted, the Progressives were busy taking over the culture—universities and high schools, subverting newspapers, magazines, networks and the cables, infiltrating the churches....In order to take over, we needed to destroy the old culture.

"Haven't you noticed how novels and Hollywood dream factories portray businessmen as shallow, selfish, crude and pathetic? Traditional male figures are depicted as either effeminate or bumbling idiots. The military has become feminized. God has left the building.

Decriminalize prostitution, legalize drugs, mock God, mock anything that's traditional. Let down your hair, live it up. Give them cakes and circuses. It takes their pathetic minds off what's really happening. The average middle-class Homer loses hope once he realizes that it doesn't matter what he does."

The man's candidness surprised Nail. "People are starting to fight back," he asserted.

"Are they indeed?" Wiedersham barked that annoying sound that served as laughter. "You conspiracy theorists are all a bunch of Rightwing kooks. Nobody listens to you. Men like George Zuniga have the real power. They pull the strings while you stand around bickering among yourselves or hypnotized in front of the TV. Marxists are masters of misdirection and deception. The socialist infrastructure has been building for decades. While you think you're fighting back, we're waiting in the shadows ready to take over. It doesn't matter whether a few old stalwarts fight back or not. You've already lost.

"Don't you know it makes no difference whether you elect Republicans or Democrats? We could have elected a trained seal to the White House for all that Anastos influences *anything.*" Wiedersham barked in disgust. "The emperor of hope 'n change! Anastos can't even read a teleprompter without stuttering. Useful idiots are, well, *useful*, during the de-stabilization stage of subverting the target. Afterwards, when their jobs are done and the *real* power takes over, you take 'em all out and shoot 'em."

"It's not going to happen here," Nail exclaimed, bitterly unconvinced.

"It already *is* happening. Total transformation is only days away. Capitalism will be destroyed from within. Be realistic. Look at what has already happened, all according to plan: deficit spending in the trillions; a national debt that can never be repaid; government control of natural resources, energy, transportation, agriculture, the military, law enforcement, communications; heavy taxation for redistribution; government underwriting of employment, food, housing, education, medical care... No one can stop it now. Anyone who stands in the way of progress must be eliminated."

Nail said nothing. The recorder was getting it all.

"The countdown to the end has started," Wiedersham said. "I predict it will all be over in two weeks. Everything will collapse within ten days from when China refuses to buy any more U.S. debt and closes off our credit. Wall Street spooks and loses a thousand points in twenty minutes as rumors spread. Europe raises interest rates, but it's already too late. Markets worldwide close. The plunge of the dollar causes global economic meltdown. People break into banks, ATMs are dry, food is rationed. Worldwide panic. Anastos declares martial law. The invisible government is no longer invisible. The IMF and G-20 led by Zuniga and his worldwide players redistribute all the debts and declare a New Global Order centered in The Hague."

Nail was stunned at how well it all seemed to have been orchestrated.

"The purpose of your meeting this week is to bring all this about? Nail presumed.

"Watch it all play out, Detective—" Wiedersham offered. "Oh, I forgot. You won't be alive to see it."

Nail rose slowly to his feet and stood over Wiedersham. "You are more despicable than the communists because you do their bidding out of self-interest."

Wiedersham opened his mouth to say something.

"Shut up!" Nail snapped, swallowing the lump in his throat. "You and your commies murdered my daughter. You're barely worth the bullet to blow you to hell. Remember that when you answer this next question. Where is Sharon Lowenthal?"

Rain began falling harder, pattering in the pine boughs and beading and running down Wiedersham's pale, fat face as he looked up into the cop's menacing features. He muttered a few last words before a single shot cracked in the forest, all but muted by the low rumble of thunder. A lone figure holding his side limped out of the pines in the rain and stood next to the logging road, the Beretta hanging loosely in his hand. His head lifted. Rain mingled with his tears and washed them away.

## Violence Disrupting Nation

***(Washington)***—*According to Harvard's Department of Sociology, this summer has been the most disruptive in the nation's history. The following is a representative summary of some of the violence during which scores of people have died or been seriously injured:*

*On the Gulf Coast, protests instigated by Tea Parties against President Anastos' ban on offshore oil drilling following the AP oil spill turned nasty and had to be dispersed...*

*Demonstrators displaying anti-Muslim signs had to be broken up in Manhattan after they disobeyed a New York law that forbids hate groups from congregating...*

*Detroit. Yoga teachers, soup kitchen volunteers, university students, public schoolteachers, union members and ACOA community organizers demanding the end of capitalism were attacked by rightwing militia and Tea Baggers, who burned police cars and broke out street windows before police restored order...*

*In Phoenix, a "Festival of Resistance" against sweeping new Arizona anti-immigration laws exploded in violence when racist groups confronted undocumented Hispanic protestors...*

*Portland, Oregon. PEIU union members peacefully picketing a branch of CitiBank were fired upon by drive-by shooters...*

*San Francisco police broke up a clash between the peaceful New Black Panther Party and a White Aryan Movement...*

*Homeland Security police firing automatic weapons and hurling concussion grenades broke up a police uprising in Los Angeles that was prompted by a Federal proposal to nationalize city and county police departments. The unrest began when hundreds of angry policemen called for a nationwide police strike to shut down the government. At least four LA policemen were killed and eight wounded. Several hundred were arrested...*

*There have also been militia attacks against Homeland Security and AmeriCorps members in Arkansas, Oklahoma, Colorado, Wyoming, New York, Florida, and other states across the nation as Rightwing terrorism spreads...*

*Responses to the increased violence have been vocal across the country.*

*"I don't see why we even got a discussion in the black community over whether or not we should arm ourselves against the crackers,"*

*said Aziz Muhammad, leader of the New Black Panthers in Los Angeles. "The answer is: Yes! We are arming ourselves for survival."*

*"We got to take to the streets like we did in the 1960s," said Matthew Underall of New Weather Underground. "We got to force the government to move toward peace and social justice."*

*The World Socialist Web predicts worse times ahead: "The whole global fabric centered on the U.S. for 60 years is collapsing, generating turmoil of all sorts. What is this social unrest? War! It's as simple and horrifying as that."*

*"Anastos is my man because he can change America," declared a PEIU union member, whose last job was as a Federal census taker. "I pray to God America will listen to Patrick Wayne Anastos. He is the true salvation for America, to bring us beyond the negative, nasty and injustice."*

*White House spokesman Dewey Gubbins said internal security forces such as AmeriCorps and Homeland Security must be further beefed up to counter growing civil unrest...*

# Chapter Eighty-Four

## Colorado

The gravel road that led to the "mental health facility" made a sharp, narrow bend between a ridge and a noisy canyon creek. Whippoorwills were starting their mournful tri-syllable exchanges in the purple twilight of evening when Dennis Shook on watch from high on the ridge gave the signal by flashlight that the buses were coming. Big C and several other Defenders got to work on a massive boulder to get it moving. Once they got it moving, it thumped the short distance downhill in a shower of dust, gravel and smaller rocks and came to rest in the middle of the road. The bus drivers would have to stop to clear the mini-avalanche.

Headlights cut through the gathering darkness as the buses eased into the curve at the base of the ridge. Militiamen scurried out of sight. The lead bus locked its wheels at the last moment and skidded to a halt only a few feet short of the obstruction. It appeared the second bus might either ram the first or pitch off into the canyon. The driver managed to brake his coach mere inches from his leader's rear bumper.

The two big vehicles sat rumbling while the dust cleared. From concealment, Big C heard the whoosh of air brakes released and saw *Gray Travel Charters* emblazoned on the sides of the carriers, below which appeared happy illustrations of families vacationing at Mount Rushmore and Monument Valley.

Hydraulic doors opened. A hefty man crammed like a sausage into a gray bus driver's jacket stepped out onto the road. Big C heard him swear. He walked up and glared at the boulder. He slapped it with his open palm in frustration. Swearing like the proverbial sailor on shore leave, he turned around and motioned toward his bus.

Two AmeriCorps Green Shirts wearing holstered sidearms got off and walked up to the driver. One of them made a joke and they laughed. The driver was in no mood for it.

"Don't stand there, assholes!" he snapped. "Help me push it off into the creek."

"Watch who you're calling assholes, asshole," one of the Green Shirts warned.

They put their backs into the rock, but could not budge it. Panting, the driver straightened and beckoned toward the second bus. That driver and two additional guards got off and strode to the front. Falling rocks in the Rockies were not an unusual occurrence.

Enough light remained in the western sky for Big C to observe that passengers on the buses appeared to have no interest in what was going on. Heads behind the tinted windows remained as stiff and unmoving as department store mannequins. The guards seemed unconcerned about their charges escaping.

Once Big C issued the order, his band of armed rebels leaped out onto the road, brandishing weapons and shouting like savages. They rushed the surprised drivers and guards, yelling and shoving and throwing them face down on the road while skillfully relieving them of their weapons. Other militiamen scurried aboard the buses. Little Tump Kinsey, the old Vietnam vet in charge of boarding, looked stunned when he stuck his head out the bus door a few moments later.

"Brown, you need to take a look at this," he called out.

Big C's was an imposing large figure in the road. The captives clearly understood by his demeanor that he meant business and was prepared to execute the lot of them if necessary. He made sure his men had the situation under control before he climbed on the bus to see what Tump was clamoring about.

Tump had switched on the interior lights. Bus seats were packed with men and a few women, none of whom exhibited the slightest curiosity about what was going on around them. Several who had been thrown from their seats remained sprawled in the aisle or jammed unresponsive in the leg spaces between seats. For all their reaction, they might have been zombies staring into the void, without emotion or intelligence.

"They drugged!" Big C realized.

"They're in Heaven, for all they care," Tump noted, overwhelmed.

"Or hell."

"They ain't what I wanted to show you," Tump said. He pointed to a seat about halfway back.

Big C's breath caught in his throat. "My God! Sharon!"

Sharon Lowenthal didn't even look at him when he rushed back and grabbed her in an embrace, repeating her name. She wore jeans and a light yellow jacket. Her dark hair looked used and there were bags underneath her eyes. A bruise on her cheek suggested she may have resisted arrest.

"Sis? It's me. Corey. What happen to James? Have you seen him?"

There may have been a flicker of awareness in her dark eyes when she heard Nail's name, but that was all. She was completely disengaged, passive. On her way to the "death camp" and she didn't even know it.

Earlier, before Big C's militia ambushed the charter buses, a Humvee occupied by three AmeriCorps goons had passed on the road outbound toward State 160. The Green Shirts inside it were buttoned up against the chill of arriving evening, smoking and joking. Clearly, they expected no trouble. Who would be interested in a nut ward kept secluded for the Public's safety?

"That hummer be coming back," Big C had predicted.

Sure enough, he was still inside the bus trying to revive Sharon when Dennis Shook came bounding back down the ridge with the Devil hot on his ass. He attempted to leap the drainage ditch, stumbled and fell flat in the gravel on the road. He scrambled to his feet, his nose skinned and bleeding and the whites of his eyes walling.

"The Hummer!" he shouted.

Big C bounced from the bus. "How far back?"

"Maybe three miles. It just rounded the bend near the State 160 junction."

Four minutes. Perhaps less. Big C was already moving, barking orders. "Leave the boulder in the road. Drag those people in the woods. Gag 'em and tie 'em to trees. I take the big Green Shirt's uniform. Bias, Combs, Turner, you put on the other uniforms. Delbert, you and Headshot are bus drivers, okay?"

"What about me?" Tump Kinsey interrupted.

"I got a mission for Shook and you, Tump," Big C said. "It too important for just anyone to handle."

He explained as he hurriedly shed his shirt and jacket and replaced them with the larger AmeriCorps tunic, ball cap, gun belt and pistol. The shirt stretched thin across his torso, but he doubted the Hummer patrol would notice in the dark.

"Tump, I need you and Shook take Sharon back across the mountain to where you stashed your cars—"

"Brown, she can't walk!"

"That's why Shook going with you. *Carry* her you have to. Build a stretcher. I don't care what you do—just get her out of here safe."

"Can't we wait for you to come back with the buses and the other prisoners?"

"What if we don't come back?"

That sobered him. Shook and Tump followed him aboard the bus. Sharon sat unmoving on her aisle seat. Big C picked her up in his arms and carried her off the bus like she was a child. The bus lights pooled shadow around the boulder still in the road. The other militiamen so designated were already stripped and drawing on their purloined uniforms while still others dragged trussed bodies into the tree line. The Hummer's headlights were not yet visible coming around the ridge road.

"Tump, this woman going to be our most influential voice for the underground resistance when it all break down," Big C continued as militiamen gathered around for further orders. "People know her from TV. They trust her like they did Jerry Baer. It up to the two of you, Tump, to make sure she get out."

He set Sharon on her feet. She was wobbly but managed to stand unaided. Big C pressed his go-cell into Tump's palm.

"We don't have a signal out here," he said. "James Nail and girl name Judy know this number. One them be calling when you get signal again. Go to Oklahoma and hide out in the hills. Take Sharon to Nail when he call. Understand?"

"Brown, I ain't too old to fight—"

Big C slapped him on the shoulder. "I know you ain't, Tump. Sharon will make people listen if we bring back Lieutenant Ross and some of the other survivors of that death camp to spread the word. We didn't stand up for the Jews when Hitler began rounding them up. No one paid attention to what Stalin and Mao was doing. It not going to be that way this time. If we have to fight, let the war start here. Tonight."

The old Vietnam warrior's wizened face looked gray in the yellow light from the bus headlights. Shook, then Tump, gripped Big C's hand with hard emotion.

"If we don't see one another again—" Tump choked up.

"You'll see me, man. Hurry, now."

Together, the two militiamen hustled Sharon off the road and into the trees. A halo of brighter light bounced off the sky and road as the Humvee roared around the curve, chasing its headlights. Big C ripped his eyes free of the darkness into which Sharon disappeared. He had to believe that Sharon, Nail, Judy and he would all be together again. Some day.

# Chapter Eighty-Five

## Colorado

The Humvee's headlights washed across the two stalled buses as it crunched gravel and slid to a halt behind the last carrier. It sat growling in the middle of the road like some beast of prey posed to strike, its turret-mounted Two-Forty machinegun manned and aimed at the coterie of bus drivers and Green Shirts who appeared to be struggling with a boulder blocking the road. Big C looked up, waved casually, and strode toward the new pair of headlights. He grinned and shrugged. *Hey, shit happens.*

He stepped out of the glare of the lights as he approached. The 40mm Glock that previously belonged to a Green Shirt remained holstered, but the thumb strap was loose. Just in case these guys in the vehicle didn't buy his rap.

The driver's door swung open. A shadow stepped down onto the roadbed. A black kid. "Wassup, bro?"

"Big mother rock blockin' the road. You homes wanna give a hand?"

The driver bent back inside the Hummer, said something to his passengers. Two other Green Shirts in full combat got out and moved around into the headlights to gaze down the road. One carried a 5.56 SAW, Squad Automatic Weapon, while the turret gunner was armed with a holstered handgun.

"Ain't never saw you in this 'hood, bro," the black driver said to Big C.

"Ain't never been in this 'hood. This my first transport."

"Fucked up place," the driver said.

Big C maneuvered a look inside the Hummer to make sure there were only three men in the crew. These were obviously not trained soldiers. Only a few short weeks ago they might have been hijacking liquor stores and ripping purses off old ladies in the cities. After drilling for a couple of weeks in some camp like the one in Arkansas, they were tossed out to guard detention camps or make raids on militias and obstructionists.

When the driver hesitated as though to stick with his vehicle, Big C said, "Hey, bro. It gonna take all three ya'all to help us move that big fuckin' rock."

"Dude, you the Green Hulk. You big 'nuff to pick up that rock you own self."

Big C laughed. “I promise my dear mammy I don’t be showin’ off.”

The three fell in step with C and they headed for the boulder.

“You play for Forty-Niners or what, bro?” the driver asked.

“Dude, my game’s cricket.”

“Say what? You some kind of big pussy?”

Big C chuckled. At the same time, using the chuckle as diversion, he took a quick side step to grab the SAW gunner by the raised neck rib of his battle rattle vest. He yanked back violently and slammed the guy to the ground while relieving him of his weapon. He sprang back and thumbed the SAW’s Safe lever to *Fire*. The Green Shirts gaped at him.

“Some a us pussies play rough,” Big C gibed.

The three prisoners were soon stripped, bound, gagged and stowed with the other captives in the woods. The commandeered Humvee was a valuable added asset. Big C assigned Bias, Turner and two of the Colorado fighters to man the armored truck. He huddled with his small band to amend their plans.

“Bias, follow the buses to the gate but stay back out of sight. We going on through the gate. Give us five minutes to roll in the tunnel under the hospital. Then you come up *on foot*, else Campione might open up on ya’all with the .50-cal. Take out the gate and disable the power shack to cut electric to the fence so Fullbright and his bunch can get in. Us on the buses will break out Lieutenant Ross and as many others we got time for. You cover us again with the hummer while we pick up the men from our other two elements. All vehicles rendezvous back here at the rock where we get on the highway and haul back across Wolf Creek Pass. Take out anybody that get in the way. We have one hour from when shooting starts to get across the pass before Apaches come on us like flies. Got any questions, better ask ’em now. This thing is going down fast and furious.”

“What happens if the Trojan Horse don’t work and they smell a rat?” Bias asked.

“You got the Two-Forty on the Humvee. Use it you got to.”

One of the Sons of Liberty jerked a thumb toward the buses. “What are we going to do with them folks? They already got the buses filled.”

“We need people who know what went down inside that camp,” Big C said. Those already in the buses, drugged to the point of helplessness, would have to be exchanged and left inside the compound. In war, things sometimes had to be done that weren’t pleasant.

"Let's get this operation on the road," Big C concluded when all questions had been answered.

Big C and a Coloradan named Jones took over the lead bus, with Headshot driving. Delbert, Roscoe and another Son of Liberty brought along the other bus, trailed by the Humvee back in the dark with its lights off. The tandem twin pools of headlights inched across the vast black landscape. The government had treated the raid on the Arkansas AmeriCorps' training camp as a "criminal action." Tonight's coordinated attack by militia against a federal installation could be considered only one way—as the beginning of the second American Revolution.

Armed revolt was not something Big C took lightly as he swayed with the movement of the bus, cradling the SAW in his elbow. He had devoted a lot of time over the past weeks mining his motivation and justification for the bloodshed that lay ahead.

In his mind, revolution was no longer merely an option, a topic of hypothetical discussion around the table in the Safe House. The line had been drawn "after a long train of abuses." As Thomas Jefferson so famously uttered: *Freedom must be periodically renewed by the blood of tyrants and patriots.* The watchman Paul Revere was once more riding across the land with his call to arms. To not resist at this point was to support a corrupt government and its illegal agenda, to bow to masters.

They would be relatively few, those who fought back, as they had been few who struggled through the Valley Forge Winter or crossed the Potomac with General Washington. Most of the population would take the easy way and go along with whatever the government did. Even most cops and soldiers would follow orders to fire upon and kill fellow citizens or incarcerate them in detention camps.

Desperate times lay ahead. Nonetheless, there came a time when men, in order to claim themselves men, must possess the courage to muster with the free and the brave, to either be counted among those who stood and fought with their countrymen or to live as penned cowards unworthy of a more noble existence.

Big C spotted the light from the compound ahead. They were coming upon the gate.

"Steady," he encouraged Headshot at the wheel. "This night will be long remembered."

## President Anastos On Top Of Crisis

***(Washington)****—No U.S. President in the history of the nation has had to deal with so many tough issues as has President Anastos during his first years in office.*

*He inherited from the previous administration a declining economy, continuing Middle East tensions between belligerent Israel and her Arab neighbors, Iran's nuclear threat, border problems with Mexico, kinetic overseas contingencies in Iraq, Afghanistan, Libya and Yemen, deteriorating American prestige abroad...*

*In spite of the challenges, however, public confidence in his intelligence, wisdom, experience and grasp of affairs continues to grow. Americans haven't felt this much confidence in their leaders in recent years. America is no longer just parochial, not just chauvinistic, not just provincial. America now stands for something. In a way, it's like the President is standing above the country, above the world. He's sort of God...*

# Chapter Eight-Six

## Watertown, New York

A thousand miles away from where Big C approached the gates of the "mental health facility" with his commandeered buses, James Nail stood in the rain by the side of the logging road, pistol still in hand, chin resting on his chest. He remained frozen in place, like the saddest statue in the saddest park in the world, when the limo crept back down the rough road and its headlights washed over him. Judy jumped out and rushed to his side, calling out his name as though to summon him back from a bottomless pit.

She looked around for Wiedersham. Not seeing him, her gaze settled on the gun in Nail's hand. Her face drained of blood. She suddenly had trouble catching her breath. Nail slowly lifted his head.

"Can we get out of the rain?" she gasped.

He let the cold dampness wash his face. "It does no good to make wishes on stars," he said.

She took his free hand. He followed and got into the limo's front passenger's seat. She closed his door, went around to the other side, slid underneath the wheel and started the engine. Rain drummed a muffled beat on the roof.

"Take me to the Butterfield Mansion," he instructed.

"Homies and police is as thick as ticks on a houn' dog. I don't see how we can get Sharon outa there—"

"She's not there," Nail said in a voice as thin and hard as a knife blade.

That shook Judy visibly. "What did he tell you?"

"Take me as close as you can," Nail said.

Without further question, her face still pale, she turned the limo around and proceeded to return to Watertown. She kept glancing at Nail. Rain had plastered his black hair to his scalp. Those cold blue eyes that always made her shiver stared straight ahead. Wipers hissed. Judy's headlights forced back the night. She turned up the heater.

Just before they arrived in Watertown, Nail took the digital recorder from his jacket pocket and placed it on the seat next to Judy.

"Take that and Trout's notebook," he said. "It's probably too late to stop what's happening. But maybe we can slow it down a little."

"They're looking for us, James."

"They're looking for *me*, not you. After you drop me off, I want you to go back to Washington and take the police to the motel where we left Cobb and the limo driver. Tell the police I kidnapped you—"

"I can't do that, James."

"I kidnapped you," he repeated harshly. "I threatened to kill you if you didn't do what I told you. The police will believe you. Then you get the hell out of D.C. with this tape and the notebook until you can turn them over to either Big C or Carl Patton at Zenergy News. They'll know what to do with them. There's going to be chaos for a long time when the decent people start to rise up."

He recalled a quote Sharon read to him at the Safe House, by someone with initials and the last name of Lawrence: *Men fight for liberty and win it with hard knocks. Their children, brought up easy, let it slip away again, poor fools. And their grandchildren are once more slaves.*

He wondered what Jamie would think about Hope 'n Change now if she were still alive. He thought about Connie and regretted all that had happened between them. He tried not to think about Sharon. He rode in cold silence.

"James, what are you going to do?" Judy finally asked.

"Evil is congregating in the Butterfield Mansion," he said in a voice edged so hard and sharp that it made Judy tremble. "It's the evil behind what happened at ORU and what's happening all across the country. There has to be a first shot fired to let them know Americans will fight when they're cornered. I don't know how it's all going to end. All I know is that if we give up now, there's no place to escape to."

He lapsed into another silence. Judy glanced sideways and choked up at sight of the tear—or was it a drop of rainwater?—reflected in the dashboard lights as it rolled down his thorny cheek.

"James? If Sharon's not…?" She couldn't complete the question.

The stony expression on Nail's face remained unchanged. "Wiedersham told me she had been picked up and executed for sedition."

"You believe him?"

"He had no reason to lie. At the end."

Both traveled without speaking.

It was full dark beneath low cloud cover when they entered Watertown and drove slowly through, past the city center. A sleepy little Main Street USA, except for black-clad Homies and Green Shirts patrolling the streets with automatic weapons and making the town look *occupied*. Soldiers in a Humvee made a U-turn and fell in behind the limo. Nail pointed to a gas station open ahead on the right.

"Pull in there."

Judy did, stopping at a pump. The Humvee slowed but kept going, apparently assuming the limo to be delivering more dignitaries to the Butterfield Mansion. Judy eased back onto the road as soon as it disappeared at the next intersection. A few minutes more and they were in darkness again, the lights of the town behind them.

"The mansion's about ten miles ahead," Judy said.

"Describe it to me," Nail requested. "Everything you can remember."

He debriefed her thoroughly for the next few miles. They approached timber that furred down from a hilltop toward the road. From her description, he knew the forest extended all the way to the back side of the Butterfield Mansion.

"Put me out up there ahead in the trees."

"James, you can't get to them."

As though to underscore the point, a helicopter's running lights bounced up from above the crest of a distant hill.

"Even if you get in," Judy pleaded, "you can't get back out again."

"One way's enough."

She broke down in tears. "James, I'm scared. For you...and Corey... and Sharon... For all of us."

Nonetheless, she swerved to the side of the road and turned off the headlights. She swiped at her eyes. Nail watched the helicopter's lights fade beyond the hills. He remained seated a moment longer.

"These are scary times, Judy. But I agree with Sharon. You and me, Big C, Sharon, Jerry Baer, Carl Patton, all of us. We were born at this particular time for a purpose. It's up to us and thousands of others like us to bring us through, to start sweeping up this mess and setting the table for the next generation. Otherwise, like Ronald Reagan said, the lights will dim and mankind will sink into a thousand years of darkness."

Still sniffling, she popped the trunk at his request and got out in the rain with him. He retrieved his Winchester 30.06 from the trunk and hastily buckled a bandoleer of ammunition around his waist. He checked the bolt and slapped a clip into the rifle.

"Go!" he ordered.

Neither said another word. Judy got into the limo and whipped a U back toward Washington on an alternate route around Watertown. She looked back and, in the reflection of her taillights, saw him standing by the side of the road with the long rifle in his hand and his head bowed as though in prayer. When she looked back again after getting the limo straightened out, the sniper had vanished into the rain and the darkness of the forest.

# Author's Note

This is a work of fiction ripped from today's headlines and based on actual current events. I have therefore drawn research from numerous public sources such as the media and public statements by public figures. This should not be construed to reflect upon these actual sources one way or another since they are used in a fictional context. However, I should like to acknowledge and pay tribute to these sources and thank them for their contributions. They include, but are not limited to, the following: *Associated Press; Reuters; New York Times; Tulsa World; Time; Newsweek; National Review; Human Events; Washington Post; Washington Times; Wall Street Journal; The New Yorker; Harper's; Atlantic; Fusion; The Limbaugh Letter; Fox Channel; MSNBC; CNN; Rush Limbaugh; Sean Hannity; Mark Steyn...*

*I should like to especially acknowledge and thank Glenn Beck, who was the inspiration for this novel and upon whom the character Jerry Baer is loosely drawn. A man of integrity and courage, he took it upon himself to ride the countryside to warn people of the dangers posed to human liberty when government runs out of control. He not only inspired this work, but his own novel, THE OVERTON WINDOW, paved the way for the speculative action-adventure political genre. Glenn Beck is truly the Thomas Paine of our times.*

Charles W. Sasser

www.ingramcontent.com/pod-product-compliance
Lightning Source LLC
Chambersburg PA
CBHW071155020726
47502CB00002B/425

*9780937660744*